THE KEEPER

P. S. WHITOCK

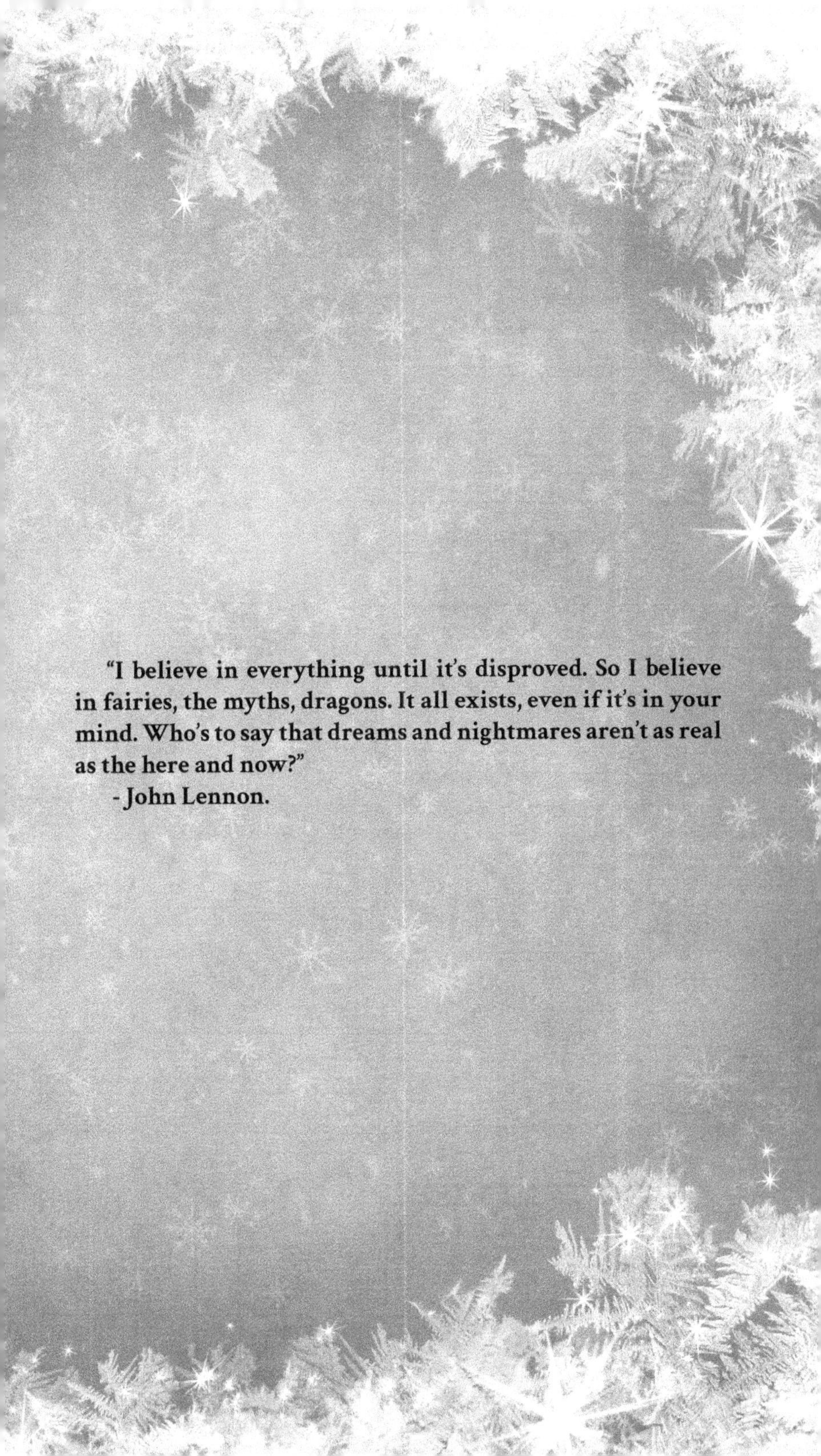

"I believe in everything until it's disproved. So I believe in fairies, the myths, dragons. It all exists, even if it's in your mind. Who's to say that dreams and nightmares aren't as real as the here and now?"
- John Lennon.

AIFABORG
Bel'onc Sea
The Fo...
Lost ...
Dauðinn Mountain
The Black Forest
Zarré City

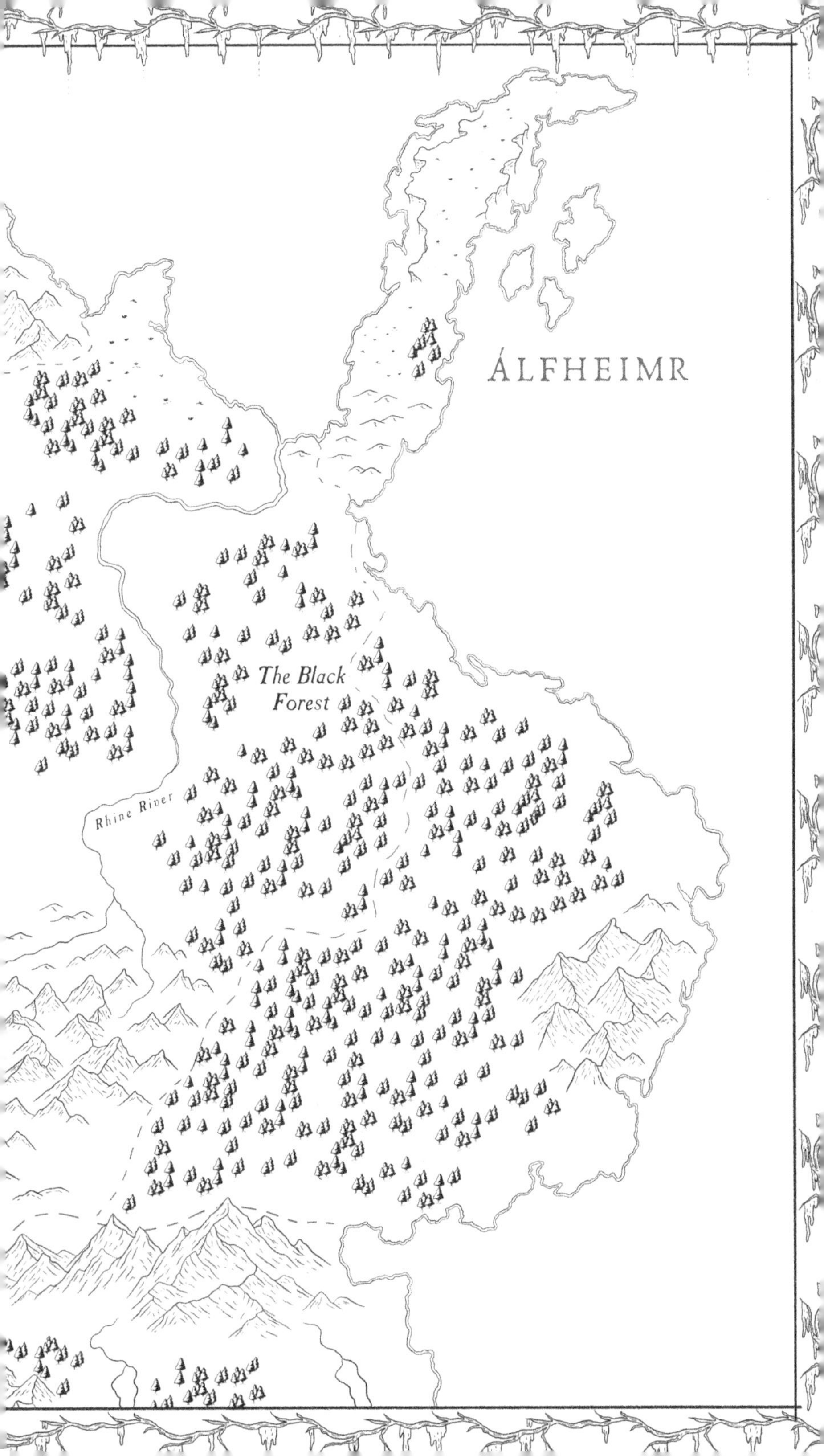

ÁLFHEIMR
The Black Forest
Rhine River

Pronunciation
Places:

Vaitarani (The Ageless River): *Vay-ter-a-nee*
Meaning: To cross over to the other world.
Origin: Hindu mythology, equivalent to Styx River in Greek Mythology.

Dauðinn: *Doi-th-nn*
Meaning: Death
Origin: Old Norse
Álfheimr: *Alf-eh-imer*
Meaning: Land of the Elves
Origin: Old Norse
Álfaborg: *Owl-va-borg*
Meaning: Elven Rock or City of the Elves
Origin: Icelandic
Thórsmörk: *Ther-sh-mork*
Meaning: Thor's mountain
Origin: Icelandic

Pronunciation Cont.
Names:

Anabelle: *Ana-bell*
Savven: *Sav-ven*
Isadora: *Is-a-dor-a*
Tatius: *Ta-tee-us*
Gallian: *Gay-lee-in*
Udiya: *You-dee-ya*
Néefar: *Ne-Far*
Valdren: *Vald-ren*
Balwin: *Ball-win*
Forndýr: *Forn-dry-er*
Lithônion: *Lith-on-nee-in*
Ezra: *Ez-ra*

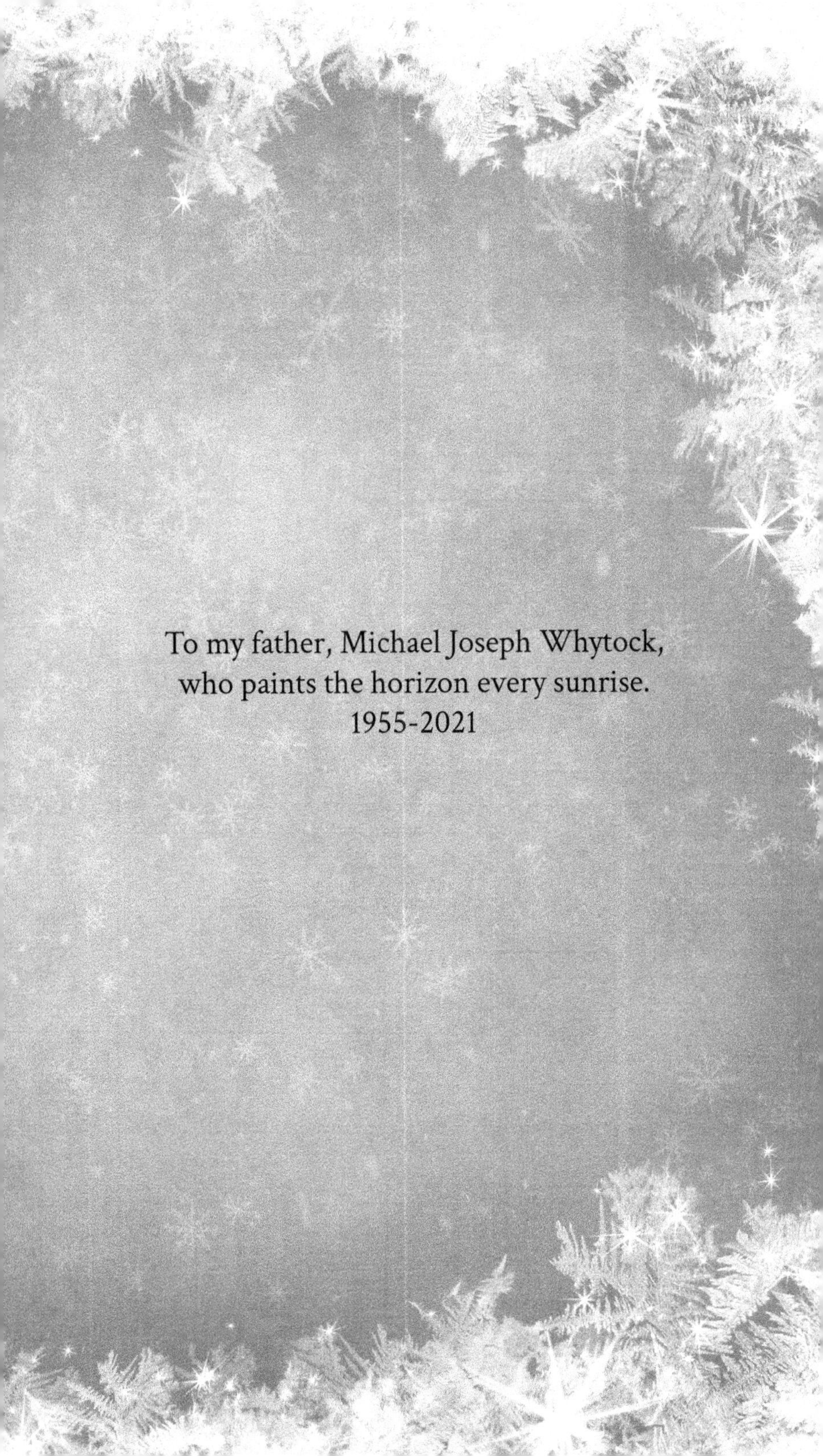

To my father, Michael Joseph Whytock,
who paints the horizon every sunrise.
1955-2021

PROLOGUE

A wet, rasping sound shuddered through the air as the Fae male sprawled on the hard earthy ground took a breath. His limbs shook, sweat dotting his brow, and his grey eyes dim in the veiled prison walls around him.

The skin on half of his face had melted. The muscle and tendon lay exposed, blood carving down the remains of his neck. His half-burned black silk tunic clung to pieces of seared flesh.

He stared at the thick, clouded walls that crawled above him with tendrils of white mist, encapsulating him. Rage burned through his chest in hot coils, but he couldn't move. His bones screamed with every twitch, his face tearing with every breath.

Chest quivering, he took in a strained drag of air. Blood sputtered from his lips, and he choked on the copper liquid, a trail of fire going down his throat. His body convulsed, drowning in his own blood, back arching and fingers clawing the ground.

He forced his body to roll onto its side and threw up. Bright red blood and saliva dribbled from his mouth as he gasped for breath. Falling onto his back again, his body went numb as he stared at the prison ceiling.

A sudden chill fell over him, slicing through the cold that had already seeped into his body. Forcing his head to turn, his eyes fell on the figure that appeared from the mist.

Bone-thin limbs were shrouded in a simple black robe and snow-white hair framed sallow skin. Deep, blood-red eyes stared at the male with a dark curiosity.

The Fae coughed again, blood wetting his lips.

Thin lips curved, and a heinous smile gleamed while blood eyes darkened.

'Wha...?' The male's words were brittle, his throat contracting with every sound. 'What are—' His words faltered with another cough.

The creature's head cocked and walked over to the Fae, hovering over his body.

'Death becomes you,' it said quietly in a low, haunting voice.

Looking into the bloody depths of the eyes that watched him, the Fae forced his words out. 'Save...me.'

A savage gleam lit up its red stare. The creature vanished into black mist, appearing at the Fae's feet on all fours. It crawled up the burned body with quick movements, hovering over melted flesh. A black tongue poked between razor teeth, and it dragged it across the exposed muscle with a hiss. It left a glistening trail, cackling when the Fae jerked under him, a cry of pain snapping through the air.

'It will cost you,' it said.

The male's eyes raged with a burning hatred. 'I...don't...care,' he bit out with a gasp.

Dragging the crooked ridge of its nose across the male's face, the creature asked, 'What do I get in return?'

'Everything.'

Fingers lengthened with bony ridges; nails turned to claws that dug into the melted flesh. The creature forced the Fae's jaw open, smiling at the cry of pain.

'Deals with the dammed and dead are soul binding, Elf.'

A low hissing echoed around them, and the air became a capsule of ice as it opened its mouth. Its jaw expanded to unnatural lengths, bones cracking, and a thick black tar sapped from its mouth into the male below it.

Gagging, the elf sputtered and choked. The tar slid down his throat like hot coals, his body igniting in a scorching blaze before turning glacial. His eyes screwed tight, limbs contorting, back arching off the ground.

Dragging a claw across the male's lip, the creature smiled, licking the tar from its finger. Standing, it watched the male take a steady breath, his limbs shuddering once, then stilling.

Grey eyes turned black, opening to stare at the creature looming over him with predatory intent. He sat up, his fingers going to his face, ghosting over the ridges of scars that puckered the once-melted flesh.

Standing, the male was eye-level with the creature, and something pulsated beneath his skin, dragging razor-sharp talons across his bones. His skin rippled with anticipation, a cynical smile turning up his mouth.

'I tell you this, Elf,' it said with a voice that echoed around them. 'I will collect my pets. And when I do, I will collect your debt.'

The male's black eyes faded to grey, the scars pulling at his mouth when he spoke. 'What is my debt?'

The same heinous smile gleamed coldly, and the creature ran his claws down the male's face.

'*Everything,*' it hissed.

Whorls of black spiralled under the male's skin. He felt those talons carve into his bones, but he didn't feel pain. He felt starved. The demons inside him whispered with promises, wants, and need. A chill went through his limbs. They wanted blood.

'Your name, Elf,' the creature demanded quietly.

A jilting smile lifted the Fae's mouth. 'Balwin.'

'From light to dark, you are now soul-bound to me, Balwin of the Fae. You will see me again, and I will collect what is mine.'

The creature vanished into a black mist, the remnants of its pointed smile lingering before disappearing entirely.

Balwin lunged for the creature, falling through the shadows, grasping at nothing. He was alone, surrounded by the walls of white fog that slithered around him.

Like an iron in the fire, his blood boiled with ravaging anger. A snarl cut through the silence, and he swiped a scarred hand through the fog. Their spindled fingers teased him as they parted, only to knit back together.

His hands sliced through the walls, digging his way into the white abyss, only to return to the patch of dirt he had started from.

Balwin's chest heaved, nostrils flaring with rage. The demons within clawed at his insides, his heartbeat ticking the seconds that went by. His head went numb, and a roaring filled his ears, fingers balling into fists. His nails cut into his palms, blood dripping to the ground.

The demons pulsed beneath his skin like a final stretch of his control, and the tether *snapped*.

His scream ripped through the prison walls that barely moved in acknowledgement. He fell to his knees, the cut of stone digging into his flesh as blinding hatred settled in his bones. And with eyes as black as night, he stared into the white mists and waited.

CHAPTER ONE

Everything burned around her. The world was ablaze, the roar of flames filled the air, and the forest threatened to collapse.

So, she ran.

Picking up her skirt, she sprinted through the tunnel of fire. The snapping of wood in her ears, branches nothing more than red-hot embers reaching for her with spindle fingers.

A ragged cry tore through her burning lungs, and she held her hands to her face as fiery sparks erupted in her path.

The roar of the fire wrecked a trail through her mind, sweat dotting her brow as the clammy tang of fear went up her spine.

Her heart leapt from her chest when the fire parted, and she could see a shadow of white in the distance. Her feet pounded beneath her, the minuscule fabric of her slippers tearing against the rocks. But she didn't care and kept sprinting for the light.

The forest around her thinned, and fire winked out like a snuffed candle. Then she was running through a black fog, the light ahead vanishing.

She screamed into the darkness, shadows surrounding her. There was nothing, and then everything, and she was falling.

Her silver-blue eyes pinched tight as she free-fell into the abyss, her dark hair a curtain around her.

Light suddenly flooded her, and she blinked rapidly. Gasping softly when she stared down at herself. The swells of her breast rose and fell against the constricting stays covered by crimson satin, the fabric flaring at her waist into a waterfall of gleaming red.

She brought a hand to her face, feeling the soft brush of velvet. Her eyes scanned the candlelit ballroom as faces hidden by masks danced to the lulling sounds of the orchestra perched on a dais in the middle of the dance floor. The cello and violin reverberated in a dark symphony.

Marble gleamed under her swaying feet as she hummed a note from the music, following the path of the stone walls dancing in and out of the marble pillars that lined the edge of the dance floor. Bodies came together and parted, circling each other in a dance of intrigue and silence. Secretive eyes, and hidden agendas, wove a tangible web like a feline looking for a mouse.

Her slippered feet brushed against the marble as she stepped into the shadows. Light from the torches hung overhead in their sconces, casting everything in a fiery dim glow.

The air was rich with perfume, shrouding her in a thick blanket. Her eyes became half-mast behind the cover of velvet, breathing in heavily the intoxicating scent of the night.

Wind blew through the dimly lit ballroom, candlelight flickering in protest. She looked at the dual iron doors at the end of the room to see them cast open. A masked man stood there with still ease, backlit by the night sky, dressed in all black. His dark hair fell in waves to the nape of his neck like ebony wine, gold skin glowing in the candlelight.

Her breath hitched in her chest, silver eyes watching him with curious fixation. He slid through the bodies like a whisper.

She watched him scan the dance floor, dipping into the horde of masked dancers when they parted. Her erratic pulse beat in her ears when she lost sight of him. She picked up her heavy satin skirt and entered the dance in step with the music. She moved to the other side of the ballroom, swaying and turning with the dancers.

Hands grabbed her waist and pulled her into the dance, and she made a sound of protest. The world around her blurred together, spinning in time with the music.

With a firm grip, she shoved the man's hands off her and spun into the crowd gathered around the dance floor.

Closing her eyes briefly, she brushed a soothing hand down her gown.

'Anabelle…'

She faintly heard her name, but it fell on deaf ears. Her eyes caught sight of the masked man slipping through an interlocked couple. Her heart stopped when he paused as if feeling her stare, and he turned, his gaze snapping to her.

With floating strides, he cut a path to her. His eyes were the same colour as his mask. Dark green with silver lining the brims. Those dark eyes held hers in their own dance, and the world around them vanished as he bowed before her.

A hand outstretched to her as he straightened, and the slight upturn of his lips caused Anabelle to smile back when he looked at her.

'Shall we?'

His voice was deep and warm, but she still felt a shiver run down her back. Placing her hand in his, he took her in his arms just as the dark lulling sounds of the waltz filled the air. Her body was flush with his, his arm a steady band around her back. The other couples melted away.

Turning them in time with the music, Anabelle's eyes never strayed from his until crisp winter air touched her exposed skin, and the swells of her breasts prickled with gooseflesh in protest against the frigid chill.

He took her hand, but she hesitated, eyeing the forest that fenced the paved garden. A tug on her hand was all it took when she looked at those green eyes.

She followed him down the stone steps into the open air, her hand on his arm. Bare forest thicket surrounded them, dead leaves covering the floor like a graveyard. The pale full moon was high in the cloudless night sky.

His thumb brushed against her knuckles as he pulled her into his arms and danced with her against the pale starlight. The romanticism of the dark waltz clung to their every step as it took them deeper into their own private world, held tightly together by a thread of unknown longing.

The waltz ended, and Anabelle dropped her gaze to their intertwined hands, his skin like gold next to her alabaster complexion.

'My sweet, Anabelle,' he whispered in her ear, bending to place a chaste kiss on her bare shoulder.

His breath fanned over her skin, and she shuddered.

With skilled fingers, one hand slid up to her knotted curls, and he released her hair in gentle waves down her back.

'My beautiful Anabelle.'

Her lips parted, and the skin where his lips had been tingled with anticipation. Knots of wanting and intrigue wove their way through the fibres of her body, heat pooling in her stomach.

He lifted her hand to his mouth and brushed a kiss on her knuckles. Her pulse was like molasses in winter, and she felt the swells of her breasts push against the stays that bound her, the friction maddening against her skin.

His eyes flickered with promise, letting her hands go when he stepped back.

'Until our next.'

The world around him shifted, and he disappeared into a cloak of shadows.

She stood there under the pale moonlight, a hand resting around her waist, the other at her heart. Then the chill swept through her like a knife, and she took the path inside, her mind still in a haze.

'Anabelle?'

Silver-blue eyes shot open against the light peeking into the room through the crack in the cotton drapes. With a groan, Anabelle stretched, rolling away from the sliver of light.

Remnants of the lulling waltz whispered through her mind, and then the roar of fire and the numbing cold of the darkness took its place. Blinking at the ceiling, she screwed her eyes shut, rubbing them vigorously before opening them.

Her nightmare had turned into such a lovely dream, and she could still see the candlelit ballroom and bodies floating in unison across marble floors, music filling the air.

Sighing, she pushed her hair over her shoulder and sat up.

Her quiet humming filled her little room as she stepped onto creaking wood floors. Traversing across her room on light feet, she grasped the dark blue fabric and pulled back the drapes with a flourish, sunlight spearing through the shadows.

Beyond her windowpanes, the lush green forest beckoned. The colourful array of green and blue encompassed the world from her windows, with greying fields laid at its feet.

Undoing the locks, she pushed the double-pane windows open and felt the chilly touch of autumn's breath upon her cheek. The mid-October wind brushed her hair across her face.

Seasons came and went as they pleased, but the earth around them never sullied at winter's touch and spring's rainfall. It thrived.

Surrounded by hills and beckoning woods that seduced her with adventures, they were alone, nothing for miles in every direction. She had been too young to remember when they had plotted the earth and built this home. Still, the isolation surrounding them was something she enjoyed, craved, even. The frivolous matters of the cities and towns weighed on her heart. She begged for the freedom the world around her provided and the untouched and untainted beauty.

'Anabelle?'

Anabelle turned and found her mother staring at her, a brow raised in question, hands crossed in front of the wool of her dark green dress. Anabelle gave the slightest smile and turned back to the window. Looking back to the forest, Anabelle let out a breath of annoyance when she found the restraints of her cottage confining.

Leaving the window ledge, she danced to her small vanity, nothing more than a wooden table with a porcelain bowl, a comb, and a cloth hung neatly over the lip of the bowl. She heard her mother start straightening the unmade bed, and she could almost feel her amusement. She would always be a child in her mother's eyes. Although with tired attempts of ageing with a mature grace requested by society, she still felt like a child, even though she had long surpassed those years. Her twentieth year was only a week away.

'It's almost noon, Anabelle. What could have possibly kept you in bed for so long? Do you feel unwell?'

Her mother pressed a hand to her forehead, and Anabelle pushed it away with a purse of her lips. Grabbing the wooden comb, she hummed the hypnotic lull of the waltz, running the teeth through the near-black waves and pulling it back with a copper ribbon. Her eyes stared back at her in the mirror, alight with curiosity that made them glow in the mid-morning sunlight.

'Anabelle?'

'Oh, it's nothing, Mother. I'm not sick, do not worry yourself,' she said, pulling out an indigo-blue cotton dress from her wardrobe. Simple by nature and social stature. Cream lace lined the modest scoop of the bodice and edges of the sleeves that fell just shy of her elbows. Anabelle took one look at the taut stays that sat primly at the bottom of her wardrobe and gave it a terrible scowl before shutting the doors on it.

Her mother chuckled, noticing the look she gave the garment.

'You're going to be the death of us in society, love,' she said, walking over to help her daughter dress. Holding the neck open, Anabelle slid her arms into the sleeves. Turning her daughter around, she laced up the back.

Anabelle glanced over her shoulder, trying to get a look at

her mother. 'I don't need to go out into society. I can stay right here, with you, with the forest, where I can be a heathen without judgment! I'll dance naked with pixies for all I care. Damn them all! I thought 1740 was supposed to be progressive?'

Her mother gave her an incredulous look. 'Language, Anabelle.'

She tucked the loose ends into her dress's skirt, grabbed a lone cotton apron, and secured the cream fabric around her daughter's waist with a bow.

'You spend more time in those trees than in this cottage. I'm surprised you're not a wild thing.'

Anabelle let a laugh slip through as she pictured herself swinging from branch to branch.

'Is that so wrong? To be a wild thing? To be a creature of freedom, bound to no socialite needs and wants.'

She smoothed a hand down the front of her apron, her fingers finding the dried remains of a flower in the pocket at her waistband.

Isadora smiled to herself, emotions clouding her eyes as she rested a hand on her daughter's shoulders.

'I find that ladies of your age have wed and bred their own wee babes or are seeking a husband at the very least. My daughter wishes to become an ape.' She mostly muttered the last bit for herself, but Anabelle heard her.

With a deep sigh, Isadora tucked her hands behind her apron as she stared at her daughter. 'You do wish to marry?'

Anabelle gave no hesitation because she knew the answer, just as her mother knew the answer. They had this conversation many times prior.

'No, I find men of this world to be barbaric.'

Her mother gave a short laugh, busying herself around the room as she straightened non-existent flaws.

'Oh? Then in what world, dearest, would you find the right man? Because I'm afraid, this is the only one I know of.'

Anabelle's fingers rubbed the dried petals between her fingertips, studying them. 'I don't know. Perhaps between the pages of my novels, one filled with magic or something close to its existence.'

Flashes of candlelight and the overhang of rich perfume filled her vision.

'I know it is,' Anabelle said. 'I dream of it. It's like the stories of Avalon. How can a world like that not exist? If they write about it, then there must be a fragment of truth somewhere.'

Isadora's steps were silent as she faced her daughter, turning her chin with gentle fingers. Seeing Anabelle's face full of so many emotions, she touched her cheek gently. 'Who do you see?'

She bit her lip, releasing it as she met her mother's identical silver-blue eyes peering curiously at her.

'I don't know,' she said with a shake of her head.

'Oh, my darling,' Isadora sighed, bringing her close and hugging her tight before stepping back. 'Dreams are funny that way. They have a way of altering reality. One must never confuse the two.'

Anabelle looked away and stepped around her mother to pick up a pair of black boots.

'You're right, Mother. After all, it is just a dream.' She gave her mother a small smile and disappeared from the room.

The brightly-lit drawing room greeted Anabelle as she slipped into the quarters.

Shelves upon shelves were stacked high with books, between fiction and science, fairy tales and romantics—and she had read them all. Those books knew her well, and she, them; every page, every tear, every scent. Anabelle let her body fall back into a well-cushioned armed chair, taking the time to slip her boots on. The chair's high back obscured her from the view of the windows behind her.

Anabelle stood, strolling to the bookshelves. Lithe fingers trailed lovingly across the stiff spines.

'Are my dreams the same as you? A memory of a memory imprinted into my bones, fictitious tales my mind has woven to escape this world of marriage and expectation. If only...'

'Anabelle?' called her mother from down the hall.

'I'm leaving, Mother!'

She hurried her way through the maze of beige walls and creaking floors. She found her way through the cottage doors to the open embrace of nature. Happily, she stepped onto the gravel road ahead.

The wind blew suddenly, as if in greeting, and she felt it propel her forward. It spoke to her, whispering secrets she did not understand. She laughed at the freedom of it, feeling as it swept through her hair, the ribbon coming undone. Dark curls tangled in the breeze, and Anabelle felt as free as a bird.

The wind held a bite in its breath, and a shiver rolled down her body. Giving in, grasping the folds of her dress, she ran through the fields to the forest that lay just within her grasp.

With a gasp, Anabelle gave a great burst of speed. She laughed gaily at the freedom, basking in the barely-warm sun.

She stopped short at the forest edge. Sunlight could be seen streaming in through the tree's thickets, dust sparkling like drops of starlight in the glow. Gold and green covered the forest. Nature was still holding onto the last breaths of fall.

She stepped cautiously into the thicket as if not to disturb the peace found within the growth, holding her breath. Warmth enveloped her, and Anabelle closed her eyes to the feeling, inhaling the earthy scent that curled its way around her limbs.

A bird broke the silence from above, and Anabelle continued forward, a smile on her lips that was likened to a child. The chains of society loosened around her.

Townspeople spoke of this forest like it was cursed, strewn with Fae folk and magic. Perhaps they were right, but she didn't care. She would take a cursed forest over the dying societal town.

Anabelle hummed a tune unknown to her about snow melting and other magic things coming to life. Cursed forest be damned.

'The chill has gone, the frost has died, and winter has fled our sights. Come, my fairy friends, won't you dance in the summer nights? The moon is full, and the stars are bright, come and dance in the summer nights.'

A giggle broke through the melody, and she saw something flash in the corner of her eye. Her voice quieted as she turned to her right. Laughter to her left carried her in the same direction.

'Hello?'

Nothing.

Then the forms of two small bodies blurred together just ahead of her, and she chased after them.

'Wait!' she called after the shadows, her booted feet careening over roots and moss-covered rocks and across the soft dirt floor.

'Wait!'

They disappeared behind the seclusion of trees, and she followed in pursuit, rounding the corner. Anabelle stopped short. A clearing stood before her. A small pool of water lazily floated in the middle of tall grass, surrounded by massive moss-ridden stones and glimmering dewdrops.

It was new to her, yet it wasn't. It was a quiet place; something about it made nostalgia creep within her mind like a lost friend.

Carefully, she approached the rocks and sat on their mossy ledge. The water reflected the brightness of the sky. Peering down, she tried to scan the inky depths but couldn't see past the watery surface.

The mid-morning sun warmed her back, and she cupped a hand in the chilly water. Bringing it to her lips, she drank, surprised when she found a lingering sweetness that coated her tongue. She drank once more and stood, walking to the edge of the clearing. Dragging a hand across thick trunks, rough bark scraped her skin.

Movement rustled behind her, and she turned to find her copper ribbon hanging from the low limb of a tree, glinting in the light innocently.

With a tilt of her head, Anabelle stepped forward. She plucked it from the branch, turning it over and looking for any sign of someone or something, but she found nothing—much to her disappointment. She returned to where she had found the ribbon and looked closer beyond the trees.

There, laid upon the forest floor, was a path. A well-trodden trail, though Anabelle was sure no one but herself had walked among the forest for many, many years.

Intrigue made her follow it, and she soon found herself back at the forest edge, her cottage just down the hill.

Frowning, she turned back. She would have known if a trail had been there. She knew every inch of the forest. Intrigue and confusion pulled at her, edging her to return, to investigate further, but she trampled it down.

Instead, tying her ribbon tightly to the branch of a tree, she marked her hidden path.

'Anabelle!'

Anabelle looked over her shoulder, acknowledging her mother's voice. Giving one more fleeting glance to the forest, she turned on booted heels and made her way leisurely to the cottage.

CHAPTER TWO

Isadora sat idly in a chair by the kitchen bay window the following day as Anabelle strolled into the room. Seeing her cup of tea and scone across from her mother's, she took the place opposite her. Her mother had her nose in a book, and Anabelle's nose crinkled in amusement.

She had her mother's silver eyes and dark hair, though they varied in comparison to each other. Her mother had never remarried after her father died when she was an infant, much to the chagrin of gossip in town. Pity was evident behind guarded eyes when they went to town. Anabelle paid them no mind, ignoring them almost entirely if she could help it.

'Do I have a bug stuck in my nose?' Isadora questioned dryly from her book, not bothering to look up as she turned a page.

Anabelle choked on the pastry, picturing a bug halfway in her mother's nostril, wiggling about. Taking a sip of tea, she cleared her throat and chuckled.

'No, but I must admit, I would find that highly amusing.'

Isadora set the book down and broke off a piece of scone, giving her a pointed stare.

'Well, you are certainly your father's daughter,' she said, adding, 'Especially when you're being stubborn.'

Anabelle shook her head, sitting back in the chair in thought.

'Well, I'm delighted to provide you with some sort of variety. How boring your days might be if I were not so keen to destroy the normalcy of everyday life.'

'Aren't I lucky, then?' she teased. 'I have a forest nymph for a daughter. The war upon modern-day ladies' fashion has only just begun.'

Anabelle rolled her eyes. 'Yes, aren't you lucky, indeed? I might even scare off a potential husband, or perhaps, I'll gain one, via flouncing around fields in only my slip and flowers tucked wildly into my hair.'

Isadora's eyes rolled as she rubbed a hand across her face, her mouth twisting into a weary smile. 'Very well, and what would convince you to marry?'

Tapping her chin in thought, Anabelle's brow pulled tight, distaste for the notion sitting on her tongue. However, she stated nonetheless, 'I suppose one's masculinity would have to trump my own.'

Isadora blinked twice, staring at her daughter. 'I'm sorry, come again?'

Anabelle righted herself in her seat, staring down at the last dregs of her tea. Tea leaves floated lazily at the bottom.

'Anything I need in life, I can obtain without a man. I can farm and feed myself, take care of chores and, try if I might, maintain a house if I put my mind to it. They may call me a spinster, but why should my life depend on a man? If he can add to it, then by all means. If not, well, I'm afraid most gentlemen of today's standing are, without a doubt, more concerned with mating rituals and gambling their lives away for wealth. I do not want a life shrouded in that sort of madness. If a man cannot give me a life I want or need, I shall be my own woman. Social grace may rot.'

Isadora studied her daughter as Anabelle stared out the window, tea in hand. She would never force her to marry, but as any mother, she wanted to protect her. Anabelle knew her mind, and Isadora felt a mother's pride thrill inside her. Glancing to the basket she had made up, she propped an elbow on the table, head in hand.

'What do you plan to do for the rest of the day?'

'What I usually do. Find a book, and read until I forget where I am entirely.'

'Have you read all the books already?'

She hummed quietly in thought. 'I believe so, though if a book is good, you can read it over and over again without ever tiring of it.'

Finishing the last of her scone and tea, Isadora looked at her daughter. 'Would you like to buy a new one?'

Anabelle stared at her mother, surprised. 'You mean to go into town and buy one? Today?'

Isadora gave her a wry smile, standing to clear the dishes. 'Yes, Anabelle, that is where books are normally found.'

Anabelle thought hard on that proposal. She could stay home. Her mother wouldn't object and flit around the cottage. Or she could go to town and buy a new book. She had read all the novels in the drawing room and the study. She could use a new adventure. She hadn't been to town since she had bought her last book months ago.

Her lips pressed together. 'I suppose it is that time again. So I don't completely forget how to act like a civilised person.'

Isadora laughed at her daughter's disconcert for leaving their little plot of land. 'You are plenty civilised, sweet. Don't let anyone tell you else wise.'

She came to her daughter's side and kissed her brow, lightly tapping the tip of her nose. 'Don't you worry, we'll get your book and come straight home. We'll be home before the night falls, I promise.'

Anabelle let out a puff of air, brushing a curl over her shoulder. 'You must admit that this society has silly rules that should be overlooked. I mean, must I always wear a coat when I go out? What about a hat? The sun is so delightful that neither is required, yet society demands it for impiety. Dare you be labelled the town whore.'

She huffed, tucking the curl behind her ear when it slipped back over her shoulder.

'A man could walk around half-naked if he so chooses, and society would hardly bat an eye, let alone look twice. No rumours, no whispered words, a man's world indeed.'

She stood up, hands on her hips like a child, her fingers tapping against the cotton dress impatiently. She stuck her chin out after a momentary thought.

'I won't wear either into town.'

Although Isadora tried to restrain her smile and laugh, she failed to remain very serious. 'I won't make you, darling, let them talk. Who are they to judge?'

Anabelle gave a curt nod, letting her arms drop to her sides. 'I'll get ready, then.'

'Don't take too long. We're leaving soon!' Isadora called exasperatedly after her daughter as she swept from the kitchen.

Gravel crunched underfoot as the two women made their way down the pebbled path, the sun high in the sky, beating upon their brows with failed attempts at warmth. A small coin purse hung from Isadora's wrist; a basket was hooked at the crook of her elbow as she strode next to Anabelle, a wool shawl wrapped tightly around her shoulders.

Glancing at her daughter, she noted her delighted face turned to the distant sun, a satisfied smile turning up the corners of her mouth.

Anabelle felt her mother's stare and returned it. 'Yes?'

Isadora just shook her head. 'Nothing, my dear.'

'No, come, tell me your secrets!' Anabelle pleaded, batting her eyelashes.

'Hmm…' She tapped her chin in thought. 'No, I think I shall keep it to myself.'

The aghast face her daughter made caused her to chortle. She wasn't thinking anything of importance, so to tease her made for good amusement as the road stretched out beneath them.

Anabelle turned around and began to walk backwards. 'You really are a cruel mother. Although,' she said thoughtfully, 'if you gave away all of your secrets just because I asked, then I suppose there wouldn't be any real mystery, would there?'

'No, I assume not.'

Anabelle stared at the grassy bluffs around them, eyes watching the sea of grass drift in the wind.

'Mother, may I ask you something?'

She bent to pluck the stem of a semi-wilted purple wildflower from the ground, twirling it between her fingertips.

Isadora looked at her daughter as she played with the flower. 'What's on your mind, love?'

'Nothing, really, just a momentary thought.' She looked at her mother with questions in her eyes. 'What made you move us away from town, into the country, when I was little?'

Isadora's steps halted, and she looked down at the dirt and gravel beneath her feet. Anxiety gnawed at her insides as a wave of bile rose. Tugging on a thread of control, she righted herself. She smoothed a now-clammy hand over her dress and gave Anabelle a tight smile.

'Why do you ask?'

She shrugged. 'I don't know.'

Tossing the flower to the ground, she looked up at the sky, squinting against the harsh light.

'I try to remember the past,' Anabelle said. 'But I can't. I don't remember anything except for our time at the cottage. Although, I must admit that the first year is also a blur. I was very young when we moved. I suppose it isn't unusual for me not to remember. After all, I was only a babe.'

Isadora felt her heart clench, and a tightening in her stomach sent another wave of nausea as she suppressed a sigh.

'Not unusual t'all, a child of five years is feigned to remember anything. Don't worry yourself with the past, my love. Focus on the present. You're living in it.'

Anabelle grinned at her mother.

'Am I?' she asked in a hushed tone, looking about as if to make sure no one was listening. 'I thought I was living in the future. I thought I had travelled through time from a different land, mayhap a different planet altogether!'

Isadora laughed freely, swatting Anabelle on her hindquarters. 'Little minx, keep your nose out of such things when in town.'

A twinkle sat brightly in Anabelle's eyes, and she grinned. 'Don't I always, Mother?'

'No!'

The autumn day had been kind and gave them a warm day with a light breeze to keep the heat from blistering their skin. Mile after mile, they walked, the path growing smaller and now scattered with flowers, tall weeds, and grass. They hadn't travelled this road in months, and it had become overrun as nature reclaimed it.

It had been some time since they had gone to town. They didn't want for anything, keeping to their humble lifestyle. Isadora kept a garden behind the house for various fruits and vegetables that flourished all year save the winter season, and they had already begun to harvest the garden for winter.

In the warmer seasons, they ate mainly what they grew. In the winter, they hunted for meat. The town was seven miles, approximately, from their cottage. Though it was not an easy task, they could accomplish it nonetheless.

Anabelle stretched her arms above her head and groaned as she felt her muscles sigh in relief. Looking to the sky and then the path they had been on for the last hour, she felt her legs ache. Anabelle needed to run. The thought of going into town made her body protest in every way it could think. Giving in to temptation, she ran for the fields, leaving her mother behind.

Isadora wasn't the least surprised, sighing as she watched Anabelle gather her skirts and toss care to the wind, sprinting ahead. Going into town was as if she were sending her daughter into an ocean full of hungry sharks. Society never got used to Anabelle's rebellion of conforming. So, she walked on alone, quite content, knowing her daughter was somewhere in the overgrowth, unseen.

Anabelle felt as free as a bird as she ran through the mounds of grass, the weeds tall and willowy, coming to her waist. She ran her fingertips over the tops and felt their feathered touch along her skin.

Stopping, she breathed in deeply as the wind blew, caressing her. Her dress clung to her body, hair dancing behind her. If only she were a bird! Then she could fly! The thought crossed her mind, and she frowned. She glanced at the birds flying overhead, envious of their feathered bodies and hollow bones.

Rustling came from the brush and a grey rabbit ran past, an orange and cream fox in quick pursuit.

'Oh!' she exclaimed in surprise, catching her foot on a rock, falling to her hands and knees. Pushing herself up, she sat back on her haunches, dusting the dirt off her palms.

Peering through the ocean of tall grass, she saw the rabbit escape through a hole in the ground, one far too small for the fox. The fox began to dig through the dirt, and Anabelle felt her heart drop for the baby rabbit. She reached out to stop it, but it was too far.

Standing, she ignored the dirt on her dress, tripping on her hem as she stumbled forward. Her heart pounded at the thought of the rabbit, unease coiling in her stomach.

'Wait,' she whispered.

Her words were lost in the wind, and she threw out a hand as she tripped on another buried stone. The ground bit into her knees with a painful stab as the fox worked at the little burrow.

Eyes widening, Anabelle watched it shove its body into the widened opening. Its hind legs pushed its body forward as they dug into the dirt, bushy tail twitching.

With a lurch, Anabelle yelled, 'Stop!'

The world around her seemed to pause: the wind ceased whispering, and the grass halted its dance. The world waited for her command.

The fox turned to her, slowly drawing amber eyes to meet silver ones.

'Leave,' she breathed in a hushed voice.

Her word echoed around her, and the fox's nose twitched once, then twice, before it dashed off into the thicket of grass.

A second later, the world took in a breath and began once more. Sounds rushed in around Anabelle like a wave.

Running to the little burrow, she knelt and peeked inside. Huddled at the very back was a grey rabbit, its little nose twitching.

'It's all right. You can come out now.' She spoke to it as if the creature could understand her.

The rabbit's ears twitched in response to her voice, but didn't heed it. Anabelle reached in and wrapped her fingers around the small body, feeling it kick in protest. With both hands, she held the rabbit to face her. It had little ears sticking up, a tiny black nose, and the softest fur coat.

She brought the animal to her breast. It couldn't have been more than a couple of weeks old.

'Did you lose your mother?'

It curled into her chest, burrowing into the warmth her skin offered.

'Well, don't worry, you can be in my family.'

She stood and carefully walked back to the path, her mother just shortly behind her. Waiting, she sat down on the grassy slope, cooing to the small animal and stroking the space between its ears.

'What do you have there?'

'The newest member of our family,' she said, standing to show her mother the baby rabbit in her arms, safely nestled in the crook of her elbow.

Isadora raised her brows. 'A rabbit for a stew, I suppose?'

Anabelle protested, aghast at her mother's words, her mouth agape in horror.

'A baby rabbit! Not a *stew* rabbit! A fox was chasing it. I couldn't just let it be eaten!' She peered at her mother firmly. 'Don't you dare think of eating her!'

Isadora held her hands up in surrender. 'I'm only teasing. Gods forbid if I were to eat her.' She gave her a soft smile, raising a brow. 'Sometimes I think you're younger than your actual age, m'dear.'

'Is that a problem? If we all acted the age we bore, life would be dull and painful. To get older means to stop believing in the unseen. Like the unseen life of a rabbit! Look how loving she is!' She paused momentarily, her attention returning to the bundle of fur in her hands. 'Well, I think it's a "she"…how can you tell?'

Anabelle's face scrunched as she turned the rabbit over, checking for a sign of its sex, but came up short. With a shrug, she said, 'Oh well, guess we'll never know.'

Isadora rolled her eyes. 'What are you going to name it? Since you don't know its gender, you should give it a name for both sexes.'

Anabelle looked at the rabbit, which was once again sleeping in her arms. 'What about Fox?'

Isadora gave her a dull look. 'Just a little ironic, sweet, don't you think?'

'There is a case of irony in all the best things, Mother.' She chewed her lip, thinking. 'Pepper, I'm going to call it Pepper. Though I believe I am going to refer to Pepper as a girl. It just seems right. I can feel it.'

'For the colour, I suppose?'

'Well, you said Fox was ironic.'

Isadora chuckled under her breath and shook her head.

CHAPTER THREE

The looming highlands of Kinzig Valley swept ahead of them as they trekked on, reaching the top in minutes. At the bottom stood the town of Gutach, nestled at the base of a mountain. Rhine River cut neatly around its outer edge, and thick forest walls surrounded the crevice. The forest that no one dared enter except hunters because they thought they were haunted by Fae.

As they strolled down the dirt path, one could tell the advances of the century were taking over the growing settlement. Cobblestone streets, stone buildings, houses, and farms lay just on the outskirts, with fresh markets, a schoolroom, and a quaint library. Homes made grander by marble and iron sat proudly away from town, seeming to glimmer in the daylight.

It seemed odd to Anabelle as she stood overlooking the town, observing. In the middle of this high valley of land was this town. As if it had just been placed there with a wave of a hand. It didn't belong, at least in her mind's eye. It seemed foreign to her in a way it hadn't before.

'Shall we?' her mother asked.

A familiar hand flashed in Anabelle's mind, a warm smile and dark velvet-green eyes. She forced the memory of the dream out of her mind, ignoring the warmth in her cheeks. Suddenly, she wished she was sleeping so she could dream again and maybe see the masked stranger who seemed to have captured her mind.

'Just a dream, Anabelle,' she muttered.

'What's that?'

Anabelle shook her head. 'Nothing.'

'Well, come on. The day won't wait for us.'

She followed her mother down the hill, the town looming ahead.

It wasn't a comfortable feeling, walking the cobblestone streets, passing by row houses and areas of business. The shops of cobblers, blacksmiths, seamstresses, healers, and more lined the main road. Everything was grey as if winter's chill had already blanketed the town in bleakness.

The warm autumn air was nowhere to be found as they journeyed further into the maze. The sky overhead was still as blue, but the sun was absent, and a crisp breeze caused Anabelle to wrap her arms around herself, hoping it would help keep it at bay. Her skin rippled with the chill.

'It's cold.'

Isadora glanced at her daughter as they turned a corner onto a street with various bakeries and a single bookshop. 'It is autumn, darling.'

'No,' Anabelle said, shaking her head. 'There isn't any life here.'

Isadora clucked her tongue. 'Hush, darling, we'll be home soon enough.'

Anabelle followed her mother into the second bakery they came upon. *Lily's Bakery* was scrawled in simple font across the front of the window. Her mother and the owner, Lily, had become mutual partners. Her mother would give Lily vegetables from their summer crop in exchange for yearly flour and butter. The quality of her mother's fruits and vegetables had kept that trade healthy since she was a child.

'Lily?' Isadora called out into the empty room.

The bakery was dreary, even as warm, delicious scents wafted through the air. Anabelle's mouth watered, and she licked her lips.

A rustle came from the back, and a plump woman with salt and pepper hair appeared behind a curtain, blocking the doorway.

'Isadora, how nice to see you. I suppose you're here for flour?'

'Butter, actually. We still have plenty of flour at the cottage,' she said, smiling at the woman.

Anabelle looked the older woman over. She wore a faded blue dress, and her hair swept into a bun, though a few strands had come loose. Her cheeks were flushed, and there was a splay of flour under her left eye.

'I'll be just a minute,' Lily said, hurrying into the backroom again. Anabelle turned to the wooden boxes, each filled with different things, some with plain bread and others with treats.

'Do you see anything you would like?' Isadora asked.

'Hmm,' Anabelle mused, plucking a sticky roll from a crate. 'I'll have this.'

'Ah, an apple roll,' commented Lily as she returned with two large jars. 'Made with your very own apples, Isadora.'

Anabelle brought the treat to her nose, smelling the scent of apples coming through the roll's outer crust.

'Do you have a carriage or basket you can take this in?'

'I'm afraid not, Lily,' Isadora answered.

Lily shook her head, the knot atop her head wobbling dangerously. 'You never do. I'll send it to your cottage with our carriage. My husband will take you back. I'll have him wait until you're ready to return.'

Isadora smiled, reaching into her small purse and giving the woman a copper for the pastry. 'Thank you, Lily, you're too kind.'

The woman's nose twitched at the compliment. Anabelle hid her tiny bit of amusement at the woman's discomfort.

Once outside, she bit into the pastry, tasting the sweetness of her mother's apples, the flaky bread practically melting on her tongue. It was delicious, and her stomach grumbled in agreement. She pulled off a small piece and held it under Pepper's nose. It twitched at the smell, and she cautiously nibbled at it. Anabelle pulled out a slice of apple and fed that to her as well.

The clop of hooves echoed on the cobblestone street, and a woman's shriek pierced Anabelle's ears. Her heart thundered in her chest as her head jerked up. Eyes wide, she watched in horror as a small boy wobbled into the street from the walkway.

His tousled head of russet curls and pale skin glowed in the light, brown eyes gleaming as he laughed. The boy was unaware of the danger as he tripped forward, pushing to his feet and running towards one of the horse buggies.

Anabelle's heart skidded to a stop, and she was moving before she realised what was happening. Putting Pepper on the ground, she sprinted to the boy. Her toes dug into the uneven surface, balancing as she slipped on a crack, arms flailing to keep her upright. She was still half a dozen stores down from him but willed herself faster.

The horse reared, a wild neigh surrounding them as the driver yelled at the boy to move. The woman screamed again, and the boy turned to look at her, his face pulling into a frown. A strangled wail rose up as the boy began to cry.

Dodging around a man who yelled at her as she rammed into his shoulder, she only hiked her skirts higher, booted feet carrying her down the centre of the street. Her hand reached out for the boy, and her brows pulled tight as her face twisted in fear, claws of ice tearing up her spine.

The horse reared up again, its hooves cutting dangerously close to those russet curls.

With a lurch, Anabelle threw herself to her knees, jerking the boy to her body as she wrapped an iron grip around his back, twisting herself to shield him.

Fear, icy hot, tore through her body. She felt like the world around her froze over. Freezing terror seemed to seep from her flesh.

Hooves cut over her head, and she pinched her eyes tight, hands curling around the child, waiting for the break of bones and the white-hot pain she knew would follow.

Seconds ticked by into a minute that seemed to stretch into eternity. Anabelle finally pried her eyes open, limbs shaking. A wall of gold and blue ice shimmered around her like a dome. She blinked at the shimmering veil. With a trepidatious hand, she unfurled her fingers and reached for it, but the moment she brushed the veil, it disappeared like a mirage.

The woman's screaming filled Anabelle's ears again, forcing her body to uncoil around the boy. She looked down, and large chocolate brown eyes stared back up at her, filled with tears. His cheeks were splotchy and red, his nose turning pink, and his mouth wobbled as a cry broke loose.

'*Gustav!*'

The boy shoved out of her grip, stumbling to the hysterical woman who must be his mother. Still, Anabelle's gaze wasn't on their reunion. Her eyes fixed on his back as he ran away, and the retreating curl of frost splayed across his back like a handprint.

An iron grip wrapped around her arm and jerked her to her feet.

'Are you bloody mad?' yelled the driver of the buggy.

His breath was rancid, his brown teeth bared, fear and anger in his eyes. Anabelle jerked out of his hold, raising her chin.

'I would mind you, sir,' Isadora said, voice cutting through his shouting, 'to not lay your hands on my daughter.'

Anabelle's head whipped to her mother as she neared, lips pressed into a thin line.

He rounded on Isadora, his rotund belly barely concealed by the brown wool work shirt that stretched across it. 'Keep a tighter leash on her!'

He rounded to the woman and hysterical boy, pointing a meaty finger at the child. 'Mind your child, or you may find him in a box before he grows tired of yer tit!'

The driver stormed back to the skittish horse, laying a flat hand on its large cheek, before climbing back into the buggy.

Anabelle and Isadora quickly moved out of the way as he snapped the reins.

Isadora stroked a soft hand down Anabelle's back, eyeing her carefully. 'Are you okay, love?'

'Yes,' she said softly, watching the mother pull the boy down the street. He fought her, another object or beast catching his eye as he pulled in the opposite direction.

'We can go home?' Isadora offered.

Anabelle shook her head, taking Pepper from her mother's hands. She cradled the tiny creature to her breast as her mind whirled with questions.

'No,' she said, finally. 'I would like a new book since we are already here.'

Isadora eyed the bookshop on the other side of the street, lips tight as she nodded.

'Very well.' She tucked a hand around Anabelle's arm. 'What kind of book would you like, darling?'

'One that has a little bit of everything in it?'

'Is it possible to have such a book?'

Anabelle shrugged. 'Is it possible to fly?'

'Not for people.'

'Nonsense. Of course, people can fly. They just don't try hard enough. Maybe I'll cover myself in feathers and jump off the cottage roof just to prove it to you.' Her lips quirked at the thought, and she glanced at her mother from the corner of her eye.

Isadora shook her head, muttering, 'That would be the day.'

The bell on the bookshop door chimed as they entered, the smell of dust lingering in the air. Anabelle wrinkled her nose, her mother sneezing beside her.

A man with round spectacles perched at the end of his nose popped up from behind a pile of books yet to be shelved—there were many such piles strewn around the bookshop.

'May I help you?' His voice was as covered in dust as the bookshelves.

He stepped out from behind the pile and straightened his dark green vest, flattening a hand over his powdered wig that tilted on his head.

'Yes,' said Anabelle, speaking before her mother could, using as much formality as she could conjure. 'I wish to purchase a novel.'

The man raised a brow, stating dryly, 'Well, certainly, miss. As you can see, we have many.'

Anabelle restrained herself from rolling her eyes. 'I can see that, clearly, thank you, but I don't want just *any* novel. I want one filled with romance and adventure, something new?'

The man coughed. 'Well, we have novels that cover those different elements, but I don't think we have one with all of them together, miss.'

'How disappointing.' She glanced around the bookshop, eyeing the stacks of novels.

'Anabelle, behave, please,' whispered her mother, low enough so the gentleman could not hear.

Nodding absentmindedly, Anabelle moved further into the store, the man and her mother watching as she wandered the aisles. She ran her fingertips over the titles as she passed, noting the various sizes and bindings, old and new. One could say this was the only good thing about the town—and perhaps Lily's exchange with her mother. She couldn't allow herself to be ungrateful.

All the books looked the same; choosing one over another would be difficult.

'Do you categorise them by genre?' she asked in the quietness of the shop. No matter how soft her voice had been, anyone could have heard her.

Footsteps followed her question, and the man appeared behind her. 'I'm afraid not, though I know where each book is and its genre. I catalogue them myself.'

'I see,' she said.

Pride could be heard in his words. He pushed his spectacles up the bridge of his nose as they began to slide, clearing his throat. 'What are you looking for?'

You know what I am looking for, she thought with a sigh, biting the words back. 'A fairy tale?'

He pursed his lips, judgement behind those spectacles. 'I'm afraid we don't have those here. Devil's work within those pages. You will find no such thing upon our shelves.'

Anabelle barely contained the look of annoyance as she looked down the many dust-ridden shelves.

'A romance, perhaps?'

A light lit in his dull eyes. 'That, we might have. Only one, I am afraid.'

He moved down the aisle, turning right and disappearing.

'Hello, miss.'

Anabelle turned, stepping back from the man who stood behind her. It wasn't the small book clerk who stared down at her with startling blue eyes. She swallowed her surprise, her hand wrapping around her waist, looking up at him. 'Can I help you?'

A whisper of a crooked smile tilted his lips, and Anabelle found herself staring at his firm mouth, snapping her eyes back to his.

'Are you looking for a book?' he asked casually.

Anabelle glanced at the rows of novels. 'Well, we are in a bookshop, so one can assume,' she said satirically.

His lips curled, and Anabelle's hand tightened around her waist, shifting her feet.

'You like to read?' he asked, his fingers grazing against the leather and cloth spines.

She followed his fingertips as they travelled across the novels, the fabric of his cream shirt stretching across the solid muscle of his forearm.

Anabelle felt herself blush and cleared her throat. 'I do,' she said. 'Do you have any recommendations?'

'Miss?'

Anabelle's head snapped to the little book clerk who stood behind her, novel in hand. 'Yes, apologies,' she said, smoothing a hand down her dress front. She turned back to the man, pausing when the empty aisle was the only thing she saw.

'Miss?'

Her eyes scanned the row of books quickly, disappointment furrowing her brows. A low cough had her straightening as she turned back to the book clerk.

Holding out the novel to her with a critical eye, he pursed his lips.

Anabelle stared at the title, *Rosalyn's Kiss,* flipping the book open and skimming the pages. Pepper peeked her head over the novel, and with a snap, the book closed, and Anabelle gave the little man a tight smile. 'I'll take this one.'

Following him to the front, she found her mother waiting, paper note in hand.

'Would you like a bill of sale, madam?' he asked, taking the money.

'No, thank you. This will be all.'

'Good day to you both.' He nodded to them as they left, not deigning a glance in their direction.

As they exited the shop, the bell rang overhead, and both women breathed in the fresh air.

'I do believe that shop needs to be dusted,' muttered Isadora discreetly as a man and woman passed by.

Anabelle chuckled and leisurely strolled down the street towards the bakery with her mother, people passing them from every direction. And yet, Anabelle found herself looking over her shoulder for the briefest moment, back at that dusty bookshop.

CHAPTER FOUR

The hushed wind blew through tree branches as it travelled the length of the forest. Light shone through the canopy. Flowers bloomed in masses of different colours, all wild and perfect in their own way.

Children's laughter could be heard from beyond a clearing of trees as a boy and girl sat at the edge of a pond, patches of moss quilting the cut of rocks beneath them. A young woman sat behind the girl, running a wooden comb through the girl's dark chestnut hair. The summer air was thick, but the three hardly noticed, the wind cooling their skin and leaving them content in the sun's ever-present midsummer heat.

The children laughed in each other's company, making odd faces at one another. Tiny, winged Fae sat on branches and roots of surrounding trees, watching in rapturous entertainment.

'Anabelle,' said the boy as he dipped a finger into the pond, making patterns in the water.

'Yes?' she replied, her bright silver-blue eyes staring at her friend. She felt her mother pull her hair gently as she braided it.

'What do you think will happen tonight?' His midnight-black hair shone under the sunlight, and equally dark green eyes stared back at her in question.

'The Fae will choose who will be the Keeper of the Forest.' She looked back at her mother. 'Right, Mamma?'

Her mother smiled down at her. 'Right, my little one.'

Anabelle turned and gave an affirmative nod to the boy. 'But you know this?'

He ducked his head and peeked at the trees where they could see the Faeries sitting, then glanced back at the water before puffing out his chest with pride. 'My father told me I was to be the Keeper, that the ceremony is uncalled for.'

Anabelle tilted her head. 'Do you want to be the Keeper? Even if one of us is to be chosen, we won't be Keeper for many moons.'

She felt her mother squeeze her shoulders.

'Oh, what wise children I have in my midst!' her mother said with a sigh, coming to kneel in front of them. 'Do not fret, loves, on what is to come tonight. Enjoy yourselves.'

The boy looked at her mother, his eyes staring into hers. 'You're already the Keeper. You don't have to worry.'

Her mother smiled gently at the boy, cupping his cheek softly. 'I am the Keeper, but my mother told me the same thing I am telling you.'

Anabelle frowned as her friend's face looked lost; she dipped her fingers into the pond and flicked water at him. He yelped in surprise. Laughing gaily, she shot off the rocky ledge of the pool as he, in turn, splashed her. Her mother stood swiftly to avoid being splashed.

Anabelle ran from the boy as he chased her around the clearing. Laughter once again filled the air as they went round and round. Giving up, Anabelle collapsed to the ground, out of breath. A broad grin covered her face as her chest heaved. The boy fell beside her. Anabelle pulled fistfuls of grass up and threw them at him. He sat up, pulling grass from the ground in retaliation, laughing as the wind picked it up, carrying it off.

Noticing a purple wildflower by her tangled skirts, one of the many *flowers blooming in the willow grass, she plucked it quickly. Gathering her skirt, she got to her knees and pushed herself up, running over to her mother. The skirt of her violet dress caught under her feet, and she stumbled but made it to her mother's side without falling.*

'Yes, love?' her mother asked.

'For you, Mamma,' she said, holding out the purple wildflower.

Her mother gave her a smile as bright as the sun and took the flower, holding it to her nose and smelling it. 'It's beautiful. Thank you, little one.'

Anabelle beamed at her, and her mother bent down, brushing their noses together.

Giggling, Anabelle turned, ready to play some more, but stopped.

Standing at the clearing's edge was a handsome man with black hair and dull grey eyes, his pretty face arrogant and frigid against the sunshine.

'Balwin,' her mother said, coming around to stand before Anabelle.

Anabelle peeked from behind her mother's skirt, glancing at her friend. The laughter that had been there was gone. She frowned.

'Isadora,' Balwin greeted. 'I've come for Gallian.'

'Oh, come, Balwin, let the children play. Tonight is a significant night for them.'

Balwin ignored her mother, snapping at his son. 'Come, Gallian.'

Anabelle turned to Gallian and watched him amble slowly to his father's side, shoulders bent in defeat. Pursing her lips, she ran from behind her mother's skirts and into the forest.

'Wait!' she called to the two.

They stopped, and she went to Gallian, taking his hands in her own, looking at him.

'Don't worry, Gallian, everything will be all right tonight. I promise.' She smiled at him, and he smiled back at her in return. Light, however dim, filled his eyes again.

Satisfied he was happy again, she kissed his cheek and ran, giggling back to her mother.

'Sometimes, I believe you are far older than your five years, little one,' said her mother.

Anabelle took her mother's hand as she led them out of the clearing. 'Will Gallian be all right?'

'Yes, Gallian is strong. He faces many challenges with his father, but

he is strong and will prosper if he follows what he knows to be right. Despite how much he loves his father.'

Anabelle's mind tried to process what her mother had said and looked over her shoulder in the direction of Gallian and his father.

Be strong, Gallian, *she thought.*

The Fae sat upon the branches of the trees, watching them progress further into the thicket, having heard her silent prayer.

CHAPTER FIVE

Anabelle stared at the wall across from her bed, blinking away the haze of sleep. Her brows scrunched, and she rubbed a hand across her face before rolling over. She noticed her new book lying neatly on her side table and came face-to-face with Pepper.

'Good morning, Pepper.'

Pepper's ears twitched as she burrowed into the pillow beside Anabelle.

Anabelle stroked her fur gently and sighed. 'Pepper, I'm starting to think these dreams are more my reality than what surrounds me.'

The image of her mother's face wafted across her memory, but it wasn't her mother's face, not really. It was different.

She gave a side glance to the rabbit, expecting some sort of reply, then gave a tired chuckle when she noticed the rabbit was asleep. With one last yawn, she sat up, eyeing her room. Her boots and dress she wore yesterday were gone, left only in her shift.

Slipping from the comforts of her bed, Anabelle flitted around her room quietly. Pepper had awakened from the movement and hopped to the centre of the mattress, watching Anabelle walk about the room.

Noting her shoes by her wardrobe, she opened the space and found her dress hanging neatly next to her others.

Her brows furrowed. 'Come on, Pepper, let's go find my mother.'

She scooped the little rabbit into her arms and whisked her from the room, wooden floors groaning under her feet.

Turning into the kitchen, she found her mother at the table, watching the sunrise with a distant longing she hadn't seen before.

'Good morning.' She leaned over and gave her mother's cheek a quick peck.

Isadora smiled. 'Good morning, love. I set aside some carrots and greens for Pepper. Fresh bread is on the counter for you.'

'Do you hear that, Pepper? Food!' She put the rabbit on the counter, pushing the small selection of vegetables in front of her. She watched as Pepper began to nibble at the offerings.

Anabelle cut a thick slice from the warm loaf, spreading fresh preserves. 'How did I get into bed last night?' she asked, sitting opposite.

'Lily's husband, Adam, was kind enough to carry you to your room after you fell asleep.'

'I hope you thanked him for me. I couldn't help it. The stars were so inviting. They just begged me to dream with them, so I fell asleep, and then dream I did.' She took a bite of her bread, watching her mother.

Isadora's lips turned up. 'Did you dream of anything special?'

Anabelle set her bread down, the memory replaying. 'Mayhap not special, but nonetheless intriguing.'

Confusing, more like, she added silently.

'Was it the same gentleman as before?'

'I don't know.' Confusion crossed her slight features as her mouth twisted in thought. 'I think it was him, only we were children…and you were there.'

Curious amusement made Isadora laugh, ushering her daughter to explain. 'I was? What was I doing in your dream?'

Anabelle's nails clicked together as she stared out the window, deep in thought. 'I don't think it was a dream.'

'Then what was it?'

'I think it was a memory,' she muttered, primarily to herself. 'The boy was named Gallian. He had the same eyes as….' Her words trailed off before she stood, grabbing Pepper and setting her on the floor.

'You were brushing my hair. It was summer, and we were sitting by a pond in a clearing. Gallian and I were playing, and then his father came—Balwin—and took him.' She turned her head to glance at her mother.

Isadora had gone silent. The colour in her face had drained, and she looked sick as she stared at her hands. Feeling their sticky surface, she clenched her fists, taking in a deep breath and schooling the features of her face to hide the panic coiling in her stomach.

Anabelle rushed to her mother's side, dropping to her knees beside her. 'Mother? Is everything all right?'

Isadora rubbed her eyes and nodded, her chest tightening. 'My head just hurts, love. Why don't you take Pepper to your room, dress for the day, and spend some time outside.'

She pasted on a reassuring smile, patting Anabelle's cheek lightly.

Anabelle picked Pepper up, laying a hand on her shoulder. 'Are you sure everything is all right? Do I need to send for a doctor?'

She waved a hand, brushing the concern away. 'No, no need. I promise I'm fine. Now go on,' she said encouragingly, ushering her daughter out of the room.

When Anabelle was gone, wariness suddenly weighed down on Isadora, and she sagged in her chair. Her heart raced, and her breath quickened as fear settled in.

Anabelle was starting to remember.

Anabelle paced her room while Pepper watched her from the bed. Still in her shift, her ivory dress was strewn across her bed. A look of deep concentration was written across Anabelle's face as her bare feet swept over the wooden floors.

'It doesn't make any sense,' she muttered, the corners of her mouth pulled down into a frown. She turned to Pepper and dropped to her knees, laying her arms at the edge of the bed, cradling her head in her hands. 'I don't understand it, Pepper. It must have been a dream. I would have remembered…'

Pepper's nose twitched as Anabelle ran her fingertip lightly over her soft face. 'There were Faeries in my dream, Pepper, watching us. The boy reminds me of my masked stranger. Hair as black as night, and eyes as green as fresh spring leaves.' Her words were barely a whisper as she stood. 'He did not appear real.'

Picking up the dress, she donned the soft cotton garment. It hugged her bust and then flowed out, brushing the floor as she walked. She grabbed the apron and tied it around her waist.

She picked Pepper up and sat on the bed. 'I feel Mother is hiding something from me, Pepper.' She held the rabbit in front of her. 'What do you think?'

Pepper's ears twitched, and Anabelle nodded in agreement.

She kissed her twitching nose and placed her on the floor to roam. Grabbing her boots, she shoved her stocking feet into them and hurried out of her room.

Anabelle slipped past the study, her eyes catching the sight of her mother sitting in a cushioned chair turned toward a large open window, one leg tucked under her, head rested in her hand. The autumn breeze blew, and she saw her mother breathe deeply, her eyes closing. For a brief moment, her mother looked utterly content. When the slight wind left, that look of happiness went with it and was replaced by a wistful stare.

Anabelle's heart sank at the thought of her mother being unhappy. Turning away with a sigh, she left her mother to her solitude.

Being outside lifted Anabelle's spirits as she walked through the fields as quietly as the wind. She didn't run or dance. She simply walked slowly and peaceably to the forest's edge. She let her hands float atop the tall grass, her palms tingling with their feathered tips. The wind danced through her hair, tangling it around her limbs as she continued.

She felt the need to return to the little pool she had found, memory and intrigue guiding her steps as she crossed over rocky ground.

Reaching the place where she had left her copper ribbon, she found it still securely tied to the tree branch, wafting helplessly in the breeze.

She touched the soft material, glancing beyond the trees. She stepped forward with hesitant footfalls and found the path to the clearing, but it had changed.

Confusion, an emotion now well-known to her, pulled her brows tight. Stepping further into the forest, she stared at the path. It looked as if no one had walked it in many years, though it had been freshly lain just two days prior. She could still see the way, but it was covered by overgrowth. Plants and scattered flowers alike tangled over the trail. Even a little yearling tree had sprouted forth.

With a determined shake of her head, Anabelle stepped onto the rough trail, weaving through the overgrowth to avoid tangling her skirts.

As the path continued, she imagined herself in a dance with her masked stranger.

'Oh!' She put a hand to her breast. 'You wish to dance with me?' Smiling, she reached out as if to let the gentleman take her hand.

Flowers tangled under her boots as she spun in and out of the trees, dancing away. She was amused with her own imagination. With a giggle, she stopped at the edge of the clearing. Her laugh was silenced, and her mouth let out a soft 'oh'.

'It wasn't a dream,' she mused aloud. 'It *was* a memory.'

She lied to me?

The pond gurgled, and her eyes flicked to the noise. The water made lazy circles as she walked to the edge, staring down at her reflection.

Just as before, she couldn't see the bottom. Glancing up at the clearing, she noted every detail, taking images from her memory and putting them in place. She and Gallian sat by the pool...then on the grass, laughing at nothing. Balwin in the shadows...her mother. Anabelle sighed heavily as a cool wind brushed through the tall trees, making her shiver, and she turned back to the dark waters.

A splash caught her attention as the water was disturbed by something along the opposite bank. She could see nothing past the surface. Another splash to her left made her turn, but she saw nothing but the disturbance of the water rippling across the surface.

She spared only a momentary thought for what could be down there before she shoved her arm into the water, trying to feel for a wall or bottom. Feet stumbling out from under her, her heart skipped a beat as her face came inches from the water. Gripping the rocky ledge, she steadied herself.

Pulling back, Anabelle sat upon the rocks, eyeing the now sodden sleeve of her dress. Nothing for it, she began peeling off her boots and undoing the laces of her dress. Peeling off the wet sleeve, the dress fell to her feet. Taking her garments, she laid them neatly across the rocks.

In nothing but the flesh she was born with, her dark hair fell over her bare shoulders in soft tendrils. The wind whipped up, and her breasts tightened at the chill. Ignoring the frozen nails that trailed down her spine, she dipped one foot in, sealing away her discomfort as her skin rippled in shock. The cold water encompassed her legs as she slowly lowered herself to the rocks, legs dangling in the open water. She still felt nothing beneath her.

Using her arms as support, she lowered the rest of her body into the water. A sliver of strangled breath slipped past her lips, just her head above the surface. She held the ledge with her fingertips until her feet brushed against something hard and rough. Pressing diligently, she let her toes rest on it.

She gave a triumphant smile, thinking she had found the bottom of the dark pond until that hard surface rocked once, then twice, before she fell all the way through and found herself wholly submerged.

The pond was as clear as air beneath the surface. Yet as Anabelle floated in place, her eyes straining through the water, she saw nothing but darkness below her. An unknown fear jolted her at the idea of something coming from those depths, pulling her down to a watery grave.

Lungs straining and heart hammering, Anabelle kicked her way up to the surface. Her head broke free, and she took in a lungful of air. Grasping at the bank, she sucked in a ragged breath as she held onto them with white knuckles, staring at the water that was once again as dark as ink.

Any sane person would crawl from that watery trap, dress, and forget there was a lazy pond of unknown origin bating them to enter. Anabelle, at that moment, did not feel very sane. Her mind whirled with thoughts of Fae, sunshine, and green eyes.

Somehow, in her foggy mind, she wanted to know what was behind the fear of the bottomless pond. To understand what was below the waters or if it truly was just water, and she was nought but an imaginative fool.

Squeezing her eyes tightly closed, she took in two controlled breaths, willing her heart rate to slow. Then she submerged herself with a deep breath before she could convince herself to jump out.

It was as bright as sunlight beneath the crystal waters, the day above her shining through. Anabelle twisted her body, looking for anything that could provide answers. She found smooth walls and a shadowed bottomless pit below her. Looking up, she saw only the bright blue of an autumn sky. The illusion made her feel like she was floating among the clouds.

Pushing her body backwards, grinning as her fear slid away, Anabelle stared into the open boundaries. Her grin faded when she saw a flicker of blue light in the distance. She swam to the surface, taking in another lungful of air before she slipped back under.

Swimming towards the blue glow, tunnels carved their way into the smooth walls. Anabelle floated in front of them momentarily, uncertain, before kicking forward into the darkness.

She followed the tunnel for a few feet until blue drops of water began to dot the shaft, first scattered, then cloisters trailing like veins. It covered every inch until the whole tunnel surrounded Anabelle in a glow of blue light.

She stared at the water, gliding her hand across it. It felt slick, like slime. Feeling her lungs strain, Anabelle glanced at the way she came and couldn't see the entrance anymore.

Bubbles escaped from her mouth as panic erupted. Frantically, she kicked through the water, looking for the end of the tunnel.

The blue water disappeared, leaving her alone as darkened walls closed in. The tunnel that had once been wide now felt like the eye of a needle. The last of her breath left her, and her lungs screamed in protest. The pinch of fear came in waves, washing over her, limbs shaking, heart beating in her chest like a wild drum.

Anabelle struggled through the water, her mind heavy, sharp pains stabbing at her chest, black spots dotting her vision. She gave a desperate scream before she gave in, sucking water into her lungs, limbs convulsing. The sounds of her choking were lost in the watery depths. White hot pain exploded through her body as her muscles contracted, and her lungs were engulfed in fire.

Without realising, she fell from the tunnel. Her last sight was of the sky above her.

CHAPTER SIX

A wet, staggering cough wrenched out of Anabelle, and her eyes flew open as she heaved to her side and retched out a lungful of water. She gasped in a ragged breath as she let her body fall back. Chest heaving, Anabelle lay strewn on the grassy floor of the clearing, fire burning her lungs with every breath. Her right arm lay limp across her damp stomach, mind growing heavy as a fog settled in.

It took her last dregs of energy to glance at the rocks with blurry vision. Her head throbbed as her eyes tried to focus, images moving in and out of each other. Anabelle's eyes landed on the shadow of a man, emerald eyes staring at her. It was the last thing she saw before tumbling into a black void.

When she awoke next, she was curled on her side, knees to her chest. The sun was setting, and the once-blue sky was now filled with pink and orange bursts. She shivered, and gooseflesh erupted against the cold wind.

The image of the man watching her made her scramble to sit up and survey her surroundings, eyes wide. Her damp hair fell down her back in chilly tendrils, clinging to her exposed flesh. Straining her neck, Anabelle cast a wary glance at the water. It floated lazily, appearing all the more innocent.

Standing, she walked to the rocky ledge, staring down at the black, watery mirror, knowing that her life had been within its grasp. Images of the tunnels and the blue glow made her body tense, but not in fear. She wanted to know where the tunnel led and if there were more of them—where they led, too.

'Fool,' she scolded herself.

Taking one last glance at the water, she pulled her dress on and laced up her boots, leaving the black waters and greying grass behind, trying to forget the blurred vision of green eyes.

Glancing at the sky, she saw twilight approaching, and the last few rays of the sunset followed her through the forest.

'How swiftly the days end when winter begins.'

Her words carried on the wind, and she never noticed the patch of frost as it curled around the base of a tree where her fingers had skimmed.

Night had fallen by the time Anabelle reached the cottage door. She pushed it open and stumbled through, catching herself as her exhausted limbs fought the urge to collapse. Leaning against the wall, Anabelle shut the door tightly behind her. Dropping her head back against the wood, exhaustion swept over her as she yawned, her lungs still raw and painful.

'Anabelle?'

Her mother's concerned voice preceded her out of the study. A stern look etched across her face, worry clouding her eyes.

Anabelle felt the ache deep in her bones and glanced at the door leading to the hall, longing for her bed.

Isadora crossed her arms and looked at her daughter, brows raised and her mouth pressed into a thin line.

'Where have you been? You've been gone all afternoon. I even entered the forest, trying to find you!' She reached out and touched one of her damp strands of hair. 'And why is your hair wet?'

The words held an edge to them that she rarely heard from her mother.

Closing her eyes briefly against her mother's penetrating questions, her limbs began to shake. Letting loose a sigh, she opened them, glancing at the door leading to her escape. 'I fell asleep.'

It was partially the truth, she thought, not wishing to cause her mother worry.

'My hair is wet due to my own clumsiness. I found myself to be the unlucky individual who fell into a brook.' She saw the look of concern on her mother's face and waved it off. 'Please, Mother, I'm exhausted and wish to go to bed.'

Isadora did a once over of Anabelle's body, looking for any distressing signs, the tightness in her face slowly melting. Lifting a hand to cup Anabelle's cheek, she gave her a small smile. 'I was worried about you. I thought something had happened. Please don't scare me again.'

There was an age in her mother's eyes Anabelle had never seen before. She nodded, leaning forward to place a kiss on her cheek. Her body screamed at the movement, threatening to drop her. 'I love you, Mamma. Goodnight.'

Walking around her mother, she escaped to her room. Shutting the door firmly behind her, she kicked off her boots.

A small thump was heard from behind her door, and she opened it to see Pepper there. Giving the little rabbit a smile, she picked her up, shutting her door again and carrying Pepper to her bed.

Pepper went to her pillow and flopped onto her side as Anabelle pulled back her blankets, stripping her dress off quickly, each pull of her laces seemingly harder than the last. Her body melted as she settled between her sheets, limbs becoming lead. Her mind was a hazy fog, and her dreams overtook her.

It was dark in the forest, the trees blurred together as if painted in the air, and the night shimmered with untouched promises.

Anabelle stepped forward cautiously. She could not see the forest floor before her. Stumbling on an upturned root, she reached out to the trees and felt them waver.

Regaining her balance, she frowned and brought her hand up to the base, waving her fingers through the mirage. It quivered as if made of water. Stepping back, she stumbled again upon a rock and fell backwards. With a cry, her body submerged into the water.

Her head hit a hard floor, and she moaned, stars flashing across her eyes. Sitting up slowly, she rubbed at the tender bruise. Opening her eyes, she was met with bright golden sunlight. In front of her was the same pond she had nearly died in, though it stood proudly before her, mirroring the dark forest trapped on the other side. Mouth agape, Anabelle turned, and her eyes widened.

Golden light filtered through every space. Everything was alive. The wind danced through the treetops, leaves shining like emerald drops fluttering in the breeze. Flowers dusted the roots of trees, weaving in and out of their bark as they crawled towards the sky.

Anabelle felt the very essence—the soul—of the forest thrumming around her. Within her, a spark seemed to ignite and burn with a familiarity of something Anabelle hadn't realised she had been missing. It fell into place, and her heart began to beat with the same rhythm as the forest. They were one, and she had the power to control it as the air swept up around her.

Stooping, she touched one of the pale pink flowers that wove within the tree bark and felt its life hum through her veins. With her hand still on the thick trunk, small pale flowers of different colours bloomed under her touch. Surprise made her yank her hand to her chest, and a startled laugh left her lips.

Footsteps met her ears, and she whirled.

The figure of a tall, lithe woman in a pale green dress of soft flowing fabric stood before her. Her silver-blonde hair gleamed under the light like white fire, and pink lips turned up in curiosity while icy green eyes gazed at her.

'Anabelle.'

The woman's voice flowed over Anabelle, and her confusion melted against the whispered melody. 'Who are you?' she asked.

The woman gave her a small smile. 'I am a Fae of the forest. I have many names, but most know me as Winter.'

'Winter? The season?'

Winter nodded patiently. 'I am the Spirit of Winter.' She reached out, plucked a pale pink flower from its place among the others, and closed her hand around it.

Anabelle drew in a sharp breath when Winter opened her hand to reveal a perfectly frosted sphere in the middle of her palm. In the centre, the very same flower floated, consumed by ice.

'You see,' Winter said, 'I come and go when the season calls and the Keeper is away or not of age.'

'What is a Keeper?'

Winter stepped forward, gliding past Anabelle and weaving between two trees. She eyed the large mirror of water briefly. 'A Keeper is linked with the life of the forest and everything in it.' She turned to peer at Anabelle. 'She is the guardian of the forest and protector of the veil.'

Anabelle's head tilted in thought. 'The Keeper is a woman?'

A smile that held many secrets glowed back at Anabelle before Winter continued walking. 'Yes, this one is, as well as the one before her…Walk with me, Anabelle.'

Anabelle followed, falling into step with her as they strolled through the summer-lit forest.

Anabelle opened her mouth to speak but closed it promptly.

'Say what you wish, Anabelle. You may speak freely with me.'

She paused to collect her thoughts, glancing at the woman. 'Is this all just a dream?'

A soft laugh escaped Winter. 'This is not a dream, Anabelle, but a new reality. Although, yes, you are sleeping.' Winter waved a hand to the watery mirror. 'Just as this is not a pond, not traditionally as you may know it. Rather a reflection of your life.'

'A dream but not a dream? What kind of magic is this?' she demanded.

Winter glanced at Anabelle, seeing the many questions she yearned to ask. 'You let your doubts consume your mind, Anabelle. You will know the answer to your questions soon enough. For now, dear girl, relax your mind and *truly dream.*'

Winter's words echoed in Anabelle's ears, and the world around her vanished like dust in the sky as she was cast into a new world. A world in which dark music played, and she wore a blood-red satin gown.

Her fingertips brushed against velvet, and she knew a half-mask adorned her face, her dark hair pinned up. The dark waltz began its hypnotic melody, and her eyes scanned the mass of dancing bodies. They landed on her masked stranger, and the world became quiet as he caught sight of her. Anabelle's heart slowed to a silent thud thud thud. He glided toward her this time and found her in the darkness of her corner, cast into shadows.

'Hiding, my sweet Anabelle?' His lips teased her with a curled smile.

A blush formed on Anabelle's cheeks, and heat bloomed in her chest. 'Never from you. I never wish to hide from you.'

He held his hand out to her, and she took it. Pulling her close, he brought her into his embrace. Dancing quietly into the mass of waltzing bodies.

He took her out into the cold and led her down the stone steps.

Her breath fanned out and disappeared into the night as she stared at her masked stranger. 'Who are you?'

Curiosity glinted in his eyes. 'You know who I am.'

CHAPTER SEVEN

Anabelle awoke with a start as her eyes flew open, and a chill crept over her. Her breath could be seen with an exhaled gust of icy air. She felt a quiver by her stomach and pulled back her blanket to reveal Pepper pressed up next to her.

'Pepper?' She scooped the baby rabbit into her arms and swung her legs out from under the blankets. Her limbs ached from yesterday as she lowered her feet to the wooden floor. The stinging bite of ice shocked the pads of her toes, and she yelped, quickly drawing her legs back. Scrambling, she tucked herself into the farthest corner of her bed.

Glancing down at the floor, she found it covered in a layer of frost that crawled up her walls and everything in its path like diamond spiderwebs. Her room glistened in a layer of winter crystals. Her bed remained untouched, much to her relief. A shiver slithered down her spine as she pressed Pepper to her chest.

Anabelle glanced at her window, hoping to find them open, but they remained tightly locked, sealing out the elements and covered in glimmering crystals. Ice erupted through her veins as she took in a shaky breath, her skin freezing. Gritting her teeth, she shook off the fear and scooted to the other side of the bed, glancing at her door.

'Pepper, what is happening to me?' The words almost held a plea of insanity in them.

Anabelle eyed the door with a sigh, taking a deep breath and readying herself to dash across her room and escape. She placed her feet on the floor and felt the cold bite before it disappeared. Glancing down, Anabelle saw the frost give way under her and vanish. Setting Pepper down on the bed, she crawled back over to the other side and looked down, and there on the floor were two dry spots where her feet had barely touched.

Raw panic overwhelmed her, and she grabbed Pepper. Running for her door, she threw it open in a frenzy and slammed it shut as she left the chill behind her. Her body acted as a barricade, leaning heavily against the wood, half expecting the door to fight against her weight.

'Anabelle? Come here.'

She barely registered her mother's words, her heart hammering in her ears. Glancing back at the door with distrust, she straightened her shoulders, wiping her sweaty palms on her shift.

'Anabelle?'

Taking in a shaky breath, ignoring the sting in her lungs, she followed her mother's voice into the kitchen. She found her standing by the counter with a well-worn apron around her waist and a bright smile.

'Good morning, love.' She moved and let Anabelle see the small cake sitting neatly on the wooden counter.

The tension in Anabelle's shoulders slowly ebbed away. 'Oh, it's lovely, thank you.' She hugged her tightly. 'You really didn't have to.'

She thought about telling her mother of the icy palace that

transformed her room but bit her tongue, schooling her features, lest she sounds crazy.

Isadora crushed her to her chest, whispering into her hair, 'Happy birthday.'

Anabelle laughed lightly and stepped back from her mother's embrace, sniffing the cake. It smelled divine. She plucked a berry from the top, plopping it in her mouth.

Isadora moved her apron aside, looking at Anabelle, her eyes seemingly guarded. 'I also wanted to give you this.' She held out a white envelope.

Taking it from her, Anabelle broke the wax seal and read it over. 'It's an invitation to a masked ball…When did you get this?' she questioned, peering up at her through thick lashes.

'When we went into town. Lily gave it to me. She said the Schulez's came to her and instructed her to give it to me directly if she were to see me. It's tonight. I thought you would like to go.'

Anabelle grinned slowly. Part of her had half a mind to reject the offer but brushed it away. Disappointment clouded her decision when she thought of her closet.

'Of course, I would be honoured to go, but I'm afraid I have nothing to wear.'

Isadora took a mask from her apron pocket and held it out to Anabelle. 'I made this for you last night after you went to bed. I have a gown of mine. Granted, it's dated, but I think it would look beautiful on you.'

'Thank you,' she whispered as she took the mask. The dark blue velvet with gold filigree was soft under her fingers, and a black satin ribbon hung from both ends.

'It's lovely, Mother.' She threw her arms around her neck, pulling her close. 'Thank you.'

Laughing, Isadora gently pushed her daughter away. 'Now, I drew up a bath for you. The water is still warm, so I suggest you make use of it.'

Smiling, Anabelle kissed her mother's cheek and set the mask down. 'When I'm done, we can eat cake.'

She left her mother's side and hurried off. The thought of a warm bath enticed her aching body.

The water felt like heaven on her skin as steam rose and curled in the air, her muscles melting in relief. Anabelle laid her head against the copper tub and gave a content sigh.

Anabelle stared at the golden orange of the metal, her distorted reflection staring back. She turned her attention to the water. Her palms floated over the top before dipping her finger and making ripples on the smooth surface.

Cupping her hands, she filled them with the warm liquid, letting it dribble between the crevices of her fingers.

'Why is the simplest thing…always the most dangerous thing of all?' she questioned to no one.

Thoughts of her dreams and now her memories flitted through her mind, and she closed her eyes to them. She willed them away as she tried to relax.

Making quick time, she washed and stepped from the tub, taking the linen towel her mother had laid out for her and wrapping it around her body.

Anabelle glanced at her shift thrown over a wooden chair and frowned. The garment had splotches of dirt on it. Thoughts of the pond bubbled to the surface, and she shook her head. She would think about it later.

Opening the door, she followed the path to her room and found Pepper sitting in front of the door.

Anabelle's nose twitched, and she took a deep breath, slowly reaching for the doorknob. Taking three quick breaths, she opened her door and held the last breath in her throat, letting it out when she saw her room as it usually looked. Like frost had not etched its way across every inch of it. It appeared as it did every morning prior.

A groan rose in her throat, and she pushed inside and shut the door. Pepper hopped along the floor, her nose brushing the wood now and then.

Anabelle dropped her towel to her bed and opened her wardrobe. Taking out a clean shift, she pulled it on, the simple edges of lace feathering against her skin. Shutting the doors, Anabelle flopped onto her bed, picking Pepper up. She set her on her stomach as she laid back, stroking her fur absentmindedly.

'Am I going insane?' she whispered.

Images of the summer forest and the dark forest muddled together and winged Fae lining the treetops as two children played. Green eyes stared at her from within a hazy fog, and a room stood covered in ice. It all seemed like a far-off memory. One she felt inclined to remember but hesitant all the same.

Her face pinched in thought. Candlelight and melodic music filled her head.

'A masked...'

Anabelle sat up with a start. Bewilderment cascaded through her, and she looked at the rabbit.

'Pepper, I have been invited to a masked ball tonight...' Anabelle bit her lip, thoughts reeling.

Without a second thought, she set the rabbit on the floor and bolted from her room.

Her mother still remained in the kitchen, where she had left her. She sat at the table with a cup of tea and her nose in the same book as before.

'Can we have some cake now?' Anabelle asked, walking over to the dessert and plucking the knife beside it. She carefully kept her face clear of the emotions churning below her skin.

Chuckling, Isadora set her book aside and walked over to Anabelle. She pulled two small plates out of a cupboard. 'By all means, please.'

Anabelle took the knife and sliced two pieces, handing one to her mother with a fork from a drawer. Both took a bite at the same time, and Anabelle smiled.

'It's delicious, Mother.'

Isadora grinned with pride. 'I'm so happy you like it.'

Anabelle used her fork to move a berry around her plate, nibbling at her lip.

'What colour is your dress? The one I will wear tonight?' she asked, staring down at her piece of cake as she took a small bite, chewing slowly, waiting.

Isadora thought carefully, tapping her chin. 'Mm, I believe it's red. Although I haven't set eyes upon it in some time.'

A small smile feathered over Anabelle's lips as she took another bite of cake. 'It sounds lovely.'

Anabelle sat before her mother's vanity, staring at her reflection in the mirror. Her lips and cheeks were stained red from rouge, and her face was powered lightly with white chalk. Her mother had done up her hair into an elegant, intricately woven work of art. Her slender neck was bare of jewels as she sat in only a shift, a bustling petticoat, and her red satin slippers on her feet.

Isadora appeared a moment later; the ridged stays in her hands, noting the evil eye Anabelle gave the piece. She chuckled, motioning for her to stand and hold the bedpost.

'It's not that bad, love.'

Slipping the unfastened stays over her head, Anabelle used one hand to hold it against her breasts while using the other to grip the post. The soft material her mother had applied to the stiff linen inside made for small comfort against the tight restraints.

'It really is that bad, Mother,' she retorted. 'It gives us no freedom to breathe. We're so busy concentrating on whether or not we can exhale or inhale that we forget to enjoy ourselves.'

She felt the first pull of the strings, and she pursed her lips into a disapproving line.

'Absolutely the worst, Mother, the worst,' she gritted through her teeth as the laces were pulled tighter and tighter.

'They wouldn't make a man wear such a torturous contraption. Preposterous dandies with their silly frills and peacocking. Let us see them wear a shackle around their monstrous gut,' she muttered darkly, primarily to herself.

Anabelle took her last deep breath for the night as she felt the last knot pulled and tied.

Isadora clucked her tongue at Anabelle's muttered words, keeping her amusement contained.

'I didn't tie it so tight, so don't be dramatic. You can breathe. I dare you to try,' Isadora mused in a light tone.

Scowling, Anabelle took in a deep breath and was content when she felt her ribcage expand with ease. She slid her hands over the ribbing, and her lips twitched in disapproval as her mother took a wooden busk and slipped it down the front. Her breasts strained against the fabric, rising with each breath. She pushed away her discomfort when she heard the rustle of cloth from behind.

Her mother stood with a deep red satin dress in her hands.

'Oh,' Anabelle whispered. 'It's beautiful.'

Smiling, Isadora brought the dress forward and opened it wide for Anabelle to step into.

Obligingly, Anabelle stepped in and let her mother fasten the back. Isadora looped the ties until they created a seamless finish, tucking the strings into the dress as she knotted them at the base.

Isadora leaned close to her daughter and softly said, 'Look.'

She turned Anabelle to face the mirror and heard her daughter's intake of breath.

Standing before them in the mirror was a woman with creamy white skin and alluring silver-blue eyes that stared innocently back, the curves of her body accentuated with every dip of fabric.

The neck of her gown fell, clinging to the tips of her shoulders, dipping to the crevice of her breasts; sleeves were tailored to her arms until satin ruffled at her elbows. The rich material fanned out into a beautiful ball gown at her waist. It was a simple gown comparable to modern fashions. Yet, it was the most beautiful dress Anabelle had ever seen and worn.

She turned to her mother and hugged her tightly, pulling back. 'Thank you. It is the loveliest thing I have ever worn.'

She returned to her reflection, admiring the woman standing before her. She was no longer just a girl, nor did she feel like one.

'You look like a rose at midnight,' Isadora said. 'Now come, my dearest, we must get you to your ball!'

Her mother whisked her from the room into the hall as a rap on the front door echoed throughout the cottage.

Isadora vanished and reappeared seconds later, slipping the invitation and mask into Anabelle's hands.

'Be careful, but enjoy yourself,' she said while touching her daughter's soft cheek.

'I wish you would come.'

'This is your time, love.'

'Not that I care, but they will find it odd that I am without a chaperone.'

Isadora smiled. 'Pay no mind to what they say. This is your night. Embrace it.'

Another knock sounded, and Isadora pushed Anabelle to the door. 'Time to leave, love.'

'You hired a coach?' Anabelle questioned, somewhat surprised, as the door was pulled open and a man stood before them, carriage and horse standing proudly behind him.

'I'm your mother. I am not about to let you walk an ungodly distance in a ballgown!' she exclaimed. 'I arranged it with Lily when you left the shop.'

With a laugh, Anabelle picked up her skirts and walked the gravel path to the carriage, petting the horses' soft hide as she passed them. The coachman opened the door and helped her in. Thick yards of satin pillowed around her in a pool of crimson.

She leaned out of her small carriage window, calling out to her mother, 'I won't be too late.'

'Take your time. Enjoy yourself!'

Anabelle leaned back as the coachman whipped the reins, and the carriage jerked forward.

The sky was twilight blue, and the moon had already peeked through the clouds. With glowing eyes scanning her darkening surroundings, she caught the sight of the tree line and her breath caught in her throat.

The leaves were gone, and the forest looked cold, bare. The warmth had vanished. Anabelle felt herself shiver against the bitterness. Winter had taken its claim under the cloak of night and left them with nothing but frost. Anabelle leaned against the carriage wall and watched as the cold, barren trees passed her.

Isadora watched the carriage bounce down the road until it disappeared from sight and glanced at her surroundings. She watched as the thin air shimmered and the image before her wavered, darkness poking through. Her stomach clenched, and Isadora closed her eyes in alarm, reaching deep within herself, searching for her tether. Like a forgotten friend, she felt the familiar nudge and clung to it like a lifeline as it sparked through her veins. She drew upon the light and let it consume her. It flowed through her and gathered in the air.

Isadora lifted her eyes to scan the sky and watched as the breeze stilled, and all was once again peaceful.

Feeling the toll on her body, she leaned against the door frame, supporting her weight, and took in a deep quivering breath.

The veil was beginning to weaken.

CHAPTER EIGHT

Anabelle alighted from the carriage with the help of the coachman. Music floated outside from beyond the dwellings of the large manor before her, excitement at her fingertips as she took the mask and secured it around her face. She glanced around her as she stood at the stone steps of the entrance. Anabelle could briefly see masked faces before they disappeared inside to the festivities.

A row of male servants held lanterns, dressed in black velvet overcoats and white trousers, glossy boots shining in the pale glow. Black and white masks adorned half their faces in a diamond pattern, like a jester at a royal court. Chandeliers with flickering candles created an alluring illusion in the sweeping hall, overflowing in the darkness of the cathedral arches.

'I'll just be over there, miss,' said the coachman, gesturing to where all carriages waited, enjoying their own festivities. Some were already well influenced by the flask of liquor Anabelle noted them passing around. Stumbling by the horses as they nickered in annoyance.

Anabelle nodded and gave him her thanks, following the flicker of candlelight. The crisp air blew through her, one of her curls coming undone and wrapping softly at the nape of her neck.

A butler, bowing at the waist, greeted her when she approached the massive oak doors. With a glance at the envelope clasped in her hands, he opened the door for her, taking the invitation as she entered.

The warmth and smell of perfumed bodies pressed against Anabelle as she entered the world of faceless people. Music hummed in the air like a tightly wound cord, and she was pulled deeper into the consuming crowd.

'Anabelle?'

Anabelle turned to find a stout, plump woman with silver hair and grey-green eyes standing behind her. Her eyes watched Anabelle with a sharpness hidden behind impassive judgement. She was dressed in a sweeping magenta gown of the latest fashion and hadn't bothered with a mask as she looked at Anabelle with a raised brow.

Anabelle curtsied to the elderly woman. 'Madam.'

She gave a short nod. 'You do not know me, but I know your mother. My name is Mrs Heinrich. My daughter Ada Sommer hosts this ball. We had asked Mrs Schulez to extend an invitation to you in case you were to come to town. How fortunate it is for us that you did,' she said drily, face pinching as she looked at Anabelle's gown with a flicker of disinterest. 'I invited you here so you may acquaint yourself with society, even though your coming of age was…many years prior.'

Her voice couldn't hold back the slither of judgement in her tone. 'Your mother, last time she graced us with a visit, had said it would be your birthday during the ball—much to her little knowledge of it.'

Anabelle nodded accordingly, ignoring the cold demeanour

that rolled off the woman. 'Please don't tell anyone it's my birthday. I don't want a fuss.'

Mrs. Heinrich's nose twitched. 'I would never have thought of it.'

'Thank you.'

With one more curt nod, Mrs Heinrich disappeared into the crowd, and Anabelle was left standing there alone.

Swallowing, Anabelle smoothed a hand down her skirt, taking a deep breath.

It's fine, ignore her, she thought to herself.

A country dance started up, and Anabelle moved along the marble floors. She swayed with the quick struts of the violin as she stood along the wall, watching the people come together in time with the music.

Anabelle's feet moved with the music, swaying around a group of gaggling women. One of the women stepped back, and Anabelle twisted out of the way only to run into a solid wall.

'Oof!' she gasped, stepping back quickly, stumbling over the hem of her skirt. She rubbed the bridge of her nose where her mask bit into the flesh and made to look up when a warm arm banded around her back.

'You might want to be more careful, miss,' said an amused, deep voice.

Anabelle jerked back in surprise at the bright blue eyes staring down at her, a simple black mask adorning half of his face. Warmth seeped through her bodice from his hand, and her pulse fluttered in her chest. 'Excuse me?' she asked.

A crooked smile tilted a firm mouth, facial hair shadowing a strong jawline. The man cocked a brow, leaning forward to whisper, 'We wouldn't want to give a gentleman the wrong impression, now, would we?'

Pursing her lips, she narrowed her eyes at him. 'And what impression would that be?'

'That perhaps you're actually enjoying yourself?'

His arm was still wrapped around her, and she removed it, putting space between them. 'And what gave you that idea?'

His low chuckle sent her nerves scattering. 'You did just fall into my arms whilst dancing.'

'I did no such thing—you were simply in my way.'

He brushed a strand of his dark brown hair from his eyes, and Anabelle caught herself tracking the movement.

'If you'll excuse me, sir,' she said tartly.

He gave her a nodding bow, that same swaggering smirk marking his face. 'Go back to your corner and pretend you're a pretty wallflower.'

Her answering scowl brought another laugh.

'I think I shall!' she exclaimed with a harrumph. With that, she whirled on her satin slippers and pushed through the crowd in a shimmering cloud of red.

People gathered and moved with the pace of the dance, and others stood in groups, speaking of the latest gossip as she merged into a corner along the wall. Anabelle had no wish to converse with anyone else after her interaction with Mrs Heinrich or that roughish man, lest she becomes part of the gossip with her harsh disinterest of court and who, or what, the next scandal was—and feared she might be labelled that next scandal if she didn't keep her mouth shut. She let her eyes fall shut, and the music began to float through the air as memories wafted over her vision.

Soon enough, she opened her eyes and pulled away from the sidelines as the music changed, thrumming with soft notes. She danced in between the marble pillars like a moving flame, humming the melody under her breath. She found a shadowed spot under torchlight and stepped into it, thrown into coveted darkness. Anabelle watched the masses converse and dance, coming together like long-lost friends.

She felt the strangest feeling of deja-vu as she watched colourful skirts and masks blur. Her dream had come to life before her eyes, the one thing that had consumed her every thought. That made her nerves tingle with impatience. Anticipation swept over her, and her heart began to pound. She knew what would happen next— had hoped would happen.

Her eyes went to the massive iron doors on the other side of the ballroom. Their iron vines with blossoming flowers created the illusion of a garden, weaving together against the glass between the metal frames. The doors parted, and the cool breath of the outside world rushed in, dousing the ruse for only a moment.

He was there, standing against the darkness. Anabelle thought her heart would stop as her eyes went wide.

Just as before, just as her dreams predicated, he scanned the ballroom. His lips turned down in what Anabelle supposed was a scowl and disappeared into the masses. Anabelle felt frantic as she searched for him in the crowd of bodies. She stood on tiptoes to try and see over the heads of everyone, to no avail. And then, as if by magic, the dancers parted, and he appeared, dressed in all black.

Pulse racing, she walked through the dance floor to the other side, watching him with caution and curiosity. He leaned against the stone wall, the picture of cool disinterest, eyes scanning the dancers with a calculated gaze.

His hair was like spilt black wine that brushed his shoulders in soft curls. A green velvet half-mask cloaked golden skin, encircling green eyes that were just as dark. His figure was strong, broad shoulders pulling the fabric of his black overcoat taut across his chest. Standing among other gentlemen, he stood nearly a foot above. His height added to the aristocratic air he held.

Anabelle could see him ignoring the stares and whispers of those around him, casting an icy look to a chittering mother and her daughter who ogled him. The side glances of prospecting young ladies, and the Cheshire grins of those prospecting young ladies' mothers, made Anabelle's brows raise.

For a week now, he had plagued her sleep and her reality. And now here he was, standing before her, indignant, and she frowned slightly. She might think he was only a phantasm if she had been anywhere else. No more than her brain losing touch with reality, and maybe she was, but here...here, she felt the validity of him. She was not the only one who could see him, that much was clear. But she was afraid this was not the same man she knew from her dreams from the icy glares he gave to those around him.

A cello's dark, inviting twang vibrated through the air, and a waltz began. Anabelle's ears rang with the familiar tune she heard every day for the last week.

As the music pulsed through her veins, she took a step closer to him, eyes wide as the bodies parted like the sea, and there was no longer anyone who stood between them.

A young man in a purple overcoat bumped into her masked stranger. Anabelle's feet hesitated when she saw the curl of his lip. The young man turned to apologise, seeming to freeze in place, before shaking his head quickly, muttering something, and hurriedly stepping back into the crowd.

Green eyes swept over her, and his scowl turned up in a hint of a smile. He pushed from the wall with an elegance that made Anabelle almost step back. He strode to her in long, graceful strides; his height towered over her with a presence that commanded attention. Even with her height that fell above the ladies of the ball, she had to look up to meet his eyes.

The sight of him only inches from her took her breath away. He was, by any standard—masked and all—beautiful. She could practically feel the jealousy reeling from the women at their backs. Their glares were not so subdued as she caught one briefly from the corner of her eye.

'Shall we?'

Her attention snapped back to the leaf-green eyes that gazed down at her, holding a flicker of something she couldn't place.

He held out a hand to her, and mutely, she took it. It was warm and soft as it enveloped hers. In a daze, Anabelle was pulled into his arms as he guided her out onto the floor. Nothing existed but themselves, the glow of candlelight and the music that coated the air with thick, lulling tones.

His arms were tight around her like a protective barrier against the glares, whispers, and gossip, and she forgot her earlier trepidation. She paid no mind to the busybodies, her chest rising with every turn, his fingers splayed across her spine. She could feel the heat from his hand through her gown, leaning into him as he pulled her closer.

The pool of people parted as if commanded by an invisible force, and he swept her outside into the cold night air. Anabelle's breath clouded in front of her.

Guiding her down the steps, he quickly pulled her into his embrace, the music spilling from the tall iron doors as the party's light fell into the dark night. He danced with her under the moonlight, sweeping her across the leaf-scattered floor in long, graceful strides. The thicket of trees along the mansion's garden circled around them, enclosing them to the world beyond and creating a world of their own.

The waltz slowly faded, and so did their dance. He held her hands and gave Anabelle a slow, knowing smile.

The silence was deafening.

'Anabelle.'

It was only her name, yet it sounded like honey on his lips. Sweet and sultry. She closed her eyes as she saw him lean forward. She felt the brush of his lips upon her bare shoulder, his touch sending her heart skittering across her ribcage.

'You are as beautiful as the pale moon above.'

She swayed on her feet, transfixed.

His dark eyes held her own as he brought her hand to his lips and placed a soft kiss upon it, too.

'Thank you for the dance. Until our next.'

He turned to leave, and Anabelle felt dread well up in her at the thought of losing him. 'Wait!' Her hand reached for his.

He stopped in his path. Anabelle came up behind him, placing a hand on his forearm.

'Please, tell me who you are. I can't live in the dark anymore—all the dreams and thoughts provoking me. I cannot wait any longer. Please tell me who you are.' She swallowed as he turned back to her, eyes glowing in the darkness.

'You know who I am.'

Anabelle shook her head, staring at him, stuttering, 'No, I don't know—I *believe*, but that is different. You are different. I beg you to tell me!'

Desperate, that's what she felt. Desperation mixed with bubbling irritation. Did he not know how her reality and dreams were merging, and she felt like everything she knew was spiraling out of control?

Those full lips turned up, and he peered down at her. 'Anabelle, you know me.'

Silence poured between them, and Anabelle slowly let her hands stretch up to his face. Her fingers tangled in his soft, unruly hair; she could not find the knot to release the mask. Reaching behind his head, he helped her undo the black satin ribbon, and she gently pulled it from his face.

One, two, three heartbeats passed, and Anabelle just stared up at him at the face she had longed to see. He was the most beautiful creature she had laid eyes on. Both unreal and real all at once.

High cheekbones framed a strong jaw, a straight nose, and deep-set green eyes; dark brows contrasted against his golden skin. Anabelle had never seen a man who compared to the one standing before her.

Although she hadn't spoken, she knew he was right. The realisation struck her like a blow to the gut.

Finally, she whispered, 'Gallian?'

'Anabelle?' he questioned back, mocking her softly.

'How are—You're here?'

Not a dream, a memory. Not a dream, her mind whispered from a dark corner of her consciousness.

'I'm here for you.'

Confusion, her kindred friend, was all she knew.

Shaking her head, she said, 'How are you here? How did you find me? I haven't seen you since we were children. And even then, I don't know if you are real now.'

Doubt began to weave within her confusion, and she took a small step back.

Gallian took her hand, peering at her closely. 'Do you not remember?'

Anabelle looked to the ground. Frowning.

'What do you remember, Anabelle?' he probed gently.

Images of the pond, of winged creatures in trees, of a boy—*him.*

'I remember us in a clearing, by the pond…That's all. Before that, I didn't know you existed as anything more than a stranger who plagued my dreams of this,' she said, casting her hands in a wide arc, gesturing to the ball.

Gallian nodded, running a hand through his hair in irritation, brows pinched in thought. 'I was hoping you would know more, but I suppose your mother did her job well.'

Irritation spiked through Anabelle. 'Well, I'm sorry I don't know as much as you would like, but there isn't anything I can do about it.'

With a sigh, Gallian placed a hand on her upper arm and stroked the skin through the silk of her gown. 'I'm sorry, Anabelle. I didn't mean it that way.'

She raised a brow.

'I mean it. You don't remember anything about what happened, and you shouldn't. It's what Isadora wanted, after all. But the seasons are changing, and along with it, the ages. Things in our world are changing now that you are of age, bad things. We need you to return to the Fae.'

Her brows furrowed, and she narrowed her eyes at him. 'What do you mean it was what my mother wanted?'

The cry of hundreds of crows cut off Gallian as they flew from the bare thicket in a hoard, blacker than the night sky. The sound of hooves upon the forest floor echoed in the air.

Annoyance flickered across his face so quickly that Anabelle thought she must have imagined it before alarm contorted his features as he stared into the forest. Seconds passed before a twig snapped, cutting through the silence like a knife.

Gallian whipped around. '*Run!*' He took her hand and pulled her behind him as he sprinted towards the hall. People laughed, not noticing the two figures who ran at breakneck speed towards them.

Then Gallian's hand let go of hers, and she halted mid-step, looking back at him when she passed, tendrils of hair flying from its updo.

'Go!' he yelled. 'Anabelle, go!'

Her muscles tensed as fear of whatever he knew was coming took over. With one last look at his face, she fled, picking up her skirt, her slippers pounded into the ground. Following the amber light, she tracked it up the stone steps, not stopping until just outside the opened double doors. She stood there, watching Gallian face the winter forest, his stance rigid.

A charcoal grey stallion stepped from the shadows, black mist coiling across the ground like a slithering serpent. A figure in black emerged from the darkness, sitting high up on the back of the horse. The man jumped from the steed with catlike grace and strode toward Gallian, his figure weathered and thin. His worn, ragged garments hung loosely around his skeletal frame.

Anabelle held her breath as she saw a blue light spark at Gallian's fingertips. Even so, Gallian took a step back. Despite his withered appearance, the man must have held unknowable power.

'Gallian.'

She hadn't meant for it to slip past her lips, but his name fell off her tongue in a whisper before she could stop it, and the figure in black turned his head sharply to her. Even at a distance, she could see the dull grey and whites of his eyes.

A scream tore from her throat as the dim light fell across the disfigured face. Needle-sharp pains stabbed at her head, the images of fire flashed across her mind, and the smell of burning flesh filled her nostrils.

Her eyes rolled back into her head, and before Anabelle collapsed to the ground, strong arms wrapped around her, and a deep voice rumbled from above her, 'Gallian, what are you doing?'

She was unaware of the people who had stopped to gather around her. All she knew was the horribly burned features that haunted her unconscious state—the face of Balwin.

CHAPTER NINE

Slender limbs tangled in blood-red satin as Anabelle tossed and turned in a fitful state of unconsciousness. Down and down she went, thrown into a chasm of darkness, of memories touched by forgetfulness cloaked by a sheet Anabelle couldn't pull back.

She screamed out into the darkness as rage boiled in her blood, and like glass, the veil shattered into a million pieces. Before her stood the image of a dark forest lit by torches…

Trees were widely spaced apart, thick, tall, and dark like giant earthly columns. The sky was black and filled with thousands of stars that glittered like dust from a diamond. Fae littered the branches of trees, and various unknown figures shadowed the forest edge.

In the centre stood two children. Anabelle and Gallian said nothing, their hands clasped between them. Their eyes were wide with anticipation, their small forms dwarfed compared to the vast surroundings.

Anabelle watched the child version of herself with piqued interest, stepping further into the memory. She saw her mother only a few feet from her child self. Balwin made an imposing figure over Gallian, who momentarily looked up at his father with a small, hesitant smile. Shadows trailed around him. Anabelle frowned and noticed her younger self did as well as she glanced at the man.

Four figures emerged from the cloak of darkness, each as beautiful as the next. When Anabelle saw Winter among them, her brows rose.

Winter wore a gown of pale blue that floated around her lithe figure, but her hair was the colour of rich honey and gleamed under torchlight like liquid amber.

'Children,' called Winter, gaining their attention. 'We are the Fae of Seasons. Winter, Spring, Summer, and Autumn. We are the Keepers of Seasons until one of you comes of age to uphold the honour of becoming Keeper of the Forest.'

Spring stepped forward, and Anabelle did not think someone could be more beautiful than Winter. Her golden hair framed peach-coloured skin, and wide green and blue eyes sparkled as she spoke. Her soft pink gown draped off her thin shoulders, gold glimmering through the fabric like stardust.

With a soft voice, Spring knelt before the children. 'Tonight, we choose which of you is to be the Keeper. We do not choose by physical strength alone, but by the strength of your heart and will.'

Reaching out, she ran her hand across Anabelle's cheek. When Spring glanced at Gallian, her eyes glazed over for only a moment, becoming bright again before anyone could notice. She stood quietly and took her place between Winter and Summer.

'Both of you are remarkable in your own way,' Autumn said. His voice was rich in the night air, filling the space. Unlike the others, he stood firm against the darkness. Clad in dark leather trousers that stretched tight over muscular thighs and black flat-footed boots, a tunic of deep red billowing over a brawny chest.

His features reminded Anabelle of the Fae she had read about in her stories. Sharp, angular cheekbones graced olive skin, similar to Gallian's, but narrower. His hazel eyes were filled with mischief and flecks of gold that glimmered in the light. Chestnut hair fell just slightly past his shoulders, strands of copper adding to the rich flavour.

'Fae children know innocence that we can no longer comprehend. As we age, we are corrupted by death, temptation, and immortality, though the children to be chosen have a gift greater than we could ever understand. Born both Fae and human, you are neither one nor the other. You are more powerful than the strongest creatures in the forest. Because of your mortality, you know the weight of death and possibilities of life within a single soul.'

Summer nodded in agreement, ebony hair cascading over one dark brown shoulder. Almond green eyes stared at the children, lips turning up in an encouraging smile. Her deep fuchsia gown enlightened the night with a summer glow. The peak of her season shone from within her.

Until then, both children had been quiet, but Gallian spoke in a small voice. 'Why?'

Summer gave him a soft smile. 'You are both worlds, joined together, a union that has not blessed us in some time. Your blood gives you the power to overcome things Fae cannot. No Fae knows the extent of what power a halving holds. You may not even know of your power until there comes a time when you must call upon it.'

The wind blew softly, whispering words that only Summer could hear, and she inhaled the warm breeze, smiling.

Tilting her head in acknowledgement, she spoke clearly. 'It is time.'

A whisper drew up through the branches as the tiny, winged Fae moved eagerly with anticipation. Winter held up a gentle hand, and the forest silenced. The four spirits closed their eyes and let magic seep through their bodies. A bond of power interwove through them, connecting them. Their bodies radiated light, glowing from within as they merged together.

Silver mist drifted across the forest floor, overlapping as it swept towards the two children. Gallian laughed as it encircled him first, wrapping around his limbs like gossamer. Anabelle watched the Fae's faces as different emotions flitted across them. They were looking for something. Her younger self giggled when blanketed in the mist, limpid vines creeping across her shoulders, fingers, and torso.

Anabelle brought a hand to her neck as she watched herself laugh and felt the whisper of something tickling her flesh.

It was over just as quickly as it began. The spirits shared quiet glances, though their faces hinted at nothing. And as though a silent language was spoken between them, they all gave a slight nod.

Summer knelt on the forest floor, bending to Gallian's ear so only he could hear her words.

Anabelle weaved through the trees and stood closer to Gallian to hear what was said.

'You were born from darkness but will grow from those shadows. They will not be your ending if you so choose.' Summer stood, stepping back as Winter came forward.

Winter peered down at the boy who stood nervously at her skirts, a frown pulling at his mouth. 'Gallian, you will have the power of choice. Laid before your life are two paths, a crossroads in your fate. Follow your mind and not your heart, and one day you may become very powerful... but today is not that day.'

A whisper drew over the forest as Winter continued, gazing at the little girl. 'Anabelle, for all you are, you will be an ember in the darkness when you come of age. On this summer night, we have chosen you as Keeper of the Forest.'

A howl of outrage vibrated through the forest, and Anabelle stumbled back as Balwin stepped up to her, knowing the chill she felt was only in her head. She put space between herself and the male, regardless.

Black shadows dripped from his body like a cloak, slithering around him. The winged Fae scattered from the trees, and those on the outskirts gave startled cries and vanished. Darkness crept over the ground, stretching towards the edges of their circle as his power grew.

'You choose the girl!' he snarled at Winter, casting the girl an icy glare. 'Gallian has everything that is needed! He is powerful and strong— physically and mentally! I made sure of it! He is the keeper!'

'We do not base the keeper by strength and power,' said Winter, stepping forward. 'They are children. We look to their innocence. You conceived Gallian in lust and hatred, not just for power but for sexual desire, Balwin. You knew that if a child were born with a mortal, they would be considered from birth to be a keeper. Anabelle was conceived in love. Your greed has clouded you.'

Pure, unadulterated hatred seethed through Balwin as the shadows grew. His dull grey eyes turned into shards of ice as he shifted his attention to the girl. His stumbling steps towards her quickened until he lunged, hands grasping for her neck.

'I will kill her!' he screamed.

Isadora cried out and leapt at Balwin, pushing him out of her daughter's path.

Anabelle shrieked as she and her younger self stared at her mother and Balwin struggling against one another.

Balwin grabbed Isadora by her hair and slammed her head against the base of a tree. The tree split down the middle, and Isadora collapsed unconscious; her body slumped on the ground in a heap. Balwin stood, advancing on the girl. She screamed as he cast his shadows on her. It came at her in a raging storm, flying like razor-edged daggers.

Winter threw herself in front of Anabelle, arms spread wide, back braced for the strike as she shielded her from the abyss.

Darkness enveloped them, and Anabelle could see nothing past the opaque shadows twisting and turning like rolling clouds. As she watched her younger self and Winter disappear, she could almost feel Winter's arms tightening around her in a protective circle, a frozen kiss pressed against her forehead, and ice shooting through her body.

A whisper floated around Anabelle. 'Do not be afraid.'

The words Winter had spoken to her in the darkness.

The winds blew with a destructive force, and the darkness spread slowly. Beyond the obscurity, a white light began to peek through, and soon it grew until the spark consumed the storm, and Balwin's shadows died. The blast rocketed them all back.

With a screeching snarl of outrage, Balwin lunged at Anabelle, who remained in the protective circle of Winter's embrace. He didn't make it more than two steps before Isadora stumbled to her feet, reaching for a shining torch, and swung it at his head, his black hair igniting in flames.

Balwin cried out, whirling on her and took a staggering step towards Isadora before dropping to his knees. His hands clawed at the flames, a roar of pain crawling out of his throat.

'Father!' Gallian sobbed.

Burning flesh filled the air, and the children shrieked at the sight. Isadora looked horrified and lifted her hand to Balwin, the flames dissipating at her command.

With a stricken look, Isadora said, 'For attacking my daughter and trying to kill her, I am not sorry. But for your son, I will let you live.'

Isadora closed her eyes briefly before touching Balwin's unburnt cheek. 'I sentence you to banishment, Balwin. You will remain within the deepest parts of the Forest of Lost Souls. You will live alone with your dark spirits, for this is your chosen life.'

Balwin's eyes rolled back into his head, and he collapsed.

Turning to the Fae of Seasons, Isadora's words were forced out of her through clenched teeth. 'Take him to the forest; let him wallow in his shadows. Let them eat him alive until he is no more.'

Autumn stepped forward and took Gallian's hand in his own, though he struggled against the hold, trying to reach his father's body.

'You will come with me now.' Autumn said.

Summer laid a hand on Isadora's shaking shoulder in comfort, then on Balwin's brow. Her eyes closed, and the two of them vanished. Gallian's screams for his father pierced the air.

Anabelle watched her mother close her eyes and take a shuddering breath, releasing the tension in her shoulders. Clasping her hands together, she went to Winter's side.

Her child self ran to her mother, her face ashen, hands shaking as they bunched in her mother's skirts.

Isadora hugged Anabelle tightly. 'I'm so sorry, my little love,' she whispered. 'I'll never let anything harm you again.'

Looking at Winter, Anabelle glanced away from her mother and herself, and her eyes widened. The once amber hair now fell like silver snow around her face.

Her mother must have noticed as well. 'Your hair....'

Winter gave her a small smile with a trace of sadness in its corners. 'The light will always prevail against darkness, but it does take a toll, as all magic does.'

'Will you die?' asked Anabelle's younger self.

A small chuckle emerged from her lips, and younger Anabelle looked up at Winter with wide watery eyes. 'No, quite the opposite. I will live. I would do it again if I had to. The life of a child and the keeper is far more precious than my own.' Winter bent low and placed one snowy kiss upon her soft forehead. 'Be the light, Anabelle.'

Spring waited for Winter, who gave one final parting. The two fell into step and disappeared into the forest.

Isadora looked down at Anabelle, mixed emotions on her features.

'Come, Anabelle, it is time to leave.'

'But Mother, what about Gallian?' her younger self asked as her mother gathered her in her arms and whispered words under her breath.

As the wind began to blow, a wild pulsing hum went through the air, and the images before Anabelle started to disappear.

'Wait!' she called out and was again cast into darkness.

'Wait!'

Anabelle sat upright, eyes wild, hand outstretched in front of her. Her hair lay plastered to her skin. It took a moment to notice her surroundings; she was in a study, and a quick glance out the window beside her, told her she was still in the Manor. When she did, she lowered her hand and drew in a shaky breath, clenching her eyes shut.

'You're awake.'

Anabelle's head snapped to the door as the man from before, with the crooked grin and blue eyes, and a younger gentleman stepped into the room.

'We heard you shout and came to see if you were all right,' said the young gentleman.

Anabelle took in his features. He was ordinary but not ugly, with grey eyes and a soft mouth. His average height and smooth face made him seem boyish. The man from before righted his emerald-green coat over his fitted cream pantaloons, his black mask still on his face.

'This good fellow,' the grey-eyed man began, 'caught you before you took a spill to the ground! It was our good fortune that he was here. He claims to be a doctor!'

The man draped his overcoat on the back of a passing chair and rolled up the sleeves of his white dress shirt. 'May I?' he asked, and at her nod, he sat beside her, pushing her skirt out of the way.

'Doctor?' she questioned warily, her voice croaking.

He hummed through pursed lips, checking her pulse, though she could see the twinkle of amusement in his eyes.

'You seem to be doing fine now, m'dear.' His voice was kind and warm, not that same assuming arrogance she heard from before.

'Was I not before?' she asked, her throat raw.

'I dare say not,' said the boyish man. 'Muttering and tossing about. I feared you were having a night scare and suggested we wake you, but our good doctor here said no. You need rest no matter what ungodly terrors you may have.'

His tone suggested he'd fought the good doctor's wishes.

Anabelle nodded, putting a shaky hand on her breast. 'Yes, thank you, he was right. I did need my...rest.' It almost pained her to agree with the stranger beside her on the elaborately stitched loveseat. Something about him made her want to talk back, and it took everything in her not to.

'I'm Charles Meier,' said the other man. 'What may your name be, miss?'

She tried to smile as she said, 'Anabelle.'

'Would you care for a dance after the doctor has you back on your feet?'

The doctor made a rude noise and shot a pointed look at Charles. 'Do not go asking for a dance after she has just taken a spill—especially with youth such as yourself. Now go,' he said with a dark scowl. Charles muttered under his breath about hoarding the prettiest girl for himself.

Anabelle's lips quirked, but she didn't have the energy to fully smile as she watched the door shut behind Charles.

The doctor reached into a hidden pocket of his overcoat and produced a silver flash, offering it to her. 'Drink.'

Anabelle gave him a look that told him no. 'Do you think I take drinks from strange men, especially when it comes from their strange flasks?'

He shrugged and took a swig.

After a moment, when he appeared fine, she asked, 'What is it?'

'I thought you didn't take strange drinks from strange men?'

'And I don't believe you're actually a doctor!' she retorted, her throat protesting.

He took another sip, shrugging again. 'Smart woman.'

Anabelle huffed, crossing her arms. 'What do you want?'

'For you to drink.' He offered her the flask again.

When she didn't take it, he rolled his eyes and grabbed a crystal glass from the table behind her, pouring the contents of his flask into it.

'Water. It's water. Happy?'

She glared at him but took the glass, sniffing its contents. 'Why do you want me to drink?'

'Because,' he said, his words pausing, his jaw flexed as he glanced around the room.

Anabelle sat up a little straighter. 'Because why? Why are you here?'

His jaw twitched, and he nodded towards the glass in her hand. 'Drink, Anabelle.'

Silence spanned between them, a clock ticking endlessly from somewhere in the room. But despite herself, she tilted the glass to her mouth. The water was sweet and familiar, but she couldn't place the taste.

She handed the glass back to him. 'What's your name?'

Replacing the glass on the table, he slid her an amused look. 'If we meet again, I'll introduce myself properly.'

'Rude,' she huffed.

Pausing, the man regarded her a moment before leaning forward so they were face to face. Anabelle resisted the urge to shift back as her nerves skittered through her limbs again. He smelled like earth and fire.

'I don't like cheaters and liars. So, my dear Anabelle,' he intoned, his deep voice raking over her name like a caress. 'I have just given you an open door to your reality. Maybe we will see each other again because of it.' He paused, grabbed his coat, and threw it over his shoulder. 'Or maybe not.'

Anabelle sat there dumbfounded.

He tossed her a wink on his way out. 'Good evening.'

Alone once again, she felt wholly overwhelmed.

With a sigh, she undid the mask when she realised it was still tied around her face, dropped it into her lap, and stared through the lone window in the study. Helplessness laced her voice as she muttered, 'I'm so confused.'

Anabelle thanked the coachman and watched the carriage disappear down the gravel road. She'd left the ball soon after awakening, thanking her hostess for a lovely evening. They appeared more than eager for her to go. It seemed she had made a scene with her hysterics, and just as she feared, she had become the latest gossip.

With a sigh, Anabelle turned toward her dark cottage. A candle burned bright in the window, a small welcome from her mother. At the thought of her mother, anger and confusion flooded her. Was she going crazy, or was she a different person entirely?

Frustration rose in her stomach, and she kicked a rock as it bubbled forth. She cursed as her big toe throbbed with pain. Patience was not something she was very good at as of late.

A bitter wind tossed up the hem of her skirt, throwing it about her feet. Clenching her teeth, she picked up the heavy satin and pushed through the current to the cottage door.

Anabelle let out a great breath as she shut the door behind herself. She clutched her mask in both hands and glanced at the unlit halls of her home, remembering the darkness from her memories. The chilling fingers of terror ran the length of her spine.

She dashed for the candle in the kitchen window and hurriedly made her way to her room. She slammed the door behind her, realising too late she shouldn't awaken her mother. She pushed away from the door and set the candle on her vanity when all was still.

A quick glance told her Pepper wasn't in her room, and she eyed her door. With pursed lips and a relenting sigh, she grabbed the candle and quietly went to her mother's room.

The door creaked softly on its hinges, and she brought the candle up to light the darkness.

Her mother slept soundly, Pepper curled beside her pillow.

With a soft smile, Anabelle backed up and returned to her

room. Closing the door gently this time and setting the candle off to the side, she made to undress.

The laces fought her, bending her arms awkwardly until they finally came loose and dropped to the floor. With a triumphant sound, she worked on her rigid stays. Once off, she threw the contraption into her closet so she wouldn't have to see it. Pulling out a nightgown, she made quick work of her slip and petticoat, sliding the nightgown over her bare limbs.

The chill of the house whispered to Anabelle, and she shivered, feeling the crisp breath press against her skin. Gooseflesh covered her arms. Grabbing her blanket atop her bed, she wrapped herself in it.

Blowing out the candle, she shuffled to sit on her windowsill and pulled her knees to her chest. Exhaling heavily, she leaned against the glass pane and stared into the night.

The moon sat high in the sky amongst many stars, keeping it company in the darkness. The tall grass of the field swayed and danced in the eerie light. The bare trees stood like an imposing barrier against the world of humans. And yet, as Anabelle continued to stare at the open world of nature, she could almost sense the glow of life seeping from their barrier. Like a bright light that wanted to be seen…but only a dark gloom was present like an oily sheen.

Her eyes fought to stay open, only to lose. But just before the untouchable world claimed her, her eyes rested on a figure dressed in all black standing within the tall swaying grass. His presence alarmed Anabelle, but her mind could do nothing but drift off into unconsciousness, limbs heavy to the hypnotic lull of sleep.

The dull grey eyes of Balwin haunting her.

CHAPTER TEN

Anabelle stared across the grasslands to the barren treeline. The blanket still wrapped tightly around her body and sat in the little nook of her windowsill.

The naked trees towered like a massive wall, and the grassy moor's grey fields waved gently in the breeze.

As far as she was aware, Anabelle herself had not changed, though the world certainly had, just in the slightest. Everything was just as it was every morning, yet it *was* different. Every colour, every movement, it had all shifted. To what, she wasn't sure.

Shaking away the thoughts, she stood on stiff legs, her muscles aching as she stretched. Shivering from the cottage's bitter chill, she pulled the blanket tighter.

The wood moaned underfoot as Anabelle drifted from her

room to the kitchen. Once there, she put the kettle on the stove and got a fire going in the iron casting. She let her fingers heat by the flames for a moment before she sank into a chair at the table.

Anabelle's gaze drifted out the bay window as she watched the cuckoos fly from their nests. She could see vast mountain ranges standing old and proud just beyond the treetops. Their peaks were topped with snow, hinting at winter's impending arrival.

Feeling the water boil in the kettle, Anabelle stood, leaving the blanket tossed over the chair. Using a cloth, she placed the kettle on a cold plate. Her hand paused midair as she reached for a teacup. She had *felt* the water boil before the kettle began to steam.

Mutely, Anabelle made a cup of tea and returned to her place at the bay window. Quizzically staring at her cup, she eyed the floating herbs with reservation. She couldn't feel the water anymore; it was just tea before her.

Anabelle took a sip, burning her tongue.

Just tea.

The wooden floors creaked as her mother approached down the hall. Anabelle cleared her bewildered thoughts, straightened in her seat, and curled her fingers around the cup for warmth.

'Good morning,' Anabelle said when her mother entered with Pepper.

Isadora smiled, padding quietly into the kitchen on bare feet. 'Good morning. I didn't think you would be up so early.'

Anabelle shrugged. 'I came home early. It was barely midnight—the kettle is still hot.'

'Thank you, love.'

Isadora set Pepper on the floor and broke a day-old carrot in half for her breakfast. Then, she grabbed a cup and made some tea before joining Anabelle.

'Tell me about the ball. Did you have fun? Did you dance with anyone?'

'Yes,' she said slowly, taking a sip to buy herself time to gather her thoughts.

Memories of the ball, that dance, blue eyes, and a man on horseback made her stomach tighten.

'I did...dance with one gentleman.'

The images of their waltz made her eyes glaze over as she got lost in her memories of last night…Then reality washed away all thoughts of Gallian, and the bitter truth sunk into her skin like a weight.

Isadora peered at her, eyebrow raised, lips quirked. 'Well, aren't you going to tell me who he is?'

Anabelle looked up, and the swirling emotions from last night came back. Anger, frustration, uncertainty.

'Why did you lie to me?'

It was the only question she could ask, the one she needed answered the most. Millions of questions bombarded her, but this was the one that hurt.

Silver-blue eyes matched as Anabelle and Isadora stared at one another. A palpable silence, thick enough to chew, lay between them.

At last, Isadora glanced away with a heavy sigh.

'I suppose I cannot hide the truth anymore? I suppose it is for the best?'

The questions were aimed at herself.

Isadora straightened in her chair, holding her tea in both hands. Her brows pulled tight, and her mouth pursed.

'First, Anabelle, my darling, I am so sorry that these lies have hurt you, but I do not apologise for keeping these secrets. They have kept you safe for the last fifteen years—kept you *alive*. I will not feel guilty for that.'

Her fingers tapped the edge of her cup. Glancing at Pepper, the rabbit moved across the room toward Anabelle.

'Last night,' Isadora said, 'you came of age. As with most things in our world, when one thing ends, another begins. So, the veil was lifted. Your memories are returning.' Isadora tilted her head in thought. 'What do you remember?'

Our world.

Anabelle opened her mouth, then snapped it shut, only to open it again.

'No,' Anabelle said. 'No, you will tell me the truth- all of it. You told me once that my dream was just a dream. Now I know that it was a memory- my memory—*your* memory. So, tell me the truth,

Mother.'

Isadora rubbed a hand over her forehead, looking out the bay window. Her features were cast in a far-off stare as she began to process memories she could no longer ignore.

'You are what I am,' she said at last. 'You are fae. Though unlike myself, you bear the blood of mortals—of humans. Before you were born—or even a mere thought, I met a human, and we fell in love. Your father made me feel alive in a way I never had before. His charisma was intoxicating, and he saw the world for its possibility. He saw the truth so long ignored by humans.'

Pain and happiness lingered in Isadora's eyes as a small smile lifted her lips.

'After many years of growing a friendship I did not know I could have, with a human no less, I became pregnant with you. A child conceived out of our passion and love. He and I happily raised and cared for you until he fell ill one day, as most mortals would, and he died shortly after. No matter what I did, try as I may, fate would have him dead.' Her eyes grew misty, glazing over. 'He was handsome and kind and believed in what most no longer believed in—our people, people of the fae.'

Isadora took a sip of her tea. Her eyes fixated on the tree line. 'There was another, by the name of Balwin, who also captured the interest of a human. But be mindful, this was not love. Balwin was like all fae, painfully beautiful in the eyes of mortals. To humans, we were like stars fallen from the sky, though now society finds the idea of us less than favourable. Your father shone just as brightly to me as I did to him. His spirit was radiant, and I was drawn to him as much as he was to me. Alas, Balwin was not the same. There was a haunting beauty to him that enraptured female mortals.

'Balwin believed the fae were superior to the humans, and he took what he thought was rightfully owed to him.' Her following words were forced out with a look of disgust. 'He took a woman by force. I could hear her screaming, but it was too late when I finally found them. The child was left in a basket at the edge of the forest, swathed in a dirty blanket. Balwin took the child and raised him. Gallian was born out of lust. Lust for power, sexual desires, control…Everything the fae holds to the lowest accounts. This child had been brought into the world from a horrible outcome.'

Isadora paused, glancing at her daughter, her fingers having gone cold around the now cool porcelain. 'Anabelle, you must know that our world is a beautiful place. Life thrives within its deep roots. There is a heartbeat in our world, ancient and pure; if you listen carefully, you can hear it. That is what Balwin wishes to destroy, the death he wishes to inflict upon us.

'As the years passed, you grew into the most beautiful little girl. Your gentle and caring heart warmed even the most isolated. Whether fae or animal, even the smallest creatures, you brought life to everything around you, even Gallian.

'Balwin's corrupt nature grew over the years, morphing into shadows and chaos. Dark magic corrupted every essence of who he was. He no longer looked fae but something lesser, something evil. Gallian loved his father and strived for his own love despite being tormented by his father.

'There came the eve on the fifth year of your and Gallian's births, the sacred choosing, the first in two millennia. The ceremony is upheld by the Spirits of Seasons to acknowledge who will become the next keeper of the Forest when they come of age. Both of you were so young, but such is tradition. The Spirits chose from the innocent to be Keeper of the Forest.' Isadora glanced at Anabelle from the corner of her eye, seeing her face expressionless.

'The Keeper of the Forest protects the boundary and everything that lives within. Initially chosen by the dragons during ancient times to serve our world as guardians, he or she hold the very essence of the forest within themselves. The power to control all things, even the world's life and death. The keeper is the forest's centre, reigning for two thousand years until it is time for a new keeper to step up and take their place. The world of man and the world of fae are one. Divided by an unseen veil created by the four gods who made our world. The forest mirrors that boundary, and you are its keeper.

'The night of the ceremony, everything was as it should be, but when they chose you, everything went terribly wrong. The Spirits, Winter, Spring, Summer, and Autumn, hold the council, and their combined magic makes its selection. When Gallian was not chosen, Balwin did not react well. In turn, he—he tried to kill you.' The words caught in Isadora's throat, and she cleared it, her eyes distant, lost in memory. 'Winter risked her life protecting yours, and Balwin was banished to a region within our darkest forest, imprisoned…until now.

'After that, I took you and fled to the mortal world. This cottage belonged to your father.' She sighed quietly, rubbing her brow. 'Anabelle, we live in a world, within a world, within another world. I created a barrier around our land, around this cottage, to protect us from Balwin in fear of him escaping. We live in the mortal world, yet no living being can pass through the barrier unless I permit it. Now that I am no longer keeper, the barrier is falling, and I am afraid it will vanish altogether in the coming days. I am afraid for us. You are the keeper now, Anabelle. You have come of age, my dearest. I can no longer protect you as I once did.'

Anabelle sat in silence, watching her mother as she finished her story. The muscle in her jaw ticked, and Anabelle looked down at her cold tea.

'For fifteen years, you lied to me,' she whispered.

Isadora shook her head, her eyes wide with panic. 'No, I just masked your memories to protect you so you could grow into the woman you are now. I didn't want your life to be controlled by fear.'

Anabelle stood, her mind blank, like an open void threatening to swallow her. She turned to leave, body rigid, limbs numb. Everything about her was silent, and that frightened her. She wasn't afraid of what her mother had told her…; she was afraid of what else she might not know.

'I don't know anything about who I am,' she whispered.

Isadora stood as Anabelle walked away from the table, reaching out a desperate hand. 'Anabelle, my darling, where are you going?'

Anabelle's hands clenched at her sides, and she forced her fingers to unfurl. 'To the forest.'

Isadora gripped the ledge of the table, her knuckles turning white. 'It isn't safe.'

'I can't live my life in fear, Mother. Isn't that what you wanted?'

Anabelle had changed into a dark blue wool dress with long sleeves, a grey wool knit scarf wrapped tightly around her neck as she trudged through the tall, fading grass of the fields for the forest. Breathing in deeply, an old familiar weight lifted, and a new weight settled on her shoulders. Her dark hair whipped across her face, and she pushed it back as she stepped past the barrier.

Her footfalls were silent on the soft floor. The air peaked with ice, settling around her like a cool blanket. A gentle hum vibrated through the air, like a distant melody, interweaving through the trees, the leaves dancing in the wind as the forest came to life around her in a way she'd never felt. Anabelle tilted her face to the sky, dim sunlight sprinkling through the forest ceiling, fighting past the grey clouds. She felt something unexplainable come to life, just as it did around her.

The breeze died down, and Anabelle settled on the forest floor, leaning against the base of a tree. Her head rested against the bark as she let her eyes slide shut. She vividly recalled the morning and the previous evening, her mind flicking through each one with adamant curiosity.

She had lost track of time when a chill swept through her like a blade, and her eyes opened to a glittering white world. Trees, leaves, and flowers bloomed in the cold season…yet everything was cloaked in a blanket of glimmering frost.

In the centre of the frozen world, Winter stood in a gown of pale blue and flowing fabrics, her pale skin and icy-green eyes glowing.

Anabelle stood slowly.

Winter was the first to speak. 'It was not by chance, Anabelle, that you found the waters of the *Mer*. Your memories led you there. Just days before your coming of age, you began to remember who you are.'

Anabelle shook her head, running a finger over the frost, studying it.

'Cast in a world branded never to fit in, never be likened to those around me...' She trailed off, glancing back at Winter. 'I suppose I was right?'

Winter tilted her head. 'Not entirely. You *are* half-human. Though immortal you may be, you still have human blood. You do have a choice. You can enjoy the human world and everything in it and even become mortal. Or you can reject it. You chose the world of fae even when your memories were shadowed to believe in something despite the repercussions. That was your choice. You are not scared, Anabelle. You know you are the keeper. There is no fear in you. Not in this.'

Chewing on her bottom lip, Anabelle took a shaky breath, staring at the ground as she processed her words. Fear? No. Confusion? Yes.

'What are the waters of the Mer?' Anabelle asked.

'They are water Fae. Their waters are tinged with healing magic.'

Her memories slowly pieced together. 'Every time I drank from the water, I remembered something about myself or another. I even dreamt of you once.'

Winter smiled, the icy forest muting everything around them. 'No, that was not a dream, Anabelle.'

'I thought Balwin was banished?' she said, recalling his scarred face at the ball, the faint image of him in the fields.

'He was. His banishment was executed by your mother, who was keeper before you. Now that her reign has ended, I'm afraid he has returned from the dark forest. Her power no longer has dominion over him.'

'Haven't you tried to find him?'

Winter gave the slightest shake of her head. 'That is not my place, Anabelle.'

Anabelle clenched her teeth, looking away with a scoff. 'The ball, it happened. How did you know?'

'I did not know. Magic is a funny creature in its own right. The spirits had no play in those dreams, though. I must go now,

Anabelle.' She turned and began to walk through the icy domain, fading into the forest.

'Wait!' Anabelle called out, taking a step forward.

Winter stopped, looking over her shoulder.

Gesturing to the frozen world, she asked, 'Why did you do this?'

Winter smiled at her, and a light laugh escaped pale pink lips as she disappeared into nothing.

Her words floated through the air: 'I did not do this, Anabelle.'

CHAPTER ELEVEN

A twig snapped, and Anabelle's eyes flew open. Her back went rigid. She glanced down, her fingers wiggling on the cold dirt floor. Frost seeped from beneath her palm, travelling across the tree's base, curling around the roots like frozen vines.

Lifting her hand from the ground, she stood, glancing at where she had sat. The frost crawled up the trunk just to where her head had laid. Slowly, she reached out her hand and brushed along the coarse bark, watching in fascination as icy tendrils spread where her fingertips grazed.

Pulling her fingers away, she cradled her hand to her hammering heart. Her chest rose and fell with every shallow breath, and she stepped back as if the forest was a predator and she the prey. Her wide eyes searched the ground briefly, blood rushing through her ears like a rapid river, and then she ran.

Her feet pounded the forest floor, and bare branches reached out like spindled fingers. She pushed forward, ripping out of their grip as they caught her dress.

Just as she saw the forest's edge, the hairs on the back of her neck stood on end. Anabelle whirled, scanning the treeline. The forest slowly darkened, and she held her breath as fear twisted in her stomach. Her eyes wide and searching, Anabelle forced herself to turn back. Still, she couldn't help glancing over her shoulder.

Leaving the forest with long strides, she made her way back to the cottage, trying to shake the feeling of eyes at her back. The cold claws at her spine wouldn't let up. She gasped as her foot caught the underside of a rock, and she fell to the ground with a heavy thud, hands splaying in front of her in an attempt to catch herself. She pushed herself onto her knees, brushing the dirt off quickly with shaking hands.

With her shoulders falling, her hands became lead in her lap as her strength bled from her bones, the wind blowing recklessly behind her. Anabelle glanced at the cottage, her mother's words ringing. She pressed her hands into the black soil, her nails combing into the earth, and closed her eyes.

'I just have to listen,' she whispered.

Moments passed, and she grew impatient and a little embarrassed when nothing happened.

Shaking her head, Anabelle took a deep breath, calming her impatience, and listened.

Her pulse slowed, her mind calmed, and the fear dimmed in the background. The wind blew around her in a harmonic tune, the yellow grass playing a contrasting melody.

Then the softest hum lifted on the wind, pulsing around her. It was not the steady thumping of her own heart. Yet, even then, she felt her own begin to beat in rhythm. Peace settled on her, blanketing her mind.

And yet, just as quickly as that peace came, it disappeared. Pure, blinding panic reared into being. The winds transformed into a wrecking force. Eyes watched her, and she whirled, hair whipping behind her in tangles, stinging her flesh. Her throat clenched, and her body began to shake with white-hot terror. In one great breath, she let out a piercing scream.

The forest was dark as far as she could see. Shadows clouded every inch, their spider legs slicing through the air, searching for life to consume. Cries of the Fae pierced the forest edge, and Anabelle let out a shriek as pain stabbed her from every direction. Her limbs trembling as their pleas wrecked through her, she fell back, trying to crawl from the carnage.

The wind blew dangerously as she struggled to stand. Her body felt made of stone. Looking back, the forest was consumed by a black mist, and those shadows crawled through the fields.

Anabelle forced herself to her feet and ran as fast as she could, the wind pushing her this way and that. Something wanted to hold her there. She could feel its bitter fingers digging into her flesh. Gritting her teeth, she glanced over her shoulder, seeing the darkness come closer and closer until it was at her heels.

She propelled onward, crying out when something shoved her to the ground. Her head slammed on the earth, pain shooting through her elbow. She threw her arms over her head, trying to shield herself from the shadows, and clenched her eyes shut, waiting for the last blow.

The wind roared, whirling her hair around her face until she felt the tug of darkness vanish. Slowly, she cracked one eye open, then both, to find a wall of ice before her. The shadows on the other side crawled like spiders, trying to escape her barrier.

She scrambled to her feet as something in her roared to life. It took control of her, and she screamed, forcing the ice wall back toward the shadows.

The demons slammed against the ice and nearly knocked her down, and she yelled as they tried to tear a hole in her defences. She drove back harder, gritting her teeth as something inside her begged to be released onto the darkness.

Let me out; let me free!

So, she did. With a wild yell, she relented to the force inside her and a power seared through her limbs. In a flash of white, it speared right for the darkness like an arrow loosed from the bow.

Her aim was true as it pierced the shadows. The pressure released from her body, and the winds calmed.

Anabelle stared at her shield just before it vanished, and she realised that it wasn't just ice but blue and white light that seemed to hold flecks of stardust and veins of gold. Rubbing her fingertips together, she stared at her hands as the light vanished and looked back up at the forest. The creeping wall of shadows and mist was nowhere in sight.

A tear ran down her cheek, and she brushed it away, gasping for a breath when her lungs started to scream. Her limbs shook, her pulse shuddering through her body.

Stumbling towards the cottage, Anabelle caught sight of Balwin standing atop the field, watching her, his mutilated face prominent in the grey light. Their gazes locked. Terror gripped Anabelle, and she picked up her skirts, fleeing for the cabin. She didn't stop. She didn't look back. Falling through the cottage entrance, she slammed the door behind her and dropped against it.

'Anabelle?' her mother called, hurrying into the hall. 'Anabelle!'

Her mother rushed to her side, and Anabelle let her all but carry her to the study. Once stuffed into an oversized cushioned chair, her body melting into it, she looked at her mother and murmured, 'You were right about the barriers.'

Isadora brushed a calming hand over Anabelle's pallid cheek, her skin cold. 'What happened?'

'Balwin has returned. He's come for me.'

Her mother took a step back, a hand going to her mouth.

'Your banishment no longer has a hold over him.'

Isadora sat across from her, nodding mutely. 'Yes, I know. I had hoped—Silly, to hope for such a thing. You cannot cure evil.'

Anabelle shook her head. 'We are not born evil, Mother. It is a choice that one makes.'

Isadora felt the same slight tug of hope she had had when Anabelle was a child. 'Are you all right, love?'

Anabelle thought momentarily and tried to express her feelings: 'I have never felt so afraid in my life, so much pain. But it was not my own pain, nor was I afraid for myself. It was for the fae, for the forest. I felt this stabbing pain when the forest was covered in darkness. I heard the cries of the fae who were trapped within it. I could do nothing to help them.'

Anguish seeped through her words, and she buried her head in her hands. She heard her mother fall to her knees in front of her just before she gently pulled Anabelle's hands away.

'You are the Keeper, Anabelle. You do have the power to do something about it. You're connected to all life. You must believe in that.'

Anabelle looked out the window and saw no traces of Balwin. But he was not gone. He was there, waiting in the shadows. 'He's waiting for me. He knows I will return to the forest, ' she thought.

Isadora reached up and cupped her daughter's cheek. 'Be strong, Anabelle. I can no longer be strong for the both of us.'

Anabelle slept soundly that night, Pepper by her side, and her dreams were scarce. She felt a quietness she had not felt in some time. The moon shone full and bright through her window.

A tall figure stood in Anabelle's bedroom, watching her slumber peaceably in her bed. Bright eyes shone in the dark. The man stepped forward and rested a steady hand on her still form, shaking her slightly.

'Anabelle.'

Anabelle moaned softly.

Again, the stranger shook her shoulder. 'Anabelle.'

Opening bleary eyes, she looked up and screamed, her heart stopping. Wide awake now, she leapt from her bed to the furthest corner of her room.

'Quiet!' he snapped. Then his voice softened, and he said, 'Don't be afraid.' He stepped into the moonlight so she could see his face.

With a gasp, Anabelle took a step forward. 'Gallian?'

His green eyes twinkled with mirth as he dusted a hand over his black coat, his dark hair framing his face. 'Did you expect someone else?'

Anabelle frowned. 'Yes, I was. I'm glad it's only you,' she said in a clipped, cold tone. She felt the tension ease only slightly and was still uncertain as she watched him.

A dark look of amusement passed over his face. 'Afraid?'

'I think I have every right to be afraid,' she snapped.

Shrugging one shoulder, he glanced around. 'My father is not far, but he is not here.' He held out his hand. 'Shall we walk?'

She stared at the hand offered to her, nibbling on her bottom lip in thought. A moment passed before she nodded with pursed lips.

'Let me get my coat. I'll meet you outside.'

When the door shut behind him, Anabelle walked to her window and tested the locks—they held fast.

Sweeping her hair over one shoulder, she let out a breath and quickly put on her stockings and boots. Stroking Pepper between her ears, she grabbed her wool coat from her closet and left the room. She eyed her mother's door, waiting to hear any sounds of her stirring, and was surprised and grateful when there was only silence.

The house creaked and groaned in the night, frightening sounds and shadows appearing as if the cottage was haunted. Though some childish part of her dreaded the thought that perhaps it was her father's soul. She shivered and shook the thought from her head. Anabelle found Gallian waiting outside, just a little past the cottage walkway.

'Anabelle.' He smiled, offering his hand once more.

She glanced at it but still didn't take it. Gallian gave her a knowing smile before steering her towards the forest.

'Where are you taking me?' she asked cautiously.

'My father will not touch you tonight, Anabelle. Not while I am with you.'

Anabelle looked up at Gallian's face, noting his solid gaze on the tree line.

'Where are you taking me?' she repeated.

'I want only to introduce you to our world.'

One of her brows rose. 'Oh?'

Gallian looked down at her. 'You quite enjoyed what I'm about to show you when we were children.'

Anabelle looked away to the long path of the forest edge, the full moon lighting their way.

'There is so much I don't remember,' she murmured.

'You have a lifetime to remember now,' he said, his eyes

twinkling.

'How did you get into my bedroom?' she questioned suddenly, stopping to look up at him.

He tilted his head in thought. 'Have you yet to figure out by now, Anabelle, that magic is the centre of the Fae?'

'Is that your way of saying you used magic?'

Gallian shrugged nonchalantly. 'If it will make you feel better, then yes.'

Anabelle sidestepped a stone in her path as she continued walking. 'You scared me, Gallian.'

Gallian didn't answer, continuing to walk along the forest edge until they reached a large rock with a knotted circle carved into it.

'I have walked this path hundreds of times,' Anabelle said, befuddled. 'I have never seen this rock before.'

'Your mother did not allow you to before,' he replied simply before touching her bicep and leading her into the forest. 'This is the home of pixies and the winged fae. This rock symbolises their borderland.'

'The winged?'

Fairies. They live together in this region of the forest.'

'How big is the forest?' she prodded, her breath clouding as she walked around a thin tree sapling.

Gallian looked back at her. 'This forest is our world, and the fae are vast in number. Our world is boundless. This is just the beginning. There are strongholds, villages, oceans, and so much more.' He shook his head in irritation. 'So much you were robbed of.'

Anabelle said nothing, and they walked on silently, though it seemed they were the only quiet thing in the forest. Whispers filtered from hidden corners, and small shadows danced in and out of the trees without being seen. Anabelle watched the world around her with raw fascination.

'Here.'

Anabelle nearly ran into him as he stopped suddenly in front of a massive wall of trees, their thick bases pressed against one another like an indestructible wall.

A yellow glow shone from the treeline's cracks, filtering through the small spaces and shining brightly along the branches.

Anabelle lifted her hand to the light, letting it cast a glittering glow over her skin. 'What is it?'

Gallian slid his hand into hers. She felt the warmth slip through her palm and up her arm.

'Come and see.'

Leading her around the wall of trees, Gallian came to a clearing filled with a warm, glowing light. Holding a finger to his lips, he waited, and Anabelle padded up to one of the large trees. Laying a hand on the bark, she leaned her body on its thick trunk and watched in awe as tiny fae danced and made merry with one another. Soft, melodious music floated in the air.

'What are they celebrating?' she inquired.

Gallian watched Anabelle as he said, 'They're celebrating you, Anabelle.'

He could see her look of wonder fade, replaced by a downcast gaze as she grew solemn.

Anabelle turned from the dancing fairies, looking past the thicket of trees.

'Only two days ago, I discovered I am the keeper. Seeing the fae celebrating me, the keeper, I feel like they have been lied to, and I was the one to do it.'

Gallian reached out a hand, turning her to face him. 'Doubt will be your biggest downfall, Anabelle.'

She closed her eyes briefly to repress her conflicting emotions. 'I don't know what they want. I don't know what your father wants. I don't know what *you* want…I don't know.'

Gallian cradled her face in his hand, causing her to look up at him. 'Your fear is my father's biggest weapon. The darkness can overcome everything, every living, breathing thing. My dear Anabelle, you are the shield from the darkness. *That* is why they celebrate you.'

Anabelle shook her head, pulling away. 'I don't know, Gallian.'

He stepped in her path again, making her look at him. 'Be the light that you were meant to be. From the time of your birth, it has resided in you. Don't run from it. Accept it.'

'I don't know how.'

'You do.'

'I don't!'

'Yes, you do, Anabelle!'

'I don't know how to!'

Gallian grabbed her around the waist and pulled her to him, his other hand snaking around her neck as his lips claimed hers. He pulled her body flush with his, wrapping her into his embrace.

Anabelle's hand went to the one at her waist to push him away, fingers digging into the lapels of his jacket, when she felt a fire begin. It started as a spark, spreading across her belly in warm waves, igniting a path through her shocked limbs. It was her first kiss.

His lips were firm against her own, her body flush against his solid form. Her heartbeat began to beat faster and faster, lingering unease coiling in her subconscious until panic, like bells, warned in her head, and she pulled back quickly. His grasp on her waist remained firm.

His eyes were an icy emerald green, lit by a desire. Her silver eyes stared at him with confusion, brows furrowed, and mouth pinched.

She opened her mouth, but Gallian spoke first.

'Your emotions control your power.' Gallian glanced down at his arm curled around her waist.

Anabelle followed his gaze and discovered that part of his forearm was covered in white ice, with veins of gold running through it. The streams of gold moved around his arm like molten fire, glowing in the darkness.

'Warmth.'

Anabelle released him and stumbled back, raising a hoarfrost-covered hand between them. 'I'm sorry.'

Gallian shook his head, waving a hand between them. 'No, don't be. I thought if I could release a strong enough emotion, you would let go of your hold on your magic.'

She opened her mouth to protest, but he cut her off.

'I also wanted to kiss you.'

Anabelle stared at Gallian, glancing down at the golden ice slowly disappearing. She ignored his last statement. It had been her first kiss, stolen from her, and her cheeks bloomed with anger.

'You had no right to do that,' she bit out.

He raised a brow at her but ignored her comment. 'Winter is the main source of who you are. When Winter protected you, she gave you a piece of her essence. My father did not want her; he wanted *you*, and our powers were not strong enough. At our age, they had not matured. Winter is a part of you.' He stroked her burning cheek. 'Winter is the purest season. Untouched and unmarked. Snow falls from the sky like frozen light. It is your shield and your sword.'

Her mouth flattened at that thought, stepping out of his reach. 'How do I find it?'

'Our magic is like a lifeline. You have to reach within yourself. When you find it, hold on to it, and it will come. It might help to use your happiest memories. The emotions they evoke will guide you to your power.'

Anabelle wracked her mind for one memory but found nothing. 'I don't think I have a significant memory. I remember moments I once found to be my happiest, but now they feel like falsehoods.'

'Our past, no matter the lie, is no less real. It's what makes us who we are today, at this moment in time. We all wear a mask, no matter if we're at a ball and tied to illusions. We're bound to reveal ourselves when the opportunity arises.'

'Do you wear a mask, Gallian? Are you who you say you are?'

Gallian's brows pinched together as he thought, 'That's hard to say...Autumn raised me after my father was banished.'

Those words held an air of bitterness that made Anabelle tilt her head in thought. 'How did you find me through the veil?' she asked, wary, wrapping her arms around herself.

'No one could find you for years. The spirits searched and searched, but you were gone— until you weren't. While scouring the veil one afternoon on a hunt with my brother, I saw you. I didn't know it was you until I saw those silver eyes and how you talked to the trees. We were invisible to you; you walked right by us once.

'After that, I watched over you day and night. I watched your daily activities. I watched you daydream in the fields for hours upon hours and read many of your books more than once. I thought I had imagined it, but I had not.'

She looked up into Gallian's eyes, and her cheeks tinged pink when she saw them fixated on her. He lifted her hands between them, her palms cast upwards. She looked down, and her eyes widened as she stared at the glowing white-blue winter's breath that hovered over her palms.

It illuminated their faces, and she took a small step back, quickly glancing at the forest around them. 'Thank you.'

A tug on her hair caught her attention. There, floating in the air, was a lithe little fairy dressed in flower petals, long red hair falling nearly to her feet. Long translucent wings fluttered behind her as she gestured for them to follow, tugging once more on a strand of Anabelle's hair.

Gallian and Anabelle followed noiselessly behind the fairy, who guided them back to the Fae festivities. Anabelle stepped into the yellow glow of their celebration.

Warmth blanketed her body like summer had never left. The ice in her limbs melted, and her body relaxed. The soft music had stopped, and all the small fae gathered close, covering the trees around them. Some sat in burrows while others floated in the air.

Anabelle heard the faintest rustle and turned her attention back to the red-haired fairy. The spry fae fluttered to an entrance at the base of a tree when two other winged bodies appeared, holding a large object between them. It took three of them to lift it to Anabelle's height. The red-haired sprite floated in the middle, while the other two, with hair like sunlight and naked, agile bodies clothed in nothing but light, held either end of a thin silver chain necklace.

Anabelle offered her palm, and they glided forward, gently laying it in her open hand.

Staring down at the gift, she noted the clear-white teardrop encased by delicately intertwined silver. It was as small as the flower seeds they sowed in the summer.

Looking up at the fairies, she asked, 'Why?'

Wordlessly, the redhead fairy closed her fingers around the necklace.

'Thank you,' she whispered, sliding the necklace over her head and freeing her hair. 'Thank you,' she said again before treading softly from the alcove of trees.

Gallian waited off to the side, frowning at the necklace.

'What is it?' she inquired.

His frown shifted into a smile, and he shook his head, waving off her words.

'Do you see now?' he asked gently.

Anabelle brushed her fingers over the teardrop, saying nothing.

'Come,' Gallian said. 'It's almost dawn. Let me walk you back to the cottage.'

When they arrived, the sky was just starting to turn the slightest shade of blue, the night slowly fading. Anabelle turned to Gallian at the door.

'Why was it so warm?'

'Because they are Summer Fae,' Gallian explained. 'They cannot survive in the winter. Summer has created a place just for them in the cold season. When they must venture from it, Summer's breath will follow.'

'Are there Winter Fae?'

'Yes, and just like their kindred, they cannot survive in the summer. Winter creates a home for them in the warm seasons.'

'I see.'

Gallian caressed her cheek with a warm hand. 'All things that are lost can be found. I believe you want to be found. Tonight, I believe you chose to see your future.'

Glancing up at him, she took a small step towards the door. 'Thank you, Gallian.'

'Goodnight, Anabelle,' he whispered.

He reached out to brush his lips over her knuckles, but she freed her hand before he could. She watched as he gave her a pointed look before taking his leave.

Anabelle watched him return to the forest momentarily before entering the cottage. All was still as she went to her room, but the house began groaning and creaking again with every step. Anabelle slipped into her bed, shrugging off her coat and kicking off her shoes. Pulling off her stockings, she burrowed under the covers and laid her head on the cool pillow with a shiver.

Pepper was still sound asleep on the other side. Anabelle twined the necklace around her finger absentmindedly, her thoughts reeling.

CHAPTER TWELVE

Balwin paced the cavern's dirt-strewn stone floors, shadows licking at his heels. Orbs of fire graced the walls, illuminating the dank cave, stretching until he could only see a pool of darkness, swallowing any light near it.

Damp and isolated from any living thing within the Dauðinn Mountains, Balwin had staked his claim.

Crow-black hair hung in greasy strands around his sunken, pale face. His once-grey eyes had become lifeless and cold. His lips were thin, and his nose—once straight and narrow—had been broken and sat crooked on his withered and scarred features.

His clothes clung to his slim form. Dark brown leather trousers, secured at the waist with a leather belt and a black shirt, open at the neck, hung on him. His hands clasped tightly behind his back, he glanced at the cavern's entrance for the third time since dawn.

Impatience wrapped its claws around Balwin, and a low growl slipped from his lips.

A shadow appeared in the mouth of the cave, and a voice carried forward. 'Father?'

Balwin's head snapped to Gallian, who strolled in with an air of haughtiness, carrying two dead hares.

'Where have you been?' he snarled, stepping forward and snatching the hares from Gallian.

Gallian tilted his head in acknowledgement. 'How lovely it is to see you as well.' Stepping further into the cave, he glanced at his surroundings and grimaced at the smell of rotting death. He spotted the source of forgotten flesh and bones of previous animals his father had consumed, tossed against one wall.

'Charming,' Gallian muttered. Turning his attention back to his father, disgust underlined his voice as he said, 'I was hunting for your supper.'

'*Where* have you been, Gallian?' Balwin repeated as he sharpened a stone and began skinning the hares.

Gallian abstained from gritting his teeth, keeping his face neutral. 'Where do you think I was?'

Balwin sniffed the air, scenting copper and something *more*. A gleaming smile cut along his scarred flesh. Animal blood dripped from Balwin's fingers as he dropped the stone and slowly approached his son. Putting his face only inches from Gallian's, he inhaled deeply, eyes rolling back. A cruel smile turned up his thin lips. 'Ah, my son, your scent deceives your games. *Who* have you been with?'

Gallian picked at his fingernails. 'The Summer Fae are enchanting to simple minds,' he stated coolly.

Balwin clucked his tongue. 'Frozen lavender clings to your skin, and only one *girl* has that scent,' he replied, dragging one bloodied finger across Gallian's cheek as he circled his son. 'Does she sing your name and the name of the Fae?'

His voice echoed in the hollow cave, and Gallian's answering smirk made Balwin cackle as he turned back to the hares.

'*Anabelle*,' he said, saying her name softly. 'Tell me, son, what becomes of our dearest girl?'

A muscle in Gallian's jaw ticked as he walked deeper into the cave. He felt the darkness flood from his father, the fires vanishing one by one in the growing shadows as they surrounded them. Dark talons clawed at the stone at his feet, and he ignored them. They pushed at him from all sides until he reached a hand into the shadows and caressed the weight of dark magic that slithered over his open palm.

Pain sliced his palm, and he jerked his hand back, eyeing the blood welling up. 'You've let your pets out to play, I see.'

Balwin watched his son with darkened eyes.

'I told her the Summer Fae celebrated her return,' he said, turning away from the hungry shadows. 'That their dancing and merriment were for her coming.'

'The chit doesn't know the silly winged Fae dance every night,' muttered Balwin, chewing on a raw rabbit leg. 'Insufferable creatures.'

Gallian rubbed a hand over his jaw. 'Yes, though they gave her a necklace. That was interesting.'

Balwin chuckled lowly. 'A necklace?'

He nodded, humming in answer.

'Let her keep the silly necklace. A token for new life.'

Gallian squared his shoulders, turning his attention to the cave's mouth. 'The others sense a change.'

Balwin's face contorted into a sly smile. 'The time for change is upon us, my son. Do you not want the best for me?'

Gallian rounded on him, his eyes flashing. 'You know I do!' Dark blue sparks lit at his fingertips, and he clenched his hands into fists, containing his anger as the leash on his magic slipped.

After a moment of silence, he took a deep breath and said, 'Do you plan on hurting her?'

'Oh, my dear boy, I plan to do much more than *hurt* her. I will take *everything* from her, as she has taken everything from me. I will *ruin* her.'

Gallian's eyes flicked to the shadows. The blood on his hand turned tacky as his fingers stuck to it. Shaking his head, he gave his father a pointed stare and turned on his heel.

Balwin watched Gallian disappear down the mountainside, taking his leave without a word and felt a twisted glee rake his chest. 'Until our next, *my son.*'

When Gallian emerged from the cave, the fresh air of dawn hit him full force, and anger rose in his stomach. Hand and foot, he climbed down the mountain, the bitter wind cutting through his clothes.

He had made the descent several times, both as a child and as an adult, but it never got easier. He jumped the last hundred feet of the mountain, landing on the ground in a crouch. Standing, he brushed the dirt from his palms and began his walk back to the forest.

'Well, well, well,' said a mocking voice he knew all too well. 'What do we have here?'

Gallian gnashed his teeth in annoyance. 'Néefar,' he sniped, turning to the shifter leaning against a tree, the picture of calculated aloofness. Néefar's dark brown hair was loose around his face, affecting boredom if not for the piercing blue eyes. Néefar's white billowing blouse was open at the neck, black trousers and tall black boots fitted around his legs.

'Brother,' Néefar said with a tilt of his head.

'I am not your brother,' Gallian spat. 'We do not share blood!'

Something predatorial flashed in Néefar's gaze, but he clamped it down with a shrug. 'Whatever you say, Gallian.' He glanced up to the mountain. 'What are you doing?'

'That is none of your concern.'

'When you involve everyone else it becomes *everyone's* concern!'

'You don't know what you speak of,' Gallian said, shaking his head.

A growl rippled through Néefar. 'The ball, Gallian! What was that?'

Gallian paled. 'How did you know about that?'

Néefar scoffed. 'You think I didn't notice you slinking around the girl after we first saw her in the forest? You started changing; everything became a secret with you!' His bitter laugh made Gallian glare, but Néefar ignored it. He took a step closer to Gallian and softened his voice. 'I care for you, Gallian. We might not be blood, but I regard you as a brother. I don't want you jeopardising everything for one person only to lose yourself because of it.'

'You think I would lose myself because of Anabelle?' Gallian asked dryly.

'No, not Anabelle,' he affirmed.

'Gallian, what are you doing?'

Gallian whirled to find Autumn stepping out from behind a cluster of boulders along the mountainside.

Gallian rounded on Néefar. 'You told him to come here?'

Autumn sighed. 'Néefar is not to blame, Gallian. We are concerned.'

'He is my blood, my birthright. There shouldn't be concern for me wanting to see him.'

'Blood, yes,' Autumn said. 'Though I fear he may lead you astray.'

'That is none of your concern,' snapped Gallian. 'The Spirits have no right to interfere.'

'Gallian, I am not interfering; I am only expressing worry. And by seeing her, are you really just risking her life? I thought the two of you were friends when you were younger.'

Gallian's nostrils flared. 'Yes,' was all he could manage through gritted teeth.

'Anabelle was not raised in our world,' Autumn said. 'You trying to guide her into this world could only cause a catastrophic event.'

'You know nothing of the power she holds. She needs to be brought back to the fae!'

Autumn put a firm hand on Gallian's shoulder. With iron in his voice, he said, '*You* know nothing about the power she holds.'

Shame coloured Gallian's cheeks, and he looked away from Autumn's piercing stare. It took great effort to swallow down a sudden rush of anger.

'Don't lose yourself, Gallian,' Autumn said. 'That is what will happen. Let it go.'

Gallian gave a curt nod despite the emotions roiling in his gut. 'Come.'

It was a simple command, and one Gallian silently obeyed before Néefar halted him.

The shifter waited until Autumn was far enough away before whispering, 'Do not think me a fool, Gallian. I was there that night.'

Gallian shrugged out of his grip, raising a brow. 'She's just a silly girl, Néefar. Don't worry your pretty little shifter head.'

A warning growl slipped from him. 'That woman is an innocent. Remember that.'

CHAPTER THIRTEEN

Pepper sat at the edge of Anabelle's bed, nose twitching as Anabelle dressed in a dark green, long-sleeved wool dress. Weaving her hair loosely into a thick braid, she draped it over her shoulder before pulling on her stockings and boots. She picked up Pepper as she walked out of her room, humming under her breath and stroking the rabbit between her ears.

'Why are you so chipper?'

Her mother's inquiring voice floated in from the study. Anabelle found her with a book in hand, standing before the many shelves piled high with novels.

Anabelle joined her, staring up at the titles. 'What are you doing, Mother?'

Isadora kissed Anabelle on the cheek. 'I was just looking over an old story.'

Anabelle came closer to peer at the cover. 'Which is it?'

'*The Tale of Rose.*'

Anabelle nodded slowly, humming. 'You used to read that to me as a child. It was the story of a girl who was overcome by greed and ruled over an entire nation. When her lover saw how low she had fallen, he saved her. It was said that when she conquered the greed, she shed a single drop of blood that fell to the earth, and it healed the ruined land.'

Isadora nodded, looking up at her daughter with a small smile. 'It's the story of the first Keeper.'

Anabelle spun on her heel, eyes wide. 'Rose was a Keeper?'

'Rose was the first Keeper and full-blooded Fae, blessed by dragon fire. She is why the keeper is now half-fae and half-mortal, so they know the weight of life and power.' Isadora flipped through the pages of the novel. 'I filled the pages of these books with the history of our people. I wanted you to know where you came from, the world that would one day, hopefully, be home again…when the time was right.'

Sunlight streamed in through the window, and the glimmer around Anabelle's throat caught Isadora's eye.

'Anabelle, what is that around your neck?'

Anabelle covered the necklace, her fingers curling around the tiny gem. Hesitating, she pulled it off, looking down at it with curiosity. 'It was a gift from the summer Fae,' she said.

Isadora sounded hesitant when she asked, 'May I see it?'

Anabelle offered the necklace, the small stone catching the light. Isadora took it, holding it up to her face.

'Do you know what this is?'

Anabelle shook her head.

Isadora's mouth pressed into a flat line, her eyes going distant. 'This is the Tear of Gabriel, the eleventh keeper. His story is told through the ages by the spirits themselves. It was said that Gabriel cried for the fallen when the nether regions attacked our lands. They are a dark, isolated place within the Forest of Lost Souls, where even Winter grew cold.

'It's said that Gabriel cried for clemency—mercy for the fae. He sacrificed himself for our people.' Isadora looked at her daughter with misty eyes, hands shaking. 'Demons of the nether regions struck Gabriel down with fatal precision, and when he lay there, his blood seeping into the earth, they finally spared them. A life for their lives.

'When all was quiet, and the battlefield nothing more than a cemetery, Spring reached within Gabriel and preserved the last of his soul, his light. It was the purest kind of light, forged from self-sacrifice. I didn't think the summer fae would have it, but Spring herself…' Isadora handed it back to her daughter. 'Keep it safe. Gifts like that are not lightly given among our kind.'

Anabelle stared at the necklace, half expecting it to speak to her and tell her what to do. Instead, it remained inanimate, and she slid it over her head.

'I will, Mother.'

Isadora returned the book to its shelf, then clapped her hands together with a grin sliding into place.

'I have plans for us today!'

'Oh?' Anabelle laughed.

'Yes,' she said. 'We are going on a picnic!'

Anabelle glanced out the window incredulously. 'It looks warm, Mother, but don't believe its lies, ' she said.

'Ah, but this won't be an ordinary picnic.'

Anabelle gave her a perplexed stare.

Isadora winked at her on her way out of the room. 'You will have to wait and find out!'

It was, indeed, a bright and clear winter's day. Anabelle and Isadora wore matching dark blue wool cloaks, and a basket hung from the crook of Isadora's arm. The two women trod over hills and lands that Anabelle had no memory of. Every tree, moss-ridden ledge, and grass-covered moor was new.

'Mother?'

'Hmm?'

Anabelle picked up her skirt as she stepped over a rotting log covered in tangled moss. 'Where exactly are we going?'

Isadora looked over her shoulder at her daughter, her eyes barely containing her excitement. 'Somewhere special.'

Shaking her head, Anabelle followed, watching her step as the hills soon turned into a thick, lush forest. Full trees with bark like midnight surrounded them. Their branches reached towards the heavens, and their leaves blanketed the forest ceiling. Beams of sunlight peaked through the evergreens, and Anabelle stared open mouth around her. It was more than just a forest. Magic lived here. Anabelle could feel it thrumming.

Knotted pieces of wood wove in and out of tree bases in an enchanting dance. Pale blue flowers of all sizes dusted the roots, and the forest floor was black and soft beneath her boots.

'Where are we?' Anabelle whispered in a soft breath, feeling tingling power in her fingertips.

A knowing smile stretched over Isadora's face. 'We're here.'

'We're having a picnic *here*, in the middle of the forest? I told you it wouldn't be warm, Mother.'

Isadora set the basket down. 'You're going to make it warm.'

Anabelle only stared.

'Anabelle, you have the power to make it warm. I want you to use it.'

Anabelle shook her head. 'You overestimate my capabilities, Mother.'

Isadora took her daughter's hands. 'Close your eyes.'

Anabelle hesitated and only closed her eyes when her mother nodded for her to do so. She rolled her shoulders, trying to relax, to release the tension she felt building.

'Now picture a tether of energy. Bright and burning within you.'

She searched for the tether, picturing a bright cord of power, and something nudged her mind. Sparks cantered down her fingers when she grazed it, and she grabbed hold. Fire and ice went down her arm, making her gasp.

'Now, imagine it's the middle of summer. The sun is hot on your skin, and a warm wind blows through this forest. Imagine it's surrounding you, covering you.'

Anabelle concentrated on the image and feel of summer, remembering its warmth and the hot, sticky air she would breathe in. Power coursed through her limbs, and a warm wind suddenly kissed her skin. She opened her eyes to find her mother's approving smile. The air was warm, and it indeed looked like summer had come. Dust shimmered in the beams of sunlight, and leaves rustled in the wind.

'Your magic is a lifeline within you, easily controlled by your emotions.'

'Gallian told me the same thing,' Anabelle commented.

'Gallian?'

Anabelle touched the teardrop around her throat. 'Yes, Gallian.'

'You've seen him, then?'

'Yes,' Anabelle said softly. 'At the ball and in the forest.'

Isadora pursed her lips in thought but only said, 'It will get easier to use your magic as you grow accustomed to it and it to you. Your magic is as alive as you and I are. To know one is to know the other. You must work together.'

'Like learning to dance or to read?'

'Learning how to use your magic is far easier than either. It's all based on emotional connection. Listen to your instincts, for they will be your guide.' She unpacked a blanket from the basket and flicked it in the warm wind, spreading it over the ground. 'Unless, of course, you completely ignore your instincts, but from observation, that is a mortal trait.'

Anabelle sat on the blanket and eyed a plate of dried meats, assorted cheeses, and fruit. She plucked up a morsel of meat, chewing thoughtfully to herself. 'Why is this place special?'

Isadora popped a blackberry into her mouth. 'This is as much my home as it is yours. I had hoped bringing you here would allow you to embrace the part of you that has been hidden for so long.' She hesitated for a moment. 'I also wanted to show you something I have longed to share for many years.'

Anabelle stayed silent, watching her mother with keen eyes.

Isadora ate another blackberry. 'I am much different than I appear. You see, I masked my true image in this world—the human world and the world you knew- not just from you and myself but from all things. You are half human and half Fae. I am not.'

'What are you trying to tell me, Mother?'

'We are still outside the wall, so it should be okay, I pray.' Straightening, Isadora closed her eyes, concentrating on the magic that flowed in her veins. The power concealed for so long seemed to purr in recognition, grazing against her essence, the hidden part of her. When she felt the tug of magic, she pulled it tight, and it seared her body, reclaiming its place.

Anabelle watched her mother's features change like a mirage lifted. Her beauty took Anabelle's breath away. Her cheekbones had heightened, accentuating her narrow oval face. Her brows swept up gracefully, and her eyes had widened. Her mother had been beautiful before, but now she was an unbeknownst beauty- a creature of fairy tales.

Isadora's dark hair fell over her shoulders in soft waves of midnight black that was almost blue. The small pointed tips of her ears swept gracefully up in a delicate arch.

'Your…ears,' Anabelle said in a hushed tone.

'The Fae, Anabelle, is every living being in this world. Our people are the Elves of Álfheimr and High Fae to our realm.'

'I'm an Elf…a High Fae?'

'You are also human—as is Gallian and Balwin.'

Anabelle became puzzled. 'Gallian and I are halflings. But Keepers are to be both mortal and immortal?'

Isadora nodded. 'The time of the last keeper was coming to an end. Balwin and I were the only children in our world at that time. Children were even rarer then than they are now. The spirits made an exception and allowed me to participate in the ceremony. I was chosen above Balwin. You see, he was not always a monster but allowed himself to become one.'

Glancing into the forest, Anabelle could almost hear their secrets as she asked, 'What is this place called?'

'These are the blackwood trees. We are in the Black Forest.'

Her words slipped from her mouth before she could think. 'You're as foreign to me as this place is.'

Sadness weighed down Isadora's eyes as her thin shoulders sagged with an age Anabelle didn't recognise. 'I'm sorry, love. I didn't want to conceal myself, least of all to you, but I had no other choice. I could not risk your life.'

Anabelle looked back to the forest, where the branches swayed, and the wind whispered. She took her mother's hand in hers, squeezing it gently. Her mother was tired— she saw that now, from protecting her. Anabelle could see the fear her mother lived with daily, and she knew the emotions bubbling in her stomach were guilt. 'We can't return,' she whispered.

'Why ever not, Anabelle?'

Anabelle paused, swallowing past the lump in her throat and pushing down the fear. 'It was so easy for him to find me...I...I would never be able to live with myself if he thought to harm you, too.' We cannot keep hiding for my sake. Not with so much to lose.'

'Oh my love, I know. That same fear possessed me for the last fifteen years and still does.'

The wind whispered their secret song, and Anabelle closed her eyes to the melody, forcing herself to take a calming breath.

Isadora stared at her daughter for a long while before nodding. 'Very well. We will leave, but Anabelle, I must warn you. In the laws of the fae, taking you from our world to the world of humans is forbidden. Once we step through the wall, they will know we have returned. Do you understand? They will come for me.'

Temptation gnawed at Anabelle. She thought of changing her mind, staying at the cottage forever, and forgetting the world of the fae—living a mortal life—if it meant her mother would be safe. Anabelle shook the idea from her head.

Isadora smiled brightly, easing any tension. 'Well then, shall we finish our picnic?'

During their picnic, Isadora had Anabelle tap into her emotions more times than Anabelle felt comfortable with, reaching for the white-hot cord that bound her magic inside her. She practised until tiny beads of sweat dotted her temples, and she could make a pebble glow red in her hand.

Packing away the basket, Isadora nodded approvingly, watching Anabelle cast the blistering stone away.

Brushing her skirt off as she stood, Anabelle looked at her mother. 'I can turn a pebble into solid fire, but I doubt that will do much against Balwin.'

Isadora's lips pressed flat as she slid the basket onto the crook of her arm. 'While true, that doesn't mean you don't have an arsenal within you. Do you feel the tether of your magic without searching for it?'

Anabelle thought for a moment, letting herself become still. In the quiet parts of her, the magic cord's thrumming was nearly silent.

When she nodded, her mother gave her a pleased smile. 'Today was not about teaching you how to use your magic—That is as easy as breathing. Today was for you to find your tether, to acknowledge it until you recognised its presence without having to call on it.'

'I see,' Anabelle said, falling into step with her mother as they began the walk back to the cottage, the setting sun casting fire above them. 'Why did you hide me all these years?' she asked suddenly, stopping. 'Did you wish me to fail? To hide my memories and have me live a mortal life?'

'No!' Isadora grasped Anabelle's arm. 'No, of course not!'

'Then why?'

With a defeated sigh, Isadora ran her fingers through her hair. 'Magic…is riddled with *holes*. Holes that have laws and order woven within them. Balwin, whilst banished, had the ability to break out of that prison if he so chose because of those holes. Knowing that and not knowing if *he* knew this, I couldn't risk your life again.'

'Then why didn't you prepare me?' Anabelle exclaimed.

'Because our world is divided! Magic is forbidden in the human world because it preserves the balance they chose to implement when they fell away from the old world. Because you knowing about our world and not living in it would break my heart!'

Anabelle shook her head. 'But you used magic this whole time! You had me using magic just now!'

'Because I have already broken those laws! I can fall no further… and you…I see now that I have failed you, and this is all I can atone for.'

Isadora took in a shaking breath, blinking away her tears.

Taking her hand, Anabelle stroked her thumb over her mother's skin. 'You didn't fail me. I couldn't ask for a better mother.'

Isadora gave her a soft smile. 'I love you, dearest.'

Anabelle quickly kissed her mother's palm before clasping her hand and pulling her instep. 'When should we leave?'

'When you wish it,' Isadora said quietly.

Summer warmth left them as they pushed through the evening wind, beating at their faces like a stormy promise. Glancing up at the sky, Anabelle saw only the fading colours of fiery red and glowing orange— no storm in sight.

The cottage loomed ahead, and Anabelle felt a deep ache at the sight of it. 'Tomorrow.'

Isadora felt a slight pinch in her heart as she gave a soft nod. 'Tomorrow then.'

Anabelle didn't sleep that night. Instead, she sat at her windowsill, fully dressed for the coming day, watching the morning's red sky take its first breath. Angry clouds came closer and closer, promising rain. The wind blasted through the tall grass in the fields, and the forest swayed and moaned silently in turn.

Anabelle rested her chin atop her knees, running her fingers through her hair, her stomach churning. She would leave this life she knew so well for one she did not.

Pepper hopped over to her, so Anabelle picked her up and buried her face in the soft fur.

Her mother tentatively knocked on her door and peeked in. 'Darling?'

Anabelle kept her eyes fixated on the coming storm. 'Do you think we will ever come back?'

Isadora sighed. 'I don't know, love.'

'Will people find our home?'

'No, because you will hide it from the mortal world.'

Anabelle glanced up at her mother. 'I will?'

'I will show you how,' Isadora said with a comforting smile. 'We best go now, Anabelle.'

It would be many, many years before Anabelle looked out this same window again, and something in her squeezed with a homesickness she knew would one day come. Standing, she brushed the skirt of her dark blue dress and tightened the ivory wool scarf around her neck.

Sniffing, she straightened her back. 'It's time to go.'

Anabelle took one last glance around her room and shut the door with a heavy heart. Then, with Pepper tucked to her chest, she followed her mother outside.

'Close your eyes, Anabelle,' Isadora instructed as they faced the cottage.

Anabelle shut her eyes, concentrating her energy on the cottage and surrounding area. She imagined a massive invisible barrier. A spark built up inside her, and she grabbed hold of it. She could feel it slipping as it grew, her lack of control evident, but she let it pour out of her before it could burst.

Seconds passed before Anabelle opened her eyes. She was greeted with nothing but tall grassy fields. The cottage had disappeared.

'You did well, love.'

Anabelle turned her back to the mirage and started for the forest. She wouldn't let herself dwell on the loss she felt. Loss of what, she still wasn't sure.

Anabelle glanced at her mother, noticing the different emotions crossing her face.

'What is it?'

Isadora shook her head. 'It's nothing.'

'No, it's most certainly something.'

Isadora sighed. 'I told you that that taking you from our world into the mortal world went against the laws of our people. They will be expecting me. Once I step foot into the forest again, they will know I have come. I do not know what will happen, but please, Anabelle, know I love you.'

Anabelle took her mother's hand and squeezed it lightly. 'I promise I won't let anything bad happen to you.'

'Everything will change once we step into the forest. The veil will be broken. Even *we* will change.'

'That is why we must continue forward.'

Isadora gave her a warm smile. 'So wise, little one.'

Together, they walked forward, stepping into the forest.

The mortal world fell behind them.

CHAPTER FOURTEEN

A handsome face turned up to the winter wind as it blew through the trees of the Black Forest. Black hair danced behind the fair features of a young elf, dark blue eyes alive with merriment, surveying the forest around him.

'Savven.'

When he heard his name, he turned his face to the treetops. He smiled when he saw Lithônion leap from a tall branch and land gracefully on his toes.

'Always a show-off, Lithônion,' commented Savven.

Lithônion gave him a sly smile. His rich brown hair glowed under the last of the winter sunlight, and his brilliant green eyes contained mischief.

'Someone has to show you up.'

Savven cocked a dark brow at his closest friend. He knew that look well. 'What sort of aberrant ploy are you planning now?'

'An adventure, my friend.'

'What kind of adventure would this be?'

'Would you join me if I offered?'

'Would I be in danger of nearly losing my head, like so many times before?' Savven commented dryly.

Lithônion ignored his remark. 'What would you say to Thórsmörk, to the city of Stonehammer?'

'The dwarves of Zarren?'

'Yes, the very same. One of the few cities I have not journeyed to.'

'Álfheimr truly doesn't know any elf as enthusiastic as you to leave its city walls.'

Lithônion chuckled. 'And you are much too comfortable on that throne of yours, dear prince.'

'Are you mocking me?' Savven smiled at his friend.

Lithônion answered by bowing low.

Savven just shook his head and looked away, placing a hand on the bark of a blackwood tree. 'I suppose it—'

He cut himself off as a powerful shift sliced through the air, throwing them to the ground.

A moment passed before they looked at one another. Thunder clapped overhead, and they glanced to the sky as rain fell like a curtain.

Lithônion grew serious but never took his gaze from the thundering storm clouds, water pelting his face.

'Someone has crossed through the veil.'

Savven said nothing, his every sense on the alert. He turned on fleeting feet, Lithônion quick to follow Savven to the gates of Álfheimr. The hair on Savven's neck stood on end as magic shifted in the air.

The great hall of Álfheimr City was alive with talk about the shift they all felt, their voices rising and falling through the low-hanging mossy vines. Woven Banyan trees grew from marble floors, acting as strong pillars, their roots rising from the ground like massive anchors. Tree branches snared together, entangling at a narrow peak that arced high above their heads; flowers and cloisters of leaves hung low from their thick limbs. Long windows were cut into the raw marble walls, letting in the last daylight before storm clouds blanketed the sky. Gossamer drapes fluttered in the angering winds.

The marble thrones of King Nydeth and Queen Casvara sat proudly atop the dais at the end of the Great Hall, over which stretched creeping vines bearing blossoming purple and pink Alyssums and bright red Amaranthus. On his throne, the king wore golden robes, his pin-straight hair falling like liquid fire around him. Clear-cut emerald eyes surveyed the hall with cool assertion. The queen stood off to the side, back turned as she stared at a water-filled gold basin. Her amethyst-coloured gown hugged her agile body, flowing from her hips in soft waves.

Savven and Lithônion stopped before the dais.

'Your Majesty—'

King Nydeth held up a hand. 'We felt it as well.'

At Nydeth's nod of consent, Savven went to his mother's side. He placed a gentle hand over hers on the rim of the golden basin. The water lapped the ledge and threatened to spill over.

'Mother?' he whispered.

Pain and sadness lingered behind Queen Casvara's icy blue gaze. 'I've seen her in the water.' She dipped a finger into it, and a woman's face appeared. 'Savven, she has returned.'

Savven stared at the image of the female he had not seen in many years. 'Truly?'

'Isadora has returned to the Black Forest.'

Brushing past Savven, Queen Casvara took her place beside her mate, her midnight hair falling in soft curls over her shoulder.

She spoke in a clear, ringing voice, 'For now, all is well. I beg, do not worry yourselves. The tides of change are upon us, but I implore you all to go with a clear head. There is no danger. The walls of Álfheimr remain standing.'

Those in the hall bowed to the king and queen and quietly left. Once the Great Hall was empty, the queen focused on Savven and Lithônion.

'You two will go to the forest edge. Ezra shall accompany you.'

Ezra, the general of their armies and captain of the guard, stood hidden in the shadows beside the thrones, keeping a watchful eye over his king and queen. He nodded mutely to Savven and Lithônion.

Queen Casvara's hands twisted together in thought, her mouth pursing. 'Isadora is to be brought to Álfheimr. She broke the laws of our people, and for that, she must receive judgment. That is your task. Bring my sister back.'

Lithônion bowed low before speaking. 'What crime did she commit, Your Majesty?'

'She took the chosen keeper from our world.'

Anabelle braced herself against a tree as a shift in the air pierced right through her. When she could finally gather her bearings and straighten, she glanced at her mother with a grim expression.

'The veil is lifted,' Isadora said. 'Now you may see the world for what it really is.'

Taking a steadying breath, Anabelle looked out into the forest. The forest she once knew became something even lovelier, full of life. Towering black trunks loomed, and the storm's light filtered through the branches, casting a beautiful glow. Rain dripped from spindle fingers to the forest floor. Though the beauty was evident, Anabelle could see an underlying stain of darkness that made her heartthrob.

'What happened here?' she murmured.

'Faith was lost, and when faith is lost, so is life. No one believed the time would come when the keeper would return. Doubt took hold of the many who lost their faith and hope for the future. I'm afraid that I was to blame for that.'

'How did they lose their faith so easily?'

'They forgot what our world once was and what it could become. The worst things in the world are the easiest to come by.

Unfortunately, many succumb to this, with doubt being the centre of it all.'

A fairy flew from her perch on a tree limb and came to dance in front of Anabelle, twirling this way and that way. Her lithe body barely existed in the dim light.

Anabelle stared, mesmerised. With the veil lifted, she could see the fairy's true nature. Like a living flower, her skin glowed brightly.

Anabelle held out her hand, Pepper still tucked in her other arm, and the fairy landed gently on her fingertips. Bowing her head at Anabelle and Isadora, the fairy's large eyes were almost black. Her chin was a narrow point, and a coy smile lifted her cheeks. Her long, pointed ears twitched as the breeze brushed past them. Anabelle nodded her head in turn to the creature, as did Isadora.

The fairy leapt from Anabelle's fingertips and curtsied before her.

Isadora's voice broke through the silence as she said softly, 'You're a messenger.'

She waved for them to follow.

Even through the grey light and rain, Anabelle could make the fairy out as she walked the forest path. They walked for perhaps an hour, treading through the wet forest growth, their breath clouding in front of them from the chill until she brought them to the trees of the Summer Fae.

The rustle of foliage was their only warning before Gallian stepped out from behind the trees. He wore dark brown leather trousers, matching boots, and a white woollen shirt. His dark hair framed his face, and his green eyes bored into her own with an easy smile.

Anabelle sucked in a breath. He truly was beautiful. Even so, she only greeted him with a cool demeanour. 'Hello, Gallian.'

Isadora stared at Gallian as if he were a figment of her imagination. It had been nearly a lifetime since she had last seen him.

'Gallian, how you have grown,' she said in awe, with a tinge of pride that only a mother could have felt.

Guilt lingered behind Gallian's eyes despite his answering smile as he stepped forward, embracing the older woman before she could object.

'Thank you for keeping her safe,' he said.

Isadora turned her attention to the wall of fairies surrounding them.

'Gallian, what's going on?' Anabelle questioned.

'We asked for them to bring you here.'

The fairies parted as four ethereal figures appeared, the wall of tiny Summer Fae weaving back together as the Spirits of Seasons stood before them.

Isadora stiffened slightly, noticeable only because Anabelle stood right next to her.

Summer gave Isadora a soft smile. 'We are not here to take you away, Isadora, nor to pass judgment on you. It is not our place to condemn you or set you free. Only your people may do that.'

Winter looked at Anabelle. 'Anabelle, I'm sorry, but you are not to stay with us. Your mother will be with the Summer Fae, but you must find Tatius.'

'I will stay with my mother,' Anabelle said.

Winter simply folded her hands in front of her. 'The Pool of Immortality is a trial every Keeper must go through.'

Autumn gestured to Gallian. 'Gallian will show you the way.'

Anabelle wheeled around to her mother. 'We just got here! I can't leave you yet!'

Isadora sighed. 'Go, I will be fine.'

'What about your people? What if they take you before I get back? What if I never see you again?'

'I am prepared for what may come, Anabelle, as you will be,' Isadora said.

Her mother's words were final. Anabelle sighed and gave Pepper to her mother, stroking the soft fur one more time.

'Both of you stay safe, please,' she pleaded.

Isadora nodded once and looked at Gallian. 'She is the keeper, but she is also my daughter. Protect her.'

Gallian was silent, but she knew he understood her.

Summer Fae parted like water, and Anabelle took a deep breath, stepping forward.

CHAPTER FIFTEEN

The rain stopped an hour into their journey. Only light drizzles lingered in the air, misting the tree branches high above them.

Anabelle grazed her fingertips lazily across the black trees as she passed them, humming under her breath. Gallian trailed behind a couple of paces.

Coming to an abrupt halt, Anabelle stared at Gallian openly, head tilted to the side in thought.

Gallian's gaze darted around them. 'What are you doing?'

'Gallian, how did I have those dreams of you?'

Gallian rubbed a hand over his brow. 'You wish to discuss your dreams, now of all times? The Spirits have sent us—'

Anabelle cut him off. 'I understand the severity of the situation,

Gallian, though I find myself questioning many things. Everything has happened so quickly I fear I have forgotten to breathe through it all.'

'You worry too much,' he said with a scoff.

'Do not disregard my concern,' she retorted with a hard stare. 'It is not commonplace—Well, to you, mayhap, but to me, it is not.'

'This is neither the time nor the place, Anabelle,' he said, running his hand through his hair in exasperation.

Anabelle glared at him. 'There will never be a right time nor place, Gallian.'

Gallian began walking, but she stood there, watching his retreating back.

'I'm afraid, Gallian.'

The quiet words were just loud enough that he halted.

Gallian let out a low breath, looking up at the sky for a moment before staring at Anabelle. 'I don't have any answers for you.'

She looked down at her hands.

When she didn't say anything, Gallian began walking.

Anabelle followed behind him, humming a melody under her breath, and tried to ignore the tangling knots that only bound tighter within her.

'What exactly are we looking for?' Anabelle asked.

Gallian shook his head, causing little water droplets to fly from the ends of his hair.

'The pond, as you call it.'

Anabelle thought for a moment, her nose scrunching in realisation and distaste. 'The one I drowned in?'

That statement caused Gallian to falter a step, but he righted himself quickly. '...Yes.'

'Why?'

'Because it is the only pool I know of, the only one that houses mer-creatures if you do not include the oceans, but they are far from here and of no concern right now.' His eyes grazed over the forest before he jerked his head to a mossy patch of earth. 'We'll stop here for a break.'

A decaying log lay on the ground like an open coffin, and Gallian sat on the moss before it. He gestured for Anabelle to sit, watching her keenly as she tested her weight on the flimsy log. When it held, she relaxed, letting out a breath through her nose.

She looked at Gallian, regarding him, as he sat there casually surveying their surroundings. He held out an arm and said something so low she couldn't hear him. A raven cawed overhead, diving towards them. Anabelle nearly shot to her feet when it caught itself, wings spread wide, and landed on Gallian's arm. Gallian spoke lowly to the bird before it flew from its perch.

The air was still around them, and she bit her tongue when he fixed her with an icy gaze.

Clearing her throat, she broke the silence and said, 'Tell me of this world. How far are the oceans, and what are the creatures within?' She had never seen the ocean; she had only read of it in a book.

Gallian shifted. 'There are many oceans. They are days, weeks even, from us. Their tides ebb and flow with the moon's cycle, and in the sunlight, their swells sparkle like an uncut gem. I have only seen it a few times in my life. The sea of Bel'onc houses the city of merpeople, ruled by Queen Amatheia.'

He waved a hand in the direction they had been travelling. 'Along the cliff shores, tunnels are woven under this world, feeding the life around us.'

'Do they travel under the entire world?'

He shrugged. 'Possibly.'

Flicking his palm up, a small blue flame appeared, dancing in the middle of his palm.

'I wish my magic came to me as easily.'

A pink flush tinged Gallian's neck, and the flame disappeared. 'It will—even easier for you.'

She tilted her head. 'What do you mean?'

'As half a mortal, while our powers are innately strong, they only come to full term if chosen as Keeper.' He flicked the blue flame back to life, studying it. 'If we are not chosen and not full-blooded Fae, our powers stay as they are, though that does not make me weak. It certainly does not help when I do need it.'

'That seems awfully unfair,' Anabelle mused.

The corners of his eyes crinkled as he smiled bitterly. 'Most things in this life are fated to be unfair.'

Anabelle shook her head. 'I don't believe that to be true. Perhaps if we only looked at the downfalls, but how we rise is the hand we choose from fate.'

'That takes away the point of fate. Your life is already chosen for you.'

'A path, perhaps, but I will not allow someone or something to dictate my ending. Magic or not, how I get to the destination is my own choice.'

Gallian picked at the damp bark of the log. 'You will learn about magic soon enough.'

'Perhaps,' she said coolly, shrugging a shoulder. 'Or maybe it will learn about me.' She looked at the path they had been travelling, brow raised. 'If we are going to that same pond, why is it taking so long?'

'When you passed through the wall, it changed your perspective on distance. Everything seemed close because the forest wanted you to find the tokens of your memory. Your mother kept you protected, but once you came of age, the forest slowly began to slip into view.'

Anabelle glanced over her shoulder, looking for any sign of her old life, but she found none. They were deep within the woods, and nothing was familiar to her.

Gallian stood, brushing off his trousers. 'Come, we're not far now. We should be there by mid-day.'

Anabelle stared at Gallian's back, questions and emotions swirling in her head, but she trampled them down. Standing, she brushed her skirts, flicking off a piece of bark, and took hurried steps to catch up.

Time passed slowly. The sun would now be high in the sky, but black clouds hid it from view.

Just as she was about to question how much further, the path was made clear. It was the only familiar thing she had seen in the whole of the forest, and it filled her with relief. Just past the trees, she could make out the rocky ledge of the pond.

The meadow was open, and the once tall grass lay limp and partially covered in frost. An icy wind blew through the clearing, tangling Anabelle's hair and rippling the water.

Anabelle felt a shift of unease web its way through her bones. She shifted on her feet, clenching and unclenching her hands, trying to shake the sensation crawling down her spine like ice picks.

Run, whispered the voice of power in her head. *Run!*

Gallian left Anabelle's side to walk to the water's edge, where he watched the ripples dance across the surface with the wind.

The hair on the back of her neck stood on end, and a heaviness in the air made Anabelle hesitate before she followed his path and stood beside him.

'What are you looking at?' She kept her voice as neutral as possible.

'Myself.'

Glancing down, she saw the perfect mirror images of themselves in the water's glassy reflection.

'This pond is called the Ageless River or Vaitarani. The righteous who drink from it will find nectar, while the impure will find blood.'

Anabelle's stomach rolled with unease. 'Ageless River?'

'The tunnels from the sea cliffs feed this pool.'

That would explain why I couldn't find an end, she thought, recalling her last encounter.

'Have you ever drunk from—'

'Oh, look, you have a friend with you!' came a gleeful voice behind them.

The two spun around to find Balwin standing at the edge of the clearing, a contorted smile on his features that twisted his mottled scars, hands clasped together in delight. He stared at Anabelle with hatred, eyes gleaming in the low light.

Anabelle took an unconscious step back, and the back of her legs hit the rocky ledge. Her heart raced, and cold fear flooded through her veins.

'Balwin,' she said. She should have run when the voice inside of her told her to.

'Keeper,' he acknowledged, giving a mocking low bow.

Gallian stepped in front of Anabelle, but not before she saw the flicker of annoyance on his face. He bared his teeth in disgust and spat, 'What do you want?'

Balwin's eye twitched as he shifted his gaze to his son.

'Oh, we're going to play games? But you made it so easy, Gallian.' His face shifted with irritation. 'Come, come, hand her over.'

Anabelle seized Gallian by his shoulder and hauled him around to face her. 'What is he talking about? What does he want?'

Gallian looked away as his father came closer. He let out a low warning growl, but his father only flashed a manic smile.

Blue lightning sparked from Gallian's fingers, and his hands shot out as pure energy travelled across the clearing.

Balwin flicked away the attack with a wave of his hand.

'Try again, my son. Let us see your great and mighty power,' he leered mockingly.

'You cannot have her,' he said and clenched his fists, trying for control as rage blew its fire through him.

Anger flashed across Balwin's eyes, and black mist began to form at his feet, crawling across the ground towards Anabelle and Gallian. 'Do not test me, Gallian!'

Gallian stepped forward and spat out between clenched teeth, 'You. Cannot. Have her!'

He shot out his hands, letting go of his control. The energy was brighter and stronger than before, fuelled by anger as he aimed for his father until the icy clearing was filled with blue light.

Balwin guarded against Gallian's attack with his own black magic. The two collided in a shower of sparks. Anabelle recoiled at the tension in the air, the stone edge of the pool digging into her legs as she pressed against it. The moment of chaos between the two magics was short-lived, Gallian's power faltering under his father's.

Balwin's powers struck through the air like a perfectly poised arrow. Gallian was thrown across the clearing like a limp doll and impaled on a branch.

Anabelle heard the crack of bone and the wet, gasping moan before he dropped to the ground, unconscious and bleeding out.

'Well done.'

Anabelle shot toward Gallian. Balwin's shadows overtook her. Their whispering tendrils were like cold daggers on her skin, branding her flesh as he hauled her across the ground.

Anabelle dug her nails into the earth, ripping the flesh under her nail beds.

With a flick of his wrist, Balwin hung her in the air like a puppet. 'Hush, little one, it will all be over soon,' he cooed.

'You killed him!' she shrieked.

Balwin shrugged. 'Haven't you figured it out yet? This is all one big game, and you its key player. Be happy he's gone. He would have broken you. It was only a matter of time.'

The familiar white-hot chill of ice covered her body as her grief overtook her, and she screamed. With a sudden rush of light, she dropped into the water.

Shocked, Balwin watched the girl break his barrier and fall into the pool. Casting out a hand, shadows lapped over the water, descending over the unsettled surface.

'You make this far too easy, Keeper,' he said in a deathly low voice, his blood rushing through his ears.

Clawing her way to the surface, her lungs were on fire, screaming for her to take a breath. She reached the surface, her hand making to punch through, but was met with a sharp pain shooting down her wrist when she hit an invisible barrier.

Panic set in. She threw her body against the barrier, but it would not break. Anabelle saw the watery image of Balwin watching from the pond's edge and screamed again. Sharp pain stabbed at her ribs; her lungs begged for release, and black dots spread over her vision.

She took a desperate breath, the water flooding her lungs. Her body began to twitch violently as she died slowly, bubbles clouding her face as the nerve-ending fire spread across her body, wracking her with convulsions. As the seconds ticked endlessly, her mind slowly shut off, the pain in her eyes faded, her pupils expanded, and her heart took its final beat.

Balwin watched with exhilaration as Anabelle slowly began to sink, her hair clouding around her pale face like spilt ink, her hollow eyes staring up at him. The delight in watching her die at his hands rushed through him.

'Wonderful,' he muttered, turning away from her body.

With a cold stare, he looked at the lifeless shape of his son, and he smiled, everything falling into place. 'Wonderful.'

CHAPTER SIXTEEN

Eyes, vibrant and glowing in the dark, pierced through the water like golden orbs. Pale limbs followed by glittering scales appeared as two merwomen swam through the tunnels and into the open water of the Vaitarani. Their waif figures wavered in the light that beamed through the water's surface. Where legs would be, beautiful tails sparkled gold, copper, and silver; gossamer tendrils flowed with every movement where the fins split.

Their gazes fixated on the female body, floating lifeless in the water. Pale lips parted, eyes open and void, her skin transparent in the dim, watery light. A blue, waterlogged dress floating around her.

Without hesitation, they wrapped long fingers around her arm in a firm grip; dark hair clouded the vacant face as they pulled her from her open grave and slipped back into the tunnel they had come from.

Vibrant blue water began to dot the passage as it opened for the three bodies. One merwoman was at the front and back, dragging the female between them.

The blue dots glowed brightly in the darkness, lighting the way. The shaft opened into an air pocket beneath the world. The merwomen swam to the surface and gently raised the body to the plant-covered stone floor.

Vines crawled up the rocky, uneven walls of the pocket. Ferns grew in cloisters where the wall met the stone floor, and lilies and moonflowers dusted over the arcing peak of the cave. The twisting length of the vines trailed over the floor like a spider's web, vibrant green moss cushioning the cold, wet stone. The vines tangled within the moss until they webbed together, hanging over the stone ledge and floating atop the water. Orbs of fire lined the cave in a glowing crown; a dais rose from the middle with a carved stone basin of water standing proudly at its core.

A small child stepped out from the shadows of the cavern, her skin pale and ghostly in the dim light. Drifting lightly over the lush floor, she stopped to pluck three dark purple berries from the vines clinging to the walls.

Black hair spilt over one shoulder as the small girl knelt beside the limp body. She quietly acknowledged the two merwomen with a glance before turning her nearly black eyes to the inanimate girl.

'Do not give up on life so easily, Anabelle. It has not given up on you,' said the girl, her voice soft in the echoing chamber.

She brushed a hand over Anabelle's face, gently moving her sodden hair away from her cheeks. Then she parted Anabelle's lips with one hand and placed the three berries into her mouth one by one with the other.

The berries dissolved almost instantly, disintegrating the feeble outer shell as the liquid centre rushed down her throat.

'Will it work? Will the Keeper come back?'

The child looked at the one who had spoken. The merwoman had dark auburn hair tossed over pale shoulders. Her black eyes were lined with thick lashes. Rich gold and silver scales scattered across her skin, shadowing her cheekbones and the alcoves of her clavicle.

'Yes, Lilla. She will return, though she will be faced with a choice. A difficult choice, but one nonetheless.'

Lilla looked at the dead form of what was once the Keeper and silently pleaded she would come back.

The time passed slowly. Lilla stayed mainly on the green-covered surface. Resting her arms on the ledge, she laid her head down on them, watching Anabelle with curious eyes.

The girl-child came and sat next to Lilla, tucking her legs beneath her. 'Why do you worry so much about her, Lilla?'

'I cannot help it, Tatius,' Lilla sighed. 'She is different. She is not like most mortals. I feel the energy of her heart, though it no longer beats. It cares far more than most do, and that is a light not often seen anymore.'

Tatius gave a whisper of a smile. 'Ah, you see, that is why she is the Keeper. Because she is neither one nor the other, she is both all the good and the bad. Her light is the light that our world is guided by.' Tatius grazed a hand over Anabelle's, feeling the almost non-existent thrum of life. 'She is there. I can feel her.'

Lilla looked at Anabelle. 'Please do not give up on us.'

Anabelle's heart finally beat soundly again at mid-dawn the next day. By then, only Lilla had returned. Her sister had grown bored, and Lilla was left watching Anabelle intently, observing the rise and fall of her chest, waiting for her to open her eyes.

'Patience, Lilla,' said Tatius as she drifted into the cave. 'Only time can heal what has been done.'

'Patience is something I have never been good at,' Lilla admitted sheepishly.

Tatius looked at Anabelle, her eyes distant. 'We all must learn to have it.'

Anabelle's fingers twitched as she came to, her eyes opening slowly. Images blurred, weaving in and out of each other before forming a clear picture. When her eyes focused, she breathed in and tried to sit up but felt her head swim, and her vision went spotty. She felt like she was floating.

Nausea welled up in the pit of her stomach, and she threw herself onto her side just as she spewed up water. Heaving for air, she rolled onto her back and stared at a rocky ceiling, blearily noticing a dark cave before passing out.

Tatius knelt beside Anabelle, pushing her dark hair away from her pale face, and rubbed soothing circles on her back.

'Anabelle, the time for sleep has passed,' she whispered.

Placing her hands neatly on her lap, she waited for Anabelle to stir, letting out an impatient breath when she didn't move.

'Anabelle…Anabelle…'

There was only silence. Placing one small pale hand on the side of Anabelle's head, Tatius let her magic thrum through her and into Anabelle.

Closing her eyes, she whispered, 'Anabelle.'

Anabelle's eyes flew open. The world around her was hazy before she focused on the child's face. Startled, she sat up and felt her head swim and body sway, so she braced a hand on the floor.

Tatius grasped her by the shoulders to steady her. 'Slowly, Anabelle.'

'Who are you?' Anabelle's voice was raw, her throat sore, but her muscles did not scream when she breathed, so she dared to take another breath.

'My name is Tatius.'

Slowly, like a blanket being lifted, everything came back. Balwin, Gallian—

'He killed him…and me.' Her words were barely a whisper.

Tatius' face grew stern, and her black eyes seemed to darken. 'You are not a victim, Anabelle. Do not allow Balwin to mould you into one.'

Sucking in a lungful of air, Anabelle's memories engulfed her as they replayed over and over again until—

'…I died?' Anabelle asked quietly, the reality settling within her.

'You were near death,' Tatius acknowledged, then paused. 'In your mortal form, yes, you were dead.'

'So, I'm not dead?'

'Immortality is a funny thing. You cannot be both mortal and immortal. You must choose. Your body is mortal, but your heart is immortal.'

Tatius got up and padded over to the berries, which hung innocently on the creeping vines. She plucked one and rolled it between her fingers.

'I gave you vættir ber—spirit berries—to restore your body, mind, and soul. Had I not, you would have succumbed to eternal hibernation.'

Anabelle looked at her surroundings, the lush green plant life that thrived within the cavern and a pool of water beside her. 'The Pool of Immortality. Gallian was right.'

'Yes, he was, in a sense.'

'I had to die to find you.'

Tatius regarded her quietly for a moment. 'Your body must know death before it can know life.'

Anabelle's brows pinched, her mouth pursing. She forced in a breath and looked at Tatius. 'You said I have a choice to make?'

Tatius dropped the berry, and it vanished before it hit the ground. Her footsteps were silent as she walked up to the stone basin on the dais, gazing down into the water it held.

Lilla emerged from the pool and smiled when she saw Anabelle awake. 'I'm happy to see you are up and breathing now.'

Anabelle stared at Lilla, subconsciously filtering her words and ignoring the statement, *breathing now* and the wince it produced. 'You're a mermaid?'

'Indeed, I am,' Lilla said with a tilt of her head.

Noticing a gold and silver tail lazily grazing the pool's surface, Anabelle peeled her eyes away and looked back at Lilla's face. She was a striking beauty that would surely lure men to their deaths if she so chose, but her eyes were kind and warm, her face soft and inviting with plush pink lips and full cheeks. When Lilla smiled, Anabelle couldn't help but smile back. There was a kindness in her gaze that Anabelle recognised and instantly trusted.

Tatius observed the exchange silently before speaking up. 'Lilla was human once.'

'You were?' Anabelle blurted.

Lilla gave a slight nod. 'Yes, I came from France in the year thirteen forty-eight.' She tapped a finger thoughtfully on her lips. 'I believe nearly four hundred years have passed since then.' Her eyes lit up suddenly, and she swam closer to the ledge, crossing her arms on the green surface. 'What is the world like now?'

'I can't say if much has changed in four hundred years. I haven't lived that long. There are more people, I assume. I lived in the country just outside the forest, surrounded by moors and valleys.'

Anabelle's mind drifted, picturing her family cottage, mother, and Pepper. 'From what I have seen, the world is full of beauty if you look for it. Though, in my experience, people corrupt the things they touch. Nothing is ever enough for anyone.'

'That is a shame,' said a quiet Lilla. 'Maybe if we pray to the gods, they will show the humans not what they want but what they need.'

'Perhaps,' Anabelle said, giving the mermaid a small, tight smile before turning her attention to Tatius, who watched them by the basin. 'What is that?'

'Come, I will show you.'

Anabelle stood slowly. She was no longer dizzy, the earth didn't tilt when she moved, and nothing hurt. Instead, her body seemed to sigh in relief.

Brushing a hand over her now-dry skirts, she walked carefully to the basin, the moss cool under her feet. 'May I ask you something, Tatius?'

Tatius nodded slightly. 'You may.'

'What are you?'

'I am the God of Immortality, the Spirit of Life and Death.'

Anabelle didn't conceal her shock when she asked, 'You're only a child?'

'You were chosen as the Keeper when you were just five years old. Why is that?'

Anabelle shook her head.

'It is because a child is simply a child. Nothing more. It does not strive to be anything but a child, and that innocence is why we both were chosen for the roles we play. I was born into my duty, created. It is all I know. I balance both life and death in this world. I am the Guardian of Immortality because only a child can see someone's true reflection.'

'You seem much older than any child.'

'I am, girl, but my essence is not. I have grown with time, but time has not changed me.' Tatius returned to the basin, dipping a finger into the water and stirring it once. The image of Gallian and Balwin appeared, and Anabelle gasped.

'He's alive!'

Tatius nodded. 'In a sense.'

Anabelle turned to her. 'What do you mean?'

Tatius didn't reply and only gestured to the image so Anabelle would watch it. Gallian turned, and Anabelle put a hand to her mouth.

'No,' she whispered, stumbling away from the basin.

Tatius watched the water for a second more before joining Anabelle at her side.

'He—he's gone! Gallian, as I knew him, is—is gone!'

A part of her rippled with pain, the other with guilt. His eyes were ice-cold, the light in them was gone, and his face was taut and expressionless.

'What did Balwin do to him?' she whispered.

'I'm afraid Gallian,' Tatius said, 'is as much at fault as his father. This is his future. The Gallian you once knew is gone, Anabelle, though I doubt you knew him at all.'

Anabelle felt a tear run down her cheek. 'What do you mean?' she asks, falling to the ground.

Tatius placed a hand on Anabelle's head, trying to provide some semblance of comfort. 'You have the power to change Gallian's destiny.'

Anabelle glanced at Tatius through damp lashes. 'How?'

'Fate cannot be altered; the path has already been created, but you can shape the stones that pave it.' Tatius stepped around the basin. 'Some people are born from darkness and, in turn, born with it. Those who wish to act on it become darkness themselves. Then there are some, like Gallian, who know right from wrong but are so clouded by their need for something else that it leads them into an abyss. Gallian was thrust into darkness by his father and is near death, just as you were. Balwin took Gallian's love of him and moulded it to his advantage, only to gain his son's power and allegiance. Balwin knew that Gallian would never be strong enough to stand against him. Gallian wanted his father's love so badly that he allowed himself to be corrupted, whether or not he knew it.

'The only way to save Gallian is to bring him out of the shadowlands his father cast him into. You are the light in this world, Anabelle. You can bring all things out of the darkness…so long as that is what they want.'

Anabelle stared at a small moonflower bloom. 'You said I must choose between being mortal or immortal. What do I gain from either? Can I not stay the way I am?'

Tatius took a seat beside Anabelle. 'To be the Keeper, you must be immortal to reign for two thousand years,' she said, adding dryly: 'We have yet to have a corpse ruling the forest and its denizens. Personally, I would like to avoid that.'

'What happens if I choose to be mortal?'

'To be mortal? Simple, you will die when this is all over.'

Anabelle blanched. 'I will die?'

'The fight will be too much for a mortal body to handle. This battle is a battle against the essence of iniquity in our world. Although your heart will remain beating, that is the only part of you that will survive. Soon, that too will die.'

Anabelle looked at Lilla, almost envious of the merwoman and her freedom. She looked away, pursing her lips. 'You're not giving me an option, are you?'

'I am,' rebutted Tatius, 'You will live forever with one, and with the other, you will fight for as long as you can, but I cannot say for how long.'

'Being mortal isn't a bad thing, Tatius.'

Tatius put a hand on Anabelle's wrist as she fidgeted with her skirts. 'I know, but you were not born to be mortal. Your heart is not mortal. That is why you were only the appearance of death when you came to me.'

Anabelle turned to Lilla again. 'If given a choice…would you be human again?'

Lilla looked back at her tail, flicking it in the water. Then she turned back to Anabelle. 'No. I would want to walk amongst humans again, maybe for a day or a week, but to be mortal is something different. This world is always changing, but it is always pure. The mortal world changes—not always for the best.'

The cave was silent. Anabelle's heart, steady and strong, thrummed in her ears, and she wanted to hold onto that feeling for as long as possible.

'What must I do?'

Tatius stood and conjured a simple iron chalice from the air. Padding quietly to the basin, she dipped the chalice in and filled it to the brim. When she returned to her side, she offered the chalice to Anabelle. 'To be immortal, you must first die.'

'I must die?'

'To be mortal is to be subject to death at any given time. It is not forever. You will rise.'

She thought again of the Gallian she had seen. 'Everything will be different, won't it?'

'Yes.'

'Do you regret it?' she asked Lilla.

Lilla played with the curl of a vine that fell over the water ledge. 'I did not have a choice when I was a little girl, but my heart wanted it, even if my mind did not grasp it then. I wish sometimes it had not happened, but only sometimes, and only because the rest of my family was left behind. I still have my sister with me. I am thankful for that.'

Anabelle's heartbeat was like a war drum in her ears. She looked down at what was to be both her death and her life and swallowed thickly as fear tried to trickle its way into her mind. Taking a deep breath, Anabelle brought the iron chalice to her lips before she could change her mind and drank deeply from it.

Tatius closed her eyes and began murmuring the ancient language of the Spirits under her breath. The air became heavy, and the light faded from the chamber. Tatius's voice grew into an old song, her voice echoing in the wind that swept through the cave as the divide between the realm of the living and the dead opened.

Lilla shrunk back into the water as the air froze over, only her eyes visible.

Anabelle gasped, the chalice falling from her fingers as she tried to breathe. A fire raged through her body, white-hot and blinding, as she dropped to the ground. Her limbs contorted, her back arching, as veins of ice webbed up her neck and across her face in a frozen tattoo.

One hand dug into the stone floor, the other clasped at her throat. Her eyes went wide and then rolled to the back of her head.

The wind settled, and the light returned as Tatius's voice drifted off. Everything was as it had been as Anabelle died.

Ezra looked up at the darkening sky as the storm drenched them. Thunder crashed, and lightning struck the ground in the distance.

Lithônion quietly approached Ezra, tilting his gaze to the sky. Their presence was firm against the wind.

'Do you feel it?' Lithônion asked softly, eyes skimming over the forest bed.

Ezra gave a barely audible hum in response. 'The darkness has grown…and death is present now. I can feel it when I touch the life of the forest.'

'This is nothing I have ever felt before, Ezra. I believe it to be different. I do not think death has passed through the forest.'

'How can you be certain?'

'The swallow still flies in the storm, the river still runs calm, and light is still present in the growth of darkness. Not all is lost, Ezra.'

Ezra watched lightning splinter across the sky. 'I believe the Keeper will guide us into the light, but I fear this darkness is a new evil. I fear this darkness is capable of destroying the hearts of many. I fear for the Keeper.'

'You are wise, Ezra, but the Keeper is strong, and the Spirits chose well. We can only hope that her will to overcome is greater than her desire to succumb.'

Ezra said nothing, and the storm above raged on.

CHAPTER SEVENTEEN

Wild as a banshee's screams, the wind blew fast and unyielding in the night, raging through the mountain gorge. Torches hung in their sconces along the cavern's slick walls as water and moss residue dripped through the cracks overhead. The darkness seemed to loom even over its own shadows, gripping every ounce of light that entered and engulfing it until it was no more.

The bitter air cut through the cave like a knife, and the stone floor provided no comfort as Gallian lay on his back, shirt torn and caked in blood, now browned with age. A fever touched his brow, beads of sweat dotting his skin regardless of the cold air. Gallian showed no other signs of life.

Balwin stood at the mouth of the cave, watching his son, as

he had done so for the past two eves. Gallian refused to wake, his heart barely beating. The only part of Gallian fighting to hold onto life was his immortal heart. Still, even then, every part of his mortal body vibrated with the thought of death. He would be lost in a shadowland forever.

Balwin pursed his thin lips, his eyes flashing, his magic slipping. Part of the mountain's side exploded, and chunks of rock fell to the earth's floor. Even as the mountain quaked, Gallian didn't stir.

'Awake!' Balwin screamed with impatience and was, in turn, answered with silence. The demons trapped within him clawed at his bones, their talons seeming to scrap against their restraint.

Release us, they whispered.

Balwin ignored their request.

A dagger appeared in his grasp, black mist wafting off its edges, and with a savage snarl, he hurled it at his son. The blade embedded in his chest, but Balwin felt his need for chaos go unfed. The demons showed their disappointment, egging him on to finish what he started. Disgust curdled at the lack of gratification, and he let the knife vanish into black mist.

Pondering the idea of using an actual dagger, Balwin gave a low chuckle as he approached Gallian's lifeless body.

'You are worth more to me alive...for now. Soon, that blade will be all too real. Then, my son, you will feel death.'

Hunger tore at his insides, and Balwin felt his irritation rise when he saw the bones of past meals in a pile around the extinguished fire pit. He looked down at his son again.

'Worthless.' And like the black mist of the blade, he vanished from the cave.

Hours passed as Gallian lay on the stone floor, unmoving. His breath began to slow as life slipped away from him, and Gallian's mortal soul passed from his body in the loneliness of rock and bones.

Lightning struck, lighting up the entirety of the cave for a brief moment.

Tatius glided softly towards Gallian's body, going to her knees, eyes scanning his pallid face.

'You have laid your path,' she whispered. 'Though as she dies, you must also die…but you must also live, as she will.'

With a single twitch of her fingers, the same chalice Anabelle had drunk from appeared in her grasp. She lifted Gallian's head gently and put the rim of the chalice to his mouth, slowly pouring the contents into his mouth.

He gave no sign of life, but it was to be expected as she lay his head back down.

'He will try to kill her,' came a voice from the cave's mouth. It floated like the wind. It was the calm in the darkness that filled the cave.

Tatius did not acknowledge the Spirit of Elements but stood and turned to face her.

A female stepped out from the shadows, her eyes the colour of fresh leaves. Whorls of silver swept up from her fingertips and over her shoulders and collarbones in long, graceful lines, bright against her midnight skin.

'Why do you come, Udiya?' Tatius asked.

Udiya entered the cave, glancing down at the unresponsive male. 'I came to watch, ' she said.

Tatius folded her hands in front of her. 'Observe is what we must do, for when they awaken, we cannot interfere. No matter what happens.'

Udiya knelt, her long black hair falling gracefully over one tattooed shoulder. She dragged a fingertip from Gallian's temple down his cheek to his jaw. A trail of silver, matching what was branded into her skin, webbed down his face as if marking him. They watched it slowly sink beneath the surface, disappearing entirely.

'Know your own heart, dark prince,' said Udiya. 'For the voices that speak will try to deceive you. They will not be your own. When you awaken, you will be consumed by a darkness that wishes to overtake you.' Udiya leaned forward, her lips pressed to his ear, whispering: 'Do not forget who you are.'

Thunder crashed overhead, and Udiya stood. Lightning briefly penetrating the shadows. Gallian's face was still pale and sweaty.

'What of the dragons?' Udiya asked quietly.

Tatius's face was unreadable. 'Anabelle has been separated from our world for too long, and the escalation of Balwin's movements will hinder the Blessing. If she survives this battle, then Valdren will go to her.'

'If she survives this battle, does that mark the beginning of the prophecy?'

The child God's face turned grim. 'Aye.'

The two stood there for a moment, their eyes fixated on Gallian. Behind them, the rain hammered against the mountain face and the wind howled in the night, almost as if in mourning for what was to come.

Without a second thought, they vanished in the wind.

CHAPTER EIGHTEEN

On the morning of the third day, a breath passed through parted lips. A gentle breeze brushed Anabelle's cheek, awakening her to the new dawn.

A new heartbeat resounded through the Black Forest, beating beneath the ribs of the woman it was caged within with a constant, unyielding force.

Anabelle inhaled the fresh scent of rain that still clung to the ground, her eyes opening. She lay on her side, cheek pressed to soft green grass, a blanket of warmth covering her.

Summer Fae? she wondered.

Her eyes scanned the forest, taking in the world covered in a layer of frost and ice that clung to naked branches. Icicles dripped from tree limbs, and crystals coated the tree bark.

Anabelle slowly stood, her muscles relaxing as they stretched, her hair spilling down her back. With a quiet mind, like the air surrounding her, she took a single step forward, her feet crunching on the thick frost. The world glittered in the sunlight. The ice beneath her feet melted away like spring had sprung, leaving only fresh, dewy grass in its wake.

She wiggled her booted feet, feeling a vibrating hum travel up her body through their soles. Following the hum, she felt the pull of magic tighten around her, freeing her all at once.

The tether brought her to a sapling that lined the clearing where she had awoken. The humming shifted the air around her, and Anabelle could feel her heart hammering in her chest.

The vibrations that coursed around her lured her closer until only a few inches stood between her and the sapling. Hesitating, she reached out and placed her hand upon the bark. Lightning struck through her. A loud crack snapped in the air as the sapling began to move and twist, its limbs contorting.

Startled, Anabelle yanked her hand back, and the sapling's movements ceased.

She swallowed thickly, her eyes wide, body overrun with the power from the tether tightly bound around her. Unfurling her fingers, she let out a breath through her nose and placed it back on the tree.

The frost and ice gripping the tiny tree melted away under her touch. Anabelle felt the tug of magic, and she seized it, her magic flowing inside her and linking to the tether that wove around her. With a sudden burst, golden veins shot up the length of the trunk. From root to branch, the sapling was tattooed in ochroid webbings.

Twisting and turning, the sapling grew and grew until it stood taller than the rest. Spring leaves sprouted along the branches, small flowers blossoming throughout. Anabelle dropped her hand to her side as she stepped back.

Amid winter stood spring.

From the corner of her eye, Anabelle saw something fall from a branch—a flower bud that had not blossomed. She threw out a hand, catching the small bulb in her palm. At her touch, ice crystals enveloped it.

She frowned. 'You cannot die, little flower,' she said softly.

Her breath brushed across the tiny sphere, and the ice melted slightly, causing the bud to twitch. With brows raised, she brought the bud to her lips and blew softly.

The flower rose from her fingers, spinning in front of her. The same golden veins from the tree encompassed the bud in a glowing shell as it spun faster and faster. Light danced across Anabelle's face as the shell cracked and fell away. She opened her hand again, and suddenly, a tiny pink flower bloomed and fell into her palm.

She watched as it moved, the flower petals fanning across her skin in an ombre of pinks that darkened to a rosy-red at the tips. A tiny leg appeared from beneath a petal; slowly, the small body of a fairy unfolded as she crawled from beneath the pink flower petals.

The little fairy stumbled on her new legs, catching herself and straightening the petals down her tiny legs. Anabelle realised where the fairy's torso ended and the flower petals began was one. The petals grew from her waist, skirting around her little legs, and her long white hair fell over her shoulders in a cascading waterfall, covering her bare chest. She watched as the fairy looked back at her wings and slowly unfurled them. She wiggled and shook until they stood proudly behind her.

'Not a flower. A fairy,' Anabelle breathed.

The fairy looked up with clear aqua eyes and nodded, a smile turning her lips.

The familiar tug of magic nudged her mind. 'Your name, is it Arie?'

Again, she nodded, fluttering her wings and hovering for a moment before she fell back into Anabelle's hand.

Chuckling, Anabelle gave her an encouraging smile. 'Try again.'

Again, Arie tried, her small profile pinched with concentration as she lifted herself into the air. After a moment, Arie looked down, and the tinkling bells of laughter poured out of her from excitement as she flew higher and higher with ease.

Anabelle watched the little fairy with amusement until she noticed the pond's rocky ledge. The events in the clearing rushed through her mind as her memories slammed into her.

'Gallian.'

Forcing her legs to move, she half-stumbled, running to the rocky ledge. Falling to her knees, she looked into the frozen water. Her hand reached out and touched the ice, melting it. She tried to see past the black waters for some sign of Lilla or Tatius but to no avail. Leaning back against her heels, she gave a frustrated sigh.

Arie came and stood on the rock in front of her, slipping on the slick surface before she caught herself.

'Arie, what do I do?'

The tiny fairy took small leaps, springing into the air on the last step, and Anabelle opened her hand as Arie flew onto her palm. The image of her mother floated in her mind, and she pursed her lips in thought.

'I need to find the others…but how?'

Arie placed a meaningful hand over her heart.

'With my heart?'

Arie nodded, flying to the tree that blossomed in the middle of winter.

The fairy looked at her expectantly, and Anabelle stared at the massive tree looming over everything around them. She could feel the tether between her and that tree thrumming with life, like a—

'Heartbeat…You want me to follow the heartbeat of the forest?'

Arie twirled with acknowledgement.

There is a heartbeat in our world, and if you listen closely, you can hear it….'

'I just have to listen.'

Rolling her shoulders back, Anabelle walked towards the tree, holding the tether between them. She looked up at the highest peak as she took one last step, inches between her and her creation, and placed her hand on the dark bark. No more twisting or moving, just the thrumming of magic around her. She let her fingers slide down the trunk as she knelt on the forest floor, her hand travelling the length of the roots before sliding to the icy grass that turned green under her touch. She closed her eyes and breathed deeply, feeling the soft grass under her skin. Her breathing slowed, and she sensed everything as it all fell silent. She pictured her mother and Winter.

Her palm grew warm, and she felt the rush of life around her, the forest opening itself to her. Every movement, every being, every living thing was like music to her ears. She opened her eyes and saw the path ahead of her to the east, pink spring flowers dotting every few trees to guide her.

Arie dropped to the root in front of her, and they shared a smile. However, it was short-lived when a branch snapped behind them. Anabelle stood quickly, scanning the area with wide eyes.

She found a black beast walking through the thicket of icicles hanging from the branches. Its massive body of matted fur starkly contrasted with the glittering white surrounding it. The beast had twisted black horns sprouting from the top of its head, and tangled black fur covered its large body, with hooves in place of feet. A menacing double-edged axe was strapped on its back, and another lay in its beefy black hands.

Fear pierced through her. Anabelle threw herself behind the cover of trees. She had only read about minotaurs; never had she seen one before. She didn't think they existed, but the nightmarish creature of her books had become a reality.

She heard the beast come closer, its heavy footfalls rocketing her pulse faster and faster with every step. Pressing her back into the tree, she clamped a hand over her mouth, terrified it could hear her heart hammering. She knew it followed her footprints in the white frost, the vibrant grass a clear marker until it stood on the other side of where she was hidden.

Silence ticked in prolonged seconds. She held her breath. The sound of something cutting through the air met her ears, and she threw herself to the side, scrambling out of the way just as an axe embedded itself where her torso had been.

A deafening roar shook the trees around them, jarring Anabelle to her core. The beast freed the axe, baring its teeth in a savage snarl. Its black eyes flashed with hunger, and it lunged for Anabelle.

A cry of terror flew from her lips as she flung herself to the side. The beast's hands missed her by inches, claws slicing the air. She scrambled to her feet, the hair on the back of her neck standing on end as she narrowly dodged the axe.

Her feet pounded over the ground, Arie right beside her as she ran past the cover of trees and into the clearing. She skidded to the rocky ledge of the water, her heartbeat racing as the minotaur charged into the clearing.

Its massive body crashed through the ice and frozen branches around it.

Her mind screamed at her to run, but every fibre in her body stood still. It knew—some ancient part of her knew what was to come. Deep within the dark abyss of her mind, Anabelle felt the cord of clear, vibrating power rush through her. The tips of her fingers tingled, and Anabelle looked down to see a golden light spark from her hands, ice climbing up her wrists.

Courage engulfed her, slipping in like a long-lost friend as the minotaur charged. She could feel the earthquake as it thundered nearer. With a shout wrenched from deep inside, she threw out her hand. Ice speared through the air, encased in golden light, striking the minotaur straight on just as it reached her a hairsbreadth away.

The beast flew back through the air, landing in a heap on the other side of the clearing, its axe sinking into the ground a few feet away.

She didn't wait. Gathering her skirts, she fled into the forest.

CHAPTER NINTEEN

Gallian stared at the ceiling of the barren cave. Although it was dawn, light fought to penetrate the cave's gloom, dimly filtering into the damp space.

He listened for movement and heard none, yet he felt the eyes of something bore into him. Gallian glanced at the cave mouth from the corner of his eye and saw his father standing there, watching him, waiting. He glanced back at the cave ceiling, his mind a black void. Blinking, he pushed himself to his feet.

Gallian's strides were silent and steady as he approached his father. His face the picture of aloofness and uncaring. He took note of the chaos slowly gathering behind his father's dull eyes.

Balwin watched Gallian walk calmly towards him, his presence unwavering after awakening from the void. His eyes were now dull, cold, and uncaring, his clothes still torn, blood caked across his chest.

'Gallian,' Balwin said.

'Father,' he said tonelessly.

Balwin cocked his head, a sly smile slipping into place. 'The Seasons gather with the Fae, according to my spies. They think to overthrow me. They do not know that Anabelle has fallen into the void.'

A sadistic laugh cackled in the echoing chamber.

Gallian looked at the earth below the mountain, the wind whipping through his hair. Hatred pooled in his heart, and his lip curled in disgust.

Savven wandered the dense forest with ease, stepping around a low-hanging icicle. The wind whispered a quiet melody through the woods as he wove in and out of tangled limbs. He placed his hand on the damp bark of an old and twisted tree. He closed his eyes when he felt the melodic vibrations coming from the life of the forest.

He let his fingers slide from the tree as he continued forward. The frost at his feet had begun to melt, cushioning the sound of his steps, leaving footprints in his wake.

Anabelle tore through the forest, her heart pounding in her ears, breath ragged. A roar came from behind her. A strangled cry escaped her throat as she sprinted faster.

She focused on the path ahead, swerving in and out of trees. The bitter air stung her bright red cheeks, burning the corners of her eyes. Her hair tangled behind her as she worked her legs to their breaking point.

Arie flew ahead of her at speeds that Anabelle could not reach, even with her new sense of speed. Even as she tried, her toes barely touched the forest floor.

The minotaur crashed behind her, tearing through the forest at almost double Anabelle's pace. Its lumbering footfalls caused the ground to quake, vibrating through her with every step closer it took.

Branches whipped out from all directions, and she dodged around them, even as they reached out to seize her. Another roar came as the sharp end of an axe lodged itself into a tree as she passed it. She glanced over her shoulder to see the minotaur dangerously close. She pushed herself, making her legs move faster than they ever had before, ignoring the burning screams of her muscles.

Savven heard a faint roar echo through the blanket of trees, so soft he thought it was only his mind playing tricks on him. But it came again, and he sped towards it.

Running through the thicket of trees like wind, he kept his steps light and agile to avoid roots and fallen boughs. The roar jarred the forest. He could hear the beast's heavy footsteps crashing through the trees, knocking against roots and trunks, shaking the earth with every step.

His eyes widened as he eyed a flash of colour and limbs that turned into a girl shooting towards him, a minotaur close behind.

She threw her body to the right as the beast's axe arched through the air, the sharp edge missing her by inches.

Savven lunged, his hand going to the blade strapped across his back. But he froze, watching the girl throw out a hand, magic rocketing through the air. The beast flew back, its body slammed into a tree, a loud *crack* echoing through the forest.

The girl forced herself up. The minotaur regained itself, shaking the ice and dirt from its body, baring its fangs. With a snarl, it charged forward.

Leaping forward, Savven threw himself at the minotaur. His sword was held down at his side. Reeling it up, he swung it over his head in a deadly arch, paring the blow from the minotaur's axe and pushing back with matched strength. Dodging the swipe of its long claws, Savven slipped into the opening, sliding his blade deep into the gut of the beast.

A cry of outrage echoed, shaking the branches overhead. The beast swung at Savven, knocking a massive fist into the side of his angled jaw just as Savven ripped the sword from his body, and it fell to the ground.

The minotaur staggered, its wound spurting blood.

He glanced at the girl, seeing anger and fear cross her face. Power surged through the air, striking like a poisoned spear that found its mark, piercing the beast's heart.

At last, the minotaur toppled over, dead.

She stared at the minotaur, her hands shaking as she lowered them to her side, sparks of red and gold igniting her fingertips.

Savven briefly looked at the minotaur to ensure it was dead before returning to the girl.

He watched her step up to the beast, wrap two hands around the sword's hilt, and brace herself as she pulled it free from where it lay trapped beneath the carcass.

Looking at the bloodied object, wincing, she thrust it, for good measure, into its heart. Pain flashed across her face.

'I'll take that back,' he said lowly, approaching her.

Disgust shuddered through her, and she glanced up at him silently. She pulled the blade free of the beast's chest and stepped around its body, holding the sword out to him.

He took it by the hilt and wiped the soiled blade on his dark pants, looking at her quietly.

She glanced from him to his blade. He knew what she would see. Hair black as night hung down his back in knots and interwoven braids, stark against his pale skin. Tall, lean, and dressed in all black, he watched her carefully with his dark blue eyes.

He slid his blade back into the scabbard.

Ice crunched softly underfoot as she shifted her weight. Her voice was raw, scraping against her throat when she spoke. 'My name is Anabelle.'

'I know who you are,' he said. And he did, now that he had seen her up close. There was no denying their resemblance.

Anabelle nodded, not bothering to question it. She was too tired, mentally and emotionally. 'Did it have to die?'

'We all end at some time.'

'We do,' she agreed, chewing on her lip. 'I never thought I would take a life. It was so easy.'

'All life comes to an end, Anabelle. None have a choice in the matter.'

Anabelle knelt and placed a cold hand upon the rough fur. Fear was replaced by sorrow. 'Death is not natural. It was created by man and beast out of anger and spite...I do not believe the Gods wanted death or created it—I cannot believe it. But I would rather live for those I love than die to satisfy those who hate me.'

She stood and turned to him. 'What's your name?'

'Savven.' He moved to Anabelle's side, putting a gentle but firm hand on her shoulder. 'You did well, Anabelle.'

'I did not do anything well, not at that moment. He is dead, and I feel it. I feel his death like a stain on my skin.'

Arie flittered in front of Anabelle and touched her hand to her heart. Anabelle nodded in understanding.

'I know, Arie, listen to the heartbeat. But there is one less heartbeat, and I can hear its silence.'

'Then listen to those that still beat,' Savven said. 'You must remember that with one less heart, there are many more to take its place.'

Anabelle gave him a curious look. 'A bird with a million feathers is still a bird; yet, when it loses just one feather, its flight is disrupted. This world is so filled with darkness that one cannot even see the world and its beauty, even in a single soul. The importance lies in that one small part.'

She looked at the beast once again, bitterness underlining her words. 'Even so, that this beast was consumed with hate and darkness, no doubt by Balwin's hand as he spreads that foulness to every corner he can reach.'

Savven nodded and offered his hand. 'Come, Anabelle. It's time for us to go.'

'Where are you taking me?' she asked, taking half a step back.

He pursed his lips in understanding. 'Somewhere safe. I give you my word as high Fae that I will not harm you.'

She stared at him for a long while before nodding shortly and looking down at the dead beast. 'May your spirit sleep in the heavens,' she murmured before taking Savven's hand.

Arie flew beside them as they trekked through the snow.

In the dim, frosty forest, encompassed in the bitter air, dark green vines sprouted from the earth when no one was present. The ground cracked and shuddered beneath the minotaur's body. Wrapping and weaving themselves around the beast, white flowers blanketed the tangles.

Silence enveloped the forest once more, and the wind blew its soft breath over the grave.

CHAPTER TWENTY

Footprints marked Gallian's path through the snow as he treaded through the bleak forest. The depths of his eyes had become something that even Gallian himself—if he had the chance to see—would not recognise.

Deep in the Black Forest, trees were as wide as they were tall, their leafless branches tangling together high above his head. The world was eerily quiet, as if it held its breath. The wind did not blow, the birds did not speak, and Gallian was greeted with silence.

He knew this place faintly, like a memory diluted. Faint images of a long-forgotten childhood roamed his mind. The land was ancient, its age seeping from the massive trees that guarded the very thing Gallian and Balwin had come for from wandering eyes.

The air around him crackled, the forest waiting with bated

breath. The looming trees creaked and moaned, their deep roots pulling from the ground. Their trunks twisted until rough faces were etched into their centres, and their limbs contorted into bludgeoning weapons and long gangrenous arms. They ripped wood staffs as long as their trunks from their cores, poised with jagged ends.

His father's low laugh of amusement sounded behind him.

'The Tree Guardians.'

Five Guardians towered in a circle, guarding the way beyond, and magic sparked at Gallian's fingertips.

With a deafening roar, the Guardians raised their staffs above their heads and stabbed them into the frozen ground. The earth shook from the impact.

'You are not worthy to pass beyond!' Their voices boomed through the forest, ancient and all-encompassing, shaking the trees around them. 'Go back from whence you came!'

As if sensing Gallian's thoughts, the ground splintered beside him as roots shot through the dirt and ice. Spinning around the bulbous limbs that came from above, his magic shot through the air. The nearest Guardian's roar was deafening as a glowing blue flame wrapped around its trunk, flames igniting the ground along its roots.

The floor was tattooed in blue fire that lit up the world around them in an intricate web.

Their spindled branches plucked Gallian from the ground. His snarl cut the air, and his arm shot out, flames wrapped around the one that held him.

'You really are wasting time, Gallian,' drawled his father from a safe distance.

Grunting as he was dropped to the ground, his right side slammed into a rock. Pushing to his feet, numb to the pain, he ducked as a wooden spear shot through the air.

The leash on his magic slipped. With a parting glance to the Guardian that charged him, Gallian let the leash go.

Blinding blue fire erupted from within him. He cried out as the world was engulfed in flames, and the fire ran the length of his body in a scorching kiss.

The Guardians' roars were unending as the fire ate them from the outside until the world was filled with ash, and the charred ground beneath their feet no longer shook.

Gallian stepped past the encompassing scorched trees that still stood, slipping through the narrow space between two of them into a circular clearing. Grey light filtered through the tree branches, ash falling like snow in beams of silver that pierced through the gloom.

Four withered, grey trunks entangled, coming together in a snarl of knots to form the singular leafless structure before him. Tightly woven together, weaving in and out of each other, their branches formed a dome within the clearing, webbed through the air.

Gallian approached the mangled tree and placed his hand against the smooth grey bark. A dark glow illuminated his fingertips, and he could feel life pulsating beneath his palm. Without a thought, he latched onto the magic tether around the tree, the one that thrummed with life like a siren's call.

A ripple went through the air, and a thundering crack ripped through the tree in a shot of light. The tether wavered against the cold, dark power ebbing from Gallian, and the smooth shell grew frigid, wrinkling as the grey went white. The blood of the tree webbed across the snow like black ink, the roots bleeding dry in a permanent tattoo upon the earth.

'The Tree of Souls,' said Balwin. 'Just as I remember it.'

The tether flickered, struggling to hold onto its lifeline, but the attempt was feeble. With a sputter, its life went dark in Gallian's grasp. Gallian didn't acknowledge his father's bitter voice as he studied the now dead tree. He felt nothing, barely feeling the cold or even his father's hand on his shoulder.

'What are you going to do with it?' Gallian asked, watching his father circle the large trunk.

Balwin scoffed. 'Do not be naive, Gallian. All things in this forest have a purpose. And this is the Tree of Souls, said to be the first creation by the Gods, blessed by the dragons that helped forge this world. There are four Gods—Taleana, Naleen, Tatius, and Udiya—and four Spirits of Seasons—Winter, Spring, Summer, and Fall. These four trees represent each of them, intertwined and connected to each other and every soul in this world. A bond.'

Black flashed across Balwin's eyes, and the brittle tip of a branch broke off, falling to the snow. Thick, dark blood blackened the white ground.

'A tree that bleeds must be important.' Balwin eyed his son. 'Do you not agree, Gallian?'

Gallian kept quiet, knowing his father didn't expect an answer.

Balwin spread his thin fingers over the trunk. Midnight veins began to creep around the tree, curling and spreading over it. Thunder rolled overhead, and clouds formed as a stale wind picked up. Lightning spiderwebbed across the sky as thunder boomed.

'Come! Come join me, you beings of darkness, you souls of the night! Come and fight for me!' Balwin screamed into the sky, and thunder roared as if in acknowledgement.

With a flick of the wrist, Balwin sliced his forearm open with the tip of his sharp nail. With fire in his eyes, he grabbed his son by the jaw, forcing his head back.

Gallian didn't fight as Balwin pried his mouth open, his father's fingers digging into his skin, drawing blood.

Balwin held his wound to Gallian's mouth, watching in fixated fascination as black blood slipped past his lips.

Like liquid ice that burned through his body, he felt his father's blood brand him from within. A roar ripped out of Gallian as flames engulfed his muscles, and his skin burned like hot iron. Whorls and webs of shadows branded his flesh. Darkness filled his eyes entirely as the soul of death settled within him. It whispered through his mind with sharp talons.

Balwin's face contorted as the demons inside him raged, feeling the shadows that now settled within his son.

'Patience,' Balwin said to them. 'Now we must wait.'

Without uttering a word, Gallian simply turned away and began the walk through the forest.

Anabelle stepped into Savven's camp, halting when two elves stood and watched her with asserting eyes.

'This is Lithônion,' Savven said from behind her. 'One of the finest warriors in Álfheimr, the city of the high Fae.'

Lithônion carried himself with an air of ease and power that made Anabelle shift on her feet. His physique was defined clearly under his ivory tunic, and his powerful thighs were wrapped in leather. Golden-brown hair fell pin-straight past his shoulders in a shining curtain, and his vibrant green eyes watched her every move.

'And this is Ezra,' Savven added. 'General to the royal armies and Captain of the Guard to the king and queen.'

Where Lithônion was the day, Ezra was the night. Midnight hair framed Ezra's pale face; sharp cheekbones and angled brows gave him an unearthly beauty. His body, while strong, was lean and agile, clothed in all black like Savven. His coal eyes surveyed her with open curiosity, a small, friendly smile lifting the corners of his mouth, softening his features.

The two elves bowed their heads.

'Are you the one called Anabelle?' Lithônion asked, an inquisitive look on his face.

'To a friend, I am,' she answered.

Lithônion's gaze travelled the length of her body, assessing her and meeting her eyes with an inquisitive stare. 'The forest speaks your name.'

Savven took her elbow gently and guided her to the fire. 'We are your friends, Anabelle.'

Anabelle raised a brow. 'That has yet to be determined. I find men to be the least discerning when it comes to friendship.'

'Males,' Ezra corrected. 'We are not men.'

Savven gestured to a log close to the fire. 'Sit. We need to gather herbs for supper.' He gave her a long look, gently touching her shoulder. 'You're safe here. We won't be long.'

And they weren't, as Anabelle sat watching them prepare the meal.

Savven picked up a dead hare from beside the fire and drew a hand over the icy ground to open a perfect hollow in the soil, the width of two hands. He lined the hole with stalks of herbs and plants, neatly placing them around the edge. Gathering snow and chunks of ice, he filled the hole and murmured, 'Saji.' Snow and ice turned to crystal clear water.

Anabelle watched Lithônion grind the herbs rhythmically against a rock anchored in the ground. Ezra skinned the hare in silence.

Anabelle felt entirely useless.

Noon turned into twilight, and Anabelle held a wooden bowl of hot stew.

She glanced at Ezra, who was sitting beside her, as she sipped the stew. 'You know who I am, ' she said.

He remained quiet.

'You're here for my mother,' she concluded.

'It is our queen's request,' Ezra said.

She pursed her lips. 'She warned me you would come, but I won't let you take her.'

'That is not your decision to make, I'm afraid.'

'I will not let my mother pay the price of her freedom for saving my life,' she said through clenched teeth.

After a moment of silence, the elf simply started to laugh. Anabelle scowled.

'I'm sorry, Anabelle. I understand your love for your mother, but we cannot disobey our queen. Your mother is also the queen's sister; she knows the consequences of her actions.'

Anabelle's brows shot up, but she quickly masked her shock. 'My aunt must not know the love between a mother and child.'

Ezra's sharp features softened. 'Savven is her son—you two share blood.'

Anabelle's eyes flicked to Savven. She could tell the two other elves were trying not to listen to their conversation, though their heads turned at Savven's name.

'Regardless,' Anabelle said, 'she does not rule over me and holds no authority that I must obey. Isadora is my mother. She both gave me life and saved it. I owe her the very freedom you wish to take away.'

'We will cross this mountain when we come to it, dear one. Now finish your stew. The air is growing colder.'

She picked up her bowl. The pit of her stomach grew warm and full as the air around them became hollow and bitter. She stared at the fire, remembering Tatius and Lilla's faces.

'I died last night,' she said suddenly, blinking in realisation. 'Is immortality supposed to feel different? My power is stronger. I see differently—I see the life of the forest beneath the forest. Does that make sense? Like lifelines that ebb and flow and tether to each other.'

'You see what binds us all, what others cannot see.'

'I'm no longer just Anabelle.'

'You will always be Anabelle. Never lose sight of her.'

The air grew stale later that night, slowly turning to the dim hours of dawn. A low-hanging fog drifted through the trees as Anabelle lay curled on her side, her back to the camp. Her limbs felt like stone, anchored to the ground, and with a struggle, she dragged her hand over the dirt. A sudden stab of pain woke her. Her eyes shot open.

A golden web strung tightly together stretched out beneath the forest floor, pulsating with life. She nearly sighed in relief until she saw shadows slowly making their way over the golden tethers. A tightness in her chest seized her, and she took in a strangled breath, fighting the hold on her. The world around her narrowed, her vision becoming pinpoints, and her chest screamed for release.

She couldn't breathe, she couldn't breathe, she couldn't—

Strong hands jerked her hand from the ground, releasing the hold on her body as she twisted upright, taking in ragged breaths of air.

'Anabelle?'

She rubbed a weary hand across her face, looking up at three pairs of eyes. She pushed herself off the ground and straightened her skirts with a shaky hand.

'Something is terribly wrong.'

Ezra reached out a tentative hand, concern evident in his eyes. 'What's wrong?'

'The land, it's dying. I saw shadows and darkness. I couldn't move, I couldn't breathe. They were dying, and I could feel it—I was dying with them.'

Her brows pulled tight, mouth pursing to a flat line as the ache in her chest worsened. Screeching in the distance pulled her attention.

'What was that?'

Lithônion glanced up at the sky. 'I will see.' He leapt for the nearest branch of the tall, black tree behind him. With swift speed, he climbed the towering tree, reaching the pinnacle in just moments.

Lithônion scanned the sky, cold winter air slicing through his skin as he gazed over the treetops, distant mountain peaks, and storm clouds overhead. A massive black cloud moved swiftly in their direction. He muttered an oath under his breath, noticing the trees shaking just beyond them, then jumped for the ground and landed nimbly on his feet.

'What is it, Lithônion?' Savven asked.

'Ravens, a cloud of ravens, and with them fly winged beasts that...' He trailed off as he focused his sight to the north.

The large, matted body of a minotaur came into his vision, followed by many more. Their ugly, twisting horns and thundering hooves crashed through the bramble of tree branches.

'There is an army heading straight for us,' he said, checking his weapons.

'An army!' Anabelle pushed past Lithônion, eyes focusing

beyond the trees, and there, she saw them.

Hundreds of creatures, their eyes colourless, as if blinded—blinded by what she didn't know. Centaurs, minotaur, satyrs—

'Satyrs are supposed to be creatures of peace,' Ezra commented, adding under his breath, 'Despite their heathen tendencies.'

'As are centaurs, I'm afraid,' said Savven, giving Ezra a quick look.

Ezra took a closer look, his hand going to the blade strapped to his leg. 'There are harpies and a Cerberus amongst them. We must reach the others before they reach us.'

Anabelle's heart beat faster, magic coursing through her blood at the thought of a fight.

Overhead, a thousand screams could be heard as thousands of ravens passed over them, blacking out the barely visible sun.

'Run!' Savven yelled.

Her feet barely touched the floor as she flew through the forest, keeping pace with the others. Her heart raced as the army approached from behind, thoughts of her mother and the others unknowingly at their mercy. Her fear pushed her faster, her breath slowing as she focused on the forest beyond her, weaving in and out of the tree line. Ezra kept pace with her. Lithônion and Savven were several feet ahead.

Her fear slowly faded, and her heart began to ease into a steady pace. A secret enjoyment came from the rush she felt. Anabelle looked back to see the ravens had become a distant—but still visible—cloud in the sky. A flash of pink caught her eye, and she slowed, then stopped altogether.

Ezra called for the others to halt. 'What is it?'

Anabelle stared at a bundle of pink flowers that lay at the base of a tree.

The canopy towered over the rest of the forest, and the trunk was the width of three trees. The flowers lay beside a set of footprints in the little snow covering the ground, trekking to the east.

Ignoring everything around her, she dashed in the direction of the footprints. The cries of her companions fell on deaf ears as she followed the marks in the ground, skidding to a halt moments later. A figure stood with its back to her, shadowed in a dark blue cloak, the hood drawn over its head.

'Who are you?' she said tentatively.

Suddenly, the forest was filled with warmth and light as the sun penetrated the bleak overhang.

The figure moved, turning to face her. Heart hammering in her chest, she watched as they drew back their hood. A strangled breath lodged in her throat.

Gallian looked just as she remembered him.

She didn't notice the others behind her, keeping their distance as they watched.

'What is she doing?' questioned Lithônion in a low voice. 'There is nothing there.'

'Something is there. We just can't see it,' said Ezra calmly, watching her intently.

Anabelle took a hesitant step forward, her breathing shallow.

'Are you real?' she whispered, reaching out for him.

His eyes were warm and vibrant, and his softly falling black hair reached his shoulders. He was still wearing dark brown leather trousers and a white woollen shirt, free of the bright red blood Anabelle vividly remembered. Her voice quivered when she spoke again.

'Are you real, Gallian?'

Gallian only smiled.

'Tatius said you would live.' She took a step closer, her eyes searching his. 'I thought your father had you. I thought he took you the day he killed me. That you died because of me.'

Gallian mirrored her, stepping closer, a sad smile pulling at the corners of his mouth. 'I'm only a memory now, Anabelle. I'm not dead, not in the traditional sense, but who I am is a shell of what I was, and even that, I'm afraid, was not much. This is the good you saw in me, the kernel of light.'

Tears formed in Anabelle's eyes. 'You're alive...but you're not. You're saying I will see you again, but I will not see *you*.'

'Anabelle,' Gallian whispered, taking another step forward, 'you must listen to me. The future holds a darkness that will try to overthrow you. Within that darkness, you will find me. We will meet as enemies. This will be the last you see of me as you knew me.'

Anabelle reached for Gallian's arm, but it went through him as if he did not exist.

'I told you, I am only a memory now.' His face pulled tight with pity. 'Please do not cry.'

She felt her cheeks. Tears streamed down her face, wetting her fingertips. 'Why are you here? Why can I see you?'

'You can see things others cannot, Anabelle. That is the gift of the Keeper. Embrace what you have become. You will do great things, but please, forgive me.'

He glanced over his shoulder. 'Trust him. My brother was an advocate for you when I was ill-intending. He will stand by you.'

With that, he leaned forward and placed a kiss on her forehead, one that she couldn't feel. And then he was gone, and with him went the sun's warmth, and the forest was once more grey and cold.

Glancing at her feet, she saw a single pink flower. She brushed the back of her hand across her face, drying her tears, then kneeled and plucked the flower from the ground.

Ezra stepped forward. 'Are you all right?'

She faced them, rolling her shoulders back, chin held high. 'I'm fine.'

'These are dangerous times, Anabelle.' Savven said.

Anabelle rounded on Savven, eyes flashing. 'You don't think I know that, Savven? I'm the Keeper. I know that better than anyone. My life is threatened every day, and those who die die because of me.'

'I apologise for—'

His words cut off as he looked over her head. His blade was in hand before Anabelle could blink. Lithônion and Ezra stepped in front of her, shielding her from whatever had stepped from the shadows.

Anabelle gave no mind to the wall they made and marched around them.

It was a man—*male.*

Trust him.

'Who are you?' she demanded.

The male stepped forward, heedless of the blade pointed at him.

His eyes roamed down her body slowly. Anabelle flushed under his appreciative stare despite her better judgment. Her stomach tightened when his gaze returned to hers.

'Look at you,' he said with a crooked smile. 'Not so helpless.'

Anabelle narrowed her eyes. 'I beg your pardon?'

Amusement flicked on the male's face. 'It's begged.'

He took another step towards her, and Ezra made to step in front of her, but she held up a hand. The elf stilled, and she tilted her head in regard.

'Who are you?' she asked.

'A friend of the family,' he replied with a sweeping bow.

'I don't know you.'

'Ah,' he said, the swagger in his strides relaxed, and he looked down at her, only a couple of feet separating them. 'But I know you.'

Savven stepped forward with guarded eyes. 'How can you prove that?'

The male raised an unbothered, dark brow, looking at Savven over Anabelle's head. 'That's for you to decide, Elf.'

Savven glanced at Lithônion and Ezra, lowering his blade but keeping it ready at his side.

Anabelle watched the male, who stared at them with an amused regard. 'We need allies. He will have enough opportunity to prove his friendship.'

Lithônion studied her but dropped his hand to his side.

Taking a deep breath, she closed the distance between them and stared at the male as he looked down at her. His pale blue eyes turned bright as light filtered across his face, twinkling with humour. His hair lay in dark brown waves at the nape of his neck, and a light coating of stubble shadowed his jaw, covering the expanse of sun-browned skin.

'What's your name?'

He adjusted the bow slung over his back, the quiver of arrows shifting. 'Néefar.'

Her gaze wandered over the black wool shirt that opened at the neck to reveal a toned chest and a dusting of dark hair. A black vest, tight over his torso, secured down the middle with bronze clasps. He wore black trousers tucked into worn boots.

She returned her gaze to his and immediately scowled at the smirk she saw. 'Are you a man?'

He crossed his arms over his chest. 'I am neither man nor beast.'

'Then what does that make you?'

'A shifter.'

'I have never met a shifter before.'

'I have never met a Keeper before. One could say you do not exist.'

She ignored his teasing. 'We go to the Summer Fae. Will you come with us?'

'I will follow you, Keeper, and your friends.'

'My name is Anabelle.'

Néefar gave her a small smile. 'As you wish.'

Anabelle stared a moment longer before motioning for Savven and the others. 'I trust him, for now.'

They said nothing, but she knew they heard her, and she could hear Savven slide his blade back into the sheath.

'We're close to the Summer Fae,' Néefar said in the silence.

'Yes,' she said. 'I recognise these woods...faintly.' Her brows furrowed, eyes noting familiar pieces now merged with unfamiliar forest.

'Then we must not waste any time,' Néefar said, unfazed by the hard looks the three fae males gave him.

Ezra, Savven, and Lithônion followed behind him, hesitating for only a moment.

Anabelle was the last to follow. She turned back to where she had seen Gallian, his eyes flashing through her mind.

'Goodbye,' came as a whisper against her ear.

She closed her eyes briefly and silently whispered goodbye to her old friend.

CHAPTER TWENTY-ONE

Hot steam wafted across Isadora's face as she stirred the bubbling broth over a blazing fire. Stray strands of hair curled around her face, and she brushed a hand across her cheek. She was tired, mentally. The weight of the last fifteen years settled on her shoulders like an old friend she did not wish to know, and with Anabelle gone, her body was wound in unmanageable knots.

She closed her eyes briefly and instantly regretted it as images of fire flashed across her memory. The night of Anabelle's choosing was still burned into her mind, and she wrenched her eyes open, concentrating on the bubbling broth.

Voices rose, and Isadora looked over her shoulder to see bodies emerge from the treeline. Her eyes focused on one, widening before she threw the long wooden spoon onto her chopping table. She picked up her skirts and dashed through the summer keep barrier.

Gallian was not among them. Anabelle stood beside faces she thought she would never see again. She recognised Ezra, his features the same as they had been nearly thirty years ago, and Savven and Lithônion. Her gaze went to Néefar. She had not seen him since Gallian was a boy; even then, he had been scarce.

'Anabelle,' she whispered into the bitter cold, her breath clouding her face.

Anabelle's face lit up, and she sprinted for her.

Isadora's arms wrapped around Anabelle tightly, and tears pricked her eyes.

'I'm so glad you're safe,' Isadora whispered into Anabelle's hair.

Anabelle tightened her hold. 'I had to come back to you.'

Stepping back, Anabelle gave her mother a grave look. 'We must speak, all of us.'

Isadora glanced at the males standing on either side of her daughter before she nodded briefly and turned towards the keep.

'This way, quickly,' she said, cautiously peering through the thicket of trees.

The summer heat warmed them to their bones as they stepped through the veil. Golden light filtered in through leafy canopies, and particles sparkled in the sunlight. Temporary huts were crafted from branches and mud, forming dome lodgings. Dwarves and satyrs mingled as they worked on making another dome hut, hacking away at fallen branches. Fairies buzzed from tree to tree overhead, no more than a small gleam of light flittering in the sunshine.

'Summer cast a veil over the summer keep,' Isadora explained. 'They expanded it to cover a vast area of the forest so we may grow our defences. After you and Gallian left for the Vaitarani, dwarves and satyrs came to us at the Spirits' beckoning. Though their numbers are few, we won't turn away the help.'

Trees were littered through the refuge, but a towering blackwood tree stood at its core. Its base was the expanse of four trees, its branches stretching and twisting higher and higher until they were tiny peaks in the sky, covered in dark emerald leaves that glinted in the light.

Isadora pressed an open hand to its coarse bark. A crack formed in the trunk, slowly revealing itself as a narrow doorway. She pulled the door open and disappeared inside.

The five followed her in. A narrow staircase, carved from the tree and anchored into its side, spiralled through its core. Nothing but shadows surrounded them. Down and down they went until light peaked at the bottom, and the narrow staircase opened into a vast underground dwelling.

A sizeable room expanded into many corridors, webbing in many directions. A large, round table made from blackwood stood proudly at the centre. A series of knots were carved into its edge, and in the middle, four trees wove together, merging to form a single growth, beautiful and twisted.

'Welcome to the Summer Fae's stronghold,' Isadora said. 'Take a seat. The others will be here soon.'

The chairs were equally beautiful, made from the same blackwood, with knots and whorls carved in the low backs and armrests.

One by one, the Spirits of Seasons glided silently from a corridor just beyond Isadora's seat. They were just as Anabelle remembered, laced with strength and ethereal beauty. She glanced at her companions and noticed no surprise on their faces.

The spirits circled the table and took seats among them. When they looked at Anabelle, she shifted in her seat.

After a moment, Winter said gently, her eyes warm, ' Anabelle, tell us what happened.'

Anabelle fiddled with a loose thread on her skirt, feeling very small as all eyes turned to her.

Glancing at each face, Anabelle paused at Néefar. He stared at her openly, his eyes like a depth of water that calmed the turbulent emotions in her. Tearing her gaze away, she stared at the carved tree, focusing on its roots that wove together.

'When we arrived at the Vaitarani, Balwin was waiting. Gallian tried to protect me from his father, but he wasn't strong enough.' She felt hot tears prick her eyes and angrily forced them back. Gritting her teeth against her emotions, she told them everything that happened, and at the mention of her death, a small gasp echoed in the council room.

Isadora placed her fingertips over her mouth.

Anabelle pursed her lips in a grim frown, her brows pinching as light and blurry images tried to solidify, small pieces of a puzzle slowly merging.

'I thought I had died. It felt like death. Cold, dark, everything you expect it to be. I believed I had died until I awoke in a cavern. I had found the Pool of Immortality. With this discovery, though, I had to choose between being mortal and immortal, just as you said I would.' Anabelle glanced at Winter and then her mother. 'When I awoke, days had passed. I lay alone in the forest. Neither Gallian nor Balwin were anywhere to be seen. I came across Savven sometime after.' She gave the male a slight smile. 'He and his companions Ezra and Lithônion were a great help.'

Anabelle smoothed a hand over her skirt, her palms sweaty as she remembered this morning. 'Balwin is moving quickly. I don't know what he is planning—none of us do, but this morning, there was a horde of creatures careening through the forest, a cloud of ravens overhead. Friend and foe were together, their eyes blinded by Balwin. We believe he has gathered them to raise up an army. Our haste to make it here is how we met Néefar.'

'An army? Are you certain?' Autumn inquired.

Lithônion straightened in his seat, his face turning serious. 'Yes, I saw it. We all did.'

Spring took in a deep breath, her pert mouth twisted in thought. 'I wish it had not come to this,' she said, her tone delicate among the talk of war. 'So many souls will be lost in this chaos.'

Anabelle glanced at Spring, the spirit's blue-green eyes downcast, her gold hair a halo around her face.

'A price I do not want to pay,' Anabelle said, 'but one that will be forced from all of us.'

Spring gave Anabelle a soft smile. 'You have grown, Keeper.'

Anabelle lowered her eyes to the image of the tree.

'We will need to gather forces of our own. We need to be able to retaliate once the time comes,' Autumn said. 'We do not wish for bloodshed, but we will have it. Unfortunately, this is not the first war we have fought to protect our land and people. We are creatures of peace, but we will not—cannot—stand idly by.'

Summer nodded. 'Yes, if one wants peace, one must be willing to fight for it.'

Savven stood silently, capturing everyone's attention. 'I'm sorry, we cannot fight with you. We have come for a separate matter.'

Anger flooded through Anabelle, and she stood abruptly, her chair threatening to topple backwards. 'You cannot seriously mean to take her! After everything you have seen?'

Savven stood calmly, unaffected. 'I have a duty to my queen.'

'A *duty*? I have a responsibility to uphold!'

'Then you know as well as I,' he replied smoothly.

Her rage only grew, and she pushed her chair out of the way as she stalked around the table. 'I will not let you take her. I told you that before, and I'll tell you this now. You will not take her!'

Ice crawled up her hands, and her eyes became molten gold as anger coursed through her. She bit down on the power that threatened to spill out, holding on to the tight rope of magic that promised to snap.

She didn't notice as Néefar approached her side, pressing his hand to her lower back.

'Do not do something in anger. You will come to regret it, Anabelle,' he said quietly enough that everyone else had to strain to hear him. Still, his words punctured through her emotions like a hot knife.

Anabelle narrowed her eyes at Savven, but she released the hold on her magic, which slipped back into the far corners of her soul. Her eyes returned to their silver-blue, and the ice faded from her fingertips.

Isadora stood, resignation on her fair face. 'I will go with you.'

Anabelle stared. 'No, you can't!'

Isadora smiled softly. 'I am needed elsewhere, my dear one. Just as you are needed by many, I am expected to uphold the responsibility of my actions.'

'You only did it to save me,' she retorted weakly.

'I did. I also knew this would come, so I have had many years to prepare.'

Anabelle felt tired, and the weariness in her bones made her feel brittle. Shaking her head, she turned her back, unable to talk, fearing she would say something awful.

After a moment, she stiffened her spine and said, 'If this is what you want, then leave. Go as soon as you are ready.'

She left them there, ignoring her mother's protests. She felt guilt rise but ignored it, climbing the spiral staircase to the surface.

Ezra found Anabelle nearly hidden by the cover of trees that lined part of the veil's outer edge. The cold air sliced through him as he stepped from the warmth of summer's shield, though he barely noticed. The Keep disappeared as soon as he stepped through the barrier, but he paid it no mind.

'What do you want, Ezra?' Anabelle asked, not taking her eyes off the tree line.

Seconds passed into minutes, the silence numbing until Ezra spoke up. 'Anabelle, I will make sure your mother has a fair trial.'

She snorted. 'She will still get tried as a criminal. She is anything but.'

'It's not your fault.'

'Yes, it is. My mother wouldn't have broken your laws if it were not for me. She wouldn't be a criminal in your eyes.'

'Look at me.'

Anabelle turned sad, guilt-ridden eyes to him.

'In my eyes, she is no more a criminal than you are. She did something out of a mother's love. I cannot make a decision as to whether she is to be charged or not with treason. Your mother is the sister of my queen. I do not believe my queen is cold and uncaring.'

'My mother is all I have left in this world. Please do not take her away from me.'

It was a desperate plea, a child's plea.

The sound of hooves upon snow reached their ears, and they both turned.

'Where may I find my sister, Keeper?'

CHAPTER TWENTY-TWO

Ezra bowed and moved to the side as his queen came forward on a magnificent golden mare. The picture of nobility in an evergreen robe, she wore a diadem on her brow. Raven hair spilt over her shoulders while icy blue eyes stared down at Anabelle with imperiousness. Her skin was as fair as the barely-there snow around them, and her brows slanted like wings.

Anabelle stared at the queen before her. The queen was beautiful, just like her mother. They were the same in every way except their eyes.

'Keeper, where is Isadora?' she asked again, dismounting her mare. Her dark plum gown contrasted against the evergreen of her cloak.

'I may be the Keeper, but my name is Anabelle. You will call me as such.'

The queen glanced at Anabelle with faint curiosity. 'You have her spirit. You look just like her, just as she did in her youth. Forgive me, Anabelle. My name is Casvara.'

'I know who you are.'

'Then please show me to my sister.'

Anabelle said nothing but turned to lead her into the Keep.

The steady thump of horse hooves and the quiet steps of Ezra and the queen followed her through the veil. Warmth soothed their bitter skin as Anabelle led them further into the refuge.

The queen draped the reins over her mare's neck and left her to graze by the trees, following Anabelle as she led them to the blackwood tree. She waited while the doorway opened and guided them down the narrow staircase.

Anabelle entered the large room and saw that none had left. 'We have a visitor.'

When Casvara stepped into the room, Lithônion and Savven stood at once, bowing their heads.

Isadora blinked at her sister in surprise. Taking a slow breath, she stood with her hands at her sides and her back straight.

'Hello, Casvara. It has been a while.'

Casvara didn't waver regarding Isadora, frankly. 'It has, Isadora. You have changed.'

'All things change, although you do not seem different. You are always one to take command. Could you not wait for them to collect me?'

'I realised that we had not seen each other in many years. I wanted to see you before all else. I didn't want our meeting after so long to be one filled with anger.'

Isadora glanced at Anabelle, then back to Casvara. 'May we talk in private?'

Casvara nodded and let Isadora guide them into one of the surrounding tunnels.

Once the two sisters left, all was quiet. Savven opened his mouth to speak but was cut off by Anabelle's words.

'I think I will take a walk.'

'You will get lost in these tunnels, Anabelle,' said Summer.

Néefar stood. 'I will accompany her.'
Anabelle bristled. 'I am not a child.'
'Nonetheless, I shall walk with you.'

'You've always been so impatient,' Isadora said. 'Coming here without so much as a guard to escort you. What would Nydeth say?'

The door clicked shut to Isadora's simple but comfortable room. Roughly carved walls surrounded a bed big enough for herself pushed into a corner, and a wooden desk with a chair was against the wall across from it. Torches were mounted beside her door and bed, their flames casting the room in a vibrant array of yellow and orange.

Casvara smoothed a hand down the front of her gown. 'I almost didn't come,' she said.

'Then why did you?' Isadora asked.

'As I said,' she said slowly, her voice soft, 'I did not want our first meeting in nearly thirty years to be one filled with disdain.'

Isadora laughed softly. 'Thirty years is nothing to us, Vara.'

'You have not called me that in some time.'

Shoulders relaxing, Isadora walked over to her sister, placing a gentle hand on her arm. 'I have missed you, sister.'

The first hint of emotion rolled over her sister's pristine face, and she looked at Isadora with weary eyes. 'I wish you hadn't come back,' Casvara said. 'I wish that my hand was not bound by Fae law.'

Isadora nodded. 'I can't fault you for what must be done, and I couldn't allow Anabelle to venture forth without me. My path had been made. There was no choice but to follow.'

'The love a mother holds for her child is beyond comparison. I would do the same for Savven.'

'He will make a fine king one day.'

Casvara laughed, her facade cracking and her eyes dancing with merriment. 'I don't know if Savven would share that opinion. He'd rather fight on the battlefront than sit on a throne.'

'I think he and I have much more in common than I realised,' mused Isadora.

'Oh, truly,' agreed Casvara.

The space between them quieted, and the air grew solemn.

Casvara took a deep breath. 'We must discuss your departure. Fae laws are binding, their magic is strong, and the longer you wait, the worse it will be.'

'I know,' Isadora said, pulling out the desk chair for her sister and taking a seat on the bed. 'Let us talk.'

Anabelle didn't wait for Néefar. Instead, she turned her back and chose one of the many tunnels, avoiding the one her mother and the queen had taken.

Néefar caught up with her quickly, keeping pace easily. Their steps ricocheted off the stone, the only sound they could hear.

After a moment's thought, Néefar's voice was full of mirth as he said, 'You pout like a child.'

Anabelle halted in her steps and looked at the man with indignation. 'Excuse me?'

'Maybe that was the wrong description?' he mused as he continued walking.

'I do not pout like a child,' she said crossly as she caught up. 'To be watched over like I am just a wee babe is absolutely ridiculous. I have learned I am more than capable of caring for myself.'

'You may be able to care for yourself, but that doesn't mean we will not watch over you. You are, after all, the most valuable piece in this game.'

'Do you consider this a game?'

Néefar weighed his thoughts for a moment. 'Yes, I do. War is a game played by kings and queens and their subjects. Whether any of us like it or not, someone has to win.'

They fell into silence again.

She took a moment to really see him. His cheekbones were high, his nose straight. He had a small scar above his lip, barely visible in the dim light. He had removed his cloak when they entered the keep, and she couldn't help but notice the cords of muscle in his arms and his muscular chest. Leather encompassed his strong thighs and narrow hips.

'Are you quite finished?'

Anabelle's cheeks burned at her inappropriate observation. 'I was only looking at the one who claims to be a friend.'

Néefar stopped, his face turning serious. 'I do not claim to be a friend. I am a friend. I would give my life If needed…which I hope it isn't.'

'That's foolish to say for somebody you don't know.'

A series of emotions mingled together behind Néefar's eyes. 'Some things you just need to accept, Anabelle.'

'Who are you, Néefar?'

Néefar smiled down at her and lifted his hand to her face, tucking a stray hair behind her ear. The pad of his thumb whispered over the flesh behind her jaw, and without a word, he continued down the path.

Her skin tingled where he touched her, but she didn't push him for an answer. Instead, she fell back into step beside him, letting him lead her through the cavern tunnels.

A dim blue glow appeared at one end of the tunnel as it curved to the right.

'What is that?' Anabelle murmured.

'I don't know.'

They followed the light and found the tunnel stopped at an archway. Slowly, the two walked through it, and the room opened up. The dim light covered the entirety of the ceiling above them, a pool of water reflecting the light like a mirror.

Anabelle knelt and dipped a hand into the water.

'It's warm,' she commented, glancing at the blue glow above

them.

She saw past the shimmering light, staring at the jellylike substance covering the ceiling. With a plop, a dollop fell into the water. It dissolved, and steam rose from the surface, filling the air with the smell of lilacs.

'What is this place?'

'I believe it's a bathing chamber,' Néefar said.

Anabelle made herself comfortable on the stone, tucking her legs beneath her as she leaned forward, dipping her fingers into the water. Her body craved to sink into the bath.

'You asked me who I really am,' Néefar started softly as he sat beside her.

Glancing at Néefar, Anabelle said, 'Your past is yours alone. You don't need to share it with me if you don't wish to.'

His brow furrowed, he stared at the water, his fingers absently tracing the rough grooves in the stone ledge. 'I want you to trust me. The first step to that is allowing you to know my past.'

'Very well,' Anabelle said quietly, turning her attention back to the water. 'I'm listening.'

'I was human,' he said, pausing, the word *human* almost foreign on his tongue. 'My mother and father were Travellers or Romani. Humans blessed with the ability of sight, though still common folk in the guise of cobblers and blacksmiths. They did what many could not and found land to build a home for me. Whilst they did settle, they never forgot the old ways. As a child, I was told stories of magical things that to any other person would seem dark or unbelievable.'

His brow furrowed as if in thought.

'In my tenth year, villagers came to my family's cottage demanding we leave. They ruined our gardens and burned our fields. My parents told me to run and hide until they came to get me. I remember the ground was soft beneath my feet; it had just rained. The forest was so quiet that I felt fear for the first time in my life.'

Anabelle put a soft hand over his. 'You don't have to tell me.'

He gently tugged on a curl of her hair. 'I want to tell you.'

Anabelle let out a soft sigh, nodding.

'They called us "gipsy," "forest rats," "thieves." We were none of these things. I wanted the words to stop, but they were all I could hear in my head. I needed an escape, and then the air grew thick. I couldn't breathe. It was like suffocating in the very thing that gives you life. I lost consciousness, and when I awoke, I was in the forest, but it was so much more. The forest was alive in ways I had never known before.'

He drew a rough hand through his hair, swallowing the lump in his throat. 'I tried to go back...but my parents were murdered that night. I watched from the tree line as villagers came to my family's home and slaughtered them for witchcraft, then hung their mangled bodies from the rafters as everything burned around them.'

His voice hitched with unshed tears, and he took a moment to compose himself, staring blankly at the water. 'My parents showed nothing but love and peace to the villagers and anyone they met. For that, they died. Autumn found me there, curled in the dirt, wishing I was with my parents. He picked me up and told me he would watch over me. For a boy of ten, I felt the age of a thousand men.'

Anabelle stared at Néefar's profile as he watched the water. She didn't know if she should hug him or sit there silently, so she settled for taking his hand. He turned to look at her.

'I'm so sorry,' she whispered into the quiet.

'I have come to live with the memory, Anabelle,' he murmured.

'No one should live with a memory like that,' she said.

He said nothing, turning back to the glowing blue water. 'You have lost much, Anabelle, but you are not the only one. You have not lost your mother; she will come back to you.'

'You cannot be certain of that. Life is fickle...as you know.'

Néefar stood, pulling her to her feet with him. 'Nothing is ever certain.'

'Yes, but if you lose those you love, who's to say you'll ever see them again?'

'I have to believe we will.'

Anabelle searched Néefar's eyes and found her own honesty staring back at her.

'Very well,' she said with a slight nod.

He absently brushed a curl over her shoulder, his fingers grazing her neck, and she shuddered involuntarily.

He cocked a brow, tilting his head with a darkened expression, and her breathing turned shallow as those blue eyes encompassed hers. Her stomach tightened involuntarily, filled with something warm and achy she didn't recognise.

She swallowed, licking her lips, flushing when she saw his eyes watch the movement.

'Do I know you?' she asked, her voice breathless.

His eyes were familiar, a tug on the back of her mind that she tried to tug back, but it slipped from her fingers.

His low laugh broke the tension in her. 'You should bathe. It'll help.'

Anabelle watched him turn to leave but said, 'May I ask you something?'

'Of course.'

'How long ago did it happen?'

'Almost eighty-nine years now."

'You're almost a hundred years old?'

'Aye, I am,' he said.

'Then you knew Gallian?'

'I do.'

'So why haven't we met until now?'

Néefar laughed lowly. 'Bathe, Anabelle, you're starting to waft,' he said, brushing the dirt from his pants.

Anabelle gave him a frozen glare, sticking her tongue out at his back as he left her to the solidarity of the cave.

CHAPTER TWENTY-THREE

Anabelle stared at the water, her thoughts reeling as she stripped off her dress. The layers of her gown clung to her skin, grime and sweat knitted into the fabric, and she shivered in disgust.

Naked, she slipped beneath the water, her feet searching for the bottom, and let go of the ledge when she found it.

The scent of lilacs surrounded her, and she took a deep breath, trying to ease the ache in her muscles. The water rippled around her as she rolled her head back, stretching her arms above her and sighing as her muscles eased. Memories and thoughts travelled through her head, and she pinched her eyes closed, humming quietly under her breath:

'*If I shall die, under the sky, fire within me*

, my love, do not forget me. Like wildflowers,
we bloom, and we wilt we go back to the earth.
With fire in the sky, if I die tonight. If I die
...If I die.'

'You have a beautiful voice.'

Anabelle whirled. Winter stood there, unfamiliar clothes folded neatly in her hands.

The spirit gave her a slight smile. 'I didn't mean to startle you. Néefar let me know you were here. I brought you fresh garments and oils for your hair and skin.' She set the items down by the ledge. 'Take your time.'

'My mother—'

'—is still here. She and her sister are speaking for now. Relax, Anabelle, you will not have the chance in the future.'

Anabelle watched Winter leave before swimming to the ledge to pick up one of the two oils. One was minty, and she poured a small pool into her palm. She rubbed her hands together before she drew her oil-covered fingers through her black hair, massaging her scalp and leaning her head back into the water.

The other vial contained rose oil, and Anabelle smiled. It smelled like the perfume her mother used to wear when she was younger.

She smiled as she rubbed the rose oil over her skin. It brought back memories of clinging to her mother's skirts. As a child, she spilt the oil all over herself and smelled like roses for days. It was the last time her mother had worn it.

'Anabelle, my little one, I'm afraid you have used too much rose oil. I have grown tired of the smell. One would even think I have grown sick of it!'

Leaning back, she floated in the water until her skin wrinkled and her body was thoroughly relaxed.

She glided to the ledge, crossing her arms on the stone with a sigh. Something hard cut into her skin, and she looked down. The Tear of Gabriel glimmered between her breasts.

Anabelle brushed her fingers across the gem. She slipped it over her head and held it before her, eyeing it. She had forgotten about it. Now, dangling in front of her, she saw the clear teardrop glint against the blue glow above. The silver weaved around it like a cage. Something so fragile needed so much confinement.

'You sacrificed yourself so the entire world may have a chance to live,' she murmured aloud. 'How will I live up to that? I want nothing more than for them to live in peace. Yet, Balwin wants blood. Will my blood fall for all of this to end?'

The teardrop sparkled back at her.

'I have to protect them, but how can I protect them if I will be the cause of their death? How did you choose what was right?'

When she found no answer, she sighed and pulled herself up, draping the necklace around her neck.

Stretching, Anabelle bent over the clothes Winter had left for her. Her lips quirked as she held out the trousers in front of her. She had never worn men's clothing before and quite liked the idea.

The water on her skin had dried almost immediately in the warm air. She wrung out her hair before slipping into the brown leather trousers. She knotted the ties and tucked them in, admiring the snug fit around her thighs. They fit comfortably on the curvature of her hips, and she hurriedly donned the dark blue wool blouse, tucking it into the waistband as she slipped the brown leather boots on, pulling them over her calves.

She felt oddly free in her new garments, wiggling her legs one at a time and watching them with amusement. She quite liked men's clothing.

With a smile, she left the oils for the next visitor and left the bathing chamber.

Anabelle followed the path carefully, staying straight and refusing to wander down different tunnels despite her keen interest to do so. When she found the council room empty, she made her way up to the keep.

Dusk had already fallen. The moon peeked above the horizon, and stars barely shone in the fresh breath of winter's early nights. Savven sat by one of the fire pits, staring intently into the flames with a frown.

'You know,' she said, walking over to him, 'the fire isn't going to suddenly jump up and start dancing—no matter how hard you stare at it.'

Savven glanced up at her.

She just shrugged. 'I thought it was worth trying to see if I could make you smile.'

He turned back to the fire. 'Watching it helps me think.'

'How very cryptic of you, ' Anabelle said, looking at the sky. 'Come with me.'

Savven hesitated but stood all the same.

Anabelle led him to the edge of the veil, which shimmered in the firelight but remained invisible to the outside world. She grabbed the lowest branch on a nearby tree, jumped easily to it, and quickly flipped herself onto the first ledge. She looked down at Savven, who stood below her.

'Are you afraid?' she challenged when he didn't move.

'No,' he replied.

He looked back at the Keep before quickly bringing himself to her level. Swiftly and quietly, they climbed up the massive tree, weaving in and out of tangles of branches and leaves. They reached the top of the blackwood tree and settled themselves in the grooves of the thick branches, their feet dangling in the air.

'Climbing trees helps you think?'

Anabelle smiled faintly. 'No, but it's fun. What helps me think and clear my head is this.' She lifted her face to the sky and the million stars. It was like gazing upon an ocean of stardust; they were floating, weightless, in the middle.

Savven stared at the sky, his face relaxing as he breathed deeply.

'What's troubling you, Savven?'

'What we saw this morning.' He pursed his lips. 'The only way Balwin could have gathered such forces is by something that controlled them all.'

'He couldn't have gathered that control over time?'

He shook his head, his face pale in the moonlight as he leaned against the branch. 'I saw Satyrs among them. They are lazy and carefree and only care about their most primal needs. They are not a race to freely hand over the very thing that makes their lives so peaceful. They are not creatures of chaos.'

'Then what do you think made them change?'

'The only way to control an unwilling soul is to go to the very thing it is connected to and take control. Then, they have no choice but to follow blindly, without knowledge of their actions.'

Anabelle furrowed her brows. 'Is there such a thing?'

Savven looked down at the ground far below. 'The Tree of Souls. The tree that was carved into the table.'

'Four trees, intertwined, to make one.'

'Each tree represents the four Spirits of Seasons. The Fae of our world reside in separate seasons that house them, the four Gods that created our world, and the Spirits that guide us.'

'Do you think Balwin has taken over the tree?'

'You cannot take over something that is not yours to take, but he can corrupt it. He can use it for what he wishes if he has enough power to do so.'

Anabelle felt an uneasy knot in her stomach. 'He can't just get away with hurting and abusing so many innocents.'

Savven looked at Anabelle, observing her silently. She stared up at the sky, her brows creased in frustration.

'You are much like my people, Anabelle—*our* people. You have Elvin's blood that courses through you. We are blood.'

'I do not feel very much like an elf. How is one supposed to feel? You're noble and graceful….' She looked down at her hands. 'I am only Anabelle.'

'*Only Anabelle*, you're far greater than you know, and one day, you will live to see it.'

'Perhaps one day. I don't know if I wish to see it.' She sighed. 'How will I choose right and wrong if I am to lead them into battle, and many will die? They depend on me as the Keeper. How will I choose what is right for them?'

'That can only be answered by you alone.' Savven tilted his head as the crunch of leaves below them met their ears. 'Come, he has something for you. Don't be afraid to jump,' he said before he swung down from the branch.

Anabelle watched as he landed neatly on his feet far below, and fear gripped her heart. She took a deep breath, steadying her nerves. She wasn't mortal anymore. She couldn't cling to human fears. Closing her eyes, Anabelle took a deep breath and leapt.

Tree branches snapped past her, and her body felt weightless as she fell through the night, the ground rushing to meet her.

It was over before she knew what had happened, and an exhilarating rush went through her as she righted herself.

'Not bad.'

Anabelle looked at Néefar, whose appreciative smile made her stomach flip. She turned to Savven and said, 'Thank you.'

He bowed, inclining his head. 'I bid you both a goodnight.'

They watched him walk away before turning back to each other.

'You have something for me?'

Néefar's smile lit up the night.

Néefar led Anabelle through one of the many underground tunnels. Several doorways cut into the walls, and Néefar opened the second one on the right.

'This is your room.'

Anabelle raised a brow at him. 'Is it?'

'I picked it out special for you.'

She gave him a flat stare.

Néefar chuckled, pushing her forward gently. 'Your mother showed me.'

'That's not any better,' she mumbled.

'Well, I saw her in passing, so I was given the task.'

It was a small room with a single bed pushed into the corner, a simple wooden desk, and a chair. Two torches hung on opposite walls in iron sconces, filling the room with a yellow glow.

'She finished speaking with the queen?' Anabelle asked.

'When I last saw her, they were together, but she did pass along something for me to give you. A little furball I find quite amusing that you're keeping as a pet.'

He went to her bed and picked up a small furry body from the feather pillow.

'I think she belongs to you,' he said.

'Pepper!' She carefully took Pepper from Néefar. Holding her close to her chest, she stroked her soft fur and buried her face into her little body.

'I take it you two know each other?' he asked, amusement clear. 'I would have eaten her already.'

'Pepper is my rabbit!' she gasped. 'I left her with my mother when I went with Gallian to the Vaitarani.' She nuzzled the fur between Pepper's ears. 'You've grown, Pepper. You can't do any more of that if I'm gone.'

'Anabelle, I also have something for you.'

Anabelle looked up as Néefar offered a slim object wrapped in fabric. He draped back the material and revealed a handheld oval mirror.

'I found this in my room. I wanted you to have it.'

Anabelle gently put Pepper on her bed and picked up the mirror. It was embedded in silver, with flowers etched on the back.

'Because I need to know what I look like?' she quipped, turning it over in her hands.

'So you can see what everyone else sees.'

Anabelle felt herself flush. She slowly raised the mirror to her face. Her reflection stared back at her, and she nearly dropped the mirror.

'Do you know yourself, Anabelle?'

She glared at him. 'What is this?'

'You chose to become immortal, and in that, you chose to cast away the mortal part of you. *All* mortal parts of you.'

Her blood rushed through her ears. 'How do you know all of this?'

'Tatius, the child, told me to find you. She said to watch over you, to stay by your side.'

Trust him.

Gallian's words from the forest rang back in her ears. 'Thank you for returning Pepper to me.' She paused, peering down at the mirror. 'And the mirror, but I need to rest now.'

Néefar gave her a soft smile and strolled out of the room.

Anabelle sat on her bed, Pepper hopping over to her side and curling against her thigh.

She lifted the mirror again. She looked like herself, and her mother joined into one. Her face was ovular yet had become more defined. Her cheekbones were high and prominent, her brows curved gracefully, and her eyes were a bright, deep blue, nearly violet. Her fair skin was like porcelain, and the black of her hair was so dark it was almost blue, the tips of her pointed ears peeking through. She looked like a Fae princess from one of her books. All mortal traces of her had vanished.

Swallowing, she stood, placed the mirror on the desk, and ran a shaking hand through her hair. Closing her eyes, she breathed through her nose before picking Pepper up and holding her close as she lay back on her bed.

'So much has changed, Pepper. I don't know if you can see it, but I have seen enough for the both of us.'

Pepper wiggled out of her arms and hopped onto her pillow, asleep within moments. Anabelle smiled and stroked her fur before closing her own eyes. 'Goodnight, Pepper.'

CHAPTER TWENTY-FOUR

Hints of dawn peeked over the mountain ridge. The whiz of an arrow sliced through the forest trees before it embedded itself into a tree trunk.

Néefar watched the arrow lodge into the wood, shook his head, and plucked another arrow off the boulder beside him.

He licked the tips of his thumb and forefinger, running them over the edges of the stark white feathers at the end of the shaft. Notching the arrow, he pulled back the taut bowstring, inhaling through his nose. He could feel the feathers tickling against the stubble on his cheek, and the forest around him disappeared entirely. He let go with a breath.

The arrow flew straight and narrow, cutting through the air with deadly accuracy before splitting the first arrow right down the centre.

With the bow still in his hand, he strode through the trees to retrieve both arrows. He cast the first to the ground as movement caught his eye. Looking up, he saw a grey squirrel stop on a branch overhead, its bushy tail sweeping the ground, nose twitching as it sniffed the air, unknowing of a threat.

He felt his stomach twist in hunger, mouth watering at the idea of food. The winter had been sparse, animals few and far between. Notching the arrow, he pulled it back—

'Will you really take its life, Néefar? When it's not its time to die?'

The male spun around. It was only a little girl. His brows pulled tight, but he kept his aim steady. He rarely trusted anything in the forest, even those that looked like children.

'Who are you?' he demanded.

The girl stepped forward. 'You may call me Tatius.'

'Yes, but who are you?'

Tatius only tilted her head. 'Who I am does not matter, but I must speak with you, Néefar, regardless.'

'And why should I speak with you, girl? I do not know you. What is worse: you made me lose my breakfast.'

He lowered the bow, sensing no threat.

Tatius's eyes flashed, and the once-forgotten, broken arrow on the earthen floor was now pointed at Néefar, the arrowhead directly between his brows.

'You will show respect where respect is due, Romani! I am the Keeper of Immortality, the decider of life and death. Do not tempt me to change my mind on the value of your life.'

With a heavy breath, he grasped the broken arrow before his face. 'What do you want?' he asked, turning on his heels and stalking across the frozen ground.

Tatius watched as Néefar placed his unbroken arrow on a rock and leaned his bow beside it. He then picked up his quiver and ignored his visitor.

'Do you know the woman Anabelle?'

He stopped, his fingers frozen over the tip of an arrowhead. He set aside the quiver and turned to face Tatius, carefully saying, 'In passing.'

Tatius's black eyes sharpened, flashing in the light. 'Do not play me for a fool, Néefar. Do you know her?'

His jaw worked, clenching tightly. 'Yes,' he ground out. He did not like *being questioned by anyone, even this tiny God. 'In passing,' he clarified again. 'My brother was...Gallian was fixated on the woman.'*

Tatius waved a dismissive hand. 'Gallian, unfortunately, is a starving fool.'

'Starving, eh?' he asked with a wry smile.

She cocked a brow at him. 'Yes. Starving. He begs for the attention of his father like a starved animal and, in the process, loses his soul. Starving fool.'

Néefar shook his head. 'Call it whatever you like. But she has only met me in passing, and through almost all of it, I was concealed by a mask.'

He remembered the distraught sound she had made when she had run into his chest and how she had quickly retorted against his comments. Néefar's lips quirked, and he rubbed a hand over his mouth to hide his reaction. She had been feisty, and despite the sour turn of events, he quite enjoyed himself that night.

'Gallian's motives are less than favourable, Shifter. You must know this.'

Her adolescent face exuded an exasperated tone that made him swallow his laughter. 'And do you think I'm a fool, too?' he asked.

Her face turned stormy.

'Aye, I do know this,' he resigned with a sigh.

Tatius folded her hands in front of her simple black dress, her calm eyes assessing. 'Anabelle makes headway for the Summer Keep. From there, she will have only days—weeks if she is lucky—before Balwin seeks her out.'

The beasts in him rumbled at the mention of Gallian's father, and he stroked a mental hand down the tether of his magic, soothing them.

'Weeks or days, huh?' he mused. 'Seems like an unfortunate circumstance.'

Tatius's expression gave way to irritation. 'Balwin had control over Gallian in a way we have never seen before, and in turn also controls the Tree of Souls, the Guardians having been turned to ash.'

'Sounds like a problem for the Gods.' He paused and breathed before turning to look at her again. 'Why don't the Gods step in and be done with it all?'

'We and the spirits cannot directly interfere in worldly matters. We gave free will when creating our world; because of it, we cannot interfere. We can only suggest...lightly.' The last part came out bitterly. 'If I could,

Shifter, Balwin would be turned to ash. But alas, I can only twiddle my thumbs like an obedient God to my own silly rules.'

Néefar glanced between the girl and the forest. 'Days or weeks, huh?' he mulled.

'With Balwin's control of the Tree of Souls, dark armies arise and he has an arsenal of them at his disposal.'

'Where is she?'

'You'll go to her, then?'

He gave her a pointed look.

Understanding coloured Tatius's face. Her voice became a resounding echo that surrounded them, the forest vanishing as her visions flared to life.

Dark trees and rolling clouds of black mist wavered in the vision. Néefar clenched his jaw when Gallian's cold face came into view. 'Gallian resides deep within the Black Forest,' Tatius said, 'bordering the Forest of Lost Souls.'

'What of Anabelle?'

The world around them flashed with another image of a woman. However, the silver eyes he remembered were near violet now and wide with caution, a bowl of soup tucked between her fingers. 'She travels with the elves within the Black Forest, heading into the southern territories of the forest towards the Summer Fae.' The vision faltered and vanished, Tatius's eyes meeting Néefar's. 'You have a part to play in this, Shifter. What that is is for you to find out.'

Tatius paused momentarily, pursing her lips as she observed the shifter. 'Do not be mistaken, Néefar. Gallian is not lost entirely—yet. He has always been confused about where he belongs, even as a child. All of this will either save him or destroy him. That is entirely up to Gallian.'

Néefar sighed. 'Why does she need me, of all people?'

Tatius folded her hands. 'As a God, I do not see just the balance of life and the weight of death. I see the worlds beyond, history to come, and those who make it happen.'

Néefar felt his heart skip. 'And you see me in this future...world?'

'Your obstinacy is almost refreshing,' she noted dryly. 'Anabelle is strong, far stronger than she knows, but this is only the beginning, and many will play their parts, some now, some later.'

He let out a harsh breath through his nose, running a hand through his dark hair. 'How cryptic,' he muttered.

Tatius turned away to leave.

'You're leaving?'

'Yes, it looks that way.' She glanced over her shoulder, gazing at the rock where his bow and quiver lay. 'They were going to starve anyway, might as well make their deaths less painful.'

Néefar looked at the rock and saw two adult grey squirrels lying side-by-side in the little snow covering the ground. He turned back to Tatius, intending to thank her, but she was gone.

Néefar glanced at the dagger, balancing it on his fingertip before flipping it and throwing it. The tip sank into the dirt.

'Many things weigh on your mind, young Shifter?'

Néefar glanced up and saw the queen step from the shadows. He stood and bowed his head in respect. 'I am not so young, Your Majesty.'

Her lips quirked subtly in amusement. 'Much younger than I, Shifter.'

'It is only memories that keep me up this eve,' he explained, taking his place beside the fire as the queen sat with him.

'You are fond of my niece?'

Néefar considered this, carefully weighing his words. 'Aye, though I am more curious who she has become.'

The queen turned to watch the fire, her frame rigid, hands folded in her lap. 'Many things have changed since Isadora and I were children. I'm torn between law and duty. My duty as queen...' She shook her head. 'The love I have as a sister tells me I do not wish to sentence my blood, but it is the law.'

'Who is to say what the law is if not you? If you, The High Queen, do not believe something to be right, then change it.'

The queen looked away from the flames, her eyes piercing

Néefar's. 'I believe you speak out of turn, Shifter.'

Néefar bowed his head. 'My apologies, Your Majesty. I simply thought you sought an answer.'

She was quiet for a moment before softly saying, 'I bid you good eve and leave you to your thoughts.'

Rising from her seat beside the fire, the queen quietly disappeared into the shadows as quickly as she had come.

CHAPTER TWENTY-FIVE

Anabelle stared at the stone ceiling, tracing its grooves and lines. Her mind played back to just weeks before, stroking between Pepper's ears.

Her breath clouded in front of her as she danced in the winter night, Gallian's hand in her own, his other around her waist, pulling her closer as they floated in time with the melodic waltz. The deep, soothing hum of bow and string surrounded them.

'Anabelle...'

Gallian's voice echoed in her ears, and she closed her eyes against the guilt that followed.

'Anabelle!' a young Gallian cried as he rushed to her, his hands cupped close to his chest.

'Gallian!' Anabelle cried back, mirroring his tone as he neared her.

Coming to a stop, they bowed their heads together, touching foreheads as they formed their own little circle around his cupped hands.

'Look at what I have caught, Ana,' he whispered, slowly opening his hand.

There, sitting patiently, was a little tree frog with round black eyes that blinked up at them.

'Aw,' cooed Anabelle, stroking its back.

'Do you like it?'

'Yes, he's so little! We should name him!'

She frowned as a new memory began to mix in her mind, tugging on her subconscious.

A crooked smile tilted a firm mouth, facial hair shadowing a strong jawline, and the man cocked a brow, leaning forward to whisper, 'We wouldn't want to give a gentleman the wrong impression, now, would we?'

Pursing her lips, she narrowed her eyes at him. 'And what impression would that be?'

'That perhaps you're actually enjoying yourself?'

Anabelle suddenly sat up, the memory fading except for those blue eyes that floated within her mind's eye. Pepper's nose twitched when Anabelle picked her up.

Brilliant blue eyes stared down at her, and a whisper of a smile tilted his firm mouth. 'Do you like to read?'

With a huff, Anabelle strode out of her room. Weaving through the tunnels, she sought her way to the surface. She was surprised to see the Keep so busy. Summer Fae whizzed from one end of the Keep to the other, the air thrumming with energy.

Anabelle's lips quirked when she saw the males she had arrived with huddled over a stone table with a map in front of them. Néefar conversed casually with a dwarven blacksmith by a cloister of tents. Winter alone stood beside the queen, who observed the Keep with an imperious eye.

Over a hundred had arrived under cover of night. Dwarves filled the area, bustling with materials grasped tightly in their arms. Forges burned hot throughout the Keep as those with metal and wood deposited their items to weapons masters. Other dwarves bustled around separate fires, iron cauldrons bubbling over hot flames.

Anabelle stepped forward only to jump back, saving herself from being run over by a sizeable wooden cart as it rushed by. It was pushed by a dwarven woman half her height, stacked to the brim.

Treading carefully to avoid getting in anyone's way, she weaved around bodies, finding her way to Winter's side.

'Good morning,' she said softly, eyeing the males hovering over the map.

Winter gave her a kind smile in turn. 'Good morning, Anabelle.'

The queen simply bowed her head in acknowledgement. 'I require a moment of your time, Anabelle.'

Winter gave Anabelle a subtle look of encouragement before walking over to Savven's side.

The queen didn't wait for Anabelle as she began walking for the cover of trees along the forest edge. Her velvet emerald cloak whispered across the ground.

With pursed lips, Anabelle had half a mind to turn around and march back to bed, though she begrudgingly followed her aunt to the tree line. The back of her neck tickled, and she glanced over her shoulder, finding Néefar watching her. His eyes met hers, and she quickly turned away.

The bustling noise slowly dimmed, and they were alone, out of sight behind the cover of brambles and tree limbs. Thick pines towered over them, their branches tangling together as they reached for the sky.

Anabelle waited patiently for her aunt to speak, watching her profile as she watched the Keep. She could see the resemblance of her mother in the queen's features.

'Your mother and I depart for Álfheimr come this eve. Will you join us?' The queen turned to look at Anabelle, waiting for a reply.

She nearly choked on air, clearing her throat in surprise. 'You want me to come with you, Your Majesty?'

'You are blood, Anabelle, regardless of past events. That makes you High Fae royalty. Will you come with us?'

'Regardless of past events, you want me to come with you...You want me to flee? Though you will not spare my mother the same courtesy?' A bitter laugh bubbled up. 'Tell me, aunt, do you always hide when the world goes to hell or is this new for you?'

The queen waited calmly for her to finish, though her tone was icy. 'You do not know your place, Keeper. Certain laws must be obeyed, even by me. We can protect you in Álfheimr and keep you safe. You are too valuable to lose.'

'To cower behind your walls, to leave those who would give their lives to protect mine? To run. How dare you suggest I stoop to your level of impertinence?' Anabelle turned to leave but whirled around instead to stare at the female who shared her blood. 'I cannot run from this and let your people protect me.'

'They are also your kin. Do not forget that.'

Stubbornness reared inside her, followed by a wave of ice that tickled her fingertips, whispering for her to let it out. She bit down on her magic.

'I appreciate your offer, Your Majesty...' She paused, searching for the right words. 'But I must embrace my fears. And one day, I will have the courage to face them. While you may run and hide behind your towers and kin, I cannot follow your lead. I am no longer a child in need of protection. I will be the one to protect those around me.'

She looked at the queen, her guarded eyes giving nothing away. 'My life is no more valuable than those around us. With all due respect, Your Majesty, neither is yours. We simply have a part to play. I have embraced my fears; now, I have the strength to do something about them. If I die, so be it, but it will not be in vain.'

The queen stood eerily still. 'You are much like your mother.'

'Thankfully,' she retorted.

Taking one last look at her, the queen bowed her head softly and left the cover of the trees.

Anabelle stood there for a minute, her heart thundering in her chest as the tension in her body slowly eased.

'May I ask why you look like a stubborn child?' Néefar said. 'With your chin raised in such a manner, you look like a little... nymph? Is that the right creature?'

Amusement was etched on his handsome face, familiar blue eyes lit in a mischievous glimmer.

'You're teasing me, Néefar.'

'Indeed, I am. So, tell me, what has happened?'

She took a deep breath and let it out in a whoosh, relaxing her shoulders. 'I believe I just insulted my dear aunt.'

Néefar paused momentarily before he barked a laugh, startling her.

'Oh, no doubt. You have a Romani's rebellious spirit, Anabelle.'

'You have plenty of that for the both of us, I'm sure, Néefar,' she said with a raised brow, giving him a wry smile.

He gave her a cheeky grin.

All was quiet between them before Anabelle rounded on him. 'Why didn't you tell me it was you!'

Néefar turned to her with a straight face, folding his arms. 'It's about time.'

She huffed, retorting, 'Oh, I'm sorry. I'll make sure to be much quicker about it.'

'See that you do,' he replied casually.

'You're insufferable!'

'But you like it.'

'You think too highly of yourself,' she said with an affirmative nod, staring up at him.

Néefar leaned forward, twirling a piece of her hair around his finger, his voice dropping an octave. 'Well, we wouldn't want to give a gentleman the wrong impression, now, would we?'

Swallowing, Anabelle's heart thundered in her chest as his breath fanned across her cheek.

After a moment, he straightened and guided her from the treeline. 'Come, I have something to show you.'

Néefar offered an arrow to Anabelle. The weapon was neither heavy nor light, perfectly balanced as it rested in her open palm.

'What exactly do you want me to do with this?' she asked,

perplexed.

Néefar plucked the arrow from her hand and held out a thin sword. Its hilt, made of gold and iron, was wrapped in black leather.

She took it from him, holding it up.

'I want you to choose.'

'Choose what?'

'A weapon. I had these made for you with the help of Da'arc, son of Ewrin, of the clan Stonehammer,' he said, introducing the blacksmith.

She looked at the dwarf. His beard was long and fiery, with a thick braid going down the centre, clasped with a small iron band. His hair was tied back down the length of his back. A large nose and bushy eyebrows framed deep-set green eyes.

Smiling warmly at Da'arc, Anabelle eyed the sword again. 'Thank you for this.'

Though long, it was light in her hands. As she swung it lightly, she felt uncertain of her movements.

Da'arc struck his fist to his iron breastplate. 'For you, Keeper, I serve allegiance.'

'There's a problem, though,' she said in a wry tone, eyeing Néefar. 'I do not know how to wield a weapon.'

Néefar took the blade from her. 'We can fix that, but first, pick one.'

Anabelle thought for a moment. Then, a vision of herself impaling a body with the sword made her cringe, and she shook her head.

'The bow, I prefer the bow.'

Nodding, Néefar set the sword aside. 'I thought you might.'

He reached for the bow on the blacksmith's stone table and presented it to her. It was made of ash wood, and in the centre was polished iron wrapped around the timber where her hand would lay. Thin leather straps were tied around the metal for her grip. Da'arc had carved the curves of the bow with the knotting of the Fae. It had patterns of delicate webbing, weaving in and out of each other. Da'arc had set iron into the carvings, reinforcing the wood. Anabelle trailed her fingers the length of it.

'Thank you, Néefar, Da'arc.'

Néefar stood entertained, watching Anabelle admire their work, the tip of her tongue wetting her lips. He tracked the movement before pulling his eyes away. He crossed his arms, watching her with a soft smile.

'Come, Anabelle, let us see if you can handle such a weapon.' He chuckled when she heard the challenge.

Glaring up at him, she narrowed her eyes, furrowed her brow, and pressed her lips into a tight line.

'You know, a gift is ruined when you challenge the one you give it to,' she retorted.

'Is that so? I don't believe that to be true. Let's see if the Keeper can defend herself. Or maybe you should go with the queen?' He picked up the quiver, looking down at the arrows thoughtfully.

She yanked the quiver out of Néefar's hands and stalked away. Irritated at Néefar's challenge, she growled low under her breath, 'Go ahead, Shifter, laugh.'

'Tha' was cruel, Shifter,' said Da'arc in a gruff voice, although he seemed amused by the young female.

Néefar grinned wolfishly when he said, 'She seems like she would enjoy a challenge.'

CHAPTER TWENTY-SIX

The sound of steel sliding out of flesh filled the cold encampment. The body of a satyr crumpled to the ground, blood melting the hoarfrost.

Handing the blade to Gallian, Balwin turned away from the corpse. Winter had taken hold of the camp. No light from the morning sun penetrated the bare branches as if a cover of permanent shadows surrounded them. Death and rot hung in the air, the creeping mist reaching for the living as it devoured the dead.

Hundreds of demons, lost souls, and even light dwellers had flocked to him. They lay veiled in the shadows, powerless to his commands.

A cruel smile twisted his lips as he turned back to the satyr's body. His pale eyes assessed what was left of the Fae as the mist slowly crept over it. The mist's demons slowly peeled away his flesh, devouring the remains.

'Damnable creatures. I do not want peace!' Balwin screamed at the body, his teeth bared. '*I want chaos!*'

All movement in the camp stopped as he took his blade from Gallian and, with a snarl, ran it through the head of the fallen satyr.

The satyr had come to him begging for the release of his kinsmen, and for peace. Balwin could admire the satyr's courage but had run him through the moment he had fallen to his knees, pleading with him.

'Freedom is not something you are granted here. And all that do not remember may come forward and sacrifice their lives for it!'

A raven cawed, and Gallian stretched an arm to it as his father sliced the dead satyr limb from limb. The raven's red eyes stared at Gallian, clicking its beak. Gallian murmured to the raven, stroking a finger down its feathers.

The raven cawed, clicking its beak again before flying off. Gallian stepped up to his father's side. 'The elves were spotted outside the Summer Keep. There were four of them before they were lost in the forest.'

'What?' Balwin snapped. 'Why do the elves go to the Summer Fae?'

'I had a raven follow them to the Keep...'

Balwin stabbed his blade into the ground. '*And?*'

'Anabelle is alive,' Gallian said without emotion, without expression.

Rage contorted Balwin's face before he screeched a curse and threw his blade into the back of a hapless centaur. It was dead before it hit the ground. A cry of outrage boomed out from Balwin's tongue. His body shook from anger before he controlled the sparks of darkness that webbed at his fingertips.

After a moment, he looked at Gallian with strange delight. 'This is perfect, do you not see?'

'I thought you wished her dead.'

'Oh, I do, my son, I do. Fear not; her blood will be spilt soon enough. She took everything from me! I lost my soul in place of revenge. For that, I plan to rip away everything she loves.'

'And how do you plan to do that?'

'By breaking her.'

He let out a sadistic laugh as he crossed the camp to retrieve his sword. All eyes followed him as he swept the sword through the air before dropping it to his side.

'Let us pay a visit to the Summer Fae and their guests,' Balwin declared. 'The Keeper has come home! Let us make her feel welcome!'

A roar went up, thundering across the camp.

'Gallian,' he said, summoning a black dagger with red veins and an onyx handle out of the shadows. 'A blade forged from darkness…You will be the one to give dear Anabelle her gift. Do you understand?'

'Yes, Father.'

'Go then, sharpen your blade. We march within the hour.'

The arrowhead sunk into the ground just at the base of the tree. Anabelle's frustration grew as she stomped to the tree again to retrieve the arrow.

'Bloody thing,' she cursed under her breath as she marched back to her place, picked up her bow, and notched the shaft against the string.

She pulled back the bowstring and aimed at the target she had made on the tree trunk just beyond the Keep's veil—a ball of frozen snow stuck on the bark.

Taking a deep breath, she released the arrow and watched it wobble through the air before falling to the ground. She couldn't hold back a scream of frustration.

'You're not pulling it back far enough. It doesn't have enough power to fly steadily.'

Anabelle turned to glare at Néefar, leaning against a tree, his face lit with amusement. 'I wouldn't know that, though, now would I? I've never used a bow before.'

'I could help you,' he offered.

Anabelle turned her back to Néefar. 'No.'

'Don't be stubborn, little gipsy.'

She turned at that. 'I thought gipsy was a slur to your people?'

Néefar›s lips ticked as he looked at the forest beyond them. ‹It is. But words are powerful, and I think we have the ability to take something ugly and make it beautiful.'

'I'm not a gipsy,' she said.

His smile broadened as he strolled over to her, plucking the bow from the ground and the arrow from her fingers. His skin brushed hers, sending a chill up her arm.

'You are as much a gipsy as I am. It is not your blood but your spirit. There is no denying that. Come, watch me.'

Néefar stepped forward, notching the arrow, and quickly pulled it back. When he let go, the arrow sailed true and straight right into the centre of the frozen target.

Anabelle eyed the man beside her. Reluctantly, she asked, 'How did you do that?'

'Practice.'

Anabelle took the bow with a frown, jerking in surprise when Néefar pressed against her back. His chest was a solid, warm wall behind her, hips pressed against hers. Reaching over her shoulder, he took her hands, positioning her arms with the bow.

He bent his head, his breath hot behind her ear, his fingers engulfing her own.

In a low voice, Néefar said, 'Instead of pulling straight back, aim the bow up and pull back while slowly bringing it down.' He dragged his hand up her arm to her neck. Brushing the back of his hand across the expanse of her skin. 'While immortality gives you many things, strength is one you still need to build up.'

'The one thing I might have needed most,' she managed to say, her voice breathy.

'We can't have you being perfect. It wouldn't be fair to the others,' Néefar murmured, handing her an arrow.

Snorting, she notched the arrow, shoving her protest down when he stepped away from her, her body suddenly feeling exposed.

She huffed when he nodded, watching her intently.

Anabelle did as he told her and pulled the bow back as she angled it towards the tops of the trees and centred it, aiming down the line of the bow. She counted the seconds, and with a soft breath, she released it. They watched it sail through the air and hit the base of the trunk. It was feet from Néefar's arrow but better than any shot Anabelle had made.

She turned to Néefar, grinning. 'It worked!'

'Practice, little gipsy. I'll come to spy on you in a little while,' he said with a wink.

Despite the cold wind, Anabelle wiped the sweat from her brow as she shot arrow after arrow. Her arms shook from pulling the bowstring, but her progress was evident, making the discomfort worthwhile.

'Anabelle.'

When she heard her name, Anabelle glanced around the forest, a stark reminder of spring and winter divided against the veil. A woman with sage-green skin and eyes the pink of cherry blossoms stepped from the shadows with bare feet, passing through the veil as if it didn't exist. Dark purple flowers gathered in her hair, and leaves made up a dress covering her lean and willowy body. She was beautiful in a way, both disturbing and intriguing.

Watching her closely, Anabelle kept her bow trained on the woman. 'Who are you?' she demanded.

'I am Naleen, the Lady of the Earth.'

'I have never heard of you,' she said bluntly.

Naleen smiled softly. 'You would not, either. I was created as a protector of the forest, a spirit of the earth. I am older than the world, for I helped create it.'

Her words struck a chord in Anabelle's chest, and the magic in her veins thrummed in acknowledgement. A shiver crawled down her spine as she assessed the god before her.

'I have come to warn you.'

'Warn me about what?' Anabelle demanded.

'The darkness is coming for you. You must warn the others!'

Naleen glanced past Anabelle to the Keep, something like fear flickering in her pale pink eyes.

Anabelle stumbled back. 'What?' she breathed, eyes darting around her.

A deafening roar shook the ground, rocks trembling at their feet.

'I am afraid you have run out of time. They are here,' Naleen said solemnly.

Another roar pierced the air, and Anabelle's eyes went wide with fear.

'Go, Balwin is coming!'

Anabelle turned and fled, picking up her quiver as she sprinted through the grass. She slung the quiver across her shoulders, bow grasped tightly in her hand. And then her path was cut off as a dwarf landed on the ground and rolled head over heels, dead before it stilled.

Anabelle skidded to a halt, horrified at the unseeing brown eyes that gazed at her. The dwarf's long black beard tangled around him, his stocky, short limbs disfigured from broken bones.

Chaos engulfed the Keep, blood raining down. Anabelle choked on the scream lodged in her throat, her eyes wide as her gaze landed on Balwin's pale figure. His scarred smile gleamed as he cut down a dwarf that charged at him with a bellowing cry. The dark army she had seen when travelling to the Summer Keep was here, baring down upon them like fleas to a mongrel mutt.

Anabelle's heart leapt into her throat as a satyr rushed at her. Its eyes were grey and lifeless, and its face sucked of any life. She quickly pulled an arrow from her quiver, her fingers clumsy as she attempted to notch it. She wasn't quick enough, and the satyr rammed into her, its horns crunching into her hips. Her ears rang when she hit the ground, and her vision sparkled. Pain lanced through her when she rolled to her feet, and she bit down on it.

A knife glinted in the light, and Anabelle caught the satyr's wrist just in time. They tumbled in the dirt, wrestling, their limbs tangling as her arms strained against the satyr's strength. His soulless eyes stared down at her, unblinking.

The glint of polished stone caught her eye, and she threw her head to the side, the knife slipping closer to the exposed skin of her neck. The discarded arrow lay just out of reach. With a wild scream, Anabelle bucked her hips and threw the creature off her. She rolled, plucked the arrow from the dirt as the satyr lunged, and slammed it into the flesh between its ribs. The satyr fell heavily on top of her, his bare chest and fur-covered legs coated in mud and stained crimson. With a wince and a grunt, she pushed his body off.

She looked down at the blood on her hands and felt her heart clench, face paling. The rush of metal and the slice of skin and bones surrounded her like a tidal wave. Tight-lipped, she sealed away her emotions and shook off the tremors. Snatching up her bow, she ran into the chaos.

Dwarves fought other dwarves, and goblins, with their mottled green and brown skin, pursued centaurs whose hides still gleamed brightly in the face of death. Centaurs ran down minotaurs, and satyrs fought satyrs. Blood fought blood, a tangled webbing of death and chaos.

Anabelle struggled to pull back the taut string of her bow, ducking as an axe flew in her direction. The ground became muddy with blood as she pushed to her feet. Running from the battle, she sprinted to the blacksmith's shop, throwing back the animal skin flap. Da'arc was nowhere to be seen, but the blade he had made for her still lay soundly on the blacksmith's anvil. She set her bow and quiver in place of it and picked up the other weapon. It was light, and Anabelle swung it through the air with ease.

'Anabelle!'

She spun, hearing her mother's call over the clang of battle, and she sprinted back into the chaos.

'Mother!'

Isadora fought through the masses. Dirt and blood streaked her face like war paint.

Heart leaping into her throat, Anabelle ran to her mother. 'Are you hurt?'

Isadora shook her head. 'No, a goblin fell into me as he was cut down. They came out of the mist, Anabelle! We must leave. You're not safe!'

'No! I won't leave. I won't run and hide. I have done that long enough—'

She ducked around her mother's arm, swinging her sword clumsily into the chest of a centaur, grimacing with remorse when the male fell.

'—I have hidden for fifteen years. I can no longer stay away. I am the Keeper; there is no changing my fate.'

Isadora nodded sharply. 'Then I will follow you into battle.'

Balwin's armies flooded the Summer Keep like a wall of shadows, overtaking them wave after wave. Anabelle felt a quiet calm overtake her, her magic singing in her veins as she charged a minotaur. Spinning to the left, hair whipping at her face, she cut blindly at the creature, feeling the blade connect with flesh.

Anabelle was grabbed from behind and dragged back even as she kicked and twisted her body, the sharp, stabbing pain encompassing her skull. She brought her sword up and around her head. Swinging at the hand holding her, Anabelle felt her blade go through the hair it had and drop to the ground. She sliced a jagged cut through a minotaur's neck in two quick, awkward movements, and with a cry that was mixed with terror and rage, she stabbed it through the heart.

The world tilted, and she was thrown through the air and slammed against a tree, pinned by magic. She searched for the source, and the shadows around her parted. The sounds died on the wind as Balwin emerged from the bodies, his long, lean limbs encased in black leather and a long-fitted black tunic that merged him into the shadows and mist that shrouded him.

Pure, blinding hatred seeped into his black eyes as he stepped up to her, still pinned to the tree. He tilted his head, the movement almost unnatural as a slight smile tilted his lips.

'You thought you could escape my notice, Anabelle,' he said. 'Your life, the air you breathe, is like a black mark on my soul. It torments me.'

'Balwin!' she spat, tasting copper on her tongue. 'For you to feel something, it truly is a miracle! What do you want?'

'It's not what I want, Anabelle, dear.' He nuzzled his cheek against hers, his skin like ice. He pointed to her mother. 'It's about what he wants.'

Horror curled its talons into Anabelle, watching Gallian approach her mother. Anabelle tried to call out, to warn her, but her scream choked in her throat as Balwin's fingers wrapped around her neck, squeezing.

'We don't want you to distract them, now do we, m'dear?' Balwin said mildly.

Blood rushed to her head, pounding in her ears and beneath her skin.

'Don't look away. We wouldn't want you to miss this,' Balwin tittered. 'Did my son ever tell you about your dreams?'

Closing her eyes, she concentrated on her power and felt it fight against the magic restraining her—

'I said look!' Balwin snapped, his hands tightening on her throat.

Her eyes flew open in time to watch her mother fend off Gallian's advances. She was stronger than Anabelle had ever seen. Grace and strength surrounded her every move, but dark blue magic pierced Isadora, throwing her back into a tree. He pinned her with one hand and raised his black blade with his other.

'He made those illusions. He groomed you into the perfect blithering chit.'

Amber light flared, and Anabelle watched, transfixed, as her mother dropped out of Gallian's hold, parrying his blow as it swung down on her, stopping suddenly.

'How do you think I found you in the forest with him? It has always been Gallian. It was all because of him.'

Gallian vanished into the mist and shadows that crawled through the bodies. Anabelle felt hope for a single moment before her mother clutched at her side, blood seeping past her fingers. Despite Balwin's grip on her neck, Anabelle managed to scream.

Power stabbed through her like ice. She dropped to her knees as Balwin flew back from the force. Struggling to her feet, she stumbled forward, her head pounding and hot tears burning her eyes.

She dropped to her knees at her mother's side, her hands pressing to the bloody wound at her mother's ribs. Her fingers tried to staunch the free flow of blood as it pooled into the ground.

'Mamma!' she begged, 'Please, do not pass on. Why aren't you healing? You need to heal! Please, please, *please*.'

Anabelle placed a hand desperately on the wound. She focused her energy on it despite the hot tears that fell down her mother's chest.

Isadora's eyes opened, and she struggled to smile. 'A cursed blade is a poisoned blade, and even the immortal will fall at its hands. I will never leave you. Do not let them turn you bitter, my wild girl.'

'Don't leave me! Please, Mamma, please!'

Dark tendrils crept over her flesh in a poisonous mark. She reached a weak, fading hand up to her daughter's cheek.

When her hand dropped, Anabelle let out a scream of agony as she bent forward and placed her brow upon her mother's, tears spilling down her face.

'Look who I found,' said Balwin.

Anabelle glared at Balwin, hot tears rushing down her face. Pepper lay neatly in his hands. He was petting her soft fur with his cold, sickly fingers, and she wanted to break them.

'I will tear you apart,' Balwin said, as if discussing the weather, and knelt to pinch her chin, 'and when nothing remains, I will take your last breath from your body. I will not make the same mistake twice.'

Ripping herself free of his grasp, she stood on shaking legs. 'I will die before I allow you to use a *single fibre* of my being for your own use. I will take the very thing you want from me: my life.'

'Please do. May I watch?'

Her power surged, and she lunged at him, her eyes wild and teeth bared. At that moment, every ounce of remorse in her body vanished.

Balwin's hand lashed out, wrapping around her throat. Shadows danced around his feet, crawling up Anabelle's body, encapsulating them from the world.

'Now, now,' he drawled, eyes narrowing. 'That's not very nice, Anabelle.'

Her curse was only sputtered sounds, face turning red as his grip tightened.

'I could *destroy* you,' he whispered. 'I could take everything right now and be done with it.' Sniffing, he tilted his head in thought, watching her intently. 'But that would be too easy… and I want you to suffer as I have.'

The darkness dissipated, and Balwin released her. Anabelle took in a sucking breath as she crumpled to the ground.

Balwin's jaw twitched, his eyes boring into Anabelle's as she stared up at him, the darkness blazing in his eyes as he snapped Pepper's neck.

The crack of bones tore through Anabelle like a shot, and her body jerked back as a strangled sound left her lips.

'You have lost today, m'dear. More than just a battle.' He tossed the dead rabbit into the mud before her with a cold smile.

Néefar let out a bellowing cry behind Balwin, and Anabelle's eyes shot to him.

An arrow was pointed at Balwin's head, and the shifter's eyes were filled with rage as he released it.

Balwin's gleaming smile vanished into shadows and mist along with his beasts, and Néefar's arrow sunk into the tree behind Anabelle.

Silence wrapped its talons around her, and her hands began to shake. Her heart broke into shards, cutting her insides as she took her mother's hand, a cold, bitter numbness encasing her.

'Anabelle,' came Queen Casvara, her voice weary.

'Leave me!' Anabelle snapped, glaring at her aunt, who was an image of pristine regality in a dim, bloodied world.

The queen pursed her lips and stepped back. Shaking, Anabelle turned her face into her mother's body.

The thick squelch of mud preceded Néefar kneeling beside her.

'Anabelle,' he said gently in his deep, soothing voice.

Anabelle's eyes remained transfixed on her mother. 'Leave me alone.'

He put a gentle hand on her shoulder.

She shook it off. 'Leave me!'

Her voice wavered and cracked, and she felt like her magic might burst through her skin, causing even more destruction. Standing on unsteady legs, she mutely walked away from the carnage, hot tears falling down her cheeks.

Néefar followed her, waving off the few who stepped forward to help. When finally alone, Anabelle dropped to the ground with a sob. Néefar rushed to her side. She struggled against him, trying to push him off. He didn't let her and took her firmly against his chest, arms banded around her. His cheek pressed against her head as he whispered softly, 'I'm here.'

She couldn't stop. The pain coursed through her like her own blood. Sobs wracked her, and she couldn't stop.

'It's alright, little gipsy, I'm here. You're not alone.'

CHAPTER TWENTY-SEVEN

'Wha' do we do now?' asked a dwarf in the crowd around the four Spirits. His face was smeared with dirt and dried blood, with mud caked in his dirty blond beard.

'Ye call us here from the protection of our homes, in the dead o' night, te come and fight a fight we kne' nothin' of. Me bruthr' is dead, me son too. Ye tell us te go and stand with this gel' who is supposed te lead us. Yet, she is but a babe!'

'Quiet, Notile!' Da'arc's voice rumbled like thunder. 'She is the Keeper. We 'ave all lost loved ones in this battle and many past. She has never faced the blood of war before—not as we have. Let her mourn this day. As we have lost, so is the same fur' the gel.'

'Thank you, Da'arc,' Summer said, her hands clasped in front of her pristine magenta gown, looking out of place amongst the death and ruin. Looking at Notile, her eyes softened. 'Notile, we did not call you here for slaughter. We knew what would happen, but Balwin's attack was not predicted. The future is always changing. Things will always fall into place, never as you would expect them to. As a soldier, you know this better than anyone. The death of your kin fills our hearts with sadness.'

Notile's lips were pressed thin. 'Say's the one that flees at battle!'

'Notile!' Da'arc snapped.

Summer held up a hand, and Da'arc shut his mouth.

'You know the laws. Spirits and gods may not interfere, and such has been the case for thousands of years. That is the law of the Fae.'

Notile's eyes darkened, but he jerked his head in acknowledgement. 'Then wha' do we do?'

'Bury the dead, pray, and mourn,' said Autumn, kneeling by a fallen female, brushing the matted hair from her face. With gentle hands, Autumn closed the female's eyes and stood. 'And when the Keeper comes, we will hold counsel. Da'arc, Notile, you are welcome at our table.'

Da'arc turned to the crowd. 'Now ye heard him, let us bury our dead so they may rest in the heavens.'

Casvara watched the crowd disperse and walked up to her son. She glanced at him silently, noting the guilt in his eyes as he travelled over the bodies of the fallen. The familiar press of his mouth and the set look in his eyes told her everything she needed to know.

'You have chosen, have you not?' the queen asked Savven in their native tongue, quietly enough only he could hear.

'I have,' he replied.

'You will stay and fight alongside her.' It was not a question. 'The others?'

'They will follow me.'

With a soft exhale, she nodded. 'Come home, Savven. All of you. We will wait for your return. But go with courage. If you perish, die with honour.' Leaning forward, she placed a small kiss on his brow. 'Anabelle is your blood. She has lost more this day than you will understand. Make sure she knows she is not alone.'

'Where were you in all of this?'

With a sigh, she turned to gaze at the bodies littering the ground, then turned her attention to her sister.

'This was not my battle to fight.'

Savven was quiet, but she knew he understood her.

Casvara walked silently to her sister, kneeling beside her body and ignoring the red mud pooling in the ground, staining her plum gown. Her hand shook as she laid it on Isadora's still chest, brushing the other across her pale cheek, still webbed with black poison.

'Sleep well, my sister.'

Néefar stared down at Anabelle, his chest clenching. He brought his brow to hers, stroked a hand over her hair, and used his magic to put her to sleep.

'You cannot always protect her from the cruelty of the world, Shifter.'

Néefar's head whipped up, his eyes flashing as the beasts in him reared their heads at the intruder.

A female emerged from the forest shadows. Her pale green skin glimmered with a golden iridescence, and her hair and eyes were the softest shade of pink.

Néefar calmed the beast in him that begged to shift, willing himself to relax. 'You're the Lady of the Earth? Naleen?' He had seen her once, many years ago, as a boy. He had been hunting too close to The Forest of Lost Souls, and she had scared him so terribly that he nearly wet himself.

She nodded in acknowledgement.

'What do you want?'

'Anabelle must stand on her own.'

'I fear she may not recover from this,' Néefar said.

Naleen gave him a critical stare. 'Who are you to say that? When you were young, you pushed yourself from the ground. No one else. Anabelle must now trust her ability to heal from this tragedy.'

'She just lost her mother.'

'Let her awaken. Pain can be a gift, but to realise that, one must confront it. Today, she will mourn, but come tomorrow, first light, all that has happened here will be erased. Every new day is a new beginning. You cannot see her to the end, Shifter. That is her burden to bear.'

'But Tatius…'

'You must let her walk, just as you did.' Her face softened despite her stern tone. 'I must leave now. I say this with much regard: your feelings for the young keeper are admirable but do not be afraid of her sorrow. Great things will come of it.'

The world around them seemed to sigh as the female entered the forest.

Once they were alone, he grasped the cord of magic within him and said, in the tongue of the High Fae, 'Vaka.' Awake.

Anabelle's eyes opened slowly, vision unfocused. She blinked twice and then again as Néefar came into view. Then she pulled herself out of his grasp.

Memories of her mother and Pepper hit her like lightning. Her heart landed like lead in her stomach, and the world blurred as hot tears stung a trail down her cheeks.

Anabelle let Néefar help her to her feet, too tired to resist. He guided her toward the Keep, and when she shoved him off, he walked several paces behind her.

Those in the Keep paid Anabelle no mind as she crept into the chaos. Bodies were carried and carted, graves dug, weapons stripped, and coins laid over their eyes for ferry passage.

She knelt beside her mother, Pepper lying by her arm. With a shuddering breath, she lowered her brow to her mother's chest, her hand grasping the frozen fingers in the mud. Her bones ached with a profound numbness.

A shudder rolled through her, and knives stabbed at her chest, threatening to shred the soul that claimed to be immortal. Wave after wave of sorrow crested over her in an onslaught of pain and guilt. She screamed until her throat was raw and she had no voice left—and then ice exploded out of her in a surge of magic.

The carts ceased moving, the graves being dug were halted, and even the dead waited on bated breath as the female before them keeled over her mother's body.

Ice and fire crawled up her limbs, igniting her chest to her fingertips. She was responsible for her mother's death and the deaths of those around her.

The ground shifted and cracked, crystals breaking apart. A dark blue light illuminated the ground beneath her palms, golden tendrils tattooing the earth.

Vibrant green vines sprouted and tangled together, wrapping around her mother and Pepper on either side, knotting together as they encased their bodies.

Anabelle stood on shaking knees, watching the vines shroud their existence. Ruby roses sprouted like a blanket over the top, covered in a delicate layer of frost. When the world hushed around her, the pain she felt melted away, morphing into anger—red, hot anger coursing through her body. She bit down on the magic that whispered for release— a different kind of release, one she hadn't yet known.

A cold chill cut through her, and it was like waking from a terrible dream. She whirled around to see hundreds of eyes on her. They did not hold judgment, watching her silently with gaunt faces.

'Thank you.' Her voice was hoarse, and she swallowed, speaking up despite the scratch of fire in her throat. 'You fought with me when you did not know me—when I did not know you.' She licked her lips. 'I know you now.'

Anabelle joined Summer, who stooped over a golden-haired

satyr, Ezra and Lithônion standing by. The males' faces were grim, and they shook their heads softly.

'What happened to the veil?' Anabelle asked, noticing the satyr before Summer, whose hands were cupped before the spirit. Once golden and full of life, a small fairy lay motionless in the satyr's rough hands, now grey with white eyes. 'How did this happen?'

Summer looked at her with sad eyes. 'I created the veil to protect the Summer Fae from winter. When the Keep grew, Isadora created another veil over my own. When she died, so did the veil.' She looked down at the sprite. 'Most made it to safety, but not all.'

Anabelle felt guilt rear its head.

'It is not your fault, Anabelle,' Ezra said.

'I could have prevented it.'

Lithônion looked at her. 'This is not your fault or anyone's. It is the fault of Balwin, Gallian, and every soul that falls into his shadows.'

'It was because of me, Lithônion. Because I lived.'

'Then do not let their deaths be in vain,' he commanded.

The winter chill wrapped around her suddenly, and her tongue felt like lead in her mouth. Forcing the words out, she muttered, 'Excuse me.'

She staggered into the tree, then down into her room, barely aware of anything around her, as she dropped onto her bed. The room felt quiet and empty, but Anabelle had no strength to move.

Then she noticed a folded piece of parchment on her pillow and grabbed it.

My darling,

I leave this day for Álfheimr. I know you do not wish for me to go, but I know this is what is right. I want you to know that you are all the love I hold in my heart, dear one. Be strong and go with faith. Balwin will try to take what is not meant to be taken from you. The love I hold for you and your conviction for this world can never be taken.

Do not lose that, Anabelle.

I love you.

Mother

A silent tear fell on the parchment, and Anabelle folded the paper again and placed it back on her pillow with a wracking sob that threatened to spill out. Startled, she jumped when Néefar's voice broke the quiet.

'You amaze me, little gipsy.'

He stood in the doorway with his arms crossed over his chest.

'You amaze me, opening my door without knocking,' she snapped.

He cracked a smile, though he didn't move from the doorway until she'd invited him. Anabelle tore her gaze away, running a hand through her hair. When she felt the short strands, she paused and stood up to grab the mirror from the desk, ignoring the look Néefar gave her.

She held the mirror up to her face, eyeing the hair that had been chopped clean just below the nape of her neck. The delicate arch of her ears poked through. 'Bollocks,' she muttered and set the mirror back on the desk with a sigh.

'Where did you learn such language?'

She couldn't help but laugh, incredulous. 'As a little girl, I would overhear men in town talking. I remembered a few choice words.'

'Undoubtedly,' he paused, watching her approach, before saying, 'I'm glad I can hear you laugh.'

Her mouth twisted in conflict. 'I shouldn't.'

'Everyone deserves joy in the face of Balwin's greed. Even you.'

Anabelle gave him a timid smile that held her thanks in it.

'You know, your hair doesn't look that bad.'

'Really?' she asked, twirling a finger around a short end.

'Yes,' he said positively. 'The last time I saw short hair was on a female troll. It really brought out her—'

She smacked his arm, ignoring his grin. 'Thank you, Néefar. Your compliments are ever so flattering.'

'You're welcome, Ana.' Néefar brushed a stray piece of hair behind her ear, letting his fingertips linger on her neck, stroking the soft flesh. 'I must go back. They need my help.'

Anabelle smiled softly at the name, but her smile slipped, and the weight slowly crept back in.

'I'll go with you. I can help.'

He put a steady hand on her shoulder, glancing at her hands, which shook quietly by her sides. 'No, stay here. They need you, but not right now. They will need you tomorrow, but they're okay for today.'

He placed a kiss on her brow.

Her cheeks flushed. When he pulled away, Anabelle followed him.

'Néefar,' she called out.

He looked back with a raised brow.

'You missed.'

His smile was slight but genuine. 'I won't next time.'

She watched him disappear and turned in the opposite direction, making her way to the bathing chamber.

The oils she had used the night before were still by the ledge. The blue glow overhead reflected her pale skin as she stripped and lowered herself into the hot water. A sigh escaped as her head tilted back, and she scrubbed her nails over her scalp as the blue sap dripped into the water, scattering the scent of roses.

Tears threatened as her memory played of her mother. A low growl of frustration slipped out, and she clenched her jaw, shaking her head.

Every sound and whisper echoed; even the silence was deafening. So, she sang quietly under her breath: '*When nighttime comes, I will be there.*' She floated on her back, looking up at the blue light above. '*When darkness comes, I will be there.*'

Images of today flashed through her head, and the stench of copper filled her nose. With that, she submerged herself. The water encased her as she sunk to the bottom of the pool, and she stayed there. Images wavered and floated back and forth above her, but all was quiet. She heard nothing but her own beating heart.

As the silence took over, the quiet places in her heart opened up. She had to contain the rage and pain that wanted to spill out, but when it became too much when the world seemed to crumple around her, she screamed into the watery depths. She screamed until her throat burned and her lungs strained. She screamed until she was forced to surface.

Her chest heaved as she swam to the ledge and touched the

necklace between her breasts. Anger and pain fileted her open, and her hands trembled even as her magic sang an unknown song in her veins. She couldn't control her destiny, but she could shape it. The tiny gem winked in the blue light, and when she knew what she had to do, she fell back into the water.

Néefar stared into the campfire, transfixed. Ezra sat in conversation with Savven across the firepit, their voices low. Néefar could only make out snippets of the Fae language, so he turned his attention to Lithônion, who sat staring into the fire beside him. His face was void of emotion, his body preternaturally still.

'So bloody stoic,' Néefar muttered, poking the fire with a long stick.

Lithônion didn't look up. 'Do we fail to amuse you, Shifter?'

'Not in the slightest, Elf,' he retorted.

Lithônion smiled, however faintly. 'Then what troubles you?'

'I find myself wondering if the gods truly have our best interests in mind, or if this is all just a game to them.'

The male tilted his head in thought. 'I think most of life is a game that we're forced to play for the amusement of others.'

'I'm quite amused by the blundering idiocies you call your life, Lithônion!' Ezra called across the fire, smirking.

Lithônion gave him a flat glare. 'Funny, Ezra, for I could say the same of you.'

'Funny,' Ezra drawled, resting an arm on his knee. 'I recall you setting off an explosion in the armoury once.'

'Listen,' Lithônion said in a way that implied this was a well-trod topic. 'How was I supposed to know that black powder and the salt mined from the troll mountains didn't blend well?'

Savven's loud laugh broke the otherwise quiet night. 'Maybe a drop would have sufficed, but not a whole cauldron!'

'Says the one who got trapped by the very troll guarding the entrance into their mountain.'

Now, Savven glared at Ezra. 'That was *one time.*'

Ezra shrugged. 'And a damn memorable one time at that.'

Savven stoked the fire, sending amber sparks into the air, and gave Lithônion a subtle look. 'This is quite the adventure, Lithônion, wouldn't you agree?'

Lithônion pursed his lips, taking a deep breath through his nose. 'Yes, quite invigorating. Zarren would have been dreadfully droll.'

'Do you find this to be tedious?' Néefar asked. 'Fighting for someone you don't know?'

Lithônion tapped a stick against his boot, head cocked in thought. 'I find no fault in giving aid to the keeper because they are an essential connection to help preserve the balance of the forest. Nor do I find fault with Anabelle. This is not a life she knows; essentially, she is being tossed into an arena and expected to survive. Still, she seems eager to adapt to it.'

'Much like how we are trained at an early age,' Savven interjected.

'Aye, he's right,' said Ezra.

'Trained? ' Néefar asked, adding dryly, 'You mean to say you're not this naturally skilled from birth?'

Savven leaned forward, firelight and shadow warring over the planes of his face. 'When we're young, we're taken away from Álfheimr and brought to Álfaborg, a great island connected by a land bridge that stretches to the sea. At its centre is a towering fortress of stone with an arena built into its core. On the first day, we are thrown into the arena and told to survive with only our hands and teeth. They release monsters and traps of magic and potions. We have to survive for three days without using our magic. Those who are still alive—and those who didn't beg to be pulled out—are then trained for a year in weaponised fighting.'

Néefar shook his head. 'I never understood your kind.'

'That's because you only have half a mind,' Lithônion said with a wink, tapping his temple. 'Not smart enough to understand.'

'Don't get ahead of yourself, Elf. You have the other half.'

Ezra sniggered. 'I'll drink to that.'

Savven laughed, but it wasn't before they sobered. The forest was an ever-present reminder of why they were there.

'Anabelle is trapped within her own arena,' Savven mused. 'And going through her own trials. We can't expect her to know or understand our ways so quickly if she is just now learning to survive.'

Ezra nodded in agreement. 'I like her spirit, though, and her innocence. It's refreshing to be around.'

Lithônion threw a pebble at him.

Savven looked at Néefar with amusement. 'So tell me, Shifter, what are your intentions with my cousin?'

Ezra leaned forward, firelight dancing over his cheekbones. 'We've noticed the way you look at her.'

Néefar kept his gaze fixed on the fire. 'I can't help when...' He trailed off, movement in the shadows catching his attention.

What is she doing now? he thought, watching Anabelle sneak along the edges of the Keep.

When he realised the others were watching him as if waiting for his answer, he sighed and said, 'I find my intentions are to remain a secret for now.'

Lithônion groaned in disappointment as Néefar stood, brushing a hand over his leather trousers. 'Don't strain the other half of our mind, Lithônion, trying to figure it out.'

Lithônion's muttered curse followed him as he slipped into the darkness beyond the firelight's reach, a smile on his face. He had forgotten what it was to verbally spar with friends.

CHAPTER TWENTY-EIGHT

The bark of the blackwood trees scraped underhand as Anabelle wove her way through the forest. Fear coiled tightly in her stomach, the darkness a thick blanket around her. Summer's veil kept even the faintest flicker of light from the Keep hidden, but it was well behind her, and only darkness surrounded her.

The bitterness pressed into her bones, numbing her skin despite the black wool tunic and dark brown leathers she wore. Her fingertips, nose, and ears were already numb.

She didn't know how long she had been walking. Seconds turned to minutes, and minutes stretched into an hour or what felt like more. The tether of life that bound the forest hummed almost silently through her. The taint of darkness on the lifeline felt like an icy bite that left her feeling hollow. But she followed it because what she wanted was at the core of that darkness.

The end of her hair tickled the nape of her neck, making her shiver. Clenching her teeth, she searched for her magic, hoping it might bring warmth.

Crack!

Anabelle whirled. Shadows played off the moonlight, and bare branches reached out like claws. Her breath sounded heavy in her ears, and her heartbeat was like a drum. The air was bitter and chilled her bones, making them brittle.

She reeled around, quickening her strides through the thicket of trees. Fear laced through her muscles as she took a hesitant step forward, then another, shaking the tension from her spine with every step. Darkness had overtaken the forest's tether, thrumming with an overwhelming presence that made her head pulse.

The shadows reached for her like ghosts wishing to drag her into their endless abyss. The palls began to beckon and creep closer in black tendrils. The echoing of whispers surrounded her.

She could hear her mother whisper to her from the mist, *'Anabelle.'*

Anabelle reached a hand out—and a rough hand grabbed her arm and hauled her away from the whisper, pressing her behind one of the massive trees. Shadows and mist coiled in the air where she had been.

'What do you think you're doing?' Néefar whispered, then whipped his head around and pressed his hand to her mouth as a minotaur walked by. Only once they were alone again did he drop his hand and raise a brow at her.

'What are *you* doing here?' she snapped, their chests brushing from how close they stood.

'I'd hoped to make sure you weren't doing something stupid. And yet, here we are.' Néefar peered from behind the tree and scanned the clearing. 'You'll die if you go in there.'

Anabelle turned in Néefar's grip, fingers digging into the bark as she watched a Cerberus snarl at a harpy as the harpy tried to steal the carcass of a dead dwarf. The harpy shrieked, flying to safety. The enormous three-headed watchdog of the netherworld tore viciously at the dwarf's limbs. Anabelle looked away with a grimace, but not before taking note of the creatures that lay in waiting. She had made it to the end of the tether without realising and now faced the darkness as it sat primly in the shape of beasts and monsters that blanketed the middle of the forest for as far as she could see.

'Everyone will die, Néefar.'

He let out a harsh breath. 'You will be that Cerberus's meal if we do not turn back.'

Reaching for the necklace around her neck, she pulled it over her head and held it up to Néefar. 'Gabriel would not let their blood be spilt for his life.'

Néefar took the teardrop and rubbed his thumb over it. 'But he fought for it first. When there was no more hope and blood left to spill, he gave his life back to this world to vanquish the darkness that would destroy it.'

He draped the teardrop necklace back around her neck. The hand at her waist tightened like a searing brand through her garments.

In a low voice, he said, 'War cannot be avoided when the ones we fight crave it. Come back to the Keep, Anabelle.'

She sidestepped him and then froze when a blade was suddenly at her neck. Néefar's eyes widened, his hand dropping to his belt, strangely empty. His eyes flew past her as she turned around slowly.

'Gallian,' Anabelle said lowly.

Gallian cocked his head, his eyes black.

Anabelle hissed out a breath as she felt the blade dig into her neck. Blood trickled down the curve of her neck, and she gritted her teeth against the pain, the fear.

'What do we have here? And no, *Brother*, I would not do that. Although it is so tempting to just slit her throat right now.'

Néefar let out a low, feral growl as he forced the magic back, baring his teeth in a snarl.

She could feel poison crawling from the cut, digging its claws into her. Her magic roared in her veins, coursing through frozen limbs to the poison.

Terror and rage sparked as images of her mother's face, webbed with poison, flashed through her mind.

'Gallian,' she said quietly as if trying to soothe him. Her magic slowly crawled up her hand, biding her time. 'Your father only controls what you give to him.'

Gallian only laughed, harsh and cruel. 'You are a fool, Anabelle.'

Clenching her hands, she said, 'I might be a fool, but there is one thing I am not.' And then she dove into her power, finding its white-hot ice bright, powerful, and unending.

With a surge of power, she lashed out, teeth bared in a yell, shooting gold and blue ice at Gallian and throwing his body back through the air. He landed in a heap, frozen crystals glimmering on his skin.

The beasts around them grew quiet, and all eyes were on them. Even the massive Cerberus glowered at them, a lone limb hanging from one of its bloodied maws. The Cerberus stood, others following suit as demons and creatures of the netherworld stepped forward.

Gallian held up a hand, halting them. 'They will be dealt with by me.'

And then Néefar was thrown back. No sooner had he hit the ground than he leapt, shifting into a massive black wolf mid-air.

He slammed into Gallian, knocking them both to the ground, but then Gallian's hand latched around Néefar's neck. He thrashed, and Anabelle darted forward. Gallian threw Néefar at her, sending them sprawling over the frozen ground. She landed on top of Néefar, who lay unconscious. She shifted, hands shaking, to protect him as well as she could.

'RELEASE ME!' her magic seemed to scream. She could feel it strain against her skin, bones, and every fibre of her identity. She fought it back, unwilling to kill him when this was only his father's doing.

Gallian sprinted towards them. She gritted her teeth and pushed to her feet, facing him.

'RELEASE ME!' her magic screamed in her ears, and the building pressure beneath her palms exploded in light of gold and white. Gallian flew through the air, and Anabelle reigned in her magic, holding the tether as she pinned him against a tree. Gallian's limbs trashed in the air, his face contorted in rage.

Her own rage burned through her, and her hands began to shake as images of her mother, and Pepper, and all of those who had fallen flooded her mind.

He *killed* her mother.

He killed her mother.

He killed—

Her heart raced, and she closed her eyes. Sucking in a deep breath, she unfurled her fingers, her blood cooling, and she calmed herself, her magic settling down to a icy simmer. Néefar appeared beside her, still in his wolf form, his gaze fixed on Gallian.

'I might be a fool,' she said quietly, 'but I am not a coward, Gallian. I am not you. I understand it was all a lie, but I hope there is even an echo of you still inside yourself so you feel the weight of their deaths.'

He choked out a bitter laugh, his neck bulging under her power.

'Then you will die a fool's death,' he spat.

With one hand, she yanked the teardrop around her neck and brought it to her lips, whispering softly, 'Show me the light, Gabriel.'

Two heartbeats sounded, and the silver twined around the teardrop melted with the thin chain, molten silver dripping to the ground as the dark mist wafted around their feet.

Silence enveloped Anabelle, and everything ceased into nothingness as she felt the power of Gabriel's tear thrum in her palm. It was the essence of pure, unadulterated light.

Looking into Gallian's eyes, she said, 'Lýsa,' in time with a whisper from the teardrop itself.

The teardrop glowed with a light that filled the forest, the black mist scattering to the shadows.

And with all the broken pieces of herself, she said the only thing she could. 'I forgive you, Gallian.' Then she shattered the teardrop against his chest, right over his beating heart.

A floating sensation overtook Anabelle as time seemed to stop. In the silence, she heard one heartbeat, then two, and three.

Light exploded out of Gallian and flooded the forest.

Anabelle was thrown off her feet, Néefar landing beside her.

Gallian dropped to the forest floor.

Dazed, ears ringing, Anabelle rose slowly. She didn't dare go to his side.

Pounding hooves and sword meeting sword flooded the forest, driving away silence and sending Anabelle and Néefar running.

The first rays of sunrise painted the sky, and a heavy white mist rolled through the forest as Néefar and Anabelle neared the Summer Keep. Only when it was in view did Néefar shift back into a man. He stood stark naked, and Anabelle's cheeks flamed. She whipped her head away, staring straight ahead, even as he chuckled.

And yet, Anabelle couldn't help but peek. His dark hair fell across solid shoulders, contrasting with olive skin. Her eyes followed the narrow cut of his hips and the scattering of black hair that went from his navel down to—She looked away, her body flushing.

A low growl rumbled through Néefar, though it didn't sound like admonishment. If anything, he might have hoped she'd keep looking.

She cleared her throat. 'I see.'

His lips quirked, eyes darkening. 'I would think so.'

Her cheeks reddened. Surely she would pass away now? 'I did not mean...'

Néefar put a calloused hand on her cheek, turning her to look at him. 'I know,' he murmured, brushing his thumb over her skin. Then he said, 'I don't think entering the Keep as I am would be wise.'

'I don't believe it would matter,' she countered in a rush. 'It is not as if males are unknowledgeable to how they look beneath their clothes. If they are—unknowledgeable, that is—perhaps they should look beneath their trousers and...blast, I don't know,' she said with a deflated sigh.

He only laughed and mused, 'I should enter as a wolf.'

She nodded in agreement, and despite herself, her hand reached for him. Néefar watched her hand hover over his chest, which heaved with every breath. The air between them thrummed, and he released a harsh breath, stepping back.

'Will you be all right?' he asked, ignoring the sudden rush of cold around him that damped his arousal.

'I have fallen as far as I can fall, emotionally. I have nowhere to go but up.'

Néefar took a deep breath, nodded, and stepped back again to give himself space to shift.

'Néefar?'

Her quiet voice halted him, and he glanced at her in question.

'He called you brother.'

He pursed his lips but nodded once.

'I didn't know he had a brother.'

'He doesn't...not by blood.'

When she only gave him a questioning look, he took a deep breath, letting it out slowly before he said, 'Gallian was taken in by Autumn when his father was banished. I had been under Autumn's care for some time, and when he arrived, we began to feel like brothers. I even helped raise and care for him as a brother should, but Gallian became distant as he got older—cold even. He couldn't let go of the past and blamed everyone but his father for what happened. Even you.'

That same familiar guilt roiled through her like a kindred friend.

As if sensing her thoughts, he added, 'But he's wrong.'

She nodded stiffly, and he shifted back into the wolf.

Anabelle entered the clearing first, the fog falling away as they passed through the barrier. When Ezra and Savven, seated at the campfire, spotted the wolf, their hands went to the blades at their hips.

'No,' Anabelle said quickly. 'It's only Néefar. He shifted.'

'Wha' were ye doin' out in the middle o'night, Keeper?' Notile's suspicious tone came from behind her, his left hand wrapped around the hilt of his blade.

Anabelle turned to look at the hard-faced dwarf. 'I went into the forest to find Balwin's camp.' She had nothing to hide; she would lay herself bare for them to trust her if that is what it took.

The dwarf hissed at her, and she had to calm Néefar's growling.

'I found it, the outskirts of it, and I found Gallian.'

The dwarf echoed a rumbling dark laugh, void of humour. 'And wha' were yew doin' with tha' bastard?'

'I pulled him from the darkness.'

He stepped forward, eyes hard. 'When there is a death wish upon yewr head by the very man who killed yewr mudder.' He spat at her feet. 'I do not trust yew, Keeper, not on me life.'

Néefar growled at the dwarf, his hackles raising as he crouched low.

Anabelle held a soft hand to calm him, and his growling ceased into a low rumble. 'I know I have not earned your trust yet, but I did not even know your name, yet I have fought alongside you.'

'Aye, but I know yewrs gel', and ye were the reason yew mudder died! Yew are weak! I remember when Isadora was the keeper of this forest. Yew are nothing like her!'

Anabelle flinched but refused to let him cow her. Gathering her words, she drew her shoulders back. 'You're right. My mother was a great woman, and she loved me dearly—just as she did this world. She protected me with every part of her being. That is a debt I will never be able to repay, but I am not my mother. All I ask is that you allow me to prove I can follow in her footsteps.'

Notile glanced at her with doubt, but he said only, 'As ye wish, Keeper.' Then he turned and walked away.

When Néefar nudged her toward the Keep, she shook her head and said, 'Go on, Néefar, I will be here.'

He rubbed his head gently on her leg, and she gave him a soft smile as he trotted off.

'He will come around,' Savven said, patting the log beside him.

Anabelle looked at Savven with a small smile, settling where invited. 'I suppose we'll find out.'

When the silence stretched too long, Anabelle glanced over at him. 'You're wondering why I did it.'

'I did not say anything.'

Anabelle shook her head. 'You didn't have to.'

'May I ask you something?'

'You're my cousin, Savven. You may ask me anything.'

'Are you not angry?' he asked, his gaze unreadable, the firelight playing across his cheekbones.

She stared at the flames for a moment, thinking. 'I'm *furious*,' she whispered, running a hand through her hair. The emotions she kept contained behind a smile and gentle hands— the burning hatred she felt that replaced all her empathy.

Anabelle inhaled sharply, tears stinging her eyes. 'I'm so *angry*,' she whispered again. 'But... there isn't any time for anger. My responsibilities must be prioritised. How I feel is second to that.'

If the world opened up and swallowed her whole, she would gladly go into the void, if only to end it all, but she couldn't, and the world wasn't going to consume her.

Savven put a gentle hand over hers when she took a shuddering breath. The gesture of support made her heart clench.

'What of the darkness?' he asked.

She looked up at the dawn-lit sky, the clouds pink and red as the sun rose. 'Shadows cannot be observed unless there is light. You cannot gaze upon the stars and moons unless there is nightfall. A soul that is covered in darkness was once born of light. We fail to realise that it isn't unending if you can see past it...' Anabelle trailed off as Ezra approached them.

Savven rested a hand on Anabelle's bicep. 'Hone that anger, but don't contain it. *Use it.*'

When Ezra stopped before them, he offered a sword in its scabbard. 'I believe this is yours, Keeper. I found it at the outskirts of the Keep.'

Anabelle carefully took the sword. The gold and iron hilt glinted in the firelight, and the whorls etched into the guard shifted in the light.

'I didn't spend hours helping to craft it for it to be lost,' Néefar quipped, now dressed in black armour. Anabelle found herself staring at him and quickly looked away. He reached for the blade, but not before catching her staring and smirking softly. 'May I?'

He tilted the sword to show her the hilt where her name had

been etched.

'None but you may wield it.'

Anabelle looked up at Néefar. 'You knew I would choose the blade?'

He shrugged. 'While both were crafted with remarkable craftsmanship, if I do say so myself, I thought the sword might come in handy one day.'

'Thank you,' she said, taking the sword and strapping the belt around her hips. Its weight was oddly comforting.

CHAPTER TWENTY-NINE

Balwin stood over the crumpled body at his feet, kicking Gallian's unconscious form. Gallian didn't have the courtesy to wake.

'Wake up!' Reaching out a hand, Balwin gripped Gallian's throat and hauled him into the air, squeezing tight enough that Gallian's face began to purple.

A strangled gasp of air came from Gallian as his eyes flew open, hands clawing at the grip around his throat, suffocating him.

Balwin loosened his grip and slammed Gallian against a tree. Gallian's head snapped against the trunk, and a satisfied smile tilted on Balwin's lips.

'Are you finally awake?' His smile went saccharine. 'Pray, tell me, son, what were you doing?'

Gallian clenched his jaw, his eyes narrowing as he looked at his father's pale face. His mind reeled. Anabelle's face floated in his mind, a wolf black as midnight, light, pain…

It all came flooding back. 'Anabelle, she was here—'

'You didn't bring the little bitch to me?' Balwin ripped his hand away, and Gallian dropped to the ground.

His head hung low as he stared at the dirt under his splayed fingers. Tears stung his eyes, and something stabbed him, slicing through his insides like a hot knife. He brought a hand to his stomach, expecting to find blood, but his hand came away dry. Isadora's face filled his memory, and a look of pain and betrayal twisted her features…and understanding. Pain stabbed through his chest, and he looked up at his father, hot tears running down his face.

'I took her life,' he whispered.

Eyebrow quirking in sudden delight, Balwin bowed low.

'What was that, son? Did you kill poor, sweet Anabelle?'

Gallian sucked in a breath, trying to remember what had happened, and then shook his head.

'Then who did you kill?' Balwin roared.

Gallian pushed himself to his feet, regaining his balance. 'Isadora. I killed Isadora.'

A moment passed, and Balwin felt himself begin to twitch; first, his fingers, then his eye, and, finally, the crook of his ugly mouth. 'What did that little Halfling do to you?' Balwin stepped closer, his teeth clenched. 'You are no son of mine, weak and snivelling as you are. You reek of her scent.'

Despite it all, Gallian felt an overwhelming sense of rightness as he found his mind free of his father's corruption. 'Then I guess you should have done a better job controlling me.'

Gallian was thrown back against a tree, the breath stolen from his lungs.

'What did you say to me?'

'She *shattered* your leash like it was made of glass, *Father.*'

With a snarl, Balwin slammed Gallian's head back into the tree, his body slumping as he was knocked unconscious. He let the body fall to the ground, one brow raised in disdain.

'Chain him to the rocks,' Balwin ordered the lingering centaurs around him. 'Let him rot.'

'I could take care of him for you.'

Balwin whirled, watching a succubus float toward him, her pale blue eyes filled with desire and hunger.

'Mara,' he said. 'That would be too easy. I wish him to suffer. To suffer the knowledge that everyone is dead, that he is all that is left. That he is the reason they are dead.'

Mara turned her attention to Gallian as she watched him being dragged away. 'Pity,' she said, her voice filled with honest remorse. 'He would have been delicious.'

Anabelle cleared her throat. 'I went to Balwin's camp last night.'

'It's a shame tha' bastard's dogs didn't tear yewr pretty head from yewr shoulders.' Notile muttered bitterly.

Savven had a blade to Notile's throat before anyone could even blink.

'If I ever hear those words again from you, Dwarf, I will kill you.'

'Yew, do not scare me, fair one,' Notile spat out.

'Heed your tongue, Dwarf, or I shall cut it out.'

Ezra looked at Anabelle, unfazed. 'Please, continue.'

Anabelle took a deep breath. 'This is where Balwin's camp is located.' She marked the location near the border with a small stone. 'The distance between us does not bring me comfort. He has creatures that can only come from fire— airborne and earthbound. He has them all at his command. We are outnumbered. Once Balwin sees what I have done, if he has not already, he will not let there be peace. I may have accelerated this war.'

Da'arc looked at Anabelle. 'And what have ye done?'

Anabelle held his gaze, straightening. 'I took his pawn from him. His son.'

Da'arc's brows shot up, and a murmur rose up.

'What do you suggest we do?' Autumn asked, silencing everyone.

'Our numbers have greatly increased. How so, I do not know. You seemed to have conjured masses from the air in the dead of night.'

'When I call,' Summer said, 'armies come.'

Anabelle glanced at the faces around her and let out a soft breath. 'I must apologise. I know nothing of wartime and battle. My use is limited, so I ask for your help— all of you. Lend me your knowledge.'

Savven pointed to the Keep's boundary. 'We'll post archers at the trees and on our perimeter to protect us from anything that comes from the sky.'

'I will lead them,' Néefar said. 'I know Balwin as well as I can with Gallian for a brother.'

'I will take fifty dwarves to cover this clearing,' Lithônion said, placing a stone on the open land within the Keep. 'Anything that moves—will die.'

Ezra nodded, a small smile tilting his lips, excitement glowing in his eyes. 'Savven and I take to the western perimeters.'

'And of us?'

Anabelle looked up at Autumn and the other Spirits. 'We cannot choose where you're to be. You know that better than us.'

'What will happen if Balwin gets through our defences?' Da'arc asked, hand going to the hilt at his side.

Anabelle was silent, her eyes meeting Winter's gaze. The question hung in the air as Anabelle leaned over the map again.

The Keep bustled with noise. Blacksmiths worked together

to craft new weapons. Carts were piled high with iron and silver. Néefar gathered archers to whittle more arrows, the blacksmiths fitting them with iron arrowheads. Pots brewed over fires. Summer Fae flittered here and there, but rarely were they seen now since the first attack.

'You found its use?'

Anabelle startled and looked away from the commotion she'd observed beside a towering tree. 'Its use?'

Winter stopped beside her. 'The Tear of Gabriel. The Summer Fae gifted it to you, did they not?'

Surprised, Anabelle nodded. 'Yes, but how did you know?'

'I know all things concerning you, Anabelle. You are the Keeper,' she replied gently.

Anabelle wasn't sure how she felt about that, but decided there were bigger things to occupy her and let it go. 'I heard him last night, or I believe it to be him.'

'It is not unheard of.' Winter mused. 'Spirits speaking to us from beyond our world. If in great need, help comes to those who seek it.'

Anabelle nodded, wrapping her arms around her waist. Then she looked at the dwarves and said, 'Do you suppose Notile will ever come to trust me?'

'All things take time. Notile is stubborn.' Winter sighed and looked at Anabelle. 'I do not believe others share his mistrust. '

Anabelle faced the world outside the Keep's barrier, watching the noonday sun through the bare winter branches.

'It feels like a lifetime has gone by.'

'A life can change in a single breath,' Winter said quietly.

Anabelle laid her hand upon the hilt of her sword. 'He killed my mother. That will not go unpunished.'

'The time of war will tell who lives and who shall die, Anabelle.'

Silence filled the space between them before Anabelle said quietly, 'If they breach our defences—'

'Anabelle...'

She looked at the Spirit. 'If they breach our defences, Balwin will seek only one thing: me.'

Winter reached for her, but she stepped back, shaking her head.

'You can't, Anabelle.'

'I can, and I will. If Balwin gets through, I need you to find a new keeper.'

'But—'

'Promise me,' she demanded. 'You chose me for this life. So promise me you will choose another if needed!'

Winter pursed her lips, and the Spirit took a deep breath, jerking her head. 'I promise.'

A dagger was stabbed into the stump of a tree as Balwin picked through the carcass of a hare, bitter air dragging its claws through his greasy dark hair. He glanced up, watching Gallian as he lay unconscious, chained to the stone pillar in the centre of the camp. Iron cuffs were locked around his wrists.

'My lord!'

Tearing his eyes away, he glared at the dwarf who stalked through the camp, holding a knife to another of his kind while a minotaur, axe in hand, shadowed them.

'What do we have here?' Balwin asked, delighted. 'A spy?'

The dwarf tried to talk, but his words came muted and muffled against the gag.

Balwin rolled his eyes. 'Take that out of his mouth. I can't understand a word he's saying.'

'Just before we shut 'im up, 'e spoke of the Summer Keep, my lord,' said the other dwarf, ripping the gag from his mouth.

The dwarf swallowed and looked up with hard eyes. 'I come with news from the Summer Keep,' he said.

Intrigued, Balwin waved a hand to the tent behind him.

'Come, tell me your tales.'

He made to follow suit, glaring at his fellow kinsmen as they stalked away. The other dwarf followed Balwin into his tent. In one corner sat a single table and chair with a silver pitcher on it. In another corner stood a bed.

'Do you drink, dwarf?'

'Aye.'

Balwin produced two silver goblets from the air and filled them with a dark red liquid. Handing one to the dwarf, Balwin watched him drink deeply from it, tilting his head when the dwarf coughed up the cherry-red liquid.

'What is your name, dwarf?'

The dwarf slammed his goblet onto the table. 'What did yew give me?!'

Balwin calmly looked down at his goblet, took a sip, and licked the droplet of red from his mouth. 'I find the earthy tones of your blood *intoxicating.*'

The dwarf blanched. 'Ye feast on our blood?'

Balwin bared his forearm and dragged a black claw up his flesh. Shadows swirled against his skin. 'Something must feed my pets.'

'This was a mistake!' the dwarf spat, taking another step back.

Growing irritated, Balwin grabbed the dwarf around the neck in a vice grip. The dwarf clawed at his hand, face turning red. As he spoke, Balwin tightened his hold, venom in his words.

'Tell me your name, dwarf, or your blood will be the next thing I wet my tongue with.'

He rubbed his neck, gasping in a lungful of air when he was released.

'Well, dwarf?'

Dropping his hand from around his neck, he straightened, face splotchy with fear. 'I am Notile of the Iron Clan, and I bring you news of the Summer Keep.'

CHAPTER THIRTY

Pain lanced through Gallian's side when he moved, and his head throbbed, but he forced his eyes open. The smell of rot and stale air surrounded him, and his hands were shackled, heavy chains sliding through an iron loop. He had been cuffed to a stone in the centre of the camp. He shifted on the dirt, straightening his legs and sighing as the numbness slowly ebbed away.

A low, strangled moan rippled through the air, and Gallian turned to his right, straining against the chains. A white female centaur lay beaten and bleeding from open wounds on her chest and head, an iron cuff around her throat and wrists, pinning her to the stone. Ribs protruding, half-starved, her unconscious body jerked uncontrollably, sweating with fever.

To his left was a satyr, an iron cuff tight around his neck, keeping his body aloof as he switched where he hung, slowly suffocating. Though his eyes bulged, he appeared unconscious. A small mercy.

The cold iron bit into his wrists. Although his body was drained of energy, he tried to focus his power on the cold iron. Nothing came of it, not even a spark.

A commotion caught Gallian's attention. He looked up to see his father drag a dwarf out of his tent, across the camp, and toward Gallian, tossing the dwarf to the ground before him.

Blood streamed down his face; he had several fingers broken, clothing torn, and a swollen black-and-blue eye. He pulled away from Gallian's feet, boots digging into the ground as he slid to stand, chest heaving with ragged breaths as he faced Balwin.

The dwarf lifted a meagre hand, hoping to ward off his father's anger.

'Did you think I would welcome you into my camp, into my army, after you became a traitor to your own?' he hissed. 'I thank you, Notile of the Iron Clan, for the vital information you gave me. But now I have no use for you.'

Gallian felt sick to his stomach at the dwarf's whimpering.

Balwin snarled, 'Chain him up.'

A harpy flew down and cackled as the dwarf struggled against her hold. She chained him beside Gallian and blocked his view of the dying centaur.

Balwin leaned forward, dragging his nail down the dwarf's cheek. 'Drain this one slowly. I want him to watch as I feast on his blood.'

'You can't!' he yelled, though his fight was pointless as the harpy held him down and drew a knife.

Balwin turned to Gallian. 'My son.'

Gallian clenched his jaw.

'As a child, you showed such potential,' Balwin mused. 'I thought perhaps there was hope, but you've become such a waste.'

Gallian flinched away from his father's touch as he reached for him.

'My pets have gone. She destroyed them,' Balwin murmured with an annoyed click of his tongue. 'Though they were never needed, the darkness was bred into you. After all, you are my son.'

'I only ever wanted your love!' Gallian snarled.

'Is that so?' Balwin asked, head cocking to the side. 'You always came back, even when warned not to. You chose despite knowing that love does not grow in darkness.'

A lump settled in Gallian's throat, but he said nothing.

Balwin dragged a sharp-clawed nail along Gallian's cheek, humming thoughtfully. 'I do hope you enjoy where you are. After all, you will die here.'

The harpy offered a silver cup, and Balwin dragged his tongue along the rim, eyes boring into the dwarf's. He drank the blood with a satisfied smile, his scars pulling tight.

Gallian's stomach churned. His father threw the empty cup at the dwarf's feet. The dwarf barely flinched, his head lolling to the side, blinking slowly. Balwin sniffed and walked away without another glance at Gallian.

Anger pooled in his stomach, burning like acid, and he screamed at the dwarf, 'What have you *done?*'

Notile flinched, turning his head away from Gallian. 'As you have done, I have done, as well.'

Gallian let out a harsh breath, staring at the dwarf in disbelief. 'You had no reason.'

His voice was muted and hard as he stared at the ground. 'Then tell me what *you* would have done.'

'You deserve this,' Gallian spat.

'As do you.'

The evening sky was a painter's canvas above Anabelle. She stared up at the array of colours as they slowly dimmed, her legs dangling from the high limbs of the tallest tree in the Keep. The noise below seemed muffled as she gazed up at the stars.

'A smile so beautiful it stole away the breath of the stars.'

Anabelle's smile faltered slightly as Néefar joined her, her heart thundering at his nearness. Taking his seat on a thick branch beside hers, legs dangling on either side, Néefar smiled.

'Hello, friend,' he said quietly.

'Hello, you,' she whispered back.

Anabelle looked back up at the sky. 'Look how beautiful it is. Even amidst everything, the world still finds time to paint the sky.'

Néefar glanced up. 'Maybe that is the purpose? To remind us that, even when the world dies, it begins the next day anew.'

'Do you suppose the gods made it so?'

He hummed.

They fell into silence, feet swinging gently in rhythm.

Swallowing, she held out her hand, looking at him with soft eyes. 'Give me your hand.'

Without question, he slid his hand into hers. His skin was warm and calloused, and Anabelle's heart rattled her ribs as she turned it palm up, fingers tracing the lines etched within.

She spoke softly. 'The future terrifies me.'

Néefar watched her intently, his voice low as she dragged her nail across his palm. 'Does it not terrify everyone?'

She shook her head, feeling the heat of his stare and her own flush. 'No, I would think not. I can't imagine you being afraid.'

Néefar's smile lingered as nightfall crept in around them. 'Courage comes from accepting our fears and being strong enough to face them.'

'The future is untold. You cannot prepare for that.'

'But the unknown is as terrifying as it is beautiful.'

Anabelle nodded, chewing on his words as they fell into silence, and his hand slipped from hers.

Néefar tapped his finger softly on his thigh, and Anabelle tracked the movement from the corner of her eye.

Looking up, his blue eyes caught hers, and her breath caught, lips parting softly. His gaze flickered to them before returning to her eyes.

'My mother taught me how to read palms when I was younger,' she said quietly.

He leaned back, his hair falling over one shoulder in a dark curtain, and he offered his hand to her again.

'Look.' She traced over his palm. 'These calluses show your work with the bow, your dedication through your lifetime. This line shows the length of your heart. Your heart line is very long, and you will live a full life. I do not see children in your lifetime, but you will have a great love—'

Her voice hushed as his fingers closed around her hand, and the air around them grew still.

'The map of our lives is written upon our skin, tattooed like a book,' he said softly.

Anabelle looked up at him with wide eyes, her heart thudding madly.

He turned her hand over and traced the lines on her palm. 'You too will have a great love in your life.'

'Oh?' she sighed softly. 'Perhaps that is asking the gods too much. For a moment, in the beginning, I thought Gallian might be more than a figment of my dreams, but that proved false.'

Néefar chuckled, pulling her gently towards him. 'My brother was only the step towards your future.'

She said nothing, only let herself be pulled closer. He brushed her cheek lightly with a soft hand, his fingers trailing down her neck. She shivered as he bent his head to the exposed skin, his breath whispering over it. A fire ignited within her at the press of his lips to her collarbone and spread where his lips travelled up her neck. She tilted her head, his teeth grazing her ear, and a shiver of need shook her. A need she didn't quite understand.

Anabelle pressed a hand to his chest, and Néefar pulled back. She took in a shuddering breath.

'I've only been kissed once,' she whispered.

Néefar cupped her cheek gently, shaking his head. 'May I change that?'

She took a breath, held it, and then let it out with a nod.

He leaned forward and brushed his lips softly against hers.

Anabelle's breath caught in her throat, and heat coursed through her.

He pulled back, and the soft sound of protest from her lips

surprised him.

A low groan rumbled through Néefar, and he grabbed her waist and dragged her onto his lap, her legs straddling him as he pulled her flush against him.

She reached for him, burying her fingers into his hair just as he slanted his mouth over hers. She felt dizzy as heat pooled between her legs, and she pressed herself against the hardness that prodded against her. She didn't know what she was doing but let her instincts take over. Giving over to the tidal wave flooding her senses.

A low moan escaped her lips. Néefar dragged his tongue against her bottom lip, devouring the sound with a growl. She opened for him, and his tongue teased hers, her body arching into his. His fingers tangled in her hair, the other sliding down her waist to her bottom. Anabelle pulled at his shirt, her hands reaching for the soft hair that dusted his chest.

Néefar pulled back with a groan, grabbing her wandering hand, the other still on her bottom, fingers digging into the mounds.

'What kind of man would I be if I took advantage of you in a tree?'

Anabelle pulled in a shuddering breath, blinking slowly past the haze. She took in their surroundings, the night sky overhead, tree branches barely concealing them from view if anyone chose to look up. A breathless laugh escaped her.

'That wasn't like my first kiss,' she murmured, her eyes hooded, the dampness between her legs making her throb, and she shifted, trying to alleviate her discomfort.

Néefar chuckled darkly. 'I would hope not,' he said, licking his lips as he pressed a soft kiss to her mouth.

'Will you kiss me like that again?' She shifted her hips and smiled when he growled lowly, his hands digging into her bottom.

He pressed his brow to hers, taking a deep breath. 'I'd like to do so much more than kiss you… but yes, as many times as you wish.'

Her heart fluttered with anticipation, and she let out a breath. Raking her fingers through his hair, she wrapped her arms around his neck and dared herself to kiss him. Leaning forward, she kissed him slowly and smiled when she heard him groan, feeling him rock hard against her.

She pulled back with a soft smile and looked away with a faint blush.

Néefar brushed the pad of his thumb across her cheek, and his gaze was filled with a softness she had never seen before.

'Do you know that the Fae do not have husbands and wives but mates? They share a bond that surpasses all magic in this world.'

'That sounds beautiful,' she said.

He brushed his lips over hers in a quick peck and leaned his brow against hers. 'Aye, it is, but you, as a halfling, and myself, a once human turned Fae, I don't believe we are granted that.'

'I think I would like a traditional title like being a wife. If I ever got that chance. To be fated to someone and called Mate is lovely, but to be chosen by someone, to be called wife by *choice*, is beautiful.' Anabelle pulled back slightly. 'Can I ask why you kissed me?'

'You told me I had missed,' he said simply, his gaze moving from her mouth to her eyes. 'I couldn't let that happen again—I won't ever let that happen again,' he amended.

Anabelle couldn't help the laugh that escaped her lips. Leaning back against the towering branch where it curved up, she entwined her hands with his.

'What now?'

Néefar looked up at the sky. 'Now, we face the dawn.'

Millions of stars blanketed above them, the crescent moon glowing brightly as they fell into a comforting silence.

Gallian awoke to a heavy white mist. It rolled through the camp like a searching soul, and nothing stirred in the whispered dawn hours. With searching eyes, Gallian realised he was alone. The dwarf was not there, nor were the bodies of the satyr or centaur. He looked down at the iron

bands; they were also gone.

Gallian stood, looking around. Was he dreaming?

'This is neither dream nor reality, young Halfling.'

The voice came, and a tall, regal male figure emerged from the depths of the mist. He had dark auburn hair falling down his back, a golden crown adorning his brow, and a white robe embroidered with gold. His hazel eyes penetrated Gallian with an assessing stare.

'Who are you?'

'I am Gabriel, the eleventh Keeper.'

Gallian stumbled back. 'You're dead.'

'This is not your reality, Halfling. Nothing is dead in the world of the void.'

'What do you want?' he whispered, his skin clammy as the white mist whispered over his limbs. Even he knew to fear the dead.

Gabriel stepped forward, his hands clasped.

'I heard Anabelle's plea. Her light broke through the darkness and the demons that consumed you.' He tilted his head, considering Gallian. 'I sense there is a darkness in your heart, though not from your father.'

Gallian stiffened. 'I don't know what you speak of.'

Waving a dismissive hand, Gabriel stepped towards the white mist wall behind him. 'I have given you two paths to choose from. What your future holds depends on the path you walk. Choose wisely, Halfling.'

Gallian's eyes flew open, and the noise of the camp surrounded him, the stench of rot and blood filling his nose.

'Ye were dreamin' boy.'

He looked at the dwarf.

'Yes' was all he could manage.

'Tha' bastard is gathering his beasts. I've been wachin' 'im since dawn. They ready to march within the hour.'

Gallian looked at his father, dressed in black leather and wool. The scar on his face glinted with an oily sheen.

'When they leave, we will 'ave our chance at escape, boy. Tha' satyr has a small axe at his hip on his other side. Do ya see?'

Gallian forced himself to look away from his father to the stiff body beside him.

'It's too far to reach,' Gallian said. 'And I wouldn't help you escape, even if I could.'

'Look at ye, so pure and innocent.' Notile mocked.

Shame and irritation coloured his neck. 'No, I am not.'

The same black-bodied centaur that had dragged Gallian away trotted over to them. He raised his blade to the dwarf and brought it down against the iron chains.

Notile startled. 'Where ye takin' me?' he demanded as the centaur lifted him off the ground.

Balwin stepped around the centaur, smiling calmly. 'I'm taking you back to the Summer Keep, Dwarf.'

Notile's eyes widened, and he thrashed in the centaur's grip. 'Why are ye takin' me back there?'

'You are no use to me. I could drain you, feast on you, but I have something else in mind.'

The dwarf spat at the ground. 'Then le' me go! Don' send me back there!'

The Cerberus growled quietly behind Balwin at the raised tone, its three heads baring their teeth.

Balwin pretended to think for a moment, giddy with his response. 'I suppose I could be generous.' He waved his hand at the centaur, who released him.

Notile stood up, hesitant. He took a stumbling step back and then another.

'Dwarf, I do not have all day.'

He ran as fast as his short legs could carry his stocky frame.

Balwin laughed lowly as the dwarf disappeared into the treeline. 'Go, fetch your dinner.'

The Cerberus leapt forward, jaws snapping, snarls erupting as it chased down the dwarf. From afar, a cry preceded a sickening crunch.

'That was fun,' Balwin mused. 'Bring me back his head,' he said to the centaur.

The bitter cold whipped through the camp as Balwin turned to his army, taking Notile's head from the centaur. 'Come! Let us present our gift to the Summer Keep! Let us show them our kindness! If they reject us, may their blood be spilt upon the ground and let the earth weep red for the next thousand years!'

Balwin stood still in the chaos as the army poured into the

forest with a roar. His eyes found Gallian's, and he smiled as he bowed low to his son.

CHAPTER THIRTY-ONE

The silence was almost numbing as Anabelle turned her face up to the brittle branches. The bitterness of the forest beyond the veil wrapped around her, and she let out a long sigh.

Shadows and mist wafted through the treetops, frost snaking across the ground. Everything stood frozen in time, even as Anabelle touched the blackwood tree. A shudder went down her spine when the thrum of life she searched for was barely a whisper in the distance, an echo of what was left.

She wrapped the dark evergreen cloak around her and walked through the veil, her skin flushing from the heat.

As the dawn slowly brightened the sky, so did the Keep. Fires were lit, temporary hearths ignited, and the horses fed.

'Lass.'

Anabelle turned to the blacksmith. 'Yes, Da'arc?'

He cleared his throat. 'I have something for you.' He waved to his hut, branches draped in cured animal hides across from his smithy.

Ducking under the animal flap hanging from the entrance, Anabelle straightened, the ceiling brushing the top of her head. Da'arc's hut was a simple room with a bedroll in the corner and a weathered chest opposite it. Animal skins were strewn across the floor, softening the hard ground, and a cluster of half-melted candles cloistered together on a tray in the corner.

Da'arc bent over the weathered chest, rummaging through it and emerged with a bundle wrapped in cloth.

'This is for you,' he said.

Reaching out and carefully unfolding the cloth binding, she gasped as bright steel gleamed in the low candlelight.

'It's beautiful,' she said.

'Elvin armour, forged from the flame of the dragon's belly. It is fit for a queen.'

'This is too generous, Da'arc. I can't accept this.'

Da'arc shook his head. 'It was gifted to me many years ago when I was a much younger dwarf. I have never had use for it, and dwarven bodies are built for the mountains and the earth, stocky and strong. We have no use of Elvin armour. Please, Keeper? It would be my honour.'

With a trepidous hand, Anabelle took the bundle from Da'arc and looked down at the steel breastplate. Four trees in the full bloom of summer were carved in beautiful detail.

'May I?'

Hesitating, Anabelle nodded and knelt on the animal skins. She moved the sword on her hip and straightened her black tunic as the dwarf unstrapped the bindings holding the cuirass together.

The press of the metal against her tunic made her heart lurch, and tears pricked her eyes. The image of her mother sweeping into the room with her gown and securing the stays around her waist appeared in her mind.

'It's not that bad, love.'

With blurry eyes, she stared at the fur beneath her, her face pinched as she held back her tears. She raised her arms so Da'arc could tighten the straps, lacing the cuirass tight against her chest and back.

'None have yet to wear this. It is with honour that you are the first Keeper.' He turned back to the chest. 'One last thing: I crafted these for you last eve.' He unwrapped thick, smooth cuffs. 'While they lack the beauty of the High Fae, they are forged from dwarven iron. They will not fail you.'

He fastened them to her forearms, tightening the leather bands until they fit snugly to her wrists.

Anabelle stood, moved her arms, testing their weight, and smiled at the blacksmith. Leaning forward, she kissed his brow.

'I will wear them proudly. Thank you.'

The dwarf gave a gruff cough and shooed her. 'I have work to be done. Now go on with ye, Lass. Dawn approaches.'

Anabelle bowed her head and ducked outside to take in a shuddering breath.

'I see Da'arc has finally given you the armour.'

Anabelle's eyes snapped to Néefar, who casually sauntered toward her. She couldn't stop the faint blush that crept up her neck.

'You knew about this?'

He shrugged. 'Of course.'

She smiled faintly, looking back down at her armour.

'Do you like it?'

She smoothed her fingers over the polished steel cuirass and the iron cuffs. 'I love it.'

'I thought you might.'

Anabelle glanced around the camp. 'Have you seen Notile? I wanted to speak to him.'

'About what?' he asked as they began to walk. 'That dwarf hates you.'

'I just wished to reassure him. I want him to know his son's death wasn't for nothing.'

Néefar laid a hand on her arm, halting her. 'I'm sure, in time, he will come to know that.'

Anabelle didn't reply. Instead, she pulled him into a copse of trees, sheltering them from prying eyes.

'You're ready for war, I see,' she commented, noting the boiled leather of his armour.

'I can't let you get all the attention, little gipsy.'

She smiled slyly, raising her hands to his chest to trace the grooves of the leather. His bow and quiver were strapped across his back.

'What exactly are you wearing?' she mused.

Néefar's eyes darkened, his voice lowering as he stepped closer. 'Boar's hide.'

The air around them thickened, and the space separating them was only a hair's breadth.

'Will it keep you safe?'

Néefar shuddered as if he could feel her fingers through the leather. 'It should. Do you approve?'

She bit her lip. 'If you're alive in the end, then yes.'

His gaze went to her mouth. 'I shall come straight to you, little gipsy.'

'I demand that you let me check for injuries when all is done,' she whispered.

Néefar growled low, brushing his nose against hers.

'My body is yours,' he whispered back before slanting his mouth over hers.

Gallian sat alone in the camp, surrounded by death and decomposing flesh. His jaw worked as his thoughts reeled. His father's smug face flashed in his head, and he bit down the anger and loathing he felt bubble inside him.

His chains rattled, and the creeping mists and rolling fog made his skin crawl. With a hard yank, he tested his restraints, though it was pointless. It wasn't as if they'd somehow weakened anytime in the past day. His head fell back against the stone, and he closed his eyes in concentration, searching for the tether of magic. Only frayed remains were left, shrivelled and dead from the hungry feast his father's demons had ravaged. He bared his teeth angrily, yelling and jerking against the chains until his wrists bled.

A glint of light caught his eye, and he turned, seeing the small axe peeking from behind the furry hip of the dead satyr. Gallian lunged for it, his fingers barely brushing the fur that covered the satyr's legs before he was yanked back.

Swallowing, he reached out with his foot, hooking it around one of its legs. The satyr was a smaller male, its legs shorter and frozen in a curled position. The satyr's body slipped as he tried to angle it closer; he let out an irritated huff as the leg fell away. The satyr barely moved, its body swinging lightly on the chain.

Growling, Gallian reached for the leg again. His fingers brushed at the fur, and Gallian strained against the iron, his hand feeling like it would snap. His fingers grasped onto a chunk of fur and pulled. When it was close enough, he grabbed the hoof and counted to three. He closed his eyes as he pulled with all his power, every muscle screaming, until he heard the tearing of flesh, and the satyr's body slid across his lap.

His breath heaved as he reached for the axe and shoved the body off his lap. Composing himself, he swung the weapon overhead and struck the freezing iron. Chains rattled against his arms, and he struck again. The chain snapped in two, and his hands dropped free.

With a shaky cry of triumph and disbelief, he stood. Axe still in hand, Gallian sprinted after the army.

Balwin stood in the shadows, watching the clearing where the Summer Keep sat veiled. Black mist crawled along the forest floor, spreading through the tree line. Beasts emerged from the haze, demons rearing their heads as they eyed the empty field.

Balwin glanced at a creature he had claimed, an ugly sneer on his face when he saw white eyes staring into nothingness. He turned his sneer to the clearing. His eyes darkened to bottomless black pits, and his jaw opened to an unnatural length as a roar ripped through him.

'KEEPER!'

His voice carried through the clearing, echoing through the woods like a banshee's screech. His voice was not the only one that cried out. The beasts at his back roared in like terms. Their hooves were impatient as they awaited his command, shaking the ground like war drums.

When he saw Anabelle standing beside the whelp Gallian had mentioned occasionally, he gave his army its command.

'Let us begin,' he whispered.

With the head of the dwarf gripped tightly in his hand, he reared his arm back and let it fly.

Anabelle heard Balwin's voice echo through the Keep. His voice scratched at her skin, sending icy talons down her spine. Her eyes went wide with alarm, and she whipped around to Néefar.

The Keep paused as his voice rebounded through their camp again. Then, everything erupted into chaos as males and females began shouting orders, sprinting to their assigned posts.

Anabelle turned on her heels and ran, Néefar close behind, dashing around bodies as they flooded past her. Chest heaving, she skidded to a stop at the clearing. She peered into the dense forest, seeing nothing but shadows.

An object came flying from the depths of the trees, and Néefar stepped in front of Anabelle, eyeing it. With a thud, it landed, rolling to their feet, and she put a hand to her mouth in horror, nausea churning through her.

Notile's head stared, ashen, up to the sky.

As she stared at the head, white-hot anger washed through her. Slowly, her eyes lifted to the shadows moving like a wave through the trees, and she bared her teeth in a silent snarl.

Néefar raised the order to those who stood at their backs. 'To arms!'

A horn blasted through the Keep, and the cry went up. Balwin's army of beasts charged from the shadowy depths of the forest line.

Anabelle pulled her sword from its sheath. Néefar was a solid presence by her side, his bow and three arrows in hand as he notched the first. Savven, Lithônion, and Ezra stood at her other side, weapons drawn.

With one final glance over her shoulder to her mother's grave, she whispered her promise, 'I will not yield.'

Anabelle bellowed a war cry and charged forward, sword raised.

CHAPTER THIRTY-TWO

Tree branches whipped past Gallian. His legs burned, but he bit through the pain.

His foot caught the underside of a tree root, and he stumbled, the ground biting into his palms as his axe tumbled across the floor. Fatigue caused him to sway, and he braced a hand on the tree beside him.

Taking one uneven step and then another, Gallian pushed himself forward. The world tilted as he picked up his feet and ran, shaking his head as his eyes wavered.

The forest seemed to open to him; the trees parted, showing him the way. What was left of his Fae strength edged him on, and he flew past the blackwood trees.

Gallian skidded to a halt, breathing raged, eyes searching as the screech of iron meeting iron resounded through the air. The cries of many blanketed him, and he squeezed his eyes shut, hands over his ears as it pierced through his skull.

As the noise grew deafening, he forced his eyes open, looking for where it came from. He took a step back and another as he turned to run from the noise, but as he turned, the air shimmered, and the world before him melted away.

A wall of shadows and mist rose from one side of the forest, and on the other side, Anabelle had a small army at her back.

The world melted away again, the scene changing as it blurred around him.

He stood on the battleground now, between the two armies, between darkness and light. The noise and chaos all rushed to a stop, frozen in time. He looked up at the imposing wall of black mist and shadows, threatening to block the sun. Within its veil, demons and beasts bared their teeth.

With a shuddering breath, Gallian turned to Anabelle. Her eyes were narrowed, and her mouth opened in a cry. He walked over and stopped inches from her face, but she didn't see him. He reached out to touch her, to see if she was real, but something hot and bitter coursed through him. His fingers curled in on themselves, and he retracted his hand.

He looked at the males charging at her back. Swallowing the sneer the burning emotions brought, his brows lowering and mouth pressing into a tight line, he saw one with his eyes locked onto Anabelle.

'*Brother.*' His voice shuddered out of him.

Walking around Anabelle, he strode over to the male and glanced at him from head to boot. The male had an arrow drawn, brown hair pulled back into a knot, and blue eyes that mirrored the sky.

'Oh, how you've moved up in the world from your little corner of the woods,' he muttered to the shifter.

'The battle between light and dark, the shadowlands and the realm of the living, will be eternal.'

Gallian whirled, narrowing on Gabriel, who stood there with preternatural stillness.

'You did this?'

Gabriel tilted his head slightly. 'You would not have made it in time. It seems that your father's demons depleted much of your power.'

'My apologies. I'll try to be on time for the next battle,' he sneered.

Gabriel folded his hands and looked at him with a solemn expression. 'What do you see, Halfling?'

Gallian huffed out a short laugh. 'A war that will never end.'

Nodding, Gabriel looked at Anabelle. 'I see resilience.'

Gallian looked at the wall of shadows towering over them. 'I see death.'

Then, Gabriel looked at Gallian. 'I see guilt.'

'You see nothing!' Gallian spat.

'Is that so, Halfling?'

Gabriel walked calmly to the shadows, slicing a hand through it. He turned to Gallian, and within his hand was a piece of the shadows, thrumming above his palm with its own life force.

'This was the darkness inside of you.' He moulded it between his hands, blue flames playing through the shadows. 'Minuscule compared to what you see before you, but significant all the same.'

'That was not my doing,' Gallian said.

Gabriel stared at the darkness in his hands, the blue flames lighting the planes of his face.

'It was not *all* your doing,' he corrected. 'You blamed Anabelle more than your father.'

Gallian looked beyond the shadows and found his father standing beyond the treeline. Gallian felt a familiar pull, a tug that had pulled him to his father's side countless times, a blood tie. He looked back at Anabelle, and beyond that seething hatred was a drop of guilt. His body moved on its own, stepping away from both sides.

'I have resented her since the Choosing. All I wanted was my father!'

'You never had a father.'

The words landed like a blow. 'That's a lie!'

'Is it?'

Gallian stepped towards Anabelle, jabbing a finger in her frozen face. 'It is *her* fault!' Flames grew at his fingertip, his magic growing despite his body's fatigue. He reached a flaming hand to Anabelle's throat, and Gabriel gripped his wrist in an iron restraint.

'So, you have chosen your path.'

Gallian bared his teeth. 'I have chosen nothing!'

'Will you not find forgiveness in your heart?'

Gallian looked back at his father, then at Anabelle.

'This world has no place for you in it, Halfling.'

Ice shot down Gallian's spine. He swallowed the rock in his throat, his words barely a whisper, 'You cannot mean…This is the only world I've known!'

Gabriel snuffed the darkness, the blue flame winking out, and with it, his magic.

'For your cowardice, I have given you a life of mortality. You will live with mortal men and die with mortal men. You will choose the actions of your life based on your mortality. Your existence in this world, Halfling, is no more.'

Gallian staggered back in shock as the weight of Gabriel's words fell on his shoulders.

'Go now, flee this world, as you have fled them.'

Gallian took one fleeting glimpse at his father and Anabelle.

'Go, now.'

He stumbled, tripping over his feet as he ran, his body foreign to him with the new weight on his bones.

The noise of battle rushed back in. Gallian looked over his shoulder as Anabelle countered an attack, spinning away from the blow and disappearing into the tower of shadows that fell.

He fled the Black Forest without looking back.

CHAPTER THIRTY-THREE

Darkness fell over them, and the day turned to night. Anabelle threw her sword up, blocking a swing from a centaur with a shout. She couldn't see as the weight vanished and swiped blindly with her sword. Her blade sank into flesh, and a howl deafened her ears.

In the darkness, she could hear them all around her, their cries, the screams, the tearing of flesh from bone as they fell around her, but she couldn't see them. She couldn't see anything.

Her chest tightened, breathing ragged in her ears as she turned in every direction, searching for a light source. There was only darkness, and fear burned like acid through her.

'Anabelle!'

'Néefar!' she shouted, running towards the voice.

'Anabelle!'

She stopped. Néefar's voice came from the other direction, and she turned around, ears straining.

'Anabelle?'

Her heart stopped, blood turning to ice. Her mother's voice echoed from the shadows.

'*Ana-belle*,' her mother sang again.

'No,' she whispered. 'You're not real.'

The world quelled around her, the darkness a quiet abyss.

'I could make it real,' came Balwin's calm voice behind her.

Anabelle whirled, slicing her sword into nothing.

'Come out, you bastard,' she snapped.

Balwin laughed, echoing around her, and then talons sliced into her skin and caught her arms, hauling them up and away from her to hold her in place.

'You see,' Balwin whispered in her ear.

Anabelle jerked, snarling at his voice.

'I could end it right now. It would all be so easy. Day turns to night, and the Keeper dies. But I like to play with my food.'

'Apparently, Fae males don't have the balls to fight me face-to-face!' she retorted.

Balwin grabbed her jaw between cold fingers, his nails digging into her cheeks. She still couldn't see him, even as the decay of his breath brushed over her, and she winced at the smell.

'If it's a fight you want, a fight you will have.'

Her face jerked back as he released her, and the talons tightened their grip once more before vanishing.

The abyss opened up, and a tunnel of light pierced through. Anabelle stumbled forward as her vision returned, and a blood-soaked minotaur charged through the tunnel like a black storm, massive hooves carving into the earth. The shadows fell away just as the beast reared up its sword.

Anabelle raised her sword, catching its own blade against hers with a shriek of steel. And then claws dug into her hair and shoulders. The screech of a harpy sounded overhead as it pulled her off the ground.

She twisted her body, sword lashing at the demon, and then she fell, the ground rushing to meet her. She landed with a thud, stars erupting in her vision.

The earth quaked under her knees, and she lunged for her blade, rolling onto her back and stabbing upward.

Hot blood splayed across her face, followed by a heavy body. With a groan, she crawled from under the corpse and rolled to her feet as the shadows vanished and light glared.

She froze, staring at the Keep. She was alone in the clearing, with only the wall of shadows looming behind her.

Taking a deep breath, she rounded on the darkness, ice running through her veins, eyes turning gold as she tunnelled into her magic. Her power hummed violently within her, and her hands were coated in frost, white fire igniting down her blade.

'You want a fight!' she screamed wildly into the darkness. 'Then come and get me!'

Seconds stretched to minutes, and Anabelle looked down at the ground as the pebbles at her feet rattled. She shifted, readying her sword, staring at the mass that grew as it emerged from the shadows.

Anabelle swallowed, the shadows parting, and she craned her neck to look up at the three heads of the fifty-foot Cerberus.

'Shit.'

Néefar held an arrow at the ready, bowstring taut, feathers brushing the stubble at his cheek. He couldn't see anything. He could hear his own heartbeat resounding in his ears like an echo in the abyss.

'Néefar?'

He aimed at the voice, soft and deep and familiar.

'Néefar?'

The voice came again directly in front of him, and he stepped back, watching the shadows, though little came from it.

'My son? Néefar?'

A new voice this time, and Néefar's knees threatened to buckle. He knew that soft burr.

Lowering his bow, Néefar stepped into the darkness. A dim grey light opened in the abyss. Two figures stepped into the light, and his heart stopped.

His mother's warm, round face smiled at him with rosy cheeks. Her light brown hair was a tousled mess of wild curls.

She smiled at him softly, turning bright hazel eyes to his father, and Néefar finally turned to look at the man he mirrored.

Bright blue eyes stared back at him, identical to his own. His full mouth turned into an easy smile that sat a little crooked with a strong jaw and high cheekbones mapping the plains of his father's face.

Where his mother was small and soft-natured, his father was solid and rugged, standing a head above her with an easy-going stance.

They looked exactly as he remembered them. Néefar's hands shook. Everything he was as a man of the mortal world and as a male of the world of Fae was because of them.

'My boy,' his father said, opening his arms to him.

'Néefar,' his mother said softly.

He dropped the bow and threw himself into their embrace with a wretched sob.

'Shh, it's all right,' cooed his mother, stroking his head softly.

'We've missed you,' said his father.

Hot tears ran down his cheeks, and Néefar only gripped them tighter. Committing his father's earthy scent of pine and tobacco and his mother's lavender and spice to memory.

'I'm so sorry,' he ground out, his heart racing as he held on. He was terrified they would disappear. 'I'm so sorry.'

He was no longer a shifter, or a man, or male. He was only a boy of ten, and he felt himself break.

The shadows swirled around them, a black chasm with no end. The air grew cold, and Néefar opened his eyes, lifting his tear-stained face, breath clouding. The skin on his neck prickled in awareness. His parent's hands stopped their soothing motions, their bodies going rigid.

As the void grew cold, fire consumed his parents, and their skin turned scolding. Néefar tore himself away. Their blank eyes stared into the chasm, skin bubbling and melting. Limbs broken, his father's head smashed in, and his neck snapped. His mother's throat was carved out, her mouth opened in a silent scream, her wrists bound.

Horror struck Néefar like a sword to the back. He drew in a strangled breath, his eyes widening as their unseeing gazes snapped to him.

His father tried to speak, but it came out in a garble.

'No,' Néefar wailed softly, eyes squeezing shut briefly.

His mother tried to speak, but blood spewed from her neck, and Néefar winced as it splattered across his face.

The darkness became a frozen void, but his parents' skin glimmered like a fire blazed around them.

Néefar ran for his bow, skidding to a halt as his parents' ravaged bodies appeared in front of him. He was surrounded, their faces duplicating until he saw nothing, felt nothing, but blood, fire, and ice.

He dropped to his knees, clutching his hair with both hands, eyes screwed tight.

'My boy!'

Their voices whirled around and around him, a windstorm of his name. There was no end to it, and he yelled until he couldn't anymore.

Ezra stared into the darkness, dark eyes assessing as his senses picked through the air. The boiled leather of his armour was nothing against the cold.

Lilacs and the smell of the sea drifted through the bitter air. Ezra paused, weapons drooping in his hands. He knew that smell.

The world around him opened up, and he stood on a cliff. Below him, a raging black sea, with waves crashing against the stone. His hair blew wildly around him as he stared at the pale face and wide sky-blue eyes of the female before him.

'Levina,' he whispered.

Levina cocked her head, a smile tilting up pretty, rosebud lips, dark golden hair curling in long soft waves down her back, the arch of her ears peeking through their folds.

'Ezra,' she said gently, joining him at the cliff's edge.

He slid his blades into their sheaths, reaching with a tentative hand to stroke one silk cheek. She closed her eyes, leaning her head into his palm.

'Why are you here, Levina? You can't be real?' he asked, his once steady breathing straining in his chest as he stared down at the female who captured his most primal and innate attention.

A voice in the back of his mind warred with his conscious thoughts, but he trampled down the emotions that came with the truth.

Levina lifted a lily-white hand to his chest, drawing her nails lightly down the sliver of his exposed skin.

'Do you trust me?' she asked, lashes fluttering closed as Ezra slid a hand around her waist and pulled her flush against his body.

Need washed through him, and he would do anything she asked at that moment.

He nodded. 'Yes,' he said.

She rose on her toes, lips grazing his ear as she whispered, 'Then jump.'

It was like water had doused him. He blinked, his subconscious voice rearing again, and he stepped back.

'What?' he questioned.

Levina's soft smile didn't waver as she reached for him again, taking his hand and pulling him to the edge.

'I want you to jump.'

Ezra looked down at the black water smashing against the cliffside, their murky seas turning to a shadowy abyss, their misty tendrils crawling up the shole. 'I can't,' he whispered.

Something dark flashed across her face. It was so brief that he nearly missed it, but it caused him to step back from the edge.

Levina wetted her lips, mouth parting as she reached for the white satin ribbon that held together the bodice of her pale pink gown. It fell off her shoulders. She pushed the flowing sleeves off, and the dress fell to her feet.

She stood naked before him, her pink nipples pebbled in the sea breeze, breasts supple as they sat waiting for his touch. The dip of her waist met the curve of soft hips, the apex of her thighs begging for his touch. Ezra swallowed, every part of him going rigid.

Levina floated towards him, pressing her naked body to him and grinding herself softly onto the very hard, very sensitive part of him that strained against his leathers.

'We choose you, Ezra,' she said, her voice breathy.

He growled low, his hands going to her waist, and she dropped her head back, exposing her neck to him.

Every part of him wanted to devour her neck, bite into her soft flesh, and mark her as his. The urge to rip his clothes off and take her on the grassy ledge was almost overwhelming. Still, the part of him whispering the painful truth was louder than his primal urges.

He forced her back, flinching as she laughed, her smile turning into a smirk, eyes growing cold. It was the same expression she had worn when she rejected him.

'Here I come offering myself to you, and *you* reject me?' she scoffed.

Ezra took in a steadying breath.

'*Who are you?*' he asked in a low voice, the language of his people slipping over his tongue, demanding the truth.

Levina's gaze grew pointed. The mask of beauty melted away as the creature's skin turned black. Its eyes went empty, and black, pointed teeth gleamed back at him.

A cackle rippled through it, and it stepped backwards, standing on the ledge.

'You will fall, or you will jump,' it said with a rasping voice. 'It's coming, it's *co-ming,* and you will bring it,' it cackled manically.

The whites of its eyes shone as they rolled back, and it fell over the cliffside.

Ezra ran to the edge, but all he saw was a sea of shadows.

CHAPTER THIRTY-FOUR

The ground met her, making her bones cry out, as three snapping maws lunged for her head.

Rolling out of the fall, Anabelle sprinted through the clearing, putting distance between her and the Cerberus.

Dodging to the right as the head on her left snapped through the air, fangs glinting in the dim sunlight, black tar dripping from the ends. Her breath left her lungs as its claws made contact with her chest, and her body rocketed from the ground. Jaws plucked her from the air, and she screamed as they bit down. The head on the right shook her like a leaf, its fang sinking into the flesh of her shoulder.

Searing pain lanced through her. Anabelle saw white as fire raced down her arm. Her armour concaved as they bit down. Her arms spasmed, and the sword flew out of her hand.

The magic in her body hummed, and she tunnelled it through the pain right into the middle head that snapped at her legs. A deafening roar blasted her eardrum, and the jaws loosened. Anabelle fell, slamming hard into the ground, something snapping in her chest.

A strangled gasp left her lips even as she scrambled for her sword and staggered to her feet. She wiped the back of her hand across her mouth, staining her skin red, and glared at the three heads.

White fire encased the blade in her hands again. Her heartbeat calmed as she let her magic consume her, giving away some of her control.

Ice filled every muscle, tendon, tissue, and fibre that made her. Frost crept up her skin as her bright gold eyes narrowed at the beast, and she sprinted forward, dodging around the heads as they snapped at her and latching her hand on the middle head's jowls. Swinging herself onto its neck, she held on tight as the Cerberus began to buck, trying to throw her off. She wrapped her legs tight around the neck of the middle head, arced her sword up, and speared it into the back of its skull.

A howling scream that didn't belong to their world pierced the Keep before a sudden silence fell.

The Cerberus stumbled to the ground beneath her, sliding over the dirt, and she held on tight to her sword, still buried in its skull, until the beast died. Anabelle yanked the blade free, its white fire spreading quickly across black fur in a gleaming cover of hoarfrost. Black eyes turned white, and the watchdog of the netherworld turned into ice. It became a white and blue statue glimmering in the sunlight with a wall of shadows reflecting against its surface.

With shaking muscles, Anabelle released a ragged breath. Pain speared her side, and the magic faded just enough for her to regain control.

The jump from the Cerberus was far enough that the impact shuddered through her, jarring whatever bones had broken in her. Straightening, teeth gritted against the pain, she unlatched her armour. The indented metal stabbed into her wounds, and her skin pulsed. A sigh of relief escaped when the armour fell away.

A loud crack split the air. Anabelle turned. The Cerberus splintered, and the ice spider-webbed, falling apart into large shards. Half of a head stared at her from where it lay.

Anabelle looked down at her chest, blood darkening the black wool. The tears along her bicep had already begun to heal, but the wound at her shoulder still bled freely. Black tar from the Cerberus's fangs oozed from the site. She could feel the strain of her magic, fighting against the poison, fingers twitching against the fire that laced through her.

Turning her attention to the shadows, she stretched her arms wide. 'I thought you wanted a fight!' she yelled.

A broken cry echoed from the shadows. Anabelle lowered her arms, nostrils flaring, eyes watching the darkness.

Another cry, and this time familiar.

Anabelle sprinted for the wall of shadows. Forcing her legs to work and tugging on the leash that tethered her to the magic in her blood. She became a moving wall of ice as she dove into the darkness.

Screams and tormented wails tore through her shields, claws digging into every part of her. They pulled and pried, ripping flesh and ice. She screamed, her spine arching as talons ripped down her back.

Her head jerked back as something grabbed her hair and pulled; her magic rippled in anger. Molten gold shone through the darkness, blue light erupting around her in a pulsating wave, and her body turned from woman to Fae to Winter incarnate.

Light pierced the shadows like a thousand arrows, and she was consumed with fire and ice. And for the first time in her life, Anabelle felt complete. Her magic singing a chorus of power through her body. Sunlight pooled around her as shadows vanished, torn away with screams and grasping hands.

Gentle hands touched her back, and she yelped, jerking away, only to raise her gaze and find Ezra. His dark eyes were wary, but his grip was firm, holding her upright.

Swallowing hard, she searched the field. Bodies upon bodies lay scattered, piled on top of one another. The survivors stood still, bloodied, their weapons covered in black and red that dripped from their edges.

Her eyes landed on Néefar, who lay bowed over his knees. She called his name and ran to him, stepping over the fallen.

Néefar turned at her voice, and she paused. His sun-browned skin was pale, sweat dotting his brow. His usually laughing eyes stared back at her, wide and terror-filled, as he sucked in a breath like it hurt to breathe.

She took cautious steps up to him, watching him retrieve his bow, his quiver still strapped across his back.

His blue eyes met hers, and he smiled at her grimly.

'I'm all right,' he said in a hoarse voice.

She lifted her palm to his cheek, and he turned his face into it, closing his eyes. Something caught her eye, and she brushed his cheek before stepping around him, her tenderness replaced by red-hot anger.

The forest darkened as shadows lurked through their tangle of branches.

'Stop hiding, you bastard!' she yelled at the shadows.

Balwin's scarred face rippled through the darkness and stepped into the light, just at the forest edge.

Her vision narrowed on the scarred male. Her body vibrated with power, begging for release. She ran a mental hand down the tether of her magic, and it seemed to purr, relaxing just enough for her to look back at Néefar.

Despite the haggard wear on his face, he flashed her a cheeky grin. He pulled out two arrows and nocked the first one, head nodding stiffly, waiting.

Her gaze went to Savven. Her cousin smiled grimly at her before she looked at the rest of the Keep. They all faced the forest, weapons and magic at the ready, their dead littered around them.

Stabbing her blade into the earth, frost shooting across the ground around it, she turned to Balwin.

'You came for me,' she spat, arms spread wide. 'Here I am, stop the games, Balwin!'

His hands rose from his side, the shadows rising with him, and he smiled.

Realisation hit Anabelle as she stared at the rising darkness. No matter how much she fought, no matter how much blood was spilt, no matter the light that pierced his shadows, the darkness would always come. As long as Balwin lived, the darkness would live.

Demons from the nether region crawled from the abyss, beasts and creatures of the living sprinkled through their mass of twisted black bodies. With a cascading wave, the demons let loose a soul-splitting scream, tearing through earth and bodies as they poured back into the clearing.

Though his army was a blur around them, Anabelle focused on Balwin as he bowed mockingly to her.

'Come and get me.' His voice brushed against her ear as he vanished into a black mist.

Anabelle charged into the forest, freeing her magic's tether. The power within her took control.

Her movements were fluid, and her body moved with ease. The noise from the Keep quieted the further she went.

A poised javelin of darkness came spearing toward her without warning, and gold and blue light met darkness, colliding like an eruption of energy. Ice glittered in the air as it fell. Anabelle hurtled through the air as power rippled across the ground, twisting her body before she landed on her feet.

Balwin's laugh reverberated through the trees. Behind him, a growl issued, and two black hellhounds stepped from the darkness. Their glowing red eyes were filled with bloodlust, hackles raised, teeth bared in a snarl, and claws gouged into the ground.

Something inside her pressed against her bones. A part of her opened its eyes for the first time, her magic shaping into something more, asking for release.

The hellhounds lunged. Anabelle met them mid-air, ice rocking through her and exploding between them as she grabbed at a snapping maw, the other flying back. Teeth sunk into her thigh, tearing it open, claws tearing at the leather as the other lunged back at her. Her skin burned, fingers digging into the muzzle that snapped a breadth from her face.

A frozen tidal wave of power exploded from her, and a white blur tore through the hounds. A massive snow leopard ripped through the hounds, black blood dripping from its maw. The hound beneath it dropped in a dead heap, and silver eyes honed in on the hound retreating into the forest. The snow leopard's only warning was a quiet hiss, crouching low before it flew through the air, jaw snapping around the hound's throat. Its yelp was quickly silenced, the leopard pinning it and tearing its neck open.

'Anabelle!'

She jerked her head towards her name. Her mother stood in the forest, a hand on her stomach, blood seeping between her fingers. Black marks were tattooed across her face, and blood flowed past her lips.

Rage replaced the blood in her veins, and Anabelle screamed.

The distraction was enough, and Anabelle whirled on Balwin, who had a spear of darkness twisting through the air like a javelin.

Ezra's bloodied face filled her vision suddenly, throwing his body across hers. He shielded her as shadows pierced through his heart. His body jerked, arching through the pain, mouth gaping, eyes widening.

'Forgive me,' his voice guttural.

'Ezra!' she screamed, but his eyes rolled back before he hit the ground.

Her magic erupted. Blinding light slammed into Balwin, sending him flying.

Anabelle sprinted into the forest, the snow leopard morphing into the spear of ice and fire aimed at his heart.

Balwin rolled quickly, the tree behind him splintering.

As the shadows grew behind Balwin, he chuckled lowly and got to his feet. 'Maybe I misjudged you? Maybe you and I are more alike than I realised.'

Her nostrils flared at his word. 'We are nothing alike, Balwin,' she spat.

'We both want the same thing,' he said coolly, raising his brow as he looked her over.

Her spine shivered with disgust, and her eyes flickered with apprehension. 'It's not what we want. It's how we want it. That is what separates us.'

Her only warning was the shift in his eyes, and Anabelle leapt to the side as a sudden explosion ripped through the ground. Snow, ice, and earth splintered. She found her footing, and light met dark, exploding between them.

Spindle fingers raked into her hair and yanked her head back. She cried out, and Balwin slammed her head into the tree in front of her. The trunk cracked at impact, and Anabelle's head rung violently.

His claws dug into her arm as he pinned it behind her back, the other nearly tearing her hair free from her scalp.

'What separates us,' he whispered roughly, jerking her head back against his lips, 'is your morality.'

Her neck strained painfully, her vision spotting, and her hair tearing free.

'I shed mine, and you cling to yours, and look who is the better for it.'

His fingers painfully grasped her chin, forcing her to look into the shadows.

'Look what my pet found. You seem to have lost it,' Balwin hissed and whipped her around, his grip on her neck tightening when she gasped.

He tossed her to the ground. Her hands caught her fall, and Anabelle righted herself, raising her eyes to watch the shadows as they parted.

Néefar was pinned against a tree, teeth bared in a snarl. A female dressed in a sheer, pale blue gown trailed a finger down his neck, a look of pure hunger in her eyes.

Néefar jerked his head toward her, struggling against invisible restraints. 'I'm sorry! We followed you into the forest but got lost in the shadows.'

She shook her head, tearing her gaze to Balwin. 'Let him go!'

Balwin looked at her like she was a bug at his feet. 'I thought I told you that if you're going to beg, to get on your knees.'

'I will never get on my knees for you,' she snarled, spitting blood at his feet.

With a roll of his eyes, he waved an idle hand at the female. 'Mara.'

The name was like a command, and the female lowered her

mouth to Néefar's, pinning him in place.

'Mara is a succubus. Interesting creatures,' Balwin commented mildly. 'They feed on souls, tempting their prey with pleasure before ripping them from their bodies.'

Slanting her lips over Néefar's, Mara pressed her supple body into his. She moaned into the kiss, her hands travelling down his body and cupping him through his pants. Néefar jerked, fighting against her, but it was no use. His eyes met Anabelle's as they dimmed, his brown skin paling, the flesh around his mouth slowly turning blue.

Her magic wove through her broken bones, tightening her screaming muscles and binding the blood that poured out of her. Anabelle bit down, muffling her cry as she forced her legs to move, even when she felt the skin of her thigh tear.

The air around her froze, and Balwin's hand whipped towards her, meeting a barrier of ice as she took three bounding strides and ripped the demon away.

She grabbed Mara by her hair and jerked her head back.

'He doesn't belong to you,' Anabelle snapped.

A blade of ice stabbed through her chest, and the succubus screeched. Light cut through her, and she exploded into mist.

Néefar crashed to her feet, his bindings vanishing. Blank eyes stared at a void world, hair beginning to grey as his life dwindled into nothing.

'No,' she breathed, dropping to her knees, the shield of ice encircling them both.

Grabbing Néefar's limp body, she pulled him into her arms. She leaned her forehead against his; his skin was cool and damp.

'Néefar,' she whispered, hot tears running down her cheeks.

'His soul is slipping away,' Balwin said, pacing along the wall of ice like a hound at the end of its tether. 'He is falling into the void, and soon, he will die.'

Something inside Anabelle snapped. Her anger, pain, and sorrow vanished, replaced by sheer, unrelenting power.

'They will all die, and soon, you will have nothing—'

A numbing calm catapulted through her mind, and she closed her eyes, taking in a steadying breath.

'—Just as I have nothing.'

She slammed her hand down, the frozen ground cracking under the force. 'Enough!'

A wave of blinding light burst from her, bathing the forest.

A hush overcame the forest, and Anabelle gently lowered Néefar to the ground, brushing a strand of grey hair from his face. She stood and turned to Balwin, gold eyes glowing in shadows that grew around her like a cage, her shield of ice melting away.

'You have nothing,' she said quietly, 'because you destroy everything you touch.'

Balwin's face tightened. 'Are you finally ready to fight me, Keeper?'

She took a single step forward. 'I think you should ask yourself that. Are you ready to fight me?'

Her voice was inquiring, but she stared at him like a predator eyeing prey.

Balwin's palms rose, and the shadows at his feet expanded into a wall. 'You think to challenge me, Keeper? I am the darkness, and you will bow before the day's end!'

The wall of shadows flew like pointed daggers, and she disappeared into its horde.

CHAPTER THIRTY-FIVE

She was consumed by the darkness. The wind howled around her, a storm of death at Balwin's hands, but it all fell on deaf ears.

Anabelle looked down at her feet, seeing the ground faintly. A minuscule patch of snow lay at the toe of her boot, and she kneeled. Rubbing the frozen kernels between her fingers, she watched it melt.

'Be the light, Anabelle.'

Her magic purred softly at Winter's long-forgotten whispered words that echoed through her, and the silver eyes of the snow leopard stared through the shadows.

Anabelle extended her palm, and the snow leopard pressed its nose to it, those calculating feline eyes never leaving hers.

Hoarfrost shot up her arm as the snow leopard disappeared, and a new pain lanced through her, her nails becoming claws and canines lengthening to sharp points.

She rose slowly, her body becoming living ice, her skin tattooed in crystals that crawled up the side of her face and down her fingertips in glimmering blue and white.

She wasn't human, and she wasn't Fae. She was the Keeper, and Balwin could never take that from her.

Her skin glowed from the inside out, the darkness parting around her as she walked through the abyss.

Balwin's face sapped of colour as he realised what she had become, and the shadows fell around her. Her fingers wrenched around his neck before words could leave his lips, and she slammed him into the tree behind him.

Leaning in close, her canines scraped against his scarred flesh. She could smell the sour tang of fear rolling off of him.

'I told you,' she whispered darkly. 'I will never bow before you.' Anabelle drew her hand back, nails glinting dangerously. 'I will never bow before anyone.' With that, she buried her clawed hand into his chest.

He screamed, even as black blood gurgled out of his throat. White cracks of light broke across his skin, his eyes bulging in their sockets as the light seared him. Her claws shattered his ribcage, and Balwin's jaw slackened.

His heart pulsed in her hand, and she tore it from his chest. A scream died on his lips, and he choked on the sound, dragging a stunned gaze to her, blood slowly trickling from his nose and down his jaw.

Her nails dug into the organ as it pulsed, blood dripping between her fingers and down her tattooed skin. Slowly, the blood froze, and Balwin's heart stilled, turning to ice.

She watched him with a cold gaze, bringing his heart to his still-seeing eyes, and crushed it in her grasp.

His body crumpled at her feet.

Staring down at the male who once made up her nightmares, she felt her anger melt away under the ice. A violent tremor went through her.

She turned her back on him, the remnants of his heart dusting the ground.

A small, barely heard moan came from Néefar. Anabelle ran to him, dropping to her knees. Her hands feathered over his body, feeling the cold seeping from his skin through his clothes, his face pallid.

'You can't die,' she breathed, clutching his hand, pressing her thumb to the lifeline on his palm. 'It's not your time.'

She pressed a kiss to his brow. A whisper of heat, of life, glimmered through her. Warm and bright like fire, it did not melt the ice within her but melded it.

That warmth spread through her. Icy tendrils webbed across every inch of her skin with golden veins. Anabelle grabbed that small kernel of fire within her, the part of her that raged with energy. Drawing back her hand, the small bead of life glowed brightly in her palm, and she gently slipped it between his parted lips, nudging his chin to close his mouth.

She watched him, holding her breath. Moments passed like hours, his skin still ashen and eyes void. Anabelle held him tighter and tighter, curling over him, whispering, 'Please, please, please.'

Her nails and canines retracted, the tattoos of ice sinking into her flesh, and she was once again just Anabelle, begging to not be left alone.

'Little gipsy.'

The words were strangled, but Anabelle's heart leapt at them as she tore away from his chest. The brightest blue shone back at her, that familiar teasing glimmer sparking in them. Néefar gaze softened, thumb brushing at her tears. With a sob, she flung her arms around him.

He chuckled weakly, an arm banding around her, using the other to help him sit up.

'You're alive,' she breathed.

Néefar took in a breath, feeling the expanse of his lungs, the sensation oddly comforting.

'I'm hard to kill.'

She laughed despite it all. His grin faded, really looking at her for the first time, the blood staining her black tunic and the shredded pants clinging to her legs.

She saw the shadows creep into his face and laid a firm hand on his chest.

'I'm alright,' she said.

Néefar's eyes strayed past her shoulder to the black, scarred heap.

'Are you sure?'

'Unless he intends to rise from the dead, we're safe.'

Nodding, he winced, his limbs stiff, and she helped him to his feet. As he let her drape his arm over her shoulders, he couldn't resist feathering a kiss to her crown.

The silence in the forest was all-consuming, and Anabelle turned in the direction of the Keep.

By the time they left the treeline, she hadn't seen any sign of Ezra. Worry gnawed through her. The ground was littered with bodies. Blood soaked the earth, bodies strewn as far as she could see, and eyes stared at Anabelle as she walked through them.

Her hands shook, and she balled them at her sides, jaw working as she tried not to bow under the weight of their gazes.

Survivors gathered in small groups throughout the field, subdued and quiet. Balwin's surviving army was mixed with her own. His veil lifted from them, allowing shock and horror to take over.

'Nothing good came of this,' she whispered, watching as those around her lifted shaking hands, staring at the blood that painted them.

Savven's princely face was smeared in black and red blood, his eyes tired but alert as he approached her. His fitted black tunic was torn at the shoulder, but his skin was untouched. 'It's done?'

Anabelle nodded silently.

Savven blinked, looking at the forest behind her. 'I've started Lithônion on triaging the dead from the wounded.'

Anabelle glanced at Lithônion, his honey-coloured hair dull, and caked in blood. Despite the grime drying on his skin, he offered a soft smile to a dwarf.

'Where am I?' asked a dwarf, blinking slowly as if seeing the daylight for the first time.

Pity squeezed her heart. 'You're in the Summer Keep,' Anabelle said as softly as she could manage.

His brow wrinkled. 'Why?'

Autumn stepped up to the dwarf, resting a hand on his shoulder. His clothing was immaculate, and some part of her burned bitterly. She forced in a breath, burying the spiralling emotion. Holding out a hand, Anabelle gestured to Autumn.

'You'll find your questions better answered by the Spirits.'

The dwarf turned around, and Autumn glanced at her, bowing his head, respect glinting momentarily.

'Why am I here?' the dwarf asked again.

Anabelle walked away without waiting for Autumn's answer, Savven and Néefar at her side.

Anabelle spotted Ezra watching everyone from the treeline with guarded eyes. Her heart leapt, and she ran for him, relief coursing through her.

'Ezra!' she yelled, throwing her arms around the male.

He lifted a hand, placing it on her back without moving.

'What you did for me, I owe you my life. I thought you were dead!'

Dark eyes slid slowly to her as she stepped back, his face blank.

'Are you well, Ezra?' she asked, her hands grasping his.

His skin was cool and dry, his fingers stiff and unbending.

He barely brushed a faint smile on the corners of his mouth. 'I'm well, Keeper. Go. Many have questions that must be answered.'

'But—'

He cut her a hard stare.

Her mouth shut, but she nodded softly.

A pit formed in her stomach, her teeth gnawing at her lip as she walked away to rejoin Néefar and Savven.

'You looked troubled,' Néefar said.

'I am…' Anabelle looked up at him and laughed.

Savven watched her with amusement, taking that as his cue to leave.

Néefar stepped closer once they were alone. 'What's so funny?'

She paused, her fingers covering her mouth in amusement. 'Well, your hair is a lovely shade of white. I nearly forgot.'

Néefar froze, looking down at a strand of his hair that had come loose from its knot. He appeared to search for words, opening and closing his mouth, before finally asking, 'How does it look?'

Anabelle tapped her chin, hiding her smile. 'Well, your brows are still dark,' she remarked.

He quirked one of those dark brows. 'Yes, but?'

Anabelle's lips twitched into a smirk.

'You look cute. I think you could be half troll?' she teased, remembering his jest about her hair.

His brows rose. 'Really? That good? Well, then.'

Anabelle saw Winter, whose pale green eyes watched her from the edge of the clearing beneath a towering tree.

Néefar followed her gaze. 'Go, I'll return to help with the wounded and dead.'

Anabelle felt the soft breeze of summer brush against her as she passed through the remnants of the veil. The breeze warmed her numb skin, and she shivered.

Winter stood in a soft wintergreen gown, skin glimmering like snow in the sunlight. Not a drop of blood or dirt on her. Anabelle felt that bitterness corkscrew through her, and it must have shown on her face as Winter said, 'I understand why it might be upsetting.'

Looking down at her own clothes, the blood making her skin sticky and itchy as it dried, she only sighed, teeth clenched.

'You didn't need us, Anabelle,' Winter said. 'You never needed us. We were only a comfort to you.'

'The price was great, though. Many died for this, and for what?' she asked bitterly.

'Because if they hadn't, then thousands more would have.' Winter gently laid a hand on a blood-soaked arm. 'Few must fall for many to live.'

Shaking her head, Anabelle walked away from the Spirit. She ran a trembling hand through her hair, a harsh breath escaping her nose. Her muscles ached, but she could feel her magic knitting muscle and bone back together, albeit slowly.

There was nothing left in her to give, and her body healed slowly, a small trickle of blood still soaking where the Cerberus had bitten.

'You should let me heal your wound.'

Winter's words were quiet, but they stilled Anabelle all the same. Her shoulders sagged, and she shook her head.

'No,' she said. 'I want it to scar, so I'm forced to remember.'

The Spirit looked at the wound, eyeing the black tar lingering around the edge of the bite.

'It'll fade,' Anabelle commented, seeing her gaze. 'I just need to sleep to regain enough energy to heal.'

Winter nodded. 'As you wish.'

'I wish my mother were here,' she said, glancing over at the rose-covered grave.

Winter looked at the grave, walking beside Anabelle and standing quietly as she knelt on the ground.

Anabelle ran her hand over the silky petals. She brought her fingers to her lips, kissing them softly and laying them on the floral grave.

'I will see you one day.'

She stood and looked at Winter. 'I have questions.'

Winter bowed her head. 'I have answers.'

Anabelle walked through the charred remains of their camp, past fires smouldering on embers and ash. The sun waned, and the hours dwindled into the early evening. Time passed quickly, but at the same time, it felt prolonged. She fixated on the ruby-red embers in a fire pit, fingers twiddling idly.

'Is our magic alive?'

Winter halted, mouth opening and closing before she finally nodded once. 'Yes.'

Silver eyes pierced her memory. 'Explain it to me.'

'Our magic is as alive as we are. Energy and essence become one. Who we are and what it is merged to create a living thing like an animal that can't be tamed but can be trusted.'

'Can that magic take form?'

'Yes.'

Anabelle met Winter's stare.

'Your magic is so much more than just Fae, Anabelle. Our magic is rooted in our world, in our creation, and some have the ability to connect with it in ways most cannot. As keeper, the tether to your power is more substantial than most.' Winter grabbed her hand between them. 'The bond between you and I is one that no one knows. Your magic is rooted within mine. That kind of power, Anabelle, does not just stay stagnant.'

'I saw it,' she said softly. 'It was a snow leopard. I had only read about them, but then it was there…and it saved me.'

Silver eyes burned into her memory, and despite her exhaustion, she felt the soft purr of her magic brush across her mind.

'Then know that is a blessing even the gods can't control.'

Anabelle pursed her lips. With a single nod, she walked away.

She only wanted to take a hot bath and crawl into her bed, but neither would happen anytime soon.

Eyeing the masses piled atop each other, her boots sloshed in blood and mud. Savven caught her eye, and she rolled up the tattered remains of her sleeves.

CHAPTER THIRTY-SIX

Anabelle inhaled the crisp scent of winter, turning her face to the snow-laden branches, the hood of her green velvet cloak falling back as she crept through the forest. Several feet of fresh snow had fallen in the last week, creating long translucent icicles hanging from overhead branches. Meanwhile, tiny leaf buds layered with frost sat poised, waiting for spring.

The forest was filled with light, and she could feel the world breathe beneath her palms for the first time since she arrived. Those golden veins of power thrumming through their world vibrated with life.

Warm hands wrapped around her waist, pulling her flush against a wall of muscle. The familiar dark musk filled her senses, and she relaxed into the hold.

Néefar's lips found the sensitive spot behind her ear. Anabelle let her head fall against his shoulders, a breathy sigh escaping.

'You shouldn't be out here alone, Keeper,' he murmured into her neck, hot breath fanning her chilled skin.

'I'm not alone now,' she breathed.

Néefar spun her, walking her back until she was pressed between him and a tree.

'There are beasts in these woods,' he whispered.

'You're the only beast I see,' she said, running her fingers through his silver hair.

His teeth nipped lightly at the underside of her wrists, his eyes darkening as he pulled away slightly.

'You're entirely too distracting, little gipsy.'

'I might argue you're the distraction,' she retorted, smoothing a hand down the front of her skirt as he stepped back. He wore his usual all-black, brown leather cuffs banded around his forearms.

Néefar winked, laughing when she frowned.

Her dark blue wool gown constricted around her as she took a deep breath, watching the expanse of snow-laden forest around them.

'What weighs on your mind?'

She glanced at Néefar before turning back to the forest, saying, 'So much has happened in so little time. I felt suffocated in my old life; it wasn't awful, but the constraints of society were overwhelming. I was sheltered away from the world of magic... and the world of men. Though this new life has given me so much, it has also taken everything I hold dear.'

After the battle had cleared and the dead buried or burned by their kin, Anabelle had stood there alone amongst the sopping grounds. Red still staining her skin, and her body wrecked as it slowly healed.

It was over.

Balwin wasn't coming back.

So what did she have left?

She had stood there until her legs couldn't keep her upright any longer, trying to make sense of all the pieces that remained of her. And when night finally fell, and she sat there kneeling on the ground, Savven, Lithônion, and Néefar came to her side and walked her back to the Keep.

She wished she had more: more time, more words spoken, more moments to cherish, more of everything. But she didn't—not with her mother or Pepper, and she didn't know Savven or her aunt well enough to ask for comfort.

So, she stood alone, hoping that as time went on, her wounds would heal, she'd come to love those around her, and the void would learn not to be so vast.

Blinking past her tears, she turned a small smile up to Néefar.

'I almost lost you, too.'

'Never,' he murmured, brushing her cheek.

Stepping up to him, Anabelle placed her hand on his chest, feeling his steady heartbeat. 'You promised to come straight to me.'

'Aye, little gipsy. Forgive me?'

His arms slid into the folds of her cloak, pulling her flush against him.

'I suppose I can,' she said softly, looking up at him with a small smile. 'You did almost die after all, and I did save you, of course.'

Néefar's laugh reverberated through her chest.

'You will never let me forget that?'

'Of course not,' she said with a grin, the weight in her chest easing.

Bending, he brushed his mouth against her cheek before feathering over her jaw to whisper in her ear, 'Good, because I will never let you forget it.' He leaned back, staring at her, and said, 'So you never doubt yourself again. So you remember what you're capable of.'

She felt warmth blossom in her chest, and she pressed a hand to his cheek, her fingers brushing over the stubble along his jaw.

'How did the world know to give me you?' she asked.

'They didn't. They gave me a choice, and I chose you.'

Standing on her toes, fingers curling into his hair, she pressed her lips to his.

Néefar's growl responded in turn as he slanted his mouth over hers. He pressed her back against a tree, his tongue slipping between her lips as he deepened the kiss, his knee slipping between her legs.

'Néefar!' she gasped, pulling away. 'Someone might see!' Her voice was breathless, a light giggle escaping as she glanced around the empty forest.

He chuckled, brushing his nose along her cheek.

'Let them see,' he muttered.

'Néefar!' she laughed, putting her hands to his chest, and he stepped back with a crooked grin.

Grabbing his hand in her own, she tugged gently on it. 'Shall we go for a walk?'

He paused, glancing over his shoulder.

'What is it?'

He shook his head. 'We can't. I was sent to bring you back to the Keep.'

Anabelle raised a brow.

'They didn't say *when* I had to bring you back,' he replied with a cheeky grin.

Rolling her eyes, Anabelle swatted a hand at him playfully, though she smiled all the same.

'And why do I need to go back?' she asked, swiping a hand over her hair.

'The Keeper of Dragons has come.'

Her fingers stilled. She looked up at Néefar with an incredulous stare.

'I'm sorry, did you say dragons?'

The Keep was nearly empty as they passed through the veil. Many had departed earlier, burying the dead and packing their carts full.

Anabelle had watched them leave over the course of three

days, the faint pinch of guilt lingering however much she tried to smother it. The scars marring her body from the Cerberus and hell hounds left a stark reminder of their sacrifice.

The Keep had bloomed like the first breath of summer. Sunlight filtered through emerald leaves like golden beams, vibrant leaves covering every branch, bursting with colour.

Flowers of oranges, pinks, lavender, blues, and deep shades of red littered the ground. Green grass was soft underfoot. Tiny blue flowers dusted the bases of trees, moss covering their roots and pillowing the spaces in between. Animals and Summer Fae alike flittered through the Keep with ease. Any lingering stench of fear was gone.

Néefar led her down into the depths of the council room, stepping aside for her to enter first.

'Pardon our delay,' Anabelle said.

Anabelle felt a blush crawl up her neck as Savven and Lithônion looked between them. Savven gave Néefar a pointed stare while Lithônion hid his smirk behind his hand.

Pursing her lips, Anabelle scanned the room and frowned when she didn't see Ezra.

The Spirits were quiet, seated on either side at the head of the table. They'd stood when she entered, but her gaze flitted past them to the newcomer.

Bright gold eyes stared at her with quiet curiosity. The male was both young and old. His skin was unmarked by time, but his eyes held ages. His grey hair was pulled back from his face with gold medallions woven through the silky strands. His gold and emerald tunic glinted in the firelight along the walls.

'Hello.' She greeted him with a tilt of her head.

'Anabelle,' Winter said, 'let me introduce you to the Keeper of Dragons, Valdren.'

'Hello, Keeper,' he said, his voice deep and soothing. 'I have waited patiently to meet you.'

She shook her head. 'I cannot say the same, I'm afraid, though only because I didn't realise a Keeper of Dragons existed.'

Valdren waved a hand. 'Regardless, I have come to bestow the Blessing of Dragons.'

'The Blessing,' she repeated incredulously.

'It is a ritual that has preceded every Keeper before you.' Valdren tucked his hands into the long folds of fabric at his sleeves. 'When the dragons selected the Keeper, they would receive the blessing the night they come of age, and there, they would choose between their mortal and Fae heritage. But as time passed, we have granted the Spirits this right. While you should have received the blessing, fate had other plans.'

'Why was I not informed of this?' she asked the spirits. She was tired of feeling unaware, tired of the secrets.

Winter bowed her head to hide a flicker of guilt. 'Because you have lived without magic for so long, your power has not come into full bloom. The Blessing of Dragons seals your immortality.'

Her words cut through Anabelle with realisation. 'You're saying I could have died?'

'We didn't have a choice, Anabelle,' Summer said softly.

'It wasn't your choice to make,' Anabelle bit out.

'It was at the time,' Winter said.

Anabelle straightened, tilting her chin in defiance. 'Regarding my life, it is nobody's choice but my own. I am not a puppet to be commanded nor a woman to be trifled with. I would give my life tenfold for this world and those I protect, but it will never be because of your choosing.'

Valdren held out a hand to Anabelle. 'I find with age, regardless of immortality, we become complacent. Forgive us, Anabelle. The Fae know nothing of mortality and become careless when it is present.'

Anabelle held Winter's stare, jaw working through the tension spiralling within her.

'If you follow me, you'll find there is one who is waiting to meet you,' Valdren commented, breaking the heavy tension.

Néefar's hand slid across her lower back as she passed him, though he followed close behind her and the Dragon Keeper.

Tall blades of grass covered the once-bloodied ground of the clearing. Wildflowers, in an array of yellows, swayed softly in the wind scattered through the field.

Her breath hitched in her throat as massive wings expanded in a glittering beam of molten gold across the sky. The great golden dragon arched through the air before gliding to the clearing, landing with a weight that seemed to shake the ground. It folded its long, leathery wings to its side. Black horns twisted from the tops of its head to the sky.

'Forndýr,' Valdren said calmly.

A plume of smoke puffed from Forndýr's snout, and he bowed as she cautiously approached him, hand outstretched.

'May I?' she asked, holding her breath.

He brushed his snout against her palm, and her body jerked as violent images played through her mind like unseen memories.

Death and rage swallowed the world. Shadows fell, and the forest became ash as fire consumed it. Gold eyes stared from the shadows, and a terrible roar rocketed through the world. Then, there was nothing. There was only darkness.

'Do you see, Keeper?'

Anabelle's blood turned to ice when Forndýr stepped back, and she stared at the dragon as his deep, gravelled voice brushed across her mind.

'Yes,' she said in a low tone.

Blinking once, the great dragon bowed his head and then leapt into the sky, his body showering them in golden light.

'Well, that was eventful,' drawled Lithônion.

She could hear Néefar chuckle, but she kept her eyes on Forndýr. Ash and fire burned through her mind.

CHAPTER THIRTY-SEVEN

Water dripped from the ends of her short hair, following the curve of her back. Her footsteps echoed against the stone walls, hands clasped behind her in thought.

Fire and ash reigned high, and the world burned. Where life sowed its roots, only cinders remained.

'You seem troubled.'

A whisper was Anabelle's only warning before Savven fell into step beside her.

She only shook her head. 'The world is a troubling place, cousin.'

Savven hummed as if in thought. 'It would seem that way after everything Balwin inflicted.'

Fire and ash, and nothingness.

'Yes,' she murmured, pushing the thoughts away.

'Will you travel with us?'

'No, I find I am needed here.'

Savven paused, turned to Anabelle, and gently touched her arm to stop her. 'Álfheimr is as much your home as it is mine.'

Anabelle looked at her cousin, whose deep blue eyes were nearly black in the dim torchlight. 'And I am grateful for that,' she said.

Savven nodded at the finalisation in her tone, not pressing the matter before they continued down the hall.

'Where is Ezra?' she asked.

Savven let out a heavy breath. 'He left in the middle of the night and didn't say a word to us.'

Anabelle chewed on her lip.

'You worry for him?' he asked.

She nodded. 'I do. You didn't see what Balwin did, what was meant for me, and what Ezra took.'

Savven was quiet for several long moments as if weighing his words before finally saying, 'Ezra is a noble High Fae and commander of the elven armies. He did what was expected of him.'

It made sense, yet she couldn't help but worry. 'Please, Savven, watch him closely. Duty or not, he is my friend, and I owe him a life debt.'

'He will be safe with our people.'

'I do pray so.'

The door of Anabelle's room clicked behind her, and she leaned her body against the solid frame, head falling back with a dull *thunk*. She closed her eyes, exhaustion like a physical weight.

Rubbing a tired hand over her face, she walked over to her desk and picked up her mother's letter. The seams were well worn from being opened and folded so many times, the corners bent from being handled. She reread the words, bringing the paper close to her chest. When she heard approaching footsteps, she folded the note and placed it on her pillow just before a light knock preceded the door swinging open.

'You are improving,' Anabelle said lightly.

Néefar's crooked smile answered her. His arms crossed over his chest, and he leaned against the doorframe. 'I thought I would try knocking this time and then opening the door. I'll admit, I'm not partial to it.'

She shook her head with an exasperated laugh.

His gaze softened as she laughed, and his lips tilted in a soft smile. 'I wondered if you would like to forgo sleep this night.'

She stopped and glanced at him. 'And what do you propose?' she asked in a hushed voice.

He held out a hand to her, tilting his head. 'I know I cut our time short earlier, so I wish to show you something to make up for it.'

Standing, she slipped her hand into his warm, calloused fingers, letting him pull her to him. 'What is it?'

Néefar gave her a secret smile. 'Magic.'

The winter air pressed against their cloaks as they trod through the snow. Néefar kept her hand warm in his as he guided her through the trees.

He let go and jumped to the first branch of a towering tree, helping her up when she lifted her skirts to follow behind him. The bulging tree limbs stood out like arms, forming deep alcoves that made it easy to climb to the top.

Néefar's hands wrapped around her waist, pulling her onto the branch he sat on. Pressing her back flush against his chest, his arm wrapped around her waist in a warm band.

Anabelle situated her skirt around her, one leg resting on the branch while the other dangled freely. She leaned back into the solid wall of muscle and relaxed in his hold, her head leaning against his shoulder.

'Look up,' he whispered against her ear.

She did, and her breath caught. The glimmer of stardust trailed through the atmosphere and twinkled in the cloudless sky. A sea of stars lay before them, not a single one out of sight.

'It's beautiful,' she said.

'Stars are beautiful,' he agreed, 'but I did not wish to show you ordinary stars.'

Anabelle hummed, twisting to try and look at him. 'Then what did you wish to show me?'

Néefar gently turned her chin. 'Watch the sky, my love.'

A slight shiver of anticipation rolled down her spine, and she pressed herself into his chest, his arm tightening around her waist.

Minutes passed, and she was about to say something when she saw it. One at first, then two, three, then hundreds, thousands—millions of stars streaked across the sky. It was a sight she had never seen, too perfect to describe with a glance. A million wishes came bearing down upon her as the stars fell from heaven like tears, and Anabelle felt her own tears form.

Néefar turned his eyes away from the falling stars, watching the woman in his arms, the reflection of unshed tears in her gaze.

'Why do you cry, little gipsy?' he murmured, brushing the tear away with the pad of his thumb.

'Because I am afraid,' she whispered without looking away from the sky, almost too quietly for him to hear.

'What are you afraid of?' he asked.

'What is to come,' she said in a broken whisper.

Fire and ash tore through her mind, and golden eyes peered through the darkness that enveloped the world.

Néefar stroked a steady hand through her slightly damp hair, kissing her temple. 'You cannot change what has yet to happen. Pave the path before you, and we will face the future together, whatever it may be.'

After a long moment, Anabelle took a breath and twisted her head to look at Néefar. This time, he didn't turn her away. He brushed his nose against hers, and she smiled, leaning her forehead against his for just a moment before turning back to the sky.

Anabelle pushed away the trembling in her limbs. The world above them promised a new beginning.

Anabelle dressed the following day in a gown of soft cream fabric. Hints of green came to life in the light, gathered under her bust. It flowed like water as she moved, shifting against her bare legs like satin. The sleeves extended from her shoulders, down her arms to the crooks of her elbows. Lace and embroidered flowers were scattered across the top of the dress.

She let her fingertips brush against their delicate details, sitting patiently on her bed as Summer braided her short hair with small flowers and vibrant green moss. If she closed her eyes, she could almost pretend it was her mother's fingers running through her hair.

Summer's hands stilled. 'There you are, Keeper.'

But it wasn't, and Anabelle opened her eyes.

Anabelle brought the mirror to her face and smiled at her reflection. 'It's beautiful, Summer.'

The Spirit stood. Her rich plum gown shimmered in the firelight, brilliant against her dark brown skin.

'Come, the dragon awaits you.'

Anabelle paused, watching Summer open the door to her chambers. Nerves roiled in her stomach.

Summer looked at her with a knowing smile, and Anabelle found herself following the Spirit despite the rapid pounding of her heart.

Dawn filled the forest with a new light as she and Summer walked through the Keep. Bright sunlight danced through the trees, and a warm wind played through the trees. Summer Fae gathered on the branches, littering the trees with glimmering light, watching Anabelle with rapt fascination.

A brilliant sunrise in pinks and oranges burst across the clearing. Anabelle's bare footsteps were soft on the tall grass. The tiny, winged Fae flittered into the clearing, excitement buzzing around them.

Forndýr stood tall and proud in the dawn's early light, sunlight cascading on his scales to form a magnificent halo around him. Valdren waited in golden robes, the fabric pooling around him and adorned with intricate emerald details.

Savven and Lithônion stood to her left with Autumn and Spring. Néefar stood to her right, Winter beside him. Summer joined her sister, and Anabelle was left to walk alone.

Her fingers balled into the fabric of her dress. She reached out for that familiar cord within her, feeling the taut rope of her power in her grasp. She forced her hands to slacken out of fists. Her magic brushed against her mind, settling within her bones like an old friend.

She took her first step, and the forest around her sighed. The thrum of the world beneath her feet steadied her as she began her procession.

Forndýr towered over them all, his large head tilted, and his amber eyes looked age-old when she stared up at him. Turning her attention, Anabelle stared firmly at Valdren.

Valdren held up a hand, and the excited buzz dimmed.

'Dragons and the four Gods crafted this world,' he said. 'They were the first to breathe life into it. They created the oceans, valleys, mountains, plains, and all the Fae. But because the Gods created the world, Fae magic bound them to honour the free will bestowed upon their creations. So, a keeper and the spirits alongside them were chosen to balance the forest and magic within. However, the spirits were bound by their laws, and the keeper was gifted the power to withstand the rise and fall of the ages and all that came with it. You were born to walk this world as its sword and shield. That is your duty as the keeper. Do you accept the tasks laid before you, even death, if that may come?'

Anabelle glanced at the large amber eyes staring down at her, and the muscles in her jaw twitched. She forced herself to nod. 'I accept, ' she said.

Valdren stepped aside, and Forndýr bowed his massive head.

A fairy flew from the cloister of the Fae, twirling in front of Anabelle suddenly.

'Arie?' Anabelle question in awe.

A plume of smoke billowed from Forndýr's snout, peering at the petite fairy.

Her tiny face grinned at Anabelle as she spun around.

'I thought I would not see you again, little flower.'

Arie rose to Anabelle's brow and pressed a kiss to it.

In the deepest part of her mind, Anabelle heard the tinkle of silver bells and the quiet *thank you.*

Arie disappeared into the gathering of Fae, and Anabelle looked up to the great dragon. He neared her, and she closed her eyes as Forndýr touched her brow with his own.

Golden light erupted between them, jerking her body as a deep-seated flame took root in her bones. Heat and cold wove together, melting and freezing until her limbs were coated in ice and her skin flushed in warm response. She was consumed in dragon fire and winter's breath.

Forndýr's gravelly voice washed through her mind, '*Be blessed in your days, young Keeper. But be warned, darkness is coming, and you cannot stop it.*'

Anabelle's breath caught in her throat, but she forced herself to answer. '*I will do all that I can, even if it is not enough,*' she whispered back into the abyss connecting them.

Forndýr released her, and the world around them came rushing back to her reality. Around her, the Fae cheered as they celebrated the blessing.

A new sense of power and ease settled in her, the world shifting beneath her feet. She felt ready to burst with energy but also wholly calm, like a bird that had been caged for so long and was finally free.

Anabelle lifted her hand, and the wind calmed as bluebells sprouted from the ground, covering the clearing in a field of blue—her mother's favourite flower. Anabelle knew she was with her now and always.

A new sense of purpose raced through Anabelle, and she felt reborn, her heart weightless.

Valdren stepped forward and clasped her hands in his. 'Tattooed upon your skin are the old writings, the commandments bred from the dragons.'

Anabelle followed his gaze to her arms, marked in ancient script from her fingertips to just below the sleeve of her gown. The tattoos shimmered like water on her skin.

'Keeper, the light does not last forever,' Valdren said solemnly. 'There will always be those who wish to extinguish it, but you have brought the light back into this world, and for now, it is lasting.'

Forndýr rose onto his rear legs, his wings expanding in a shower of golden light. He lifted his head and let loose a roar that shook the trees to their roots.

The cloister of Fae scattered with silent shrieks, hiding in the tree limbs.

Her friends laughed around her, and she couldn't help but join in. Closing her eyes, she felt her heartbeat in her chest, the rise and fall of her power, and the restraint slipping from her mental grasp. With a feral grin, she released the leash of her magic.

The blast of light crashed around them in a warm blaze, and the forest bathed in her power.

The noon sun bore down on Anabelle, her feet still bare as she walked alone through the clearing. Bluebells and tall, feathery grass stalks grazed against her gossamer skirt.

She settled on her knees in the middle of the clearing and played with a blade of grass as her gaze wandered over the expanse of field. What had looked like a tidal wave of death now blossomed with life, and she released the grass stalk, lying back to stare up at the sky, which was blue and clear.

Every breath she had taken, every hour of her existence, and every pondering thought came together like puzzle pieces, even in the chasm that still split her heart, where pieces lay missing.

Even as the whispered warning in her mind ushered her to be alert, she ignored it. It was safe for now.

Closing her eyes, she took a deep breath and exhaled softly. For the first time, Anabelle just lay there and breathed.

EPILOGUE

The quiet drip of water echoed in the cavern as Tatius approached the stone basin, the padding of her bare feet muted on the wet stone. Torches illuminated the dais as she looked down into the water, silent and undisturbed. Dipping her finger into it, ripples appeared, and so did the face of one elf with coal-black eyes and midnight hair.

Udiya appeared from the shadows, her dark brown skin glowing in the firelight, the silver whorls tattooed on her skin sparkling faintly.

'What becomes of the elf?'

Tatius glanced up at the female, shuddering as death filled her vision. Bodies and blood seeped into the earth like poisoned water. The innocent fell into fire and ash, their cries echoing in her ears as the vision faded. Exhaling sharply, she returned her gaze to the water.

'The time for shadows and mist has gone,' murmured Tatius.

Udiya stepped up to the basin and watched as one with coal-black eyes turned up to a stormy sky, mouth opened in a scream they couldn't hear.

'If the Keeper does not rise, our world will fall into fire and ash.' Tatius's face became void, her childlike features turning ancient. 'From shadows and mist and fire and ash, walls will fall, and darkness will reign. As one is, so shall the other be. From darkness and light, the world will rise.'

Tatius's voice echoed against the stone chamber, looming like a dark promise. The two females were silent as they watched the water. Ezra's face was the only thing they could see as shadows overtook him.

As the fate of the Black Forest spiralled out of control, the small god of immortality— of life and death— smiled faintly.

SO IT BEGINS...

Next up in the Keeper trilogy:

The Black Forest

Coming summer 2024

About The Author

P. S. Whytock is a nearly thirty something year old who's just trying to figure out life. She currently lives in Florida and is a Merchant Marine when she's not pretending to be an author.

ACKNOWLEDGEMENTS

I didn't think I was going to write an acknowledgements page, mostly because I never thought I would publish this book. It has been eleven years in the making. Eleven years of ups and downs, growing, and learning, and most importantly: evolving into the person I am today.

So, even if no one reads these acknowledgements, I'm just happy they're here.

This book, first and foremost, is dedicated to my dad. He was the first person to read this book from start to finish while it was still a first draft, and to be fair, horrible. He would always tell me that one day I'm going to be a famous author, and they're going to make movies out of my books… well, I wouldn't go that far, Daddy. He always talked about writing his own book one day of all his sea stories (he was a Chief Merchant Marine and a surfer!) and would tuck me into bed with them.

"Pop, do you know the difference between a fairytale and a sea story? One starts: Once upon a time. The other starts: Now this ain't no shit."

He passed away suddenly before he could see this published, and before he could finish chapter one of his own novel. So, the most I can do is write him into my stories, and dedicate this to him, and hope, maybe, they have libraries in Heaven.

To my mum, who told me that if I wanted to write, and write well, I had to read *everything*. Even the stuff I hated (I'm looking at you Scarlett Letter and Sherlock Holmes!). I love you so much, and as your daughter I'm so proud of you, for everything you've accomplished in this life. Everything you've done has shaped me into the woman I am today, and I'm so incredibly grateful to you and daddy.

Josiah, what an unlikely friend I found in you. You have supported my writing since you found out I wrote novels and have been one of my biggest support systems since. I can't wait to see your own novels come to life one day, and I look forward to returning that support.

To Charlie, thank you for providing me with the love and space to write and finish this because you knew how much it meant to me. If I could give you the stars I would, but I'll have to settle for thank you.

To the few people who beta read this novel before it was… this novel. Thank you so much! It truly means the world that you all took the time to look over this book and give me the feedback needed to make it what it is today.

To those who read the first draft of this novel, I'm sorry, but also, thank you. I hope your brain will forgive me.

Thank you to Charly (@designsbycharlyy) for making a beautiful cover for my paperback, and the interior design. Charlotte, for designing the hardcover, and Styro, for taking the time out of your chaotic life to help a stranger out and formatting it to fit.

Baddie (@batwingbaddie) for being an amazing PA and being so kind and helpful through all of this. You were a rock for me to rely on, whether it be support or guidance, you led me through this new process, and I'm so grateful for you.

Bianca, Gina, Izzy, Alexis, and everyone else I've met at my local B&N *thank you* for being so overwhelmingly sweet and welcoming to me. You're truly magnificent humans and I'm lucky to have met you.

And to me, I know most might think it's a little ridiculous to thank yourself but…I am a mosaic of every version of myself since writing this novel, and she is the woman who stands here today. I started this book before my first marriage and ended it a month after my divorce. Trauma does a funny thing to a person, and we can either let it consume us, or rise from it. So, I wrote a book, and it helped get me through those turbulent waters. And while my writing has evolved and matured greatly since this novel, I have to remind myself that this story healed parts of me no one ever could. So, even if this isn't the best novel in the world, or a fan favourite, it's my favourite. That's all that matters.

I'm so proud of you.